All I Want for Christmas Is a Duke

Also by the Authors

By Valerie Bowman
THE UNLIKELY LADY
THE IRRESISTIBLE ROGUE

By Tiffany Clare
DESIRE ME NOW
DESIRE ME MORE

By Vivienne Lorret
THE WALLFLOWER WEDDING SERIES
THE RAKES OF FALLOW HALL SERIES

By Ashlyn Macnamara
THE ETON BOYS TRILOGY
DUKE-DEFYING DAUGHTERS

All I Want for Christmas Is a Duke

VALERIE BOWMAN
TIFFANY CLARE
VIVIENNE LORRET
ASHLYN MACNAMARA

AVONIMPULSE
An Imprint of HarperCollinsPublishers

"The Duke and Duchess Trap" copyright © 2015 by June Third Enterprises, LLC.

"Sophie and the Duke" copyright © 2015 by Tiffany Clare.

"The Duke's Christmas Wish" copyright © 2015 by Vivienne Lorret.

"One Magic Season" copyright © 2015 by Ashlyn Macnamara.

EPub Edition DECEMBER 2015 ISBN: 9780062441515
Print Edition ISBN: 9780062441539

10 9 8 7 6 5 4 3

Contents

*All I Want for
Christmas Is a Duke*

The Duke and Duchess Trap

By Valerie Bowman

To Anne Bergeron, who knows why.

Prologue

London
September, 1810

"Lady Evangeline Hollister?" The headmistress's voice rang out across the huge banquet hall.

Evie swallowed. Oh, she didn't like this. Not one bit. She bit her lip. Being shy was such a curse. Why did *she* have to be the first to be called upon on the first day at her new school? Apparently, new students were first to be inspected and provided with a class schedule. She stared up at the monstrous carved chandeliers that hung like gargoyles from the wood-beamed roof of the hall. Attending the most exclusive school in London was her birthright. Mother had said she must be brave. She'd promised Mother. Never mind that the idea of leaving Mother, her home, her dog, her beloved horses, not to mention the servants, made Evie want to cast up her accounts.

She blinked away the tears that stung her eyes. Tears would not do. Mother said the daughter of a duke did not cry. Even at the tender age of twelve. Evie smoothed her blue skirts and glanced down at her perfectly clean and orderly white stockings, which peeped out at the ankles. She pressed her palm against the thick wooden table, preparing to stand. She tucked her book under her arm. The book had been another recommendation from Mother. "One cannot be homesick when one is reading a compelling book," she'd said. "When you're reading, it doesn't matter where you are."

Mother was right, and Evie had been clutching her copy of *The Canterbury Tales* ever since she'd arrived at Miss Hathaway's School for Young Ladies. But she somehow doubted that Headmistress Hathaway would take kindly to her reading during roll call.

"Lady Evangeline," the headmistress called again. Evie pushed herself to her feet. The short heels of her leather slippers clicked against the polished wood floor, and the eyes of all the other girls swiveled to watch her. She gulped and stepped forward, forcing herself to take another step and another, shuddering at each smack of her heels. She pressed her hand to her book, clutching it so tightly that her fingers drained of color.

"Present," she managed to force from her dry throat.

The headmistress's head snapped up, and she eyed Evie's approach over the rim of her golden spectacles. It seemed as if hours passed before Evie arrived, trembling, at Miss Hathaway's table, which was perched on a dais at the front of the cavernous hall. The middle-aged lady lowered her spectacles and glared at Evie through narrowed dark eyes. She spoke in a pinched, unhappy voice. "I'm not amused, Lady Genevieve. I said Lady *Evangeline* Hollister."

Evie gulped. "I beg your pardon, madam." Her voice trembled. "I *am* Lady Evangeline Hollister."

Miss Hathaway pursed her lips. It was an unfortunate look for her. She contemplated Evie with a suspicious glare while the giggles of the other girls grew louder. Evie swallowed and clutched the book to her chest, crossing her arms over it, desperately wishing she could disappear. There couldn't possibly have been a mix-up, could there? Mother would have seen to all the details. Mother was kind, and beautiful, and full of laughter. And Mother never made mistakes. It was absolutely inconceivable.

The headmistress's eyes narrowed further, if that was possible. "What have you done to your hair?"

Evie pushed her free hand up to her red locks. "My . . . my hair, madam?"

"Don't pretend you don't know what I mean, Lady Genevieve. You're forgetting that I was present when you decided to run off into the park without your bonnet, resulting in that unfortunate incident with the pine sap, which led to Miss Lancaster having to *cut* your hair—and seriously displeasing your father, I might add."

"My . . . my father?" Evie cocked her head to the side and stared at the headmistress as if she'd been speaking a foreign language. Evie hadn't seen her father since she was a babe. Or so Mother had told her. Evie certainly didn't remember him or their last meeting. What in heaven's name did Miss Hathaway mean? And why did she continue to refer to her as Genevieve?

"I beg your pardon, madam," Evie managed, "but to my knowledge, I've never had the misfortune to get pine sap in my hair, and I have yet to make the acquaintance of a Miss Lancaster."

There was more tittering from the other girls. Evie's cheeks heated. She clutched her book even tighter in her slick palms, wishing she could disappear into the volume. She had the distinct impression she was about to be dismissed from the most exclusive school in London before she'd even begun. What would she tell Mother?

The headmistress tapped the end of her quill against the wide mahogany table in front of her. "Lady Genevieve, as usual, I do not find your behavior amusing in the least. Now, I shall ask you for your full name one final time. I warn you, your father will hear about this if you give me anything short of the truth."

Evie swallowed and nodded.

Miss Hathaway's nostrils flared. She raised her chin and pressed her spectacles farther up her beaklike nose. "Your name, if you please."

Evie didn't blink. "Evangeline Marie Sandford Hollister." Her voice was low and weak as usual, and she silently cursed herself for it.

The headmistress's hand cracked against the surface of the table, making Evie jump. She jumped a second time when the door to the hall slammed open and an urchin with short red hair, sagging stockings, and an askew bonnet came running across the wide expanse of wood flooring. She passed the banquet tables filled with girls and skidded to a halt in front of the headmistress, her hair flipped across her brow, obscuring her face. She smelled like sherbet lemons, reminding Evie of home. Mother's favorites.

The girl was breathing heavily and seemed to be balancing precariously on one foot. Evie also noted with no small bit of wonder that the urchin was missing a button from the back of her gown, and one of her gloves appeared to be stained. Blood? Good heavens! Or was it chocolate? She wasn't sure which was more alarming. Mother wouldn't approve of Evie missing a button from her gown, let alone being in possession of a stained glove. What sort of mother did *this* urchin have? And how in heaven's name had the creature managed to matriculate at Miss Hathaway's School for Young Ladies?

"I was told you were looking for me, Miss Hathaway," the urchin stated in a loud, clear voice. "I am sorry, ma'am, but I was in the science hall feeding the lizards and quite lost track of the time."

The urchin turned to look at Evie. She swiped the unfashionably short crop of red hair from her forehead, and her face came into full view.

Evie gasped.

Miss Hathaway gasped.

The urchin's eyes (which were the exact same shade of blue as Evie's) grew wide. "Oh, my. How wonderful. You must be my twin sister, Evangeline. I cannot tell you how lovely it is to finally meet you."

Chapter One

The London town house of the Duke of Hollingsworth
Three days before Christmas, 1810

NATHANIEL DAVID MONTGOMERY HOLLISTER, the sixth
Duke of Hollingsworth, eyed the plump, sixty-year-old
housekeeper who stood staring at him expectantly across
the desk in his study. Mrs. Curtis was overbearing, insistent, and impertinent, but she'd been employed by the
Hollister family since before Nathan was born, and he
wasn't about to dismiss her. She was another of his duties.
Like his vast properties and investments, Mrs. Curtis was
something to be managed.

"Your Grace, we must discuss the menus for the upcoming week," Mrs. Curtis repeated. "It's Christmastide,
and if you and Lady Genevieve intend to remain here in
London, we must prepare accordingly."

Nathan glanced at the ledger he'd been balancing. "Of
course we must, Mrs. Curtis. It's just that . . ."

"Yes, Your Grace?" Mrs. Curtis leaned forward, her
lips pursed, her eyes watching, expectant.

Nathan tapped his quill along the paper in front of

him. "At times I wish I had a wife who would deal with these matters."

"You *do* have a wife," Mrs. Curtis replied in a matter-of-fact voice, but Nathan didn't mistake the twinkle in her eye. "Lady Elizabeth just doesn't happen to live *here*. Though I'm sure Her Grace would be quite capable of picking out excellent menu items if given half the chance."

Nathan ignored the servant's impudence. The house-keeper had never shied away from giving him her full mind, and she wasn't about to start now that he was five and thirty. She'd made it more than clear through the years that she did not agree with his marital arrangements. Not one bit.

"I'll leave the Christmastide menu in your capable hands, then," he replied instead, returning his gaze to his papers.

She opened her mouth, no doubt to give him an additional piece of her mind, but a light knock on the door stopped her.

"Come in," Nathan called, thankful for the reprieve from Mrs. Curtis's cheek.

The door opened silently and the butler stepped inside.

"Yes, Winthrop. What is it?" Nathan asked.

"The dowager duchess has come to call," the butler intoned.

Nathan scowled. "Mother? Here? On a Tuesday afternoon? What could she possibly want?"

Mrs. Curtis put her hands on her chubby hips. "Lady Genevieve is coming home today," she reminded him.

"Yes. That's it. Isn't it?" Nathan shook his head.

"Mother doesn't want to see *me*. She's merely visiting as a thinly veiled excuse to see her granddaughter."

"It's a shame she can visit only the *one* granddaughter," Mrs. Curtis added with a distinct harrumph.

Nathan eyed her down the length of his nose. "*That* will be all, Mrs. Curtis."

Mrs. Curtis bobbed a quick curtsy, sidled past the butler, and left the room, but not before giving Nathan a look that informed him it would not, in fact, be all. Not by a far cry.

"Show my mother in," Nathan said to Winthrop.

"The dowager has requested that you meet her in the blue drawing room. She said . . ." Winthrop cleared his throat. " . . . she said your study was too . . ." The jowly man looked away, his face turning red.

Nathan sighed. "Go ahead and say it, Winthrop."

"I believe the word she used was 'dark,' Your Grace."

Nathan glanced around the room. It was true that the space was filled with dark brown leather and dark brown wood, and the rug just happened to be navy, and the portraits were all a bit gloomy, if he was being honest, but what did Mother care?

"Be that as it may, show her in . . . *here*," he repeated in a voice that brooked no further debate.

The butler nodded once and turned to leave, but Nathan stopped him.

"Has Lady Genevieve returned from school yet, Winthrop?"

The butler paused, his white-gloved hand on the door handle. "Not yet, Your Grace."

Nathan waved him off, pushed back his chair, and rubbed his fingers through his dark hair. He truly adored his daughter. *Both* of his daughters. But the fact remained that he was a duke without an heir. He spent considerable time and resources setting aside money for Genevieve and Evangeline, but he'd long ago given up hope of siring a legitimate male heir. That would involve seeing Elizabeth again, *touching* Elizabeth again, and he'd as soon cut off his right arm. No, Genevieve would be well cared for financially, as would Evangeline, but his estate, the land and holdings, would all be entailed to his cousin Richard, and Nathan was just fine with that. His mother, however, was . . . not.

"Very well, Hollingsworth, I see you mean to make me suffer the dinginess of your study." His mother's words sliced through the air as she regally marched through the door. His tall, thin mother wore a purple silk gown and carried an ivory-tipped cane that she did not need. Carefully removing her kid gloves, she touched one long fingertip to a slightly graying eyebrow.

Nathan stood. "I thought it was dark, not dingy."

"It is both. Make no mistake," the dowager countered. She cocked her perfectly coiffed head to the side, presenting him with her pale cheek, and Nathan made his way around his desk to kiss it. He did love the old bird, even if she was a handful.

Before resuming his own chair, Nathan waited for his mother to take a seat in front of the desk. "Gena is not back yet," he informed the older woman.

She stamped her cane upon the carpet. "Do you

assume I came to see my granddaughter alone and not my son?"

Nathan quirked a brow. "That's exactly what I assume. Do you deny it?"

She pursed her lips. "Yes. I wanted to speak with you."

Nathan steepled his fingers over his chest. "I already told you that Gena and I intend to spend Christmastide in London this year."

"Nonsense. You will spend it with me in the country as usual. But the Christmastide arrangements are not why I've come."

Nathan leveled his gaze on his mother. He adopted his most patient voice. "Then why have you come?"

"Always direct, aren't you, my son? So different from your father that way." She regarded him coolly down the length of her nose.

"I'm different from my father in many ways," Nathan replied evenly.

"Also true. And all of them for the better, I might add. All save one."

Nathan's gaze met hers. His eyes were the same sapphire blue as his mother's. At nearly sixty, his mother was still attractive, with a sharp, aristocratic nose and strong brow, but she was also as clever and cunning as a fox. He knew better than to step into her trap. "I won't ask what you mean."

"Your father was able to sire an heir, at least."

"Ah, yes. This again. I should have guessed." Nathan pulled his ledger closer. "I'm quite busy today, Mother, and I refuse to have this conversation with you yet again.

You might have saved yourself the trip. You're welcome to return later this afternoon to see Gena, but until then . . ."

His mother held up a hand. "You're wrong again, Hollingsworth. Your lack of an heir is also not why I've come. Though I daresay you would need to at least be in the same *town* as your wife, if not the same *room*, to do so, and you've steadfastly refused to do either."

Nathan rubbed the back of his neck where an ache was beginning to form. He'd been a lad in leading strings the last time he'd done his mother's bidding, and he wasn't about to begin again now. Or rise to her bait. "I'll do us both a favor and not respond to that. Now, if you haven't come to see Gena or to lecture me about my duty, why have you come?"

The dowager pressed her gloved hands upon her cane. Her back ramrod straight, she said, "As you know, I have many contacts at Miss Hathaway's School for Young Ladies."

"If by 'contacts' you mean 'spies,' then yes, I know."

She rolled her eyes. "They are not spies. They are my dear friends, and I've been sitting on this particular rumor for nearly four months now."

Nathan stood and walked over to the sideboard to pour himself a drink. A drink was often in order when his mother paid a call. "I highly doubt that. You've never sat on a rumor a day in your life."

The dowager lifted her nose in the air and stamped her cane upon the rug again. "Be that as it may, this rumor has been confirmed, and in fact, I visited the school myself to ensure that it was true."

Nathan splashed a bit of brandy into his glass. "By God, if Gena's got into trouble again—"

"No, no. It's nothing like that. From all reports, she's been doing exceedingly well this year."

Nathan let his shoulders relax. He turned to his mother. "Care for a drink?"

"Of course not." She waved it away. "I never drink in the afternoon."

"Ah, yes. You prefer to keep your wits about you in order to flay me alive with questions, don't you?"

Her nostrils flared. "Don't be ridiculous."

"Let's see now, where were we?" Nathan scooped up his drink and returned to his seat. "It's true that I haven't had half as many letters from Miss Hathaway this term as I have in the past. But I don't like the idea of you interfering in Gena's schooling, Mother."

"I'm hardly interfering, dear. I was merely confirming a rumor."

Nathan brought the crystal glass to his lips. "What rumor?"

"That Lady Evangeline Hollister had matriculated at Miss Hathaway's this year."

Chapter Two

Kent, the country estate of the Duke of Hollingsworth

ELIZABETH MARIE SANDFORD HOLLISTER, the Duchess of Hollingsworth, tapped her foot on the Aubusson rug in the front drawing room of the giant manor house that she called home. She hadn't been able to sit still for longer than five minutes all day.

"Any moment now, Sampson," she said to the large red setter who sat on the carpet next to her feet.

Sampson made a small whining noise and tapped his paw on the rug. He missed Evie, too. Elizabeth had no doubt.

The door to the drawing room flew open, and her lady's maid and best friend, Mary, hurried in. "Your Grace, Lady Evangeline's coach is coming up the lane."

"Evie!" Elizabeth jumped from her seat and hurried out of the drawing room toward the foyer. Mary followed quickly behind her.

"It would not be ladylike, let alone duchesslike, to break into a run, would it, Mary?" Elizabeth asked.

"In this case, Your Grace, I think being duchesslike

would be highly overrated," the slender young brunette replied.

Elizabeth flashed her trusted servant a grin. Mary was right. It wouldn't hurt to pick up her skirts slightly in order to move a bit faster. Evie was coming home at last. Evie. Her baby. Save for Elizabeth's brief union with Evie's father over a decade ago, the few months that Evie had been gone had been the longest of Elizabeth's life. She had spent the autumn months keeping a stiff upper lip in front of the servants and retiring to her room at night in tears. Only Mary knew the truth—that being away from Evie for so long broke Elizabeth's heart.

Evie was all Elizabeth had. The only bright spot in her life. At the age of thirty, she lived in a gilded cage, essentially a prisoner. But she'd never allowed Evie to feel anything other than love and safety. Elizabeth had to let her daughter go. Evie was the daughter of a duke, after all, and if Elizabeth's mother-in-law, the dowager, had taught her anything, it was that anyone who was anyone in the *ton*—a young lady at least—was required to attend London's Miss Hathaway's School for Young Ladies.

A dozen years ago, after she and Nathan had had their infamous falling out and decided it was best for everyone if they lived apart, Nathan had informed her that he intended for Genevieve to attend the school. So it had been a surprise to Elizabeth when the dowager had arrived for her monthly visit last summer and informed her that Genevieve would, in fact, be going to a new, more sought-after school in London. That was just as well for Elizabeth. As a result, she was able to send Evie to Miss

Hathaway's. Elizabeth put great stock in tradition. She might have been a miserable failure as a wife, a daughter, and a duchess, but she refused, absolutely *refused*, to be a failure as a mother. At least to the one daughter she was able to mother. Elizabeth's throat clenched. She shook away the tears that always threatened when she thought of Genevieve. Regardless, if Evangeline had the opportunity to go to Miss Hathaway's, then attend the prestigious school she would.

Elizabeth had worried over the decision for months, but in the end, she'd decided she must be brave, just as she'd instructed Evie to be. Now she would have two blissful weeks of holiday with her beautiful daughter before she'd be forced to ship her back to school.

A footman passed Elizabeth on her way to the front door. "Your Grace, one of the outriders just dismounted. He says Lady Evangeline looks to be in great spirits and fit as a fiddle."

"Oh, thank you, Thompson," Elizabeth said, her heart swelling with both pride and love. She lifted her skirts a touch higher and increased her pace.

The butler opened the door as she approached. "My pelisse, if you please, Broderick."

The staid servant's eyes widened a bit, but he quickly helped her on with that garment. "Do you mean to wait *outside*, Your Grace?" His voice was tinged with surprise.

"Indeed I do." It was true that the wind was piercing and the skies were heavy and gray, but a bit of inclement weather wasn't about to stop her from seeing her baby.

Broderick quickly helped her on with her cloak, and

Elizabeth pulled a wool hat down over her ears and stuffed her hands into a fur muff. Barely breaking her stride, she marched out the door, sucking in her breath when the frigid December air found the exposed bits of her skin. She shuddered and straightened her spine, then shielded her hand over her eyes to have a look across the vast expanse of the front lawn. The coach was indeed nearing the house at a rapid pace. Evie was home. Elizabeth tapped her slippered foot against the frozen gravel of the drive and squeezed her hands together inside the muff.

Minutes later, the coach pulled to a stop directly in front of Elizabeth, and she nearly leaped forward to wrench open the door herself. A footman wearing a large, dark wool overcoat disembarked from the back of the conveyance and opened the door instead. A moment later, her daughter, a tangled mass of red wool coat, large gray bonnet, skinny limbs, and flower-scented hair came hurtling out of the coach directly into her arms. Elizabeth caught her with an *oomph*. Good heavens. When had Evie ever acted so . . . boisterously? Her daughter was normally the epitome of prim and proper behavior. Not to mention she must have grown two inches since Elizabeth had last seen her.

"Evie, dear. Wait. Let me see you." She hugged the girl closely while simultaneously trying to get a good look at her face. Was she indeed well? Happy? Healthy? Had she lost weight? Gained it? Was she—?

"Oh, Mother. I'm so, so, so, so happy to see you. You are absolutely beautiful." The girl's embrace tightened, and Elizabeth's heart swelled. Evie wasn't usually so demonstrative, but Elizabeth reveled in her daughter's hug. She'd always wished for hugs from her own mother when she'd been a child. Hugs that had never come. She squeezed the girl tightly in her arms, tears pricking her eyes.

"I'm happy to see you, too, darling," Elizabeth said.

Mary, who had tossed a shawl over her shoulders and followed her mistress outside, patted Evie on the back and squeezed her shoulder. "It's good to have you back, Lady Evie," she said. Elizabeth didn't miss the tears in the servant's eyes either.

"Come in the house where it's warm." Elizabeth ushered the girl inside while Evie kept her arm around her waist, and Elizabeth bit her lip to keep her smile from widening. Perhaps the time away had been good for Evie. She seemed much more relaxed (if a bit louder) than before.

The two entered the foyer, the servants directly behind them. Evie let go of Elizabeth long enough to assist Broderick in removing her coat. The footmen marched past, carrying her trunks. Sampson ran up and sniffed Evie, then backed up, growled, and barked at her twice.

Elizabeth stared at the dog with wide eyes. "Sampson, what in heaven's name has got into you? This is your darling Evie, back from school." The dog continued to eye Evie warily. Elizabeth paused to allow Broderick to help her remove her pelisse, then turned back to look at her daughter, who was plucking off her bonnet. Elizabeth completely forgot about the dog's odd behavior at the sight of the mop of short red curls that sat atop her daughter's head. Elizabeth gasped. "Oh, Evie. What have you done to your hair?"

Chapter Three

"LADY GENEVIEVE HAS arrived, Your Grace," Winthrop announced from the doorway of Nathan's study.

A smile spread across Nathan's face, and he quickly tossed aside his quill. The ledgers and paperwork could wait. His daughter was home. The only daughter he would come to know, at least. He scrubbed a hand across his brow. He had no idea why Elizabeth had changed her mind and decided to send Evangeline to Miss Hathaway's. Shortly after his wife had left London all those years ago, he'd drawn up extensive paperwork with his solicitor detailing the exact plan for each child—where she would go to school and what she would receive for her dowry and marriage settlement. He'd also settled a considerable sum on Elizabeth in the event of his demise. His wife might have chosen to live separately from him, but he had ensured that all three of the females in his life were well taken care of. And damn it, they'd had an agreement. The least Elizabeth could have done was inform him of her decision to change her plans.

Gena was an imp and likely to turn Miss Hathaway's hair gray before she left school, but he'd missed his rambunctious daughter. He'd missed her a great deal.

"Has she gone up?" he asked Winthrop.

"Indeed she has, Your Grace."

Nathan pushed back his chair and made his way out of the study, through the corridor, and up the sweeping marble staircase at the front of the house. Minutes later, he knocked on his daughter's bedchamber door.

"Come in," came Gena's voice, more quiet than he'd ever heard it.

He turned the handle and pushed open the door. Gena stood still as a statue in the middle of the room, her trunks stacked near the bed. She gazed at her bedchamber as if she'd never seen it before. Instead of launching herself into Nathan's arms as she normally did, she stood silently assessing him. Were those tears in her eyes?

"Oh, Father," she said softly, folding her hands calmly in front of her. "It's so very nice to see you."

"'Father'? So formal?" Nathan grinned at her, but his throat tightened. Perhaps his little girl was growing up. She was becoming a young lady now.

"Papa . . . I mean." She returned his smile.

Yes, there were definitely tears in her voice. That was unlike her, too. He'd never known Gena to be sentimental. He walked over to her and crooked his finger to tip up her chin. He looked down into her blue eyes, which were swimming with tears. They were her mother's eyes—but he quickly shook *that* unhelpful thought away. "Are you all right, Gen?"

Her hair was still short, courtesy of her unfortunate tussle with some pine sap. It had upset the proper Miss Hathaway far more than it had upset him, despite the headmistress's insistence that it should cause him great concern. Gena's hair had grown a bit. That would make her grandmama happy. The wayward curls also seemed more tamed than usual.

"I'm quite well, Father, er, Papa." Her eyes searched his face.

"Why are you looking at me like that?" he asked.

"Like what?"

"So . . . seriously."

"I want to remember your face forever."

He laughed and shook his head. "Are you feeling well, Gen?"

She scrunched up her nose. "Yes. Why?"

He reached out and squeezed her shoulder. "I've missed you, Imp." He grinned at her, waiting for her to make some equally whimsical rejoinder. Instead, she just blinked at him evenly. *Imp.* He must remember to stop calling her that. Somehow, the nickname didn't seem appropriate any longer. The girl standing in front of him was no imp. She had transformed into a regal, poised young lady. His chest tightened again.

"Have you, Papa? Have you missed me?" she asked.

He furrowed his brow. "Of course I have. And your grandmama's missed you, too. I expect she'll be by for a visit any moment now."

"Grandmama?" Gena's eyes turned into wide blue pools. "Grandmama is coming to visit? Truly?"

Nathan laughed. "Yes, and I must say I've never seen you so eager to see your grandmama."

Gena snapped her mouth shut. "Oh, it's only that I haven't seen her in so long and—"

Nathan cocked his head to the side. "That's odd. She mentioned that she paid you a visit at school."

"Oh, yes. Of course. How could I have forgotten?" Gena bit her lip. "Papa? What are our plans for Christmastide?"

"I thought we'd spend it here in London, for a change."

"With Grandmama?" Gena asked.

"Your grandmama intends to spend Christmas in Surrey."

"Why doesn't Grandmama live at the dower house in Kent . . . with Mother?"

Nathan nearly choked. Had he been drinking something, he no doubt would have choked. A thousand thoughts raced through his mind, each one more disturbing than the last. In the end, he decided a vague answer was best. "The Hollingsworth holdings include many properties, Gena. Your grandmama prefers the house in Surrey."

"And Mother prefers Kent?"

"Something like that." He regarded his daughter down the length of his nose. "Now, may I ask you a question?"

"Yes, of course. Anything."

He crossed his arms over his chest. "Did you meet Evangeline at school?"

Chapter Four

ELIZABETH HAD NEVER had such a talkative shadow as Evie proved to be. Normally, her daughter preferred to rest quietly in her room in the afternoons, reading a book or practicing her embroidery, but the new Evie, fresh from boarding school, was filled with both questions and information. Perhaps going away to London had been good for the girl. Elizabeth feared she had kept her daughter pent up in the countryside for too long, where her only friends were animals and servants instead of other children.

As for animals, Sampson continued to eye Evie with a mixture of distrust and wariness. Even now, he lay on the rug, quietly growling at Evie, when normally he would have been cuddled up to her side. Elizabeth shook her head. Perhaps the dog was getting senile in his old age. He was nearly eleven, after all. She'd purchased him when Evie was a baby, an inadequate attempt to replace a sibling. Elizabeth sighed.

"Tell me all about it, dear. Tell me everything," she prompted as she set about pouring tea from the elaborate service Broderick had laid out for them in the drawing room on their third afternoon together.

Evie's eyes sparkled, and she clasped her hands together. "Well, we learned manners and comportment and we studied the peerage and we—"

The teapot clanked against the cup. "You studied the peerage?"

"Yes."

Elizabeth pressed her lips together and refocused her attention on not spilling the tea. She tried to keep her voice from shaking. "Did you learn about your father?"

"Just a bit," Evie replied. "Miss Hathaway says Father's title is one of the oldest in the country. Is that right, Mother?"

"Yes, that's right." Elizabeth set down the teapot and picked up the silver tongs to grasp a lump of sugar.

Evie's voice was bright and loud. "And that he is one of the most vocal voices in Parliament. Is that right, Mother?"

"I've always known him to be vocal," Elizabeth mumbled under her breath.

"Miss Hathaway seemed quite impressed by Father," Evie added.

A bit more mumbling. "I'm glad someone is, dear." She picked up the teapot again to pour the next cup.

Evie blinked at her. "Mama, why does Papa never visit?"

The teapot clattered to the silver tray, its porcelain

lid popping up to sit haphazardly on its side. "Wh-what? Whyever would you ask that?" Elizabeth replied. Not to mention the fact that her formal daughter had just referred to herself and her estranged husband as "Mama" and "Papa."

"I'm curious about him," Evie replied. "He's not hurt, is he? Unable to travel? Or excessively old?" Was it her imagination, or was Evie hiding a grin?

Elizabeth shook her head. "No. Of course not." In fact, he'd been excessively healthy, virile, and, ahem, good-looking the last time she'd seen him. She tugged at the collar of her butterscotch day dress. Was it hot in here suddenly?

Evie ran her fingers through her bright curls. "Then why does he not visit? He lives in London, does he not?"

Elizabeth righted the teapot's lid and dropped the requisite two lumps of sugar into Evie's cup. "Your father is quite a busy man." There. That was vague enough, wasn't it? She handed Evie her cup.

"Yes, I know. He's a duke, and Miss Hathaway says dukes are the highest ranking of all the peers, but surely even a duke has time to visit his wife and daughter."

Elizabeth concentrated on stirring the sugar in her own teacup. "It's not quite that simple, dear."

"Why not?" Evie blinked at her.

"Your father and I . . ." She pursed her lips. "It's difficult to define, dear."

"Why?" Bright blue eyes blinked inquiringly at her.

Elizabeth's breath caught in her throat. She'd always known this day would come. She and Evie had never discussed Evie's father, at least not the reasons why he didn't live with them, but certainly as the girl aged, she was bound to have questions about him. Elizabeth merely wished she had a bit more . . . time. She did the only thing she could think to do: change the subject.

"When did you cut your hair?"

Evie's smile was downright mischievous. It made Elizabeth laugh.

"Do you like it, Mother? Please say you do."

"I'm still getting used to it, but yes, I like it very much." Actually, it was a horror, but no matter what, her daughter was beautiful. She would certainly never criticize the girl the way her own mother had criticized her. Besides, perhaps all the girls in London were cutting their hair short. Elizabeth hadn't been to London for so long that she had no idea of the latest styles.

"I met a friend, Mother, a very dear friend. And, well, her hair was fashioned just so and—"

"Oh, Evie, tell me you didn't change your hair simply to look like another girl." Elizabeth glanced at the nearby bowl, which normally held her beloved sherbet lemons. It was empty again, for the third time since Evie had come home.

Evie giggled.

"What's so funny?" Elizabeth cocked her head to the side.

"Oh, nothing. It's just that . . . I already looked quite a bit like this other girl regardless of our hair fashions."

Chapter Five

London
Christmas Eve morning

GENA HAD STEADFASTLY denied meeting her twin at school. So vigorously, in fact, that Nathan had known immediately that she'd been lying. And he had every intention of revealing the truth.

"It's time for our annual Christmas Eve morning tradition," he announced soon after the breakfast plates had been cleared away.

The book Gena had been reading toppled to the wooden floor. "Christmas Eve morning tradition?" she echoed in a voice that shook unmistakably.

She was wearing a prim white day dress, and a wide white bow peeked out of her curls. Her white stockings were suspiciously unwrinkled, and her dress remained even more suspiciously unstained at the late hour of ten o'clock. That was it. He would get to the bottom of things.

Nathan stood and folded his hands behind his back. "Yes, our walk in the park. Don't you remember?"

Gena bent down to retrieve her book. "Oh, yes, of

course. Our walk in the park. I've been looking forward to it all year."

Nathan grinned. "Perfect. I'll get my coat and meet you in the foyer."

Ten minutes later, wearing his dark wool overcoat and black top hat, Nathan escorted his daughter in her blue wool overcoat and gray wool bonnet out of the front door of their town house, down the steps, across the street, and to the entrance of the park. The cold air was sharp, and the sky was heavy with an impending snowstorm. They walked at a brisk clip while Nathan watched his daughter from the corners of his eyes.

"Tell me about your friend you met at school," he asked after they'd gone a considerable distance in silence.

"School?" Her mouth formed an O, as if she was surprised by the question.

Just then a woman walking a small dog on a leash passed them. Gena squealed and ran over to the animal. "Oh, may I please pet him?" she asked the woman.

The lady nodded, and Gena stooped to pat the little creature on the head. Nathan couldn't stop his smile. Soon after, his daughter returned to him, and they finished their walk, during which Gena did an admirable job of changing the subject each time he attempted to ask her about school.

By the time they arrived back home, the snow had begun to fly in fat, wispy flakes whisked away by the wind. Mrs. Curtis had drinking chocolate waiting for Gena and a hot toddy waiting for Nathan. They sat in the library and sipped quietly. Gena had retrieved the book she'd been reading earlier and was busily studying it.

Nathan waited until his daughter set her cup on the table next to her.

"You know, I'm awfully glad to see you again, Evangeline."

The girl froze. The book tumbled, forgotten, into her lap. She slowly turned to face him, her eyes filling with tears. "How did you guess, Papa?"

"I've had my suspicions since you came home from school. But they were confirmed today."

Evangeline lifted her chin. Her words were soft. "May I hug you now?"

"Of course, my darling." Fighting back his own tears, he set down his glass, stood, and held open his arms. His daughter stood and quietly walked into his embrace. She sniffled against his shirtfront. "I've wanted a father my entire life."

He stroked her shining red hair. "You've always had one, my darling, I assure you."

Minutes later, they sat together on the sofa. "Tell me, truthfully, how did you know?" Evangeline asked.

"For one thing, unfortunately, your sister is a much better liar than you are. For another, I've yet to see Gena read with the attentiveness you have over the last two days. Thirdly, I've never seen Gena stop to play with a dog. And finally, and perhaps most telling, we don't *have* a Christmas Eve morning tradition of a walk in the park."

Evangeline smiled shyly. "I thought perhaps Gena had failed to mention it. We tried to teach each other everything we would need to know to pretend to be each other. I suppose we couldn't think of everything."

"On the contrary, you fooled me quite easily for a while. Though I did think you were a bit more formal than Gena."

"That's true. You know, when I met her at school, I thought her the veriest urchin."

Nathan laughed. "I can believe that. She's known to be a bit . . . unconventional."

"She's wonderful, Father, and so is Mother."

Nathan stood. How should he reply to that? He crossed back to his former seat to retrieve his toddy. He turned back to face his daughter. "Who else knows about this?" He took a sip.

"Only Mrs. Curtis."

Nathan nearly spat his drink. "Mrs. Curtis knows and didn't tell me?" He closed his eyes, shook his head, and sighed. "I suppose that shouldn't surprise me."

"Don't be angry with her, Father. She guessed right away. After she saw how tidy all of my clothes were. I made her swear she wouldn't tell you."

"Of course she listens to a twelve-year-old over her employer." Nathan rubbed one aching temple. "Does anyone else know?"

Evangeline bit her lip. "Grandmama," she admitted, glancing away.

Nathan bit the inside of his cheek to keep from cursing. "Your grandmama knows?"

Evangeline shrugged. "It's as you said, she visited us at school. Grandmama always knew."

Chapter Six

Kent
Christmas Eve morning

"EVIE, DARLING, WON'T you help Cook make the Christmas biscuits?" Elizabeth asked. She and Evie sat in the front drawing room. Elizabeth had just finished going over the dinner menu with Mrs. Henderson, the housekeeper.

Evie's eyes bugged from her skull, as if she was going to retch. "Christmas biscuits?"

"Yes, the shortbread ones you enjoy so much."

"Oh, Mother. I'm sure Cook can manage without me."

"You know she always appreciates your help." Theirs was an informal household for a duke's, but Elizabeth preferred it that way. She crossed over to the settee, where her daughter was practicing her embroidery. The embroidery looked as if a two-year-old had done it, so unlike Evie's usual precise stitches. Elizabeth hid her smile. She'd guessed yesterday that Gena was here with her and not Evie. If the massive consumption of sherbet lemons and the short hair hadn't convinced Elizabeth, Sampson's reaction would have. It was surprising, but, apparently, true. The two girls must have met at school and switched places. Ingenious, really.

Elizabeth couldn't be angry. In fact, she'd snuck into Gena's bedchamber last night and watched her beautiful daughter sleep. Tears had stung her eyes, and her heart had swelled as if it might burst, but now Elizabeth was having a bit of fun attempting to get her obviously stubborn daughter to admit her identity. "Are you feeling all right, dear?"

"Oh, yes, Mother," Gena replied. "It's just that . . . do you think Cook will be too disappointed if I don't help her with the biscuits this year?"

Elizabeth patted her daughter's shoulder. "I'm sure she'll make do, dear. Now about your embroidery . . ."

Gena tossed the embroidery to the side. "Mother, why do we never spend Christmastide with Father?"

Elizabeth strode to the sideboard and poured herself a glass of wine. It seemed wine was in order this particular holiday with the number of questions her daughter had been asking, and the frightening prospect that switching the girls back might very well involve contacting (and heaven forbid, *seeing*) Nathan.

"I told you, your father and I . . . We have an arrangement, and it's a bit . . . difficult to explain. We've agreed to spend holidays separately. It's better this way."

"But Grandmama comes to visit." Gena leaned forward and braced her palms on the sofa cushions. From his spot on the rug, Sampson barked at her.

Elizabeth took a swig of wine. She might need another glass if this questioning was to continue. "Yes, your grandmama enjoys seeing you and—"

"Does that mean Father doesn't enjoy seeing me?"

Elizabeth expelled her breath, pasted a smile on her face, and turned back to face her daughter, the wineglass balanced in her hand. "No, darling. Of course not. The decision your father and I made had nothing to do with you and Ev—"

Gena's face flushed and her eyes widened. "Who?"

Elizabeth swallowed and shook her head. "Your uncle Tony is coming, dear. He's sure to bring presents and make us laugh as usual."

Gena's face fell. She retrieved her embroidery wheel from the sofa cushion and plucked at it absently. "Yes, Mother."

Elizabeth bit her lip. She didn't want it to be awkward between them. She searched about for something to change the subject, lighten the mood. "I know what we should do. Let's go down to the stables and ride Morning Glory and Daffodil."

Gena's hand froze in mid-stitch. "The, er, horses?"

Elizabeth watched her daughter carefully. "Of course the horses, silly."

Gena shook her head so vigorously that her curls bounced. "Oh, no. It's so cold out, and snowing. I don't feel much like riding."

Elizabeth put both hands to her hips. "Now I *know* you're ill. I've never heard you say you don't feel like riding a day in your life. And when has the cold or snow ever stopped you from seeing the horses?" There, that should get her to confess.

Instead, Gena lifted her chin and bravely said, "Very well. Let's go."

AN HOUR LATER, after changing into her riding habit and making her way out the back of the house to the stables, Elizabeth was securely mounted sidesaddle on Morning Glory. Gena hadn't arrived yet. Apparently, the girl was more stubborn than she'd guessed. And quite unlike her sister. Elizabeth had never beaten Evie to the stables. Elizabeth looked out across the stretch of ground that separated the stables from the house, only to see her daughter trudging along through the snow in her sister's smart green riding habit. Gena appeared to be reluctantly making her way, kicking at the ground with her boots. Sampson, who had accompanied Elizabeth outside, barked and ran in an agitated circle.

"Apparently, Genevieve isn't the dog lover Evie is, eh, boy?" Elizabeth asked the dog, shaking her head and laughing.

When Gena finally arrived, one of the grooms escorted Daffodil over to her. Gena eyed the pretty little horse warily.

"Aren't you going to greet her?" Elizabeth asked, watching her daughter stare at her sister's beloved horse as if the animal had been a fearsome dragon.

"Of course." Gena swallowed and tentatively reached

out to pat the horse on her black nose. "Good, er, girl," she said in a shaky voice.

Elizabeth watched with growing amusement as Gena straightened her shoulders and allowed the groom to assist her in mounting the medium-sized chestnut bay. The horse lurched to the side, and Gena squealed.

"Evangeline Hollister, my goodness," Elizabeth said, clutching at her riding crop and pressing her hat atop her head. Thankfully, she was facing away, so Gena couldn't see her grin.

After three more awkward attempts, Gena landed on the back of her mount and was able to sit upright.

"Ready?" Elizabeth asked, trying to keep the humor and growing bit of alarm from her voice.

When Gena was finally settled, she said, "I . . . I'm fine, Mother. Let's go." She tentatively kicked at the horse's flanks with her boot heels and shrieked as they took off out of the stable into the snow, Sampson barking at them.

Following her daughter, Elizabeth called out with a laugh, "I swear, if I didn't know any better, Evie, I'd say it's as if you were afraid of horses."

Chapter Seven

Later on Christmas Eve

THE SNOW WAS falling in huge, fluffy flakes, accumulating faster than Nathan had ever seen it. He thumped on the door that separated himself from the coachman. "Faster, man, faster," he yelled, hoping the poor servant could hear him over the howling wind. "We must get there before the storm makes travel impossible." He turned back to stare at his twelve-year-old daughter. The wrong twelve-year-old daughter. For Gena was, at present, in Kent with . . . Elizabeth.

Evie had informed him that they'd intended to continue the ruse until the end of the holiday in order that each of them might be able to spend time with the opposite parent. And while he didn't blame his daughters for being curious about the two of them, he also couldn't in good conscience allow Elizabeth to go on thinking that she had Evie. Nathan hadn't wasted time with a letter. That would only serve to protract the thing. No, he needed to switch them back as soon as possible. He'd ordered the coach put to and Evie's bags packed, and they had set off for Kent immediately.

Nathan watched Evie sitting across from him. She was as poised and beautiful as her mother. She was as lovely and intelligent as her sister, though obviously less cunning, based on the alacrity with which she'd admitted her transgression, not to mention the guilt she seemed to carry over it. Gena would have had no such guilt or compunction. In fact, he was quite sure Gena hadn't confessed, which was why he feared Elizabeth didn't know she had the wrong girl. Evangeline had emphatically insisted that no one else knew about their ruse, but Nathan had his doubts.

He cleared his throat, not entirely sure what to say to his daughter. "I suppose you were forced to cut your hair?" he ventured.

Evangeline blinked at him with her huge blue eyes, which somehow reminded him even more of Elizabeth's than Gena's did. Evie was a quiet little thing, quiet and contemplative, the exact opposite of her twin.

"Yes, we thought it would be best," she said wistfully, running a small, pale hand through the short locks. "Mother won't be pleased."

"Well, there's a surprise," he mumbled under his breath.

"What was that?" Evie asked.

"Nothing. I've just never known your mother to be pleased about much."

Evangeline frowned. "Mother does seem sad. Not daily, but overall. There's something very melancholy about her at times. But she laughs at Uncle Tony's jests, and she adores sherbet lemons, and she is ever so pleased to get a new vial of plumeria perfume each Christmas. She never says no to a glass of wine, and she loves to sing, and she even dances when she thinks no one is looking."

Nathan stared hard at his daughter. It was as if the words she'd just spoken had been in a foreign tongue. "Your *mother* dances when no one is looking?" he repeated dumbly. Surely they were not speaking of the same woman. Why, the Elizabeth he remembered was frightened of her own shadow and said preposterous things like "Wine is the devil's work."

"Oh, yes, quite often," Evangeline replied, nodding vigorously.

His mother-in-law quickly came to mind. "What does your grandmother think of your mother singing and drinking wine?" He couldn't help but ask. Nathan suspected that godly woman was the reason Elizabeth had been born without a fun-loving bone in her entire body.

Evangeline appeared to contemplate the matter quietly for a moment. Finally, she said, "I don't think she knows. We only see Grandmother once a year. On her birthday."

Nathan's brows shot up. Another surprise. He'd have thought the controlling woman would have moved into the manor house by now and would be hosting church services in the parlors.

"What do you do to celebrate your grandmother's birthday?"

Evie leaned back against the sapphire velvet seat and sighed. "She usually makes us attend a church service with her."

"I see." Now *that* sounded like the mother-in-law he recalled.

"Which Mother says we must suffer through for her sake."

Suffer through? Nathan frowned. The Elizabeth he knew would never use *suffer* and *church* in the same sentence. Why, she'd reveled in such "suffering."

"Oh, it's not that Mother is sacrilegious," Evangeline hastened to add.

"She's not?"

"No. It's just that, well, Grandmother is a bit fervent with regard to the rules, and Mother says she's stifling."

"Stifling?" This time Nathan sat back against the velvet seat and rubbed a hand over his forehead.

Was it possible that Elizabeth was no longer a straight-laced, tedious zealot who followed her mother's every command? The thought was too overwhelming to contemplate.

Evangeline folded her hands in her lap. "I understand why you're angry, Father, and why you must return me to Mother and take Gena home, but I cannot say I regret it, because I've found it ever so lovely to finally meet you. Mother often says you're wonderful, but I—I just wanted to see for myself."

Nathan could have been knocked over with a pin. "Your mother says *I'm* wonderful? Often?" He pointed at himself, nonplussed.

Evangeline nodded. "Oh, yes. She's forever telling me how handsome and intelligent and kind and generous you are."

If the girl sitting across from him hadn't looked exactly like his Gena, he'd have been convinced her mother must have been someone other than his wife.

"But what I don't understand is, why didn't Mother ever tell me about Gena? That is to say, Gena knew all about me."

"I cannot answer that, but I assume your mother didn't want you to be sad that you and Gena never saw each other. I always told Gena that someday, you two would meet. I just never imagined it would be this . . . unexpected."

"But you and Mother both agreed to never see the other daughter?"

"Evangeline, it's not that I don't—" Nathan rubbed a hand across his face. "It's not that you're not welcome with me or that Gena is not welcome with your mother. We love you both, of course, but, you see, we had an agreement and—"

"I know, Father. Gena explained it to me. She told me that Grandmama—that is, your mother—told her that you and Mother decided long ago that you weren't suited and therefore agreed to live apart and raise us separately."

"Precisely." Nathan nodded. He desperately wanted to change the subject. Something else she'd said had niggled at him. "Tell me, Evangeline. Who is Uncle Tony? To my knowledge, your mother doesn't have a brother, and neither do I."

"Oh, Uncle Tony isn't *really* my uncle. He's Mother's dear friend who visits us and brings us presents and tells the *most* clever jokes."

Nathan blinked and sucked in his breath. Damn it all to hell. Was his wife cuckolding him in the country?

Chapter Eight

ELIZABETH STARED OUT the window at the copious amounts of snow falling from the ever-darkening sky. "Evie, dear, won't you play the pianoforte? My nerves are quite on edge. If this snow doesn't let up, Uncle Tony won't make it to spend Christmastide with us."

Gena blinked. "Uncle Tony? Oh, yes, yes. Uncle Tony."

Elizabeth considered her choices. She was beginning to understand just how stubborn Gena could be. After downing another half a bowl of sherbet lemons and insisting that Sampson must be losing his sight in his old age, the girl had steadfastly refused to admit to her deception. She'd suffered through an entirely awkward horseback ride during which Elizabeth had been constantly in fear of the poor girl flying from the sidesaddle. Perhaps Gena would finally be forced to admit defeat if she wasn't as adept at playing the pianoforte as Evie was.

Five minutes later, Elizabeth realized her daughter

hadn't moved toward the instrument that sat across the room. "Evie, won't you play something for me?"

"Oh, um, Mother, I . . . I find my fingers are too cold to play at present."

Elizabeth lifted a brow. "Your fingers are too cold?" She glanced at the fireplace behind the instrument. "I daresay it's warmer over there than it is sitting here on the sofa."

Gena bit her lip and nodded. "Very well." She stood slowly, made a grand show of smoothing her skirts, and finally picked her way over to the pianoforte, approaching as if it had been a wild beast that might suddenly attack her. She finally took a seat on the bench in front of it and made an even grander show of *arranging* her skirts.

"Go ahead, Evie," Elizabeth prompted, shaking her head at the girl's obvious attempt at stalling.

Gena took a deep breath. She fluttered her fingers atop the ivory keys. Then she began to play, and the song that came out of the large instrument was a bawdy number that Elizabeth hadn't heard in years, and then only because she'd caught one of the servants singing it when he'd been in his cups.

The embroidery Elizabeth had been working on fell in a lump to her lap. "Evangeline! Where on earth did you learn that song?"

The music came to an abrupt halt, and Gena winced at her mother guiltily across the wide expanse of the instrument. "School," she offered with a shrug.

Elizabeth shook her head. "I cannot believe an establishment as renowned as Miss Hathaway's School for

Young Ladies allowed you to hear *that*." Good heavens, what was Nathan teaching the girl?

Gena plucked at her collar. "I, er, learned it from one of the girls there."

Elizabeth gave her a stern stare. "Remember, bad habits are adopted quickly."

"Yes, Mother." Gena slid off the bench and skipped back over to her seat. "Perhaps I'll just take a break from playing the pianoforte this afternoon."

"Perhaps that's best." Elizabeth returned her attention to her embroidery. Apparently, she'd be forced to find another way to get Gena to admit her identity. She grinned to herself. It would hardly be sporting to come right out and tell her she knew. Besides, the longer Elizabeth played along, the longer she could ignore the fact that Nathan would have to be summoned eventually.

Several moments of silence passed before Gena said, "Mother, why did you and Father decide to live apart?"

Elizabeth drew a deep breath. Very well. Whether Gena or Evie, the girl deserved to know the truth. "We didn't suit."

"But why? Why didn't you suit?"

Elizabeth pulled the pin through her embroidery. "Your father is quite rigid, dear, and—"

"Oh, no! He's ever so accommodating and kind and—"

Elizabeth cocked her head to the side and stared at the girl as if she'd lost her mind. "Pardon?"

Gena glanced down at her hands. She fidgeted with her fingers. "I mean, I guess that he is. I should *hope* that he is. Did you ever love him, Mother?"

Elizabeth glanced up and stared, unseeing, into the fireplace across the room. Her daughter deserved to know the truth there, too. "I did. Very, very much."

"How did you know it was love?" Gena asked in a dreamy voice, clasping her hands together in that endearing way of hers.

Elizabeth stared into the flickering flames, memories colliding in her brain. "Your father had a party. A lovely, large party—a ball, really—at his town house in London."

Gena's eyes were wide. "*Father* had a party?"

Elizabeth laughed. "Yes, does that surprise you?"

"A little," her daughter replied.

"Be that as it may, he had a party and it was absolutely beautiful. It was a Midsummer Eve ball, and there were garlands and wreaths and flowers and twinkling candles. He'd turned his ballroom into a garden on a summer night. It was the most beautiful thing I'd ever seen."

Gena sighed. "It sounds lovely, Mother."

"Your father was courting me, but I had some other suitors."

Gena scowled. "You did?"

"A few," Elizabeth replied with a wink.

Gena winked back at her.

"When I arrived at his party, your father was so debonair. He was wearing black evening attire and a snowy white cravat, and well, he's exceedingly handsome."

"Yes, he is. Isn't he?" Gena cleared her throat. "I mean, I'm sure he is."

"He asked me to dance, and it was as if we were the only two people in the entire room. It smelled like flowers, and the candles twinkled like stars in the sky. And then . . ."

Gena sat forward. "Then what?"

"He took me out on the balcony and . . . oh, I shouldn't tell you."

Gena leaned forward even farther. "What? You must tell me."

Elizabeth was surprised to discover her belly filled with butterflies. "He kissed me."

Gena nearly toppled off the settee. Her grin was irrepressible. "That's the most romantic thing I ever heard."

"I should hope so, dear. You are only twelve." Elizabeth smiled at her daughter.

"Then what happened?" Gena prompted.

Elizabeth sighed and laid her head to the side to rest on one shoulder. "And then he asked me to marry him, and I said yes."

Gena pressed her hands to both cheeks. "Oh, Mother, how could you say you don't suit?"

Elizabeth lifted her head again and shook it. Her eyes refocused on her embroidery, her mind refocusing on the present, not the past. "It doesn't matter, dear. When we met, it was lovely, but suffice it to say that we didn't make each other happy. There's more to a marriage than finding a rich, handsome nobleman."

The scowl returned to Gena's sweet face. "But you haven't seen him in years. How do you know you wouldn't make each other happy now?"

Elizabeth stared at Gena. When had her daughters become old enough and wise enough to ask her a probing question that she couldn't answer? The truth was Elizabeth hadn't thought about such a possibility before. Was it conceivable that Nathan Hollister had changed? She rubbed her fingers against her temples. No matter. There was no use in even contemplating it. She would never have the opportunity to find out.

A knock sounded upon the door, and Broderick walked in. "Your Grace, a coach is approaching."

Elizabeth smiled. "Oh, thank heavens, Tony's here. If he'd been any later, I daresay he wouldn't have made it." She stood and hurried toward the door. "Come with me to greet Uncle Tony, Evie. He's been so looking forward to seeing you."

Elizabeth and Gena made their way to the foyer. When the carriage pulled up to the front of the house and the door opened, Elizabeth's face fell. For it wasn't the grand coach of the Earl of Atwater that sat like a fat little black duck in a sea of white in the front drive. It was an even grander coach that had arrived, one with the crest of the Duke of Hollingsworth.

The blood drained from Elizabeth's face. Her hand flew to her throat. "Your father," she gasped.

"My father?" her daughter gasped even louder from behind her.

Chapter Nine

As soon as the coachman opened the door, Nathan secured his hat, adjusted his overcoat, and bounded out into the snowy drive. He turned back to the vehicle to look at Evie. She was preparing to follow him. "Wait here just a moment, won't you, sweetheart?"

She blinked at him. "Why, Father?"

He pressed his hat down farther. "Because if I know Gena, she didn't confess as easily as you did, and your mother may very well still believe she's got you in there."

Evie visibly paled but nodded. "You're right. Gena won't be happy either when she learns that I confessed."

"She'll manage." Nathan smiled and pulled the furs closer to her chin. "I'll just be a moment, and then I'll send for you."

When the door to the great hall opened, the butler looked as if he'd seen a ghost. "Your . . . Your Grace?" Nathan handed him his coat and hat and stepped into the

grand foyer of his childhood home. The place was familiar, of course, but it seemed fresher now, brighter, and it
smelled like . . . sherbet lemons.

"I must speak to your mistress immediately," he said
to the butler.

"I'm here," came a quiet yet firm female voice.

Nathan swiveled to see her. Elizabeth stood a few
paces away near the window, partially obscured by a
large potted palm. He scanned the foyer. She was alone.
Gena wasn't with her. His gaze returned to Elizabeth. At
least he *thought* she was Elizabeth, but the woman who
faced him now was no thin, eighteen-year-old girl with
a haunted, unhappy look in her eye. Instead, this woman
was a fully grown beauty with plump cheeks, full hips,
red lips, and glossy blond hair piled high atop her head.
She was wearing a pretty blue gown that brought out the
color in her cornflower eyes. The look in them was a bit
wary, but there was humor there, too. Right then, he was
convinced. She seemed like a woman who might secretly
break into dance, Nathan thought with a wry smile.

He shook his head. He'd been struck dumb at the
sight of her. He briefly wondered what she thought of
how *his* appearance had changed in the last dozen years.
"Elizabeth . . . I—"

Her smooth forehead wrinkled into a frown. "I must
say it's not a complete surprise to see you."

He cocked his head to the side, not entirely sure what
to make of her statement. "May I speak with you privately
for a moment?"

Elizabeth blushed a gorgeous peach color. She glanced

at the butler. She'd obviously forgotten he was standing there. "Of course," she replied. "Come with me."

Nathan followed her into the nearest drawing room, watching the gentle sway of her hips. Years ago, when they'd visited this place together, she'd seemed so timid in this house, like a mouse trapped in an oversized box, but now, he noted the way she gestured to Broderick to hang up Nathan's coat and how easily she glided across the parquet floor with him in her wake. She was indeed the mistress of the house now.

When they entered the drawing room, Nathan realized that her demeanor wasn't the only change. He glanced around. The room had been a deep burgundy color the last time he was here. But Elizabeth had redecorated. Now it was styled in bright blues and white, a much more uplifting space, and one that also smelled like sherbet lemons, he noted with a smile. Gena's favorite, too.

He gestured to the sofa and allowed Elizabeth to take a seat first.

"Where is Evangeline?" he asked, sitting across from Elizabeth in a nearby chair.

Elizabeth eyed him cautiously. "Evangeline?" she repeatedly slowly. "She was directly behind me when your coach pulled up the drive, but she said she'd forgotten something in her room. I suspect she was a bit reluctant to see you. I told her it was your coach. You can't blame the girl. Your visit is quite . . . unexpected, after all."

"I'm sure she was reluctant to see me," he mumbled.

Elizabeth cupped a hand behind her ear. "What was that?"

Nathan shook his head. "Nothing."

Elizabeth didn't meet his eyes. "Is *Genevieve* well?"

"She's . . . I believe she is well."

Elizabeth glanced up at him from beneath impossibly long, dark lashes. "Then . . . why have you come?"

"I will get straight to the point." Nathan took a deep breath. "It seems our girls have met. Met and tricked us, that is. The young lady you have here is Gena. Evie is waiting in my coach."

A gasp from behind the door to the drawing room made them both turn their heads a moment before they heard the sound of footsteps rushing in the opposite direction.

"Gena!" Nathan stood to follow her, but Elizabeth reached up and put a hand on his arm.

"Let her go."

"That was Genevieve," he said.

Elizabeth quickly pulled her hand away as if it had been burned. "I know that. I've known for two days, but what I truly want to know is . . . how?"

Nathan paced toward the windows. "Gena has been at Miss Hathaway's School for Young Ladies for a year now. I didn't know you intended to enroll Evangeline."

Elizabeth's brow furrowed. "But your mother said—"

Nathan turned sharply to face her. "My mother? What did she have to do with it?"

"She told me that Evie should matriculate at Miss Hathaway's. She said it was her birthright."

Nathan clenched his jaw. "I had no idea you and my mother were in contact."

"She visits regularly. She hasn't told you, in all these years?"

"No." He shook his head. "So you knew the girls would meet?"

"No, of course not. Your mother said that you'd decided to send Gena elsewhere. I never would have sent Evie if I'd thought they'd find each other. I didn't expect them to meet until their come-out." Elizabeth pressed a hand to her forehead. "Oh, Nathan. I think we've been duped by someone other than the children."

Nathan rubbed the back of his neck. "I think you're right."

Elizabeth made her way toward the door. "I suppose we should fetch Evie from the coach."

Nathan slid his hands into his pockets. "No need. If I know Gena, she's gone straight there to gather her partner."

A small knock sounded at the door just then.

"Come in," Elizabeth called.

The door opened and the twins, mirror images of each other, came walking in, arm in arm.

"Oh, Gena." Elizabeth opened her arms, and her daughter ran to her and hugged her close. She knew it was Gena only because she recognized the clothing she'd been wearing earlier. Sampson jumped up from his spot on the rug and ran to Evie, wagging his tail.

Evie bent down and hugged the dog. "Sampson," she murmured into his fur. She glanced up warily at her mother. "Are you very angry, Mother?"

"No. How could I be? I've been waiting for nearly

twelve years to see you together again. You are perfect, my darling," she said to Gena, tears pooling in her eyes. She reached out her other arm for Evie. "Come here, Evie. I've missed you."

Evie walked into her mother's embrace. "I'm so glad you aren't angry, Mother."

"Let me look at you both." Elizabeth glanced back and forth between the two. "It is so wonderful to see you together. And it's obvious how you had us fooled. With your hair this way, you look exactly alike." Tears streamed down her face. Nathan pulled a handkerchief from his pocket. Elizabeth let go of her daughters long enough to take it and wipe away her tears.

Gena stepped back and threaded her arm through Evie's again. "Father, Mother," Gena said in her characteristic strong voice, "my sister and I would like to spend the Christmastide holiday together."

"That's impossible," Nathan said. "The storm is quite bad. We must get back on the road immediately if we're to have any hope of making it home at all."

A knock at the door interrupted them. Broderick walked in. "Her Grace, the Dowager Duchess of Hollingsworth," he announced.

Nathan's brows snapped together. "Mother?"

The dowager strode in with her cane in one hand and her fur muff on the other. She shook the snow from her muff, marched over to her son, and waited for him to bend down and kiss her cheek. "I'm afraid leaving is impossible, Hollingsworth. I just arrived, and the road is completely covered by snow. It looks as if we'll all be spending the holiday together, here." A foxlike grin spread across her face.

"Oh dear," Elizabeth uttered. She slid into the nearest chair and let her forehead rest on her palm.

"Perfect. What else could go wrong?" Nathan asked.

A footman walked through the door and whispered a few words to the butler, who promptly intoned, "Your Graces, may I announce the arrival of Lord Anthony Gillette, the Earl of Atwater?"

Evie beamed. "Uncle Tony!"

Chapter Ten

Elizabeth placed a shaking hand on the arm of the chair. Dear God, Tony. Tony had been a steadfast friend to her for many years, and that was all he was to her. But she understood how it might look to Nathan and his mother to have the Earl of Atwater arriving for Christmastide. Tony lived at a neighboring estate and had paid a call on Elizabeth once or twice at the very beginning of her time here. Slowly, over the years, he'd come around more often, and Elizabeth had eventually told him about the problems in her marriage and the reason why her husband and her other daughter never came to visit. Tony was often gone to London, and when he returned, he kept Elizabeth abreast of some of her husband's doings, though usually she didn't want to hear much. Apparently, over the years, Nathan had escorted a few widows to the theater. He'd escorted a few others to the opera. Eventually, Elizabeth had asked Tony not to tell her any more.

But Tony was her closest friend here in the country, and Tony adored Evie and had been nothing but gentlemanly and honorable to both of them. He did not deserve the scene he was about to encounter.

"I nearly didn't make it, Lizzie." She heard his voice before she saw him come round the corner. "What with this weather—"

Tony, holding large gifts under each of his arms, stopped as soon as he spied the occupants of the room.

Nathan had narrowed his eyes when Tony had said "Lizzie," and Elizabeth winced. She and Tony had long ago agreed to be less formal and call each other by their given names. But it had to seem positively scandalous to Nathan and his mother.

Elizabeth jumped up from her seat and quickly crossed the fine rug to greet her friend. "Merry Christmas, Lord Atwater," she said in an overly bright voice. "Won't you join us?"

Tony glanced around the room, obviously sizing up the situation quickly. His ready smile never left his face. "Why, I'd no idea that Lady Genevieve would be here. If I'd known, I'd have brought gifts for everyone."

"Oh, no need to worry on that score," Elizabeth said in an unstable voice. She couldn't look at Nathan or his mother. It was all too awkward. She took the gifts from Tony and set them on a nearby table.

Tony turned to the other occupants of the room. "Hollingsworth, good to see you." He held out his hand, and Nathan stood and shook it. "It's been a while. I usually see you only in London."

"Right," Nathan replied in a voice that sounded as if it had been etched from stone.

"Your Grace," Tony said next, bowing to the dowager.

"Lord Atwater," the dowager intoned icily with barely a regal inclination of her head.

"It's good to see you, Uncle Tony," Evie said from her perch on the sofa next to her sister. "Thank you for the Christmastide gift."

Elizabeth winced again. From the disgruntled look on Nathan's face, he didn't appreciate Evie referring to Tony as her uncle.

"Don't mention it, dar—" Tony cleared his throat. "Don't mention it, Evie. I'm pleased to see you back from school. Your hair looks quite beautiful."

Evie beamed at him and blushed. "Thank you. This is my sister, Lady Genevieve Hollister." Evie flourished a small hand toward Genevieve.

"I could only guess she was your sister," Tony said with a small smile tugging at his lips. "There *is* a bit of a resemblance, is there not?"

Gena eyed Tony warily until her father prompted her with an obvious warning glare.

"It's nice to meet you, Lord Atwater," she said, but she didn't sound a bit happy about it.

"Please come and sit," Elizabeth said to her friend. Her eyes begged Tony to stay. He nodded nearly imperceptibly. He understood. Thank heavens. He could tell she was under duress and needed him. Elizabeth mentally sighed. She could always count on Tony. Of course, the man probably had little choice. If what the dowager said about the weather was true, he couldn't leave if he wanted to. Actually, was it true? At any rate, discussing the weather seemed the safest option at present.

"How are the roads, my lord?" Elizabeth asked as Tony took a seat to her right.

"Quite impassable, I'm sorry to say. If I'd known how dreadful they were, I wouldn't have risked it."

"A pity," the dowager remarked, her patrician nostrils flaring slightly.

Tony glanced at the older woman. "Yes, well, I left Mother at home to be safe."

"Oh, *that's* why you left your mother at home," Nathan drawled.

"Yes, er, quite," Tony replied, tossing Elizabeth a private what-exactly-is-going-on-here look.

Elizabeth counted three to steady her nerves. There was no way to make the situation less awkward, so she did what any self-respecting hostess would do. She rang for tea.

"So," Tony said, settling into his chair, his legendary smile returning to his face. "Tell me how you all decided to . . . spend Christmastide together."

"It was our fault, Uncle Tony," Evie admitted quietly. "I met Gena at school, and we decided . . . well, I decided I wanted to meet Father, and Gena wanted to meet Mother. So we . . . switched."

Tony coughed. He beat his chest with one fist. "You switched?"

"Yes," Gena said, apparently taking to the subject. "I convinced Evie to cut her hair because of the pine sap, and we taught each other everything we needed to know. Except how to play the pianoforte properly," she added with an unrepentant grin.

Elizabeth shook her head at her daughter. "Pine sap? And I shudder to ask where you learned that song you played."

"That was the only song I knew," Gena admitted with a shameless giggle.

"I think Father knew it wasn't me the moment I didn't run into his arms and hug him," Evie said.

Tony whistled. "So, you both were discovered and—"

"And I brought Evie back home immediately," Nathan replied tightly. "However, now the roads are impassable and we are stu—"

"We are planning a *family* Christmastide celebration," the dowager interjected, stamping her cane on the rug.

Elizabeth closed her eyes. There was no way Tony hadn't heard the emphasis the older woman had placed on the word *family*.

As BRODERICK SERVED tea, Elizabeth surreptitiously glanced at Nathan. She tried to guess his mood. Was he angry? Resigned? Bored? She couldn't tell. He'd always been maddeningly unreadable. That, apparently, hadn't changed. However, one thing had. The man looked better with age, devil take him. She'd always found him handsome. In fact, she'd been quite agog at his good looks when she'd first met him at seventeen. Dark, slightly curly hair, piercing sapphire eyes. He was tall and broad-shouldered and had the smallest crook in his nose that she'd dreamt of kissing. Of course, after their wedding ceremony and first year of marriage, she'd decided that dreams and reality were two *very* different things. She and he had been at odds from the moment they'd spoken their vows. Nathan had been flippant about her beliefs and had constantly quarreled with her mother, while she herself had never been good enough or happy enough for him.

The fighting had only intensified after the babies were born, and when the girls were three months old, Elizabeth had left London for the country. Nathan had demanded she return the children, and Elizabeth had steadfastly refused. Finally, he'd written her a proposal. He wasn't about to give up both of his children, but he could take Genevieve back to London and Elizabeth would keep Evangeline in the country. Elizabeth had refused the proposal at first. She couldn't give up one of her babies. She just couldn't. But as the weeks had passed and their arguments hadn't diminished, she'd realized that Nathan's offer was the best for all of them. It was the only way she could be rid of him nearly entirely without losing both of her daughters. And so Nathan had hired a wet nurse and taken baby Gena with him to London.

Elizabeth had cried so much that first year that she'd thought she could never cry again. But she'd made a life for herself here in Kent. She brought food and clothing to the villagers and tenants. She became friends with Tony and his mother. She taught her daughter how to ride, and they had a large menagerie of animals on the estate that

Evie grew up playing with. They were content here, if not happy. Oh, why oh why did the dowager have to go and ruin it all by tricking her into sending Evie to that blasted school?

Broderick arrived with the tea service just then, jolting Elizabeth from her thoughts just as the dowager said, "So, Lord Atwater, when are you leaving?"

Chapter Eleven

NATHAN STROLLED THROUGH the library with his hands in his pockets. He let out a deep breath. God's teeth, that had been awkward in there earlier with Atwater. There was really no excuse for his mother's rude behavior, but Atwater had handled it with humor to spare. "If you'll point me to some snowshoes, I can be off immediately if you wish," the earl had responded with a grin to the dowager's rude question. And while his mother had looked as if she might just be tempted to go fetch him the snowshoes herself, Elizabeth and Evie had both immediately chimed in and said they wouldn't hear of such a thing and he should stay until the roads were clear.

Tea had been served, and immediately after, Nathan had quickly made an excuse of needing a bit of exercise to get out of that room. Elizabeth had also excused herself to see to the sleeping arrangements, and his mother had appropriated both girls to show her the Christmastide garland in the dining room. That had left Tony Gillette alone in the drawing room, sipping his tea and probably wondering what the hell had happened. Nathan couldn't help but feel a bit sorry for the earl. He'd always liked Tony. They'd been friends when they were boys. But Nathan could easily *dis*like him if he thought the earl was sleeping with his wife. If Nathan found out *that* was true, he would knock the earl's teeth down his throat, childhood friend or not.

Nathan made his way out of the library and into the large corridor that housed the portraits of all his ancestors. He hadn't seen these paintings in so long. It was like coming . . . home. On more than one occasion over the years, he'd wished he hadn't promised Elizabeth he'd never bother her here. He'd wanted to come, to visit, to see the home where he'd grown up, to ride across the fields he'd ridden across as a boy, to see Evangeline. Every time he'd begun to write Elizabeth a letter telling her that he intended to pay a visit, he'd ripped it up and tossed the bits in the fireplace. He'd been too damn stubborn to come back, to admit he'd banished himself from a place he missed. Of course, he hadn't particularly wanted to see Elizabeth, but he had been curious about her over the years. His mother hadn't admitted she was visiting her regularly. She'd only told him from time to time that she'd heard a bit of gossip that Evie and Elizabeth were healthy and doing well, and as long as Nathan continued to hear that, there had seemed no need to disturb them and their life here. A life that obviously included Tony Gillette.

Nathan rubbed the back of his neck. Blast it. If Elizabeth had gone and fallen in love with his neighbor, Nathan had only himself to blame. Elizabeth was a beautiful woman. Beautiful and poised and clearly changed from the girl she'd been twelve years ago. When they'd met, he'd been dazzled by her beauty, obvious wit, and charm. But as soon as the marriage had taken place, and his mother-in-law had begun to wheedle her way into their marriage, everything had changed. Why had Nathan never considered the possibility that she had changed again over the years? It had been foolish of him. When Tony had walked into the drawing room, she'd looked nothing short of horrified. That proved she loved him, didn't it? Or at least had an inappropriate relationship with him? If they were merely friends, surely she wouldn't have been so aghast by his presence in front of her husband.

Yet Nathan knew he had no right to be jealous. Yes, they were husband and wife, but he'd made it clear when they'd decided to live apart that Elizabeth was free to do what she liked as long as she didn't give birth to a bastard and shame him. That hadn't happened, of course, but it didn't mean she wasn't in love with Tony. Why did her being in love with Tony seem so much worse than her going to *bed* with Tony? Nathan hadn't exactly been celibate all these years himself. He'd had a good time with the odd widow upon occasion, but none of them had held his interest for longer than a few weeks, and he had certainly been discreet.

Nathan moved into the music room. Evie apparently

spent a great deal of her time here. She'd told him as much during their journey today. The room had also been redecorated. It was bright and white, a happy place, much different from the dark colors of his mother's reign in this house. And she had the nerve to call his study dingy? In fact, now that he'd had a chance to look around, Nathan realized that the entire main floor had been redecorated, and every room for the better. The changes were obviously Elizabeth's doing. He never would have thought the unhappy girl he'd married so many years ago would have made this house into more of a home than it had ever been.

He glanced out the window of the music room and spied Gena and Evie playing together in the snow. Apparently, they'd finished their tour of the dining room with their grandmama. They were bundled up in their overcoats. Both wore scarves and mittens and were chasing each other around in large circles, laughing and shrieking with delight. A lump formed in Nathan's throat. His daughters, playing together. It was the first time he'd ever seen it. They'd been denied that privilege for twelve years of their lives. Had he failed them? By God, he'd do right by them now.

Chapter Twelve

ELIZABETH HAD HURRIED from the awkwardness in the drawing room to the kitchens to find the housekeeper. "Please see that rooms are made up for Lady Genevieve, His Grace, and the dowager."

"What about Lord Atwater, Your Grace?" Mrs. Henderson asked.

"Oh, yes, Lord Atwater, too." She'd nearly forgotten that Tony would be forced to stay overnight due to the weather. He normally went home at the end of the day when he visited.

"Your Grace, should I make up His Grace's bedchamber then?" the housekeeper asked, not meeting her eyes.

Elizabeth nodded hesitantly. "Yes, I think that's best, Mrs. Henderson." But her voice shook, too. Nathan's bedchamber was adjacent to her own and had an adjoining door. She couldn't very well justify not having the duke stay in his own bedchamber, and she found it far too awkward to ask the man if he preferred to stay in another room. Besides, there was no need to involve the servants in her little familial drama. No doubt they all gossiped about the fact that the lord of the manor hadn't been home in over a decade. No need to add to the talk.

There was no help for it. Elizabeth would have to go up there later, to a room she hadn't entered in over twelve years, and ensure it was acceptable. The hostess in her demanded it. Where was the Christmastide wine?

SHE KNEW SHE would find Tony in the conservatory. It was his favorite area of the house. He was partial to plants and growing things.

"I love it in here," he said, turning to face her. She noted that he had a glass of brandy in his hand. "Especially in winter, when everything is dead outside."

"It's lovely, isn't it?" She sighed, rubbing her fingers across the leaves of a potted palm.

"Where are the children?"

"They asked if they could play in the snow. I said yes. I want them to spend as much time together as they can before—" She glanced away and folded her arms over her chest, her lungs so tight she couldn't breathe.

"Before Hollingsworth takes Gena back?" Tony asked softly.

Elizabeth nodded. She lifted her chin toward Tony's glass. "Drinking early?"

He arched a brow. "I'm surprised you aren't drinking yet, what with the return of the prodigal duke."

Elizabeth slumped onto a nearby white ironwork bench and stared down at her slippers. "I can't say I haven't been wishing for wine. Oh, Tony, what am I going to do? This whole situation was a complete surprise. I mean, I realized the girls had switched, but I didn't expect *him* to just arrive here without so much as a note. I thought I'd have more time to prepare."

"So I gathered." Tony held his glass down in front of her face. "Care for a sip?"

Elizabeth began to wave it away, but then she thought better of it, took it, and downed a good fourth of the contents, coughing as the liquid burned her throat. "Thank you. I believe I needed that," she said once her coughing ceased.

"I don't doubt it," he said with a laugh, taking back his glass.

She took a deep breath. "I'm sorry. For what happened in the drawing room earlier."

"No need to apologize, Lizzie. It's not as if you could have warned me."

"Believe me, if I could have got a note to you, I would have. They'd only just arrived and—oh, Tony, this is a nightmare."

Tony met her gaze. "A nightmare, Lizzie? Or a dream come true?"

She glanced away sharply and pressed her lips together. "What do you mean?"

He shook his head and turned away. "I mean I know how desperately you've wanted to see Genevieve. I know how much it hurt you to give her up."

"I thought you meant—" Elizabeth pressed her fingertips to her eyelids. "She's beautiful, isn't she?"

Tony nodded. "Yes. Like her sister . . . and her mother."

Elizabeth bit her lip. "What if he tries to take Evie from me?" That was the fear that had been riding her since she first saw the crest on Nathan's coach this afternoon. It hurt to put it into words.

Tony took another sip. "He won't. He's not an ogre. You two just weren't suited. That's not a crime."

"I suppose that's true, but I'm dreading a confrontation with the dowager. I've been avoiding her."

A grin spread across Tony's friendly face. "Why?"

"I have reason to believe she planned this entire debacle."

Tony chuckled. "Why doesn't that surprise me? She's a wily lady."

Elizabeth pressed her hands to her cheeks. "How are we ever to have a pleasant Christmastide this way?"

"Just enjoy your time with the children. Don't worry about Nathan, or the dowager, or even me."

She reached up and squeezed his hand. "What have I ever done to deserve a friend like you?"

"Plenty," he said, beaming down at her.

A shout of laughter caught Elizabeth's attention. She stood and hurried over to the glass wall of the conservatory. Her daughters were outside, throwing snowballs at each other. Her eyes filled with tears. She felt Tony approaching from behind, and she wrapped her arms around her middle. "You know, I've never heard them laugh together before today."

Tony's voice was kind, warm. "It won't be the last time, Lizzie. It won't."

"I'm a hideous mother. I know that."

"You are not. Don't say that."

"It feels as though I am. I haven't seen Genevieve in twelve years."

"It's never too late to begin again." Tony raised his glass. "Here's to new beginnings."

Chapter Thirteen

NATHAN PUSHED OPEN the wide double doors and strode into his bedchamber. He hadn't been in this room in twelve years. The servants had dusted and polished the furniture, but otherwise it was exactly as he'd left it.

She might have redecorated the rest of the house, but Elizabeth hadn't touched this room. His large cherry-wood bed sat in the middle of the space. The matching writing desk was perched in the corner. The upholstered chairs that formed a small sitting area near the fireplace were untouched. Even the last candle he'd burned sat crookedly in its silver stick. He made his way over to the bed. The same dark blue silken sheets covered the thing. He couldn't help but think that the last woman he'd made love to in this bed had been his wife. His beautiful wife. His body got rock hard at the thought of her. They might have been ill suited, but they'd never lacked passion.

A slight movement to his right caught his attention.

He turned to see Elizabeth walking slowly toward him. He swallowed.

"Why didn't you redecorate this room?" The question was past his lips before he even knew why he'd asked it. He couldn't take his eyes off her. Her skin was like porcelain, her cheek smooth as marble. This was madness. Why was he lusting after . . . his wife?

She trailed a finger along the edge of the wooden bed. "I don't know. I just couldn't seem to . . . bring myself to."

He glanced away. "Thank you for letting us stay. I hope it hasn't been too much of an imposition."

"This is your house, Nathan." Her voice was quiet. Resigned?

"I know, but . . ." He trailed off, staring unseeing out of the frozen windowpane. He walked over to the window and looked down to see the children still running about in the snow. "They seem to be enjoying themselves."

Elizabeth joined him. The scents of lemon and plumeria wafted over him. "Yes, they do seem to be enjoying themselves." Were those tears in her eyes? They were in her voice, at least.

"I like seeing them play together," he said.

Elizabeth pressed two fingertips to her lips. "Oh, Nathan. It breaks my heart. Have we done them a disservice, keeping them apart for so long?"

He turned to face her. "I was thinking the same thing."

"I'm glad to know it's not just me."

They were only a few inches apart. He took a step closer. He touched Elizabeth's hand, squeezed it. "No. It's not just you."

"Tell me we haven't ruined them, Nathan. Tell me they'll be fine." She pulled her hand from his and rubbed the tops of her arms as if she was cold. Almost instinctively, he pulled her against him. He meant to warm her, to comfort her, but her chin tipped up at the moment he looked into her face, and he was lost. His mouth moved down slowly, inexorably, to cover hers. She leaned into him and whimpered. Nathan didn't force the kiss. He tasted her slowly, explored. When she reached up and wrapped her arms around his neck, he let his tongue meet hers and matched her thrust for thrust.

Minutes later, he forced himself to drag his lips away. He had to. If he didn't, he would kiss her cheek, her throat, her neck, and he wouldn't stop there. Or at least, he wouldn't want to. He was already imagining her full, round breasts in his hands and her long legs wrapped around his hips. They'd never had a problem in the bedroom. No. Their arguments had been reserved for every other room of the house.

He pulled himself away from her and focused on righting his breathing again.

Elizabeth braced a hand against the wall and touched her fingers to her lips. She was breathing heavily. So was he. The tiny moan in the back of her throat she'd made a moment earlier was playing over and over again in his memory, and it wasn't making it easy for his cock to stop throbbing unmercifully.

"What were we saying . . . about the children?" she asked in an unsteady voice, shaking her head a little.

He turned toward the window again and placed his

hand against the cold glass, hoping the temperature against his palm would help cool the rest of his body.

"Evie is wonderful. Polite, quiet, intelligent, a credit to the Hollister name," he said.

"Yes. She's always reminded me a great deal of her father," Elizabeth replied softly.

Nathan glanced down at his boots and swallowed the unexpected lump that formed in his throat.

"And Gena is so spirited and full of life," Elizabeth continued.

"The kind of girl who would dance around the house even when someone is looking," he said.

The hint of a smile popped to Elizabeth's lips. He liked that so much better than seeing the tears that had been in her pretty blue eyes a few minutes earlier.

"I suppose she's a bit like me—or at least, how I might have been when I was her age if my mother hadn't been so overbearing," Elizabeth replied.

Nathan narrowed his eyes on her. "I'm surprised to hear you say that."

Elizabeth rubbed her hands up and down her arms again, but this time Nathan resisted the urge to reach for her.

"What do you mean?" she asked.

"Evie told me you rarely see your mother. I thought you two were much closer than that."

"We were. Once. When I was eighteen, she ruled over me."

"And now?"

"Now I rarely see her. Letters suffice."

Nathan rubbed his cold palm against his forehead. He needed to change the subject, to say something else. "How have you been getting on, Elizabeth?"

"I make do." Her eyes were unfocused, but a myriad of emotions seemed to fleet across her beautiful face.

"And Tony?" Nathan could have kicked himself the moment he'd let the other man's name slide from his lips.

Her face froze in a mask. Her voice cooled. "He is a friend."

"Is that all he is?" Apparently, Nathan couldn't help himself. If he was trying to make her hate him, he was doing a splendid job of it.

Her back went rigid. She didn't look at him. "I don't know. What about the widows I hear you've escorted about London? Are they only *friends*?"

Nathan turned toward her and raked his hand through his hair. "Damn it, Elizabeth. That's different. They meant little to me. Tony's been my friend since I was a lad."

She braced a hand against the wall next to the window and turned her head to look at him. Her eyes pierced him. "Did he never mention me when you saw him in London?"

Nathan gave a curt shake of his head. "We didn't speak of you, no."

"Probably for the best," Elizabeth replied. She turned abruptly toward the door. "I'll let you settle in and will see you downstairs for dinner." She stalked away.

Nathan watched her go. He clenched his hand into a fist and banged it against the wall. Damn it. He wanted to know two things: how in the hell could he be so ravenous to make love to his own wife, and how could he ever ask her if she was in love with his friend?

Chapter Fourteen

"MOTHER! MOTHER, COME quickly!" Even though her daughters' voices were identical, by the strength of the tone, Elizabeth knew that it was Gena who was shouting through the foyer.

Elizabeth picked up her skirts and hurried toward the sound. "What is it, darling?" she asked as she rounded the staircase. She gasped as soon as she spied the scene in the foyer. Tony was lying on his back on the marble floor near the front door. Both girls, two footmen, and Broderick all hovered over him.

"Oh, Tony, no!" Elizabeth rushed down the last several stairs. Could they all see her guilt over sharing a passionate kiss with her husband while poor Tony took a tumble in the foyer?

"Be careful, Your Grace. There are several puddles here," Broderick warned as Elizabeth made her way toward them.

"Yes, that's how Uncle Tony slipped," Evie announced, wringing her hands.

"I didn't stamp my boots properly and the snow melted all around. I'm so sorry, Mother," Gena said, looking guilty.

Elizabeth approached Tony, careful to step over the various puddles that were already being mopped up by one of the maids.

She peered down at him. "Lord Atwater, are you all right?"

His dark eyes opened, and he looked a bit dazed. "I believe I've hit my head."

"I'm so sorry." Elizabeth turned to the footmen. "Let's carry him into the drawing room and lay him on the sofa."

"Yes, excellent idea," Tony agreed. "But I believe I can stand. If these helpful chaps would just assist me . . ."

Five minutes later, Tony was lying on the sofa in the nearest drawing room, a blue silken pillow propped under his head and his boots sitting neatly next to each other by the door. Evie and Gena had each removed one.

Elizabeth insisted on pulling a quilt over him. She was just finishing when the dowager glided into the drawing room, clutching her cane.

"I came to see what all the commotion was about. What's happened, Lord Atwater?" she asked.

"Uncle Tony slipped in a puddle and fell," Evie explained.

"He is *not* your uncle, dear," the dowager said to Evie.

Elizabeth opened her mouth to retort, but Tony interrupted, wincing. "It's my back, I'm afraid. I have an old injury from my youth. Was tossed from a horse. I was abed for a week."

"A week? That's a pity. But you cannot stay here for an entire week," the dowager replied.

Elizabeth's mouth fell open. "Your Grace, Lord Atwater is our guest and has hurt himself on our property. The least we can do is help him to recover."

One of the dowager's eyebrows made a perfect arch. She leaned over and patted Tony's hand where it rested above the quilt. "We can discuss it later, Atwater. For now, I hope your back heals . . . quickly."

"Girls, let's allow Lord Atwater some rest," Elizabeth said. She crossed over to a desk near the window, opened its drawer, and removed a small silver bell, which she placed on the table next to him. "Ring this if you need anything, my lord. Anything at all."

Tony nodded. "Thank you, Your Grace. I shall."

"I'm awfully sorry, Uncle, er, Lord Atwater," Evie added.

"I am, too," Gena managed, but she looked more sly than sorry.

The four of them removed themselves from the drawing room, and Elizabeth closed the door behind them.

"Elizabeth," the dowager said, "I've arranged with Mrs. Henderson to have my dinner sent up to my bed-chamber this evening. I'm feeling exhausted from the journey. I've asked the girls to join me. I would like to spend time getting to know *both* of my granddaughters."

"But—"

"You wouldn't begrudge an old woman time with her only grandchildren in the world, would you?" She rested both hands atop the handle of her cane.

Elizabeth glanced at the expectant faces of her daughters.

"Oh, please, Mother. I do so want to get to know Grandmama better," Evie said.

Elizabeth sighed. She couldn't say no to that request. "Of course, darling."

"You should send some broth in to Lord Atwater," the dowager replied.

Elizabeth nodded. "I agree. He should not be asked to make the trip to the dining room and sit in those stiff chairs. I suppose that leaves me to—"

"Have dinner with Papa," Gena said, a bright smile on her face and her eyes twinkling.

Chapter Fifteen

Despite the change in plans, Elizabeth donned the gown she'd already intended to wear for Christmas Eve dinner that evening. It was a silver concoction with spangles and beads that made her shine like a star. If things had gone as planned, she and Evie and Tony and his mother would have had a lovely, quiet dinner, then her guests would have returned home for the evening and come back in the morning, when they all would have had a nice breakfast while Evie opened her gifts.

Instead, she was set to have dinner with—what had Tony called him?—the prodigal duke. She glanced at herself in the looking glass. After helping her dress, Mary had placed Elizabeth's hair atop her head and left a few curls to fall along her neck in a fetching fashion. Elizabeth pinched pink into her cheeks and turned her head from side to side to view her profile. She pushed the tip of her nose. What did Nathan think of her appearance now? Did he find her half as alluring as she still found him? Perhaps. He had kissed her, after all. And she had certainly kissed him back. A shiver went down her spine at the memory of it. For a moment, she'd felt like a young girl again.

Why did her nerves jump at the thought of having dinner alone with Nathan? She was being silly. It mattered little what she looked like. It mattered even less what her husband thought of her appearance. They'd come to their arrangement years ago. It wasn't as if he was courting her. But the thought did remind her of her come-out. Nathan had been the only gentleman she'd seen that evening. The moment she'd clapped eyes on him, it had been as if none of the other gentlemen asking for a dance had even existed. She had danced with a few of them, to be sure, but when Nathan had taken her in his arms and spun her around the floor, she'd forgotten the name of every other man in the country. For a moment, earlier, just after he'd kissed her, she'd had a vision of them naked and tangled in the silken sheets of his bed. Her face grew hot just thinking about it. But then he'd asked her about Tony and completely broken the spell.

"I just checked on Uncle Tony," Evie said, walking into Elizabeth's bedchamber and jolting her from her thoughts.

Elizabeth turned and smiled brightly at her daughter. "How is he, dear?" she asked, sliding on a long white glove.

"His back is still sore. But he's in great spirits as usual. I brought him a few books from the library, and Cook sent up her chicken broth. I think he's as comfortable as can be."

Elizabeth slid on the second glove. "I'm glad to hear it."

"You look absolutely beautiful, Mother. Father is sure to think so, too."

Elizabeth gulped, nearly audibly.

"Be sure to wear your perfume," Evie added with a knowing smile.

"Why, Evangeline Hollister," Elizabeth said, shaking her head.

"Mother, why did Grandmama insist that Uncle Tony isn't my uncle?" Evie asked.

"Well, he isn't, dear, and your grandmama is rather . . . formal."

Evie worried her bottom lip. "I'm sorry Uncle Tony was hurt."

"I am too, darling." Elizabeth crossed over and squeezed her daughter's shoulder. "I do hope he's better by morning. Speaking of the morning, dear. Is it all right with you if we give a few of your gifts to Gena this year so she'll have some presents to open?"

"Oh, Mother, of course. I meant to suggest it earlier. I cannot stand the thought of poor Gena having no gifts to open on Christmas morning."

Elizabeth smiled and cupped her daughter's cheek. "You're a sweet girl, Evie."

Evie made her way toward the door. "We've also been to my wardrobe, and Gena has picked out the gown she would like to wear in the morning."

Elizabeth smiled. "That's lovely, dear."

"My clothing fits her perfectly, you know."

Elizabeth laughed out loud at that.

"I'm off to have dinner with Grandmama and Gena," Evie said. She paused in the doorway. "You know, Father is not at all what I expected a duke to be like."

Elizabeth glanced over at her. "What did you expect, dear?"

"I expected him to be formal and rigid and dukelike. He's quite personable, really. And, of course, he's very handsome, don't you think so, Mother?" She waggled her eyebrows at Elizabeth.

Elizabeth gave her a warning stare. "I'll see you later, dear."

Evie smiled at her again and ducked from the room.

Elizabeth took a deep breath. Fighting her nerves, she made her way downstairs to the drawing room near the dining room to meet Nathan before dinner.

He was standing near the window, looking out onto the dark grounds. He turned, and Elizabeth sucked in her breath. He was wearing formal black evening clothes and a perfectly knotted white cravat. It reminded her of the night they'd met.

"Good evening," he said, turning to her and bowing. "Seems I'd left a few things in my wardrobe. I suppose a certain look never quite goes out of style, does it?"

"No," she breathed.

"What was that?" he asked.

"Lucky for you," she replied a bit louder.

"You are beautiful, Elizabeth." He moved toward her,

a drink in his hand. "This is for you." He handed her a glass of wine.

"My favorite," she said, trying to ignore his compliment.

"Yes, Evie told me you never say no to a glass of wine. I must say I was surprised to hear it."

Elizabeth laughed. "Evie told you that?"

"She did."

"Yes, well. I've changed." She lifted the glass of wine in semblance of a toast.

He returned the gesture. "So it seems."

Elizabeth nervously plucked at her earlobe. "Evie and Gena are having dinner with their grandmother."

"Mother told me." He cleared his throat. "How is the invalid?"

Elizabeth took a sip of her wine. "Wrenched his back, poor thing. He's resting in the front drawing room."

Nathan's eyes took on a kind glow. "I'm glad you agreed to have dinner with me, Elizabeth. Alone. And I'm sorry—about earlier."

She watched him carefully. "Sorry you kissed me, or sorry about what you said about Tony?"

"What I said about Tony. I'm not sorry I kissed you at all." His grin was positively wicked.

She arched a brow. "You're . . . apologizing?"

He flashed his straight white teeth in a grin. "Does that surprise you?"

"Very much. The Nathan I knew a dozen years ago didn't apologize for anything. I believe you even told me that once."

"I said that?"

"Yes."

"I'm sorry for that too, then."

Elizabeth downed another fourth of her wine. She needed to change the subject. This was all a bit too serious of a sudden. And Nathan was a bit too . . . different. He was no longer the stubborn man who never apologized? What else would she discover about him?

"How could I refuse dinner with you?" she asked with a bright smile. "It's Christmas Eve."

He lifted his glass in a salute. "So it is."

He moved toward her and looked her in the eye, unnerving her a bit. "Evie tells me that you say—let me see if I can remember all of the accolades—that I'm handsome and intelligent and kind and generous."

Elizabeth nearly choked on her wine. She pressed a gloved hand to her throat. "She said that?"

"Yes."

"She exaggerates."

He smiled at her, and it made her go weak in the knees. "No, she doesn't."

Elizabeth shrugged one shoulder. "Well, I couldn't very well let her think her father was awful, could I?"

"Thank you. I never spoke a bad word about you to Gena either. Believe me."

Elizabeth sighed. "I suppose we owe them both a better explanation than they've been given."

"Now that they've met, we can't very well keep them apart," Nathan said.

"I agree. What do you propose?"

The question hung in the air, and their eyes locked. For a heart-stopping moment, Elizabeth was sure he was going to kiss her again. Her gaze dipped to his firm lips. Their kiss earlier played itself again and again in her mind. Somehow she'd blocked out the memory of their lovemaking over the years, but now it was coming back to her in vivid, bold pictures. His rock-hard, naked abdomen, his muscled shoulders, his narrow waist. His mouth on her—

"Why don't we take turns?" he asked.

Elizabeth shook her head. Take turns? Doing what? What had they been discussing?

"With the children?" he continued. "I can have them one holiday. You can have them the next. And so forth."

Elizabeth clamped her teeth together so hard that her jaw throbbed. For one moment, for one foolish, awful moment, she'd actually believed he was going to say that they should live under the same roof again. So that their children could be together. But no. He'd only meant to share them. He couldn't bring himself to live with her again, even for the girls' sake. Elizabeth pressed her lips together. She'd have to give up Evie even more if she agreed to this. But she must do what was best for Evie, not what was best for her own battered heart.

"Yes," she whispered. "That's probably the right thing to do."

Chapter Sixteen

NATHAN WAS SITTING in the breakfast room early the next morning when Atwater came limping in. None of the others had come down yet, not even the children. Nathan glanced up from his newspaper to eye the slightly younger man. "Atwater?"

"Merry Christmas, Hollingsworth."

"Merry Christmas," Nathan answered reluctantly. "How is your back?"

"Better, but only slightly, I'm afraid. I intend to leave for my house immediately. Broderick tells me the road is clear. Apparently, most of the snow has melted overnight. Mother is at home. We should spend Christmastide together. Not to mention I don't want to be a burden on Liz—ahem, Her Grace."

"How kind of you." Nathan gave him a tight smile.

"Will you tell her I said good-bye? And Evie and Gena, too? Good-bye and merry Christmas?"

"I will." Nathan folded his paper and eyed Atwater carefully.

"Something tells me your mother will be only too happy to see the back of me."

Nathan didn't reply to that.

Atwater made his way slowly toward the door, but just before he left, he turned toward Nathan again. "Take care of her, Hollingsworth. She's still in love with you, you know."

And with that astonishing bit of news, the earl was gone. Nathan narrowed his eyes on the space Atwater had just vacated. What could Tony Gillette possibly have to gain by telling Nathan that Elizabeth was in love with him? Was it true? Was it possible?

The girls ran into the room just then, Sampson on their heels, distracting Nathan from his thoughts.

"Merry Christmas, Father," one of them said brightly.

"Merry Christmas," he replied. "I daresay, with you wearing matching dressing gowns, I cannot tell you apart."

The girls exchanged catlike smiles.

"I'm Evie." She curtsied to him. "And I cannot tell you how awfully glad I am to spend Christmastide with you at last."

Nathan reached out and squeezed her small hand. "Likewise, Evie. Likewise."

"Where's Mother?" Gena nearly shouted. "I cannot wait to spend my first Christmas with her. Come, Papa. Let's go look at the gifts!"

The girls were off in a swirl of white dressing gowns

and a trail of giggles. Sampson loped out after them. Nathan folded his paper and followed them, whistling. His first Christmastide here with his girls on his estate. It felt good. It felt right.

But Nathan stopped whistling. For a moment last night, he'd wanted to ask Elizabeth if he could move back here. Live with her, if not as man and wife, at least as parents to their daughters. He didn't have to ask for permission. He knew that. He could move his entire household back here tomorrow and Elizabeth wouldn't gainsay him, but it didn't feel right. He wanted to be welcomed. He wanted to be . . . wanted. Instead, he'd offered the foolish compromise of having the children take turns between households, which he didn't want either. Not only would he miss Gena when she was here but he'd miss Evie, too. And perhaps Elizabeth now, if he was being honest. Damn his foolish pride for even suggesting it. But Elizabeth hadn't contradicted him. She hadn't offered another suggestion, hadn't offered to allow him to come back home. And he sure as hell wasn't about to beg his wife for her affections or even her acceptance. No, he'd made the best suggestion for all of them, and she'd agreed to it. It was obviously what she wanted.

When he came to the front drawing room, he paused a moment before he entered. Elizabeth was there. He heard her speaking softly to the girls. She'd been so beautiful last night. So damned beautiful in that shining gown with a soft curl brushing the smooth skin of her shoulder. And that kiss yesterday in his bedchamber . . . No. No good could come of that way of thinking.

"Merry Christmas," he said, walking into the room and smiling. The room smelled like pine needles and sherbet lemons.

Elizabeth glanced up at him. She seemed a bit startled to see him. She was wearing a pink dressing gown and looked as fresh and pretty as a spring flower.

"Merry Christmas," she replied, glancing away shyly.

The girls were busily shaking the gifts that sat on a table near the center of the room.

"I didn't bring any of Gena's gifts," he said.

"Don't worry. I'm giving her some of mine, Father," Evie called out.

Elizabeth's smile brightened her eyes. "They've already learned to share."

Nathan took a seat next to Elizabeth on the settee. "Mother should be down shortly," he said. "She's never been one for mornings."

"Broderick mentioned that Tony left," Elizabeth said quietly. "Apparently, the road is clear."

"Yes," Nathan replied. "Atwater stopped by the breakfast room on his way. He said to tell you all good-bye and merry Christmas."

Elizabeth tugged at the sleeve of her dressing gown. "I wish he would have stayed."

A knife sliced through Nathan's chest. Did she? Did she wish Tony had stayed? Did she wish he were here with her now instead of him? Did she love Atwater, despite that fact that Atwater appeared to believe that she loved *him*? Was that why she'd so readily agreed to his plan to take turns with the girls?

Nathan shook his head. He needed to concentrate on making the holiday enjoyable for the children and then get back to London. If the road was clear enough for Tony to get home, no doubt it was clear enough for him and Gena and Mother to return to London.

He stood and moved away from Elizabeth. "Girls, wait for a few moments. I'm sure your grandmama would enjoy seeing you open your presents," he called.

SIX HOURS LATER, all the gifts had been opened, carols had been sung, and a sumptuous feast had been consumed by all five members of the Hollister family. Despite the happy holiday, Nathan couldn't justify staying a moment longer.

"Gena, gather your things. We must get on the road back to town before it gets too dark."

Gena crossed her arms over her chest. "No, Father."

Nathan's brows shot up. "No?"

"That's right." The girl nodded firmly and set her jaw.

Elizabeth turned to look at their daughter. "What do you mean, no?"

The girls stood side by side, their arms crossed over their chests. They had changed into nearly identical gowns, one red, one green. They looked like adorable Christmastide elves. "We've decided we want to spend more of our holiday together."

"Gena." Nathan drew out the name in his most domineering, dukelike tone.

"How do you know I am Gena?" one of them said.

He narrowed his eyes on her. "What do you mean?"

"I may be Evie," she replied.

"Or am *I* Evie?" the other said.

Elizabeth pressed a hand to her cheek. She crossed over to the girls and bent down and stared hard at one girl's face. "This is Evie. I'm sure of it."

"Are you certain? *Truly* certain?" the girl said.

Elizabeth frowned. "This is not funny, girls."

"We have a proposal," one of them said. "We want you both to come to London with us for a special event in three days. After that, we'll tell you who is who and you can switch us back."

Nathan eyed them both. His daughters were clearly getting to an age at which they intended to rebel. But he had to admit that half of him was curious as to what sort of event they had planned in London. "What if I threatened to spank both of you until you couldn't sit down for a sennight?"

"You'll just have to spank us, Father. Because we absolutely refuse to tell you until three nights hence," one of them said, while the other nodded vigorously in obvious solidarity.

Elizabeth turned to Nathan. "I don't know what to say."

Nathan glanced at his mother, who was quietly sitting on the settee, sipping tea. "What do *you* have to say about this?"

The dowager arrested her teacup halfway to her lips. "I say Elizabeth had better pack for London, because *I* certainly cannot tell them apart."

Chapter Seventeen

ELIZABETH HAD TO admit that despite her daughters' coercion, she was actually looking forward to the trip to London. The city was always a pleasure to explore, and she hadn't been there in so long. It was a shame that she'd only be there for a short time. She would adore having the chance to do some shopping on Bond Street or take in a play at one of the theaters.

They set out the next morning. Elizabeth, Mary, and the girls rode in Elizabeth's carriage, hidden under a bundle of blankets and furs, while Nathan and his mother rode in the ducal coach. Elizabeth didn't bother asking the girls who was who during the ride. She just enjoyed their company and spent not a little time trying to guess what it was that they wanted their parents to do while together in the city. She also spent a fair amount of time fretting about Tony's back. She'd sent him a note to let him know she was going to London and not to worry about her. She'd apologized for his unfortunate accident and sent her best wishes for a happy holiday to him and his mother.

Many hours later, when the coaches arrived in London, Elizabeth stared out the window of the conveyance with as much glee and awe as the children. The coaches quickly passed through the outskirts of the town into the streets of Mayfair and finally came to a stop at the fashionable residence that Nathan called home.

Butterflies swarmed through Elizabeth's belly as she walked up the stairs to the imposing white stone town house. Would the servants remember her? Would they wonder why she'd come? Oh, of course they would.

She did not have long to contemplate it. The door to the house flew open, and Mrs. Curtis came hurrying down the steps to meet her. "Your Grace, you're home!" she said, her smile reaching ear to ear. "The dowager sent word and told me you were coming. It's been an age. Far too long, if you ask me," she whispered. And then more loudly, "I have your bedchamber all made up for you. And one for Lady Evangeline as well."

Well, that settled that. The sleeping arrangements, at least. Elizabeth had wondered if she would be sleeping in her old suite, which was—just as in the country—next door to Nathan's with an adjoining door. No doubt the dowager had made such an arrangement.

In a flurry of activity, Elizabeth was whisked into the house and up the stairs to her bedchamber, where a bath and a tray of food were waiting, and then she was promptly ordered by Mrs. Curtis to take a nap. In all these years, she hadn't forgotten how domineering the housekeeper could be. Elizabeth snuggled under the soft covers of her bed and hid her smile against the pillow.

"The dowager's orders. You're to rest and enjoy yourself for the next two days. Then, there's to be a ball, you know?"

Elizabeth blinked. A ball? No. She hadn't known. How had Mrs. Curtis known? Elizabeth opened her mouth to ask about it, but the whirlwind of a housekeeper had already gathered Elizabeth's dusty traveling clothing and exited the room.

The next two days were a blur of activity and family togetherness that tugged unmercifully at Elizabeth's heart. She and Nathan spent the days in the park together with the children teaching Gena how to ride without shrieking. The evenings were spent playing games together in the drawing room, where Nathan and Gena taught Evie how to play several questionable card games. After Evie taught Gena how to play a decent rendition of Mozart on the pianoforte, Gena returned the favor by teaching Evie how to play the bawdy tune she'd played for Elizabeth. Elizabeth shook her head and hid her smile as she watched her formal daughter sing a silly song and laugh uproariously about it afterward. They really were good for each other, the twins, which made the prospect of pulling them apart again soon even that much more heartwrenching.

For her part, the dowager duchess stayed away. Mrs. Curtis mentioned something about her having come down with a head cold. Regardless, Elizabeth did her best to enjoy the inexplicable gift of time with her daughters and the new Nathan, who, she quickly learned, *was* a man just as kind, generous, and intelligent as she'd always told Evie that he was. When the evening of the third day drew near, Elizabeth couldn't help her nerves. A ball? There was to be a ball? But for what purpose? The children, of course, weren't saying.

MARY OUTDID HERSELF. She presented Elizabeth with the most gorgeous, deep-green gown Elizabeth had ever seen and wrapped Elizabeth's hair in a loose chignon. Then Mary twined emeralds through Elizabeth's blond hair and placed a glorious matching emerald necklace around her neck.

"From the children," Mary said.

Elizabeth furrowed her brow. "The children?" She adored the children, but she highly doubted they'd been able to procure this expensive gown and these priceless jewels themselves.

Mary shrugged. "That's what they said."

"Yes, well, what else did they say? Mrs. Curtis mentioned a ball, but that is all I know about tonight."

"You're to meet the children outside the ballroom on the third floor at ten o'clock."

Elizabeth raised both brows. "The ballroom? Here?"

"Yes," Mary replied. "And that's all *I* know."

"Very well." Glancing at the clock on the mantelpiece across the room to ensure it was nearly time, Elizabeth picked up her skirts and made her way out of the room, down the staircase to the third floor, and to the double doors in front of the grand ballroom. Ten o'clock was past her daughters' bedtime. Whatever could they be up to?

She took a deep breath and pressed her hand to her middle. "I suppose I should go in," she whispered to herself. Taking one more deep breath for good measure, she placed both gloved hands on the door handles and pushed them wide.

She stepped inside the room and caught her breath. The ballroom was magnificent. It was decorated as a summer garden, just as it had been years ago on the night when Nathan had proposed, complete with the twinkling candles near the ceiling and a cornucopia of summer flowers that must have emptied several different conservatories. Tears filled Elizabeth's eyes.

The girls stood near the entrance, dressed in lovely matching gold gowns.

"Do you like it, Mother? Oh, by the way, I'm Evie."

Gena giggled.

"It's absolutely breathtaking, my darlings," Elizabeth answered, turning in a wide circle to see the entire space. It was re-created almost precisely as she remembered it.

She turned toward the door and stopped as Nathan came strolling in, his hands in his pockets. He was wearing formal black evening attire, and a sapphire winked in his cravat. The jewel matched his eyes. He, too, turned in a circle to take in the decorations. His face was inscrutable as he directed his attention back to his daughters. "How did you two make this happen?"

"Grandmama might have helped a bit," Gena admitted with a sly smile.

"A bit?" Nathan arched a brow.

"Well, quite a lot, actually," Evie replied.

"I thought she had a head cold," Elizabeth said.

"Yes, well, ah, we will just leave you to it," Gena said, backing away slowly, a mischievous grin on her face.

The girls ran off, giggling, and Elizabeth turned to Nathan. "You know what this is, don't you?"

His brow furrowed.

"They've re-created the night we became betrothed," she said.

"Ah, it seemed quite familiar," he replied, glancing about again before returning the full force of his blue gaze to Elizabeth. "And . . . you look beautiful. More beautiful than you did all those years ago." His eyes caressed her from head to toe.

"You can't mean it," she replied with a slight smile.

He stepped forward, took her hand, and kissed the back of it, causing gooseflesh to pop up along her arm. "I absolutely do," he breathed.

She slowly pulled her hand away but didn't move her eyes from his. It was as if she was caught in a spell. A spell or a memory. She shook her head. "If I remember correctly, you brought me a glass of champagne."

As if on cue, a footman walked past with a silver tray in his hands. Two glasses of champagne rested upon it.

"So I did," Nathan said with a laugh. He pulled the glasses from the tray, and the footman quickly disappeared. "And if I remember correctly, you said you didn't drink."

"I do now."

"My lady." He bowed to her and handed her the glass.

Elizabeth took the glass and sipped it eagerly. Was this fun or excruciating? She didn't know yet.

"And then you put a lily in my hair," she replied.

He turned to examine the broad selection of flowers that were arranged on the trellis nearest them. He dashed over and plucked a lily, returning quickly.

"My lady," he said with another bow.

She swallowed. He had slid it behind her ear himself all those years ago.

He must have read her mind. "May I?" he asked.

She nodded.

He cupped his hand at her ear and slid the flower behind it, and Elizabeth's breathing hitched. His hand quickly fell away. Elizabeth took another grateful sip of champagne.

"And then what?" he said softly, watching her.

She plucked at the emeralds around her throat. "You don't remember?"

"I remember," he replied, taking her empty glass and setting it with his on a nearby table. It didn't go unnoticed by her that he didn't call for another glass of champagne. The old Nathan would never have stopped at one glass, of anything. Instead, he turned back to her, and his voice was husky and sensual. "I just wanted to hear *you* say it."

Her words were a mere whisper. "You asked me to dance."

As if on cue, a soft waltz began to play. Elizabeth inclined her head toward the lovely music and realized that Evie was playing the pianoforte across the room. Gena was sitting on the bench beside her sister, smiling from ear to ear.

Nathan bowed to her. "Will you do me the honor?"

"Of course, Your Grace." She breathed the same words she'd said to him that night.

He took her into his arms then, and led her to the floor. Elizabeth closed her eyes. If this was a dream, she didn't want to wake up. She didn't want to be pinched or nudged from her cocoon of wonder and delight. She spun around and around, enjoying the music, the smell of the flowers, the feeling of having drunk a glass of champagne so quickly. But most of all, the feel of her husband's broad shoulder beneath her fingertips and her hand clasped in his.

Moments later, when she forced herself to open her eyes, Nathan was studying her face. "What were you thinking about?" he asked.

"I was thinking about the question you asked me all those years ago on a night very like this."

He pulled her against his chest, and she caught her breath. His lips brushed her ear. "Tonight I want to ask you a different question entirely," he whispered.

"What?" she asked breathlessly.

His lips remained near her ear. "Why did you leave all those years ago?"

The song ended just then, and Elizabeth was thankful for the reprieve. How could she answer that question while dancing in his arms? It was too much. Her hands fell away from him and she took a tentative step back.

Another waltz soon began to play, but they remained still, looking at each other, watching each other.

"I'd like an answer," he said. They both kept their voices low so the children couldn't overhear.

She shook her head and turned away. "Does it matter? We were young, stupid. I don't even remember what that last argument was about." He couldn't see her face. She closed her eyes, tortured. It was decided. This was excruciating.

"I do."

She opened her eyes again and turned back to him. "Then you tell me. Why did I leave?"

"I told you you had to choose. Your mother was ruining our lives together. She kept telling you how to behave. I told you to open your eyes. To see her manipulation for what it was."

"I didn't choose you?"

He shook his head. "No. And what I can't understand, especially given the fact that you've obviously separated yourself from your mother now, is why?"

An ache formed in Elizabeth's chest. She could barely breathe. "I don't know. All I remember is that I packed, and left, and well . . . you never came after me."

He took a step forward and clasped his fingers over her upper arms. He searched her face. "I never knew you wanted me to."

She shook her head to clear the tears from her eyes. She looked down at his chest so he wouldn't see her anguish. "It doesn't matter now, does it? We were both so very young, foolish, stubborn."

He nodded. "Agreed."

"And that was all so long ago."

"Not so long ago. I remember the Midsummer Eve ball like it was yesterday." He traced the outline of her ear with his fingertip. She still couldn't look at him. "And I meant it when I said that you're even more beautiful now than you were then."

"Oh, stop. I'm practically an old lady now."

"Hardly. I . . . ." He bent his head to her ear. "When I first saw you on Christmas Eve, you took my breath away."

She couldn't help her answering smile. "I'll admit I'd nearly forgotten how handsome you are."

"Truly?"

"Yes. Truly." She couldn't stop her smile. "Begging for compliments, Your Grace?"

"When they fall from the lips of such a beautiful woman." He pulled her into his arms and looked down at her. "Now I want to ask you something I never could have asked at the last such ball."

Her heart quivered in her chest. "What's that?"

His words were a sensual whisper. "May I escort you to your bedchamber?"

Chapter Eighteen

NATHAN ESCORTED HER to her bedchamber. To the door, at least. Escorted her and left her. Though he couldn't help but wonder if Elizabeth had wanted more—a kiss goodnight or . . . more. When he'd asked her the question in the ballroom, he'd fully intended to take her to bed and make love to her, to show her with his hands and body and mouth how much he felt for her. How much he wanted things to be different between them. How much he wanted to . . . try. But by the time they'd reached her door, it seemed as if the spell from the ballroom had been broken, and he felt like a complete ass, asking his wife if he could come into her bedchamber.

Damn it. He'd *be* a complete ass if he just assumed that she wanted him, but now he was kicking himself for not having at least attempted to kiss her when they'd been standing at the door. She with that gorgeous smile and sparking emeralds around her throat—he'd never been jealous of rocks before—smelling like plumeria and gazing up at him nearly like she had a dozen years ago, with that trusting, admiring look in her eye.

The children had gone to bed in the other wing. He and Elizabeth wouldn't be disturbed. He knew it. Yet, somehow, he just hadn't been able to bring himself to kiss her. What if she rejected him? Again.

With the help of his valet, he changed out of his clothing and wrapped his sapphire velvet dressing gown around himself. He spent a good ten minutes pacing in front of the windows of his bedchamber, scrubbing his hand through his hair, before he finally decided. He had to try. Once more. Tony had insisted that Elizabeth loved him. Perhaps Tony knew what he was talking about.

Nathan waited until he was sure Elizabeth had had time to change out of her ball gown with the help of her maid before he knocked quietly on the door that connected their bedchambers. There was some shuffling on the other side before Elizabeth opened the door, wrapping her pink dressing gown around her waist. A brace of candles glowed on a table near the bed behind her. She looked so young and pretty, her blond hair down around her shoulders, her face fresh-scrubbed, her cheeks rosy. His eyes scanned the room. Thankfully, the maid was gone.

"Nathan," she breathed.

He smiled. "Who else would it be?"

"It's been a very long time since anyone knocked on my bedchamber door," she said with a small, quiet laugh.

He liked the sound of that. "May I come in?"

She nodded hesitantly and moved aside to allow him to enter the room.

It smelled like her, an alluring scent that made Nathan want to close his eyes and breathe it forever.

He strode toward the center of the room, a dozen thoughts racing through his mind. Should he apologize? Should he ask her to kiss him? Should he ask her if she loved Tony? Ask her if she wanted to give their marriage another try? Ask her if she wanted him to get the hell out?

He turned to say one of those things. She was standing not a foot away from him, gazing up at him tentatively. She looked so beautiful, so beautiful and vulnerable and—oh, hell. He pulled her roughly into his arms and opened his mouth across hers.

ELIZABETH WANTED TO sob. Nathan was kissing her. Actually kissing her. She hadn't thought he would. Hadn't thought he wanted to after leaving her earlier. She'd nearly sobbed then, too, but for an entirely different reason. He was so handsome and he smelled so good, like a combination of pine needles and soap and . . . her husband. She wanted him, wanted him more than she'd ever wanted him before. She didn't care about what happened tomorrow. She only knew that she needed this man to take her to bed tonight. Her arms moved up to wrap around his neck, and she whispered in his ear, "I want you, Nathan. Make love to me, please."

Nathan bent to sweep her into his arms. His mouth never left hers. He carried her to the bed and laid her there, following her down and ripping his dressing gown from his shoulders at the same time. He was naked save for some linen trousers. Elizabeth's hands and eyes roved over his chest. Her fingertips touching him were unholy torture. He tugged at the belt around her waist, and her dressing gown opened to reveal a rather prim-looking night rail. "I didn't know you would be visiting," she whispered against his mouth by way of explanation.

"I don't give a bloody damn what you're wearing as long as you agree to take it off. Now," he demanded in a half growl that sent a wave of pure lust rocketing through Elizabeth's body.

"Yes, Your Grace." She smiled against his mouth. They were ravenous for each other, not stopping their mad kisses as Elizabeth moved up to her knees and pulled the dressing gown off her shoulders and the night rail over her head. As soon as she was naked, he pushed her back to the bed and paused only to remove his trousers and toss them to the floor. Then he was on top of her, his muscled body pressing against her softness and her long legs wrapping around his outer thighs.

"I need you, Elizabeth. Now," he groaned against her mouth.

"It's been so long. So long. I haven't been with a man since you. And I—"

That was all he needed to hear. His chest clenched at the thought that his exquisite wife was untouched by any man but him, even after all these years. He'd make it up to her; every mistake he'd ever made, he'd make it up to her tonight by making her come again and again and again.

"I'd never hurt you," he said, his tongue gliding against her ear, making Elizabeth's whole body buck.

"I know," she whispered.

"I can't wait. I have to have you." His rough, hot hands slid to her hips, and he positioned her, gliding his cock against her wet cleft, closing his eyes and groaning. "God, Elizabeth. You feel so good. So damn good."

She reached down and pressed him home. He slid inside, and they both moaned. Then he pressed the backs of her hands into the mattress, setting their rhythm, owning her, pressing against her again and again, angling his hips so that he touched her in a spot that made her cry out. It had always been good between them, but it had never been *this* good. She was mindless with lust as he pressed the little nub between her thighs with his body over and over.

She wanted to touch him, rub her fingers through his hair, hold his mouth to hers, but he wouldn't let go of her wrists. His breathing was heavy. "If you touch me, I'll come," he groaned into her ear.

"I want you to come," she whispered back, straining against his strong hands.

"You first." He pulled out of her and Elizabeth wanted to cry, but when he drew her wrists down to press into the sheets near her hips while his mouth moved between her legs, Elizabeth forgot why she'd ever wanted to be free.

"Oh, God, yes," she cried when his hot, wet tongue found the nub of pleasure between her legs. He circled her, nipping, biting, licking in deep, hot strokes until Elizabeth gave a keening cry and fell over the precipice in the most intensely sensuous feeling of her entire life.

As soon as she came, Nathan groaned, let go of her wrists, and moved back up. In one swift maneuver, he slid inside her and pumped into her again and again while she wrapped her silky legs around his hips, her tongue tangling in his mouth and her hands clutching the back of his head. Nathan pumped into her until he couldn't breathe, couldn't think. He was mindless, thoughtless. Sweat beaded against his forehead, and his balls throbbed. He opened his mouth in a growl and clenched his teeth in an orgasm that shot through his entire being, and his wife's name flew from his lips as he groaned and released himself into her sweet warmth.

Chapter Nineteen

IT WAS STILL dark outside when Elizabeth rolled over and covered her smiling mouth with her fingers. The nearly burned-out candles still twinkled in the brace next to the bed. Her body still twinged in places she had forgotten existed. Oh, God, what that man did to her. Did they really argue about things like religion and drinking all those years ago? It seemed silly now. Nathan clearly didn't drink to excess any longer, and she'd long ago given up the religious fanaticism her mother had tried so desperately to instill in her.

Nathan reached out and wrapped a lock of her hair over his finger. "You're beautiful, Elizabeth."

She startled. "I didn't know you were awake."

He pulled her hand between his thighs, where his erection proudly jutted against the sheets. "I'm awake."

"I see that."

He rose up and kissed her shoulder. "I could make

love to you all day." He moved to wrap his arm around her waist, but she pushed up to her elbows and moved away.

"That sounds . . . dangerous," she said with a shaky laugh.

"It's not." He advanced on her. "I assure you."

She moved farther back and pulled the sheet up to her neck. "Yes, but . . ."

His face fell. "What's wrong?"

"Nothing." But she'd said it too quickly.

He sat back against the pillows and watched her warily, as if she'd been a bird that might fly away if he made too sudden a move. "Elizabeth, I understand you're frightened. It frightens me, too, a little. After all these years. After all we've been through."

"It just can't be that easy. We can't just fall back into each other's arms and pretend nothing happened."

"I don't want to pretend nothing happened."

"Then what do you want, Nathan?"

He scrubbed a hand across his face. "I don't know. I—"

She took a shaky breath. "This was . . . incredible, but it doesn't mean we're suited to each other any more than we were a dozen years ago." *And it would break my heart to have to leave you again.* But she couldn't bring herself to say those words. She just couldn't.

"Damn it, Elizabeth. We were little more than children when we married. My parents were pressuring me to take a wife and—"

"And my mother was pressuring me to marry a duke."

"I loved you, though," he whispered. "Very much. At least as much as I was able to at the time. I was selfish and stubborn, and I drank like a jackass and I didn't know what a marriage entailed."

Elizabeth turned to him and pressed her palm to his warm, stubbled cheek. "I loved you, too. So much. And my mother was horrible. I did everything she said. I don't listen to her anymore. I finally realized that I didn't agree with a word she said. I'd been thoughtlessly listening to her all those years out of habit or duty or something. But then one day I heard her say something to Evie. Evie was only three years old at the time, but she told Evie she was a gluttonous sinner for eating too many chocolates. I'd given her the chocolates, of course. I realized I couldn't allow my daughter to grow up around that. I couldn't. I wouldn't. Mother and I had a huge row and she packed her bags and left, telling me the devil had obviously captured my soul. It nearly broke me to watch her go. I was lonely and alone, but I had to do it, for Evie."

Nathan clasped Elizabeth's hands. "I'm sorry, Elizabeth. I wasn't there for you when you needed me, and I'll never forgive myself for that. But don't you see? We've both changed. I no longer believe I'm always right, for example. And I do believe in an apology now and then." His smile was boyish. It stole her heart. "Not to mention, I stopped drinking to excess at least ten years ago."

Elizabeth sucked in her breath. She wanted to believe it. She did. But how could she tell him how frightened she was of herself? Of not being a good enough wife? She'd already proved to be a miserable failure at it. How could she trust that she could be better now? "We may have changed, but is it truly enough? How can it be that simple?"

"It doesn't have to be that complicated either." He scratched a hand through his short dark hair, making it stand up in delectable ways. "Don't you think we should try? For the girls' sake?"

Elizabeth's stomach clenched. There it was. The truth. He only wanted to try for the sake of the girls. That had been her fear all along. "I want them to be together, too, Nathan. Believe me. But we talked about this. They'll see each other at school, and we'll make arrangements to keep them at different times."

He faced her, his eyes meeting hers. "Is that what you want? Tell me, Elizabeth. Is that what you truly want?"

She dropped her gaze and stared down at her hands, pale and cold against the dark blue sheets. "Has it ever mattered what I truly want?"

His voice was harsh. "Maybe not before, but it matters now. Answer the question."

She pressed her lips together. Hard. She wanted him but only if he truly wanted *her*. She didn't want him back out of a compelled sense of duty. That would be no life at all. She forced herself to meet his eyes again. "Yes. I think it's for the best if we remain apart."

Chapter Twenty

THE RIDE BACK to Kent was long, cold, and bumpy. Elizabeth and Evie barely said a handful of words to each other. Evie tugged at the gold locket around her neck that her grandmama had given her for Christmas. It contained two tiny portraits of her and her twin. "I miss Gena," she said with a long, dramatic sigh.

Elizabeth pulled one of the furs up to her neck. Her heart ached and her head pounded, but she tried to make her words sound as jovial as she could. "You'll see her at school."

Evie sighed again. "I miss Father."

Elizabeth clenched her jaw and looked out the window at the cold, snowy landscape. "He's agreed to have you for the next holiday, and I'll have you both in the summer." But the joviality in her voice slipped a bit.

"Mother, I—" Evie snapped her mouth shut.

"Yes, dear?"

"You're so poised and proper and you never make mistakes, but I have to say that in this case, I believe you're making a grievous one."

Elizabeth pressed her lips together and shook her head sadly. "Oh, Evie. Who said I never make mistakes? I'm only doing what I think is best and . . . I know it's difficult to comprehend, especially at your age, but someday, I hope you can understand."

Evie opened her mouth to retort again but quickly closed it.

The rest of the journey continued in silence with only the occasional odd sigh from Evie, while Elizabeth tried *not* to remember last night, tried *not* to remember Nathan's hands on her, his mouth on her. Last night, she'd thought all she wanted was one night with him, but she'd been a fool. She wouldn't be able to banish his lovemaking from her mind. Not ever.

When the coach pulled up to the manor house, Evie jumped out as soon as the door was opened. She rushed across the graveled drive and entered the manor. Elizabeth followed at a much less hurried pace.

By the time Elizabeth walked into the foyer, Evie was twirling in a circle, obviously looking for something. "Sampson," Evie called. "Sampson."

But the dog was nowhere to be found. That was odd. Sampson was always at the door to greet Evie.

Elizabeth turned to Broderick. "Where's Sampson?"

"I believe he's in the library, my lady," the butler replied evenly.

"The library?" Evie frowned, but she handed Broderick her coat and hat and made her way to the library. Elizabeth followed her.

The door opened, and Elizabeth's heart skipped a beat. Gena was sitting behind the desk, and her father was leaning against the wall near the windows, looking out over the grounds. Sampson was lying on the rug near the fireplace.

Evie's jaw dropped. "What are you doing here?" She rushed over to hug her sister.

"Do you know how fast Papa's coach can travel?" Gena asked with a grin.

Nathan met Elizabeth's gaze. "It's true. My coach is quite fleet."

"We didn't see you on the road." Elizabeth tried to gather her wild thoughts back into some semblance of order.

"I know a shorter route." Nathan grinned, strode over to her, and took her hands in his. "Elizabeth, listen to me. You told me once that I didn't come after you. I refuse to make that mistake again. We can't pretend the last dozen years didn't happen, but we can make the next dozen years the happiest of our lives."

"Nathan, I—"

"No. Wait. Listen to me. You said it can't be that simple, but why can't it? As Gena pointed out to me this morning, how do we know we wouldn't be happy together now? I don't know, and you don't either, but I do know that I want to try. And I want you to try, too."

She searched his face. "What if I'm an awful wife?"

"Then I'll be your awful husband and we'll learn how

to be better . . . together." He fell to one knee. "We're already married, so I can hardly ask you to marry me, but I am asking you if you could love me again, Elizabeth. Can you?"

Tears streamed down her cheeks. She knelt, too, and wrapped her arms around his neck. "I already do, Nathan. I already do."

He grinned from ear to ear, picked her up, and spun her around in his arms.

"Could you love me again, Nathan?" she asked.

"I never stopped."

Nathan set her down, and they turned to their children. Elizabeth wiped away her tears with a handkerchief Nathan quickly produced from his pocket.

"Thank goodness," Evie said, wiping an arm across her forehead.

"It worked!" Gena cried.

"What worked?" Elizabeth asked. She stopped sniffing and furrowed her brow.

"Our plan, of course, to ensure that the two of you reunited. Grandmama came to Miss Hathaway's, and we planned everything."

Elizabeth's mouth fell open. "You planned every—" She glanced at Nathan. "Did you know about this?"

Nathan grinned at her. "Not a thing. But please don't stop them. I'd like to hear the rest."

"The three of us organized the entire affair," Gena continued. "Of course, it was mere luck that Lord Atwater was such a sport. He was quite convincing as an invalid, was he not?"

Elizabeth put her hands on her hips and stared back and forth at her daughters. "Tony! He didn't really slip on the puddle?"

"No," Gena replied. "It was his idea, even. Brilliant, if you ask me."

Elizabeth looked at Evie. "Evie, is this true?"

"Oh, yes, Mother. Uncle Tony was quite lovely. He said he'd been waiting for Father to return and do right by you for quite some time, and he didn't want to spoil it all with his untimely presence."

Nathan chuckled. "He did, did he? I'll have to thank Atwater the next time I see him."

Evie nodded happily.

"And what did your grandmama have to say for herself?" Nathan continued.

"She said that if she had to wait for the two of you to get about the business of producing an heir, she'd be waiting until her deathbed."

"She did, did she?" Elizabeth echoed.

"Yes, and I must say that we shall be delighted to welcome a younger brother," Evie replied.

"Yes. We shall dote upon him," Gena added. "At your earliest convenience, of course."

Nathan exchanged a smoldering look with Elizabeth and brought the back of her hand up to his lips for a kiss. "I'd be happy to see what we can do about that."

About the Author

VALERIE BOWMAN grew up in Illinois with six sisters (she's number seven) and a huge supply of historical romance novels. After a cold and snowy stint earning a degree in English with a minor in history at Smith College, she moved to Florida the first chance she got. Valerie now lives in Jacksonville with her family, including her rascally dog, Roo. When she's not writing, she keeps busy reading, traveling, or vacillating between watching crazy reality TV and PBS. Valerie loves to hear from readers. Find her on Facebook, Twitter, and at www.Valerie-BowmanBooks.com.

Discover great authors, exclusive offers, and more at hc.com.

Sophie and the Duke

By Tiffany Clare

I don't think anyone loves
Christmas more than you did, B.
I love you for being who you were and for
helping to shape the woman I grew up to be.
You are forever in my heart.

Chapter One

Kent, England
The Duke of Helmsworth's Christmastide masked ball

ADRIAN TRENTON, THE Duke of Helmsworth, was looking for a bride. Sophie Kinsley supposed he would have to eventually marry, but finding the right person to be his duchess at a masked Christmastide ball seemed . . . peculiar.

Sophie ducked her head so the stiff feathers atop her mask didn't hit the carriage doorway. A footman held out his white gloved hand to assist her down the steps. She took the proffered hand, since the voluminous skirts her cousin insisted she wear were easily tangled around her ankles. Not once in her eight and twenty years had she dressed so elegantly. And she loved every moment of it.

"Oh, my," her cousin Isabelle muttered in Sophie's ear. "I never quite imagined there would be this many attendees."

"After the open invitation that went out, I am not surprised. Half of London is likely here." An invitation for a Christmas ball had gone out only last week, announcing that the duke was looking for a bride.

Sophie had known the duke since they were both children. Their families lived on neighboring estates, and their parents had become fast friends, with their children born only four months apart. Adrian and Sophie had played together until he'd moved away to be educated in a proper school. She hadn't seen him for nearly fifteen years and couldn't even imagine what he looked like now. Would he have a gray streak through his hair like his father had? Would he be tall? Average?

It was hard to imagine any duke being average, especially the Duke of Helmsworth.

She shoved her wandering thoughts to the back of her mind. The duke needed a bride. And Sophie was too long in the tooth to court the idea. Not that she was here for the sake of marriage. Isabelle would be married in the spring, and they were merely enjoying one last grand celebration together.

While the thought of her cousin marrying and leaving her behind was enough to make her cry on a normal day, the night ahead kept the mood bright. She hadn't been to a ball in too many years to count, and never as an invited guest.

"It will be much easier for us to get lost in this melee than I imagined," Sophie said, for she had good reason to want to get lost in the crowd.

They walked into a marble-encased foyer that was grand enough to double as a spare ballroom. There were six ivory-colored marble pillars that stood as high as the house and ended at the arched ceiling. A crystal chandelier that held more than a hundred candles gave the room a soft glow that sparkled like a night sky. Artwork that was taller than her five and a half feet and wider than the panniers under her cousin's dress displayed previous generations of dukes and duchesses. Sophie remembered staring up at them when she was a child, wondering at their beauty.

Once her cousin helped her out of her mantle, she returned the favor and then handed them to a waiting footman.

"I think every eligible young lady in England is here to vie for the duke's hand in marriage. Perhaps you should, as well, cousin," Isabelle said. Quieter, she added, "After all, you do share a common history."

Sophie let out a wholly unladylike sound that was a cross between a snort and a cough. "I will do no such thing. Besides, my stepsister is amongst the ranks of women in line to steal the duke's attentions, as she wishes to win the duchess title from every other eligible young lady present. We both know no one will marry someone of my age. And the duke? Goodness, cousin, it's been *years* since we last laid eyes upon each other. It's unlikely I would even recognize him."

Though she didn't truly believe that, for she knew, deep in her heart, that she would never forget what her best friend looked like.

"I found a match at my age," Isabelle said.

"You are two years younger than I."

"That doesn't make marriage impossible." Her cousin looked around at the crush of guests as they navigated through costumed person after costumed person. Sophie had never seen so many people in one place and doubted that an average ball would be attended by so many.

Isabelle tilted her head toward Sophie, eyeing the deep-sapphire-colored gown she wore. "You are easily the most beautiful attendee, and I daresay you could steal the duke's attentions if you put your mind to it. Look at all the eyes you are drawing in our direction."

Sophie blushed. She disliked being praised by others, but when it came from her cousin, who had always been her champion, it was different . . . it was genuine.

"It's the gown, which I cannot thank you enough for."

"Anything that is mine is yours." Isabelle focused her soft brown eyes on Sophie. "And you never know whom you'll meet tonight. If not the duke, who is to say you can't meet some other dashing man who will fall head over heels in love with you."

Her cousin was ever hopeful. The truth was, Sophie had no means, no inheritance, nothing to offer any man aside from her status as a lady. And anyone who married her would have to put up with her stepmother and stepsister. She was sure that in itself was enough to keep any potential suitors away. Marriage had always been a distant dream for Sophie, so she'd never put much thought into it.

"Need I remind you that neither of us is here to make a match but to enjoy the night to the fullest?"

Sophie touched the edge of her mask to make sure it was secure before she pulled her cousin toward the ballroom. Sophie's heartbeat quickened; while nervous over the possibility of being discovered by her stepmother, she was excited to be part of tonight's festivities.

And to think she almost hadn't come!

"This will be my last grand outing as Miss Isabelle Kinsley," Isabelle said. "Sometimes I wonder why I agreed to marry Freddie."

"Because he is kind to you. I know you, Isabelle. No matter the circumstance you and your mother find yourself in, you wouldn't have said yes had you not been fond of him."

Frederick was the Earl of Carswall, and he was a good man. When Isabelle's father had died, the family had struggled to keep the lifestyle they'd been accustomed to on a fraction of the funds they'd previously enjoyed. Isabelle's marriage would give her and her mother the financial security they needed. While the union was not a love match, there was no doubt in Sophie's mind that it would grow into one.

"Freddie hates these types of affairs. What if I never attend another ball?" Isabelle pouted out her ruby-painted lower lip.

"He will give you everything you desire. And he can't avoid all social functions in his position."

Isabelle looked away. "You know as well as I that this match was my mother's doing. She feared we'd become destitute if I didn't marry a man of great wealth."

"She wouldn't have agreed had you been ill suited."

"I am always going to wonder if the only enticement she needed was his ten thousand pounds a year."

"I don't believe that for one moment. And neither should you. Your mother takes your best interests to heart." Sophie wished her stepmother cared enough about her to do the same, but her stepmother's main goal since her father's death had been to make her life miserable and lonely. "Let's promise to not dwell on anything but us for the remainder of the evening."

"It's hard to do that when I'll be moving away after the New Year. I always thought we would marry and have children of our own at the same time. I'm afraid we'll grow apart when I move."

"That's nonsense. And stop thinking that way. I will write you every day."

Isabelle visibly gathered herself, standing taller as she took in a deep breath. "Then I agree that we should dispense of this maudlin conversation and enjoy the ball."

Sophie squeezed her cousin's hand before she focused her attention on the room around them. Even though she'd been to this house plenty of times as a child, Sophie took a moment to enjoy the beauty of the architecture. The ballroom floor was an intricate pattern of dark and light hardwoods. Tall rounded pillars lined the edge of the long rectangular room. White paneling covered the walls three-quarters of the way up, and the rest was painted in gold leaf.

But none of that was what made this particular room so beautiful; it was the scene played out on the frescoed ceiling in rich oil paints, which was nearly as old as the house itself. It was in this room that Sophie had learned every Greek tragedy and victory—as depicted above their heads in vivid color—under her friend's tutelage. That was before her dearest friend, Adrian, became the Duke of Helmsworth.

She closed her eyes for just a moment and caught the faintest snippet of memory of Adrian telling her about Bacchus and Ariadne falling in love at first sight and the artist drawing hundreds of stars on the ceiling where Ariadne had been raised to the heavens; those painted stars shone in the candlelight even now.

"Have you ever seen anything so breathtaking?" Isabelle asked, drawing Sophie out of her reverie.

"It's been a long time since either of us have been here. We were too young to truly appreciate the beauty of this place as children."

"I am glad we get to see it once more." Isabelle grabbed Sophie's hand and pushed through the guests until they were a few steps away from joining the country dance that some of the guests had lined up for.

"Do you think we should try the dance?" Isabelle asked.

"Are you sure you don't want to attend the competitions in the garden or cards in the games room?" Sophie said. Of all the places her stepmother and stepsister might be, the ballroom was the likely choice. And running into them could very well ruin both her and Isabelle's night.

Sophie studied the room around them, remembering a moment from her childhood when she and Adrian had hid on the mezzanine level that jutted out over one side of the ballroom, watching a party just like this. She looked up then and saw two men standing there watching the events of the ballroom.

She squinted her eyes . . . was that the duke standing with an older gentleman?

The younger man appeared to study the crowd with little interest. With his hands curled around the upper railing, his body seemed tense and . . . unwilling. Then his gaze landed on her and paused. He had the same powerful presence his father once had, and even at this distance, she could see the resemblance. How embarrassing to be caught staring, and of all the people to be caught staring at.

Sophie ducked her head, and her fingers skimmed over the edge of her mask to ensure it was secure. Her identity was safe.

"I think we should join in for the next dance," Isabelle said, pulling Sophie to the dance floor. "No one will recognize us."

"I can't help but feel this will end badly for me." Sophie looked at the nameless faces around her, looking for the two people who had the power to ruin her and Isabelle's night.

"What can your stepmother possibly do?"

"Keep me from seeing you."

That was the last thing either of them wanted.

"How about we give each other a signal if we see either of your step-relations?"

Isabelle always knew the right thing to say to put Sophie at ease. "I'll flick my fan open if I spot them," Sophie decided.

"And I shall do the same," Isabelle said. "Now let us fill the rest of our night with more fun than we imagined possible."

Isabelle took Sophie's hand and pulled her right into

the middle of the dance floor where dancers formed two neat rows for the next country set.

Sophie looked across from her. Her dance partner was tall, his hair fair, and she had no idea who he was. That gave her comfort in knowing her identity was likely just as much a mystery. With her brown hair and dull brown eyes, there wasn't anything about her that would make her stand out in a crowd. Tipping her head, she curtsied to her partner before taking his hand and following the steps with the rest of the dancers.

"MY FATHER CANNOT possibly have expected me to pick the future duchess in a crowd of three hundred, Uncle Albert." Adrian pulled at the front of his jacket. This whole situation was strange. Tonight's purpose and outcome were to save this house and surrounding lands. He could never forget that. He wanted to keep this estate for his children.

"If it were up to me, I'd have given you some time to choose," his uncle said. "The good part of tonight is that every eligible woman in a fifty-mile radius is here. You have the pick of the crop. I suggest you make good use of the night ahead and find your bride before it's too late to save the estate."

Today marked the one-year anniversary of his father's passing. One week ago Adrian had received a sealed envelope from his father's solicitor. The writing on the outside had been his father's. When Adrian had opened it, a lot of the troubles he'd had obtaining funds from the estate had become clear. He needed to marry before the rest of the money tied into the estate could be released to him.

His father's note had been short, saying that if his son had already found someone to love and marry, he wished them a great future together. If not, Adrian had one week to fulfill that final duty as a son, or the money tied into the estate would remain out of reach until his thirtieth birthday, which was two years away. Problematic, since he could no longer hold off paying the succession duty for the estate.

His father's note had also included very specific instructions on how Adrian should go about finding this elusive bride, so here he was, holding a Christmastide ball in search of her, whoever *her* turned out to be. He knew his father had meant well, and the past year had been full of change for Adrian; no carousing and gambling into the wee hours of the morning, no more nameless women adorning his arm—and his bed. He had taken his responsibility as the Duke of Helmsworth seriously. But his father was not here to see that change.

Adrian had never been opposed to marriage; he had always assumed he would meet someone he liked well enough to court, and then eventually propose in his own time. It was almost distasteful to pick a bride in a roomful of masked guests. This was a lifelong decision, and to make it in one night . . .

What if Adrian chose someone he despised?

This was not a decision he intended to make lightly, as it affected not only his life but also the bride-to-be's.

"It's a bit . . . severe to have to pick someone I do not know. Someone I cannot even see."

"Your father did like to have the last laugh."

"That he did." Adrian raked his fingers through his hair. "Tell me whom you recognize."

"No one." His uncle laughed. "That is the point of having a masked ball."

"I'm beginning to despise that fact more and more as the night goes on. And I do believe you are lying to me. You are enjoying my predicament."

His uncle slapped him on the shoulder. "I recommend you get on with it while the night is young."

"Yes, I suppose there is no time like the present."

Adrian rubbed his hand through his unruly hair and took one last look at the clusters of attendees before descending the stairs. Though he wore a mask as everyone else did, his presence did not go unnoticed, because the guests parted to allow him entry into the middle of the room.

A young woman in a virginal blush gown and white-feathered mask stepped forward on the hand of her father. She seemed out of breath, as though her father had made her run for the opportunity to be the first to dance with the duke.

"May I present my daughter, Your Grace." The man did not give his daughter's name, as the invitation was very specific in that the bride would remain a mystery to the prince of the ball—which was him, unfortunately—until he was overcome with what . . . affection?

Adrian imagined his father would love seeing his son

rip off his mask at the end of the night and go down on one knee to press his suit to the lucky lady who should enamor him above everyone else.

The young woman curtsied as her father held her hand out to Adrian, which he took, for what else was he to do? This was likely how the evening would go. Nameless women would dance with him all evening, followed only by banal conversation that would bore him to tears before half the night was through.

Adrian walked the young woman into the middle of the ballroom. She could not have been a day over eighteen; her cheeks were red in embarrassment, her hand shook in his as he turned her to face him for the dance the orchestra started up.

"Your Grace, it is a pleasure to make your acquaintance." The young woman's voice was shaky and nervous.

"And yours, my lady. Do you live in Helmsworth?"

"Norwich, Your Grace. We are visiting relatives in Helmsworth for the winter season."

Helmsworth was a town of estates and rolling lands of green. Perfect to escape to during the heat of London's summers and an even better retreat during the cold winter months, when you wanted nothing more than to shut yourself in and sit by a warm fire. Though that was far from what was happening now.

Had the night really only just begun?

Chapter Two

Sophie knew the moment the duke entered the lower room. And he was as devilishly handsome as her imagination had built him up to be over the years. Gone was the boy she had grown up with. In his place stood a man with a strong and determined bearing. The duke was tall, his shoulders wide. His dark—almost black—hair was on the long and unruly side, with streaks of gray at the temples. She couldn't make out his eyes from the distance that spanned between them, but she wondered if a hint of mischief could still be found in them.

The duke did not wear a costume, only evening dress and a simple black mask. She supposed the purpose of the night for him was not to hide but to participate in his upcoming engagement.

Sophie focused her gaze elsewhere as he walked his dance partner out onto the floor for the next country set.

How odd was it that she didn't want to be recognized?

Even though it was unlikely he would know her, considering they hadn't seen each other in fifteen years, it was the possibility that had her heart beating a little faster in her chest.

"Might I claim you for the next dance," the gentleman next to her said, a hint of something dark and mysterious in his voice. He was dressed in Georgian costume, powdered wig and all. While he didn't have the same height as the duke, he stood taller than her and carried himself in a distinguished manner that said he was someone worth noting.

As the orchestra started the next set, the gentleman took her hand and bowed regally. His hold was firm and warm as he guided her into the right position on the floor. Before she could protest or ask for a later dance, they were moving through the steps in line with the duke. Sophie was handed off to the next partner, and then the next, until she was in the duke's arms. She was so stunned by her stupidity that she forgot every rule of etiquette she'd ever learned during her dancing lessons and uttered not one word as their steps started.

His blue eyes were more beautiful than memory served. So much so it was difficult to tear her gaze away from his. That must have been a belated and stunned reaction to having been flung into his arms.

"Good evening, Your Grace," she finally mustered. "It's interesting that we should find ourselves dancing together instead of playing spectators as we used to."

The duke searched her eyes, as though he was sifting through all her secrets. Sophie blinked. Why had she given him that much information? She had planned to pretend ignorance, pretend she didn't know him.

"There is something vaguely familiar about you," he said. "Have we met, my lady?"

She didn't dare mention that they'd had the same dance instructor, or that they'd learned to dance together.

"I have spoken out of turn." She cleared her throat. "What is it that you find familiar in me?"

"The way you carry yourself. Almost as if we have danced before."

"Maybe we have," she teased, then internally chastised herself. What was she thinking?

While she wasn't one to outright lie, she knew she couldn't reveal who she was. The duke would surely feel obligated to ask what she'd done during the years they'd been apart. It was also possible he wouldn't remember her.

"I am intrigued," he said.

She stammered a few sounds of confusion that made her want to groan at her insipidness, then she was handed off to her original dance partner.

She breathed a sigh of relief.

"I should like to find you again after this dance, my lady," her partner said.

"I think that would be acceptable." What was she saying? She didn't want to dance with nameless men all evening. Her cousin's voice rang clear in the back of her mind, telling her this was a night she could be anyone she wanted to be, be with anyone whose company she wanted to enjoy.

"Excellent," he said, bringing her a little closer than what was considered acceptable.

"That is if I can spare the time, my lord. You see, I am here with my cousin, and she will never forgive me if I abandon her for the evening."

"Then I will dance with her and keep you both company."

She ducked her head and smiled. "Your tenacity is to be admired. And you have been an excellent dance partner. I must apologize for being a poor conversationalist."

"And I should have chosen a dance that did not include the duke. Are you one of the ladies vying for his hand?"

The comment seemed to draw the duke's attention their way. Sophie tried hard to not glance over at him but failed.

She blushed at having been caught staring twice now. "I am not," she said, loud enough that she hoped the duke heard.

"Would it be too presumptuous to ask for a second dance?"

She gave him a bright smile. "I would be honored," she said as they switched partners.

It wasn't long before she was with another dance partner, giving her time to think of something witty to say to the duke on their next passing. She made idle chatter about the weather and the event with her other partners. Before she knew it—or could better prepare herself—she was once again in the duke's arms.

"And we meet again," the duke said in his pleasantly deep voice.

"We do, Your Grace." She tipped her head, not that she needed to, but more to break eye contact with him. His hand brushed against her lower back as they turned around each other. She could have pulled away, but she didn't want to.

"You know, I find it wholly unfair that you know who I am, but I do not know precisely who you are. Can you give me a hint as to your identity?"

As tempting as it was to bite onto that and tease him for not remembering her, such a revelation was impossible.

"You did call for a masked ball. I wonder what it would say about my character should I give you even a sliver of information about me."

His hand squeezed hers, their arms brushing as the turned around each other. Sophie did her best to ignore the tingling sensation that ran through her whole body whenever he touched her. He was doing it on purpose, too.

"Yet I'm sure we have met before. Surely you won't keep me in suspense indefinitely?" The duke wore a wry grin, revealing a dimple in one cheek. He really had grown into a handsome man.

"I'm afraid knowing who I am, or any of the attendees, would take the fun out of the evening." She couldn't keep the silly grin from her face. Really, she was just glad to have found her voice.

"You find me amusing," he said.

"Perhaps more than I should."

"I'll try not to take that insult to heart."

"I meant no disrespect, Your Grace."

They turned around each other, their hands almost touching when they should not for this part of the dance. Sophie was allowing herself to get lost in the moment. That would do her no favors. But it was tempting to make a friend of the duke after having been apart for so many years.

"Your silence is a form of torment. Have I upset you?"

"No, Your Grace. I was merely thinking the dance has almost concluded and I've enjoyed our time together. I wish you luck this evening. You have a difficult decision to make in the course of one night."

"What if I said I need look no further?"

Sophie's breath caught. Surely he jested. They'd had two passing conversations, hardly enough to pick a bride from.

"I see that was the last thing you expected me to say. Do you belong to another?"

Sophie couldn't help the blush that painted her cheeks. She was suddenly too hot in this packed room. Thank goodness the dance would end shortly.

"I do not. And I hope you pick your bride with more care than a few dances. She'll have an important seat next to you."

He slowed his steps, and she thought he would end their dance right in the middle of the room, where everyone watched everything the duke did. He realized his mistake quick enough and continued into the next steps.

"I would prefer to spend the evening with those I know."

And what could she say to that? She pinched her mouth shut.

"I see your game. You'll torment me with the knowledge I desire most right now."

She was saved from having to answer, for she was back in her original partner's hands and the dance ended. She wasted no time in letting him walk them off the dance floor, putting as much distance as she could between herself and the duke.

DESPITE BEING THE host of the ball, Adrian would not cater to every one of the eligible young women that seemed to be here in the hundreds. Yes, his father was likely rolling over in his grave in a fit of laughter at Adrian's predicament. Find a bride in a night, all without knowing who she was.

Wanting time to enjoy grandchildren before he was gone, Adrian's father had always wanted Adrian to start a family young. It was too late for that, so what was the rush into marriage about now? Aside from needing the remaining funds of his estate released to him, why couldn't he take a few weeks, at the very least?

It shouldn't strike him as odd that he was most interested in the lady with the least interest in the duchess seat. That might be part of the attraction he felt toward her. He was often spurred on by what was denied him. Right then and there Adrian decided he wasn't willing to let her escape just yet. He came up short of his quarry, stopped by an altogether too eager mother.

"Your Grace," she said in a voice that was shrill enough to cut glass. "I wish to present my daughter."

Adrian barely refrained from rubbing his ringing ears. The daughter in question stepped forward with a curtsy that had likely been perfected from years of practice; she was no spring chicken, not that age alone would sway his decision in a bride.

Adrian raised his hand to stop the mother from saying more. He did not want to know the daughter's or family's name. He did not want to know anyone aside from the woman who'd gotten away.

"If you will excuse me, I have neglected to be somewhere." At the pinched expression on the mother's face, he said, "I offer my sincerest apologies. Please save your daughter's next dance for me."

Words he might live to regret.

Adrian bowed and took his closing promise as an easy escape, bypassing everyone else who thought to stop him. He did not see the black feather top of the mysterious woman who'd slipped through his fingers. His height gave him an advantage in seeing over the heads of most of the guests. Oddly enough, he did not spy his anonymous lady anywhere in the ballroom. How in the world had she escaped so quickly? She'd been determined to avoid him by leaving the moment the dance had concluded, that much was obvious.

Heading for the doors that led to the back gardens, where the flowers had long ago died in the cold that had settled in at the beginning of fall, he slipped outside, hoping for some peace and quiet. Three dances, and he'd had enough of the ball.

How was he going to make it through the rest of the night?

Shutting the doors behind him, he walked toward the stone balustrade wall and stared out over the maze of hedges carved out by stone paths that covered a good two acres of his land.

The cold didn't bother him, and being out here was a better option than being hunted down by a mob of enthusiastic mothers and fathers that wanted their daughters to marry a duke. He needed just a moment to his own thoughts.

His breath fogged in the air with each exhalation as his resolve to find a suitable bride strengthened.

The rustle of material being folded came from behind him. He hated to lose his solitude so soon, but he would not be caught in a compromising position. Spinning around, his reproachful words stalled on his tongue.

His mystery lady had not escaped him after all.

"And, so, fate would have us meet again," he said.

The expression on her face was a mixture of astonishment and . . . exasperation? Was his company so terrible?

"I came out to cool off from the dance. It's been ages since . . ." She caught herself from saying more, biting into the soft pink flesh of her lower lip.

He wanted to capture that part of her with his mouth. Suck on that delicate flesh to see how it tasted.

It was her. There was something about her that drew him in, made him want something that he had been denied.

"If you haven't been to a dance in ages, why come to this one if not in search of a husband?" he boldly asked.

What he also wanted to know was why she seemed intent on avoiding the host of the party.

Adrian moved away from the stone balustrade and stepped in her direction, taking in every detail the closer he got. Her hair was dark and as rich a brown as the top of an acorn. Her dress was a multitude of thin layers of sapphire gauze, giving the impression that she floated when she walked. Her generous breasts were held by the ruching gathered there and over one shoulder in Grecian style. Gold bands of rope wrapped around her rib cage, her waist, her hips, making her look like a goddess come to life. The dress was daring and one that could not have been worn by the majority of guests that had come tonight.

Her dark eyes were inquisitive and sharp, even in the gloom of evening. Her mask was gold and crowned with two Pegasuses holding a shield, which fanned out into a tall array of jet-black feathers. She stood stoic, but he noted a slight shiver that had her hands trembling.

She pressed up against the wall, as though she could disappear into it. That made him grin; he'd caught her, and she had nowhere to escape to without causing a scene to those waiting inside the doors.

Her breasts heaved, whether from excitement or from fear, he couldn't say, though he doubted it was the latter. Her eyes darted every which way without ever making contact with his gaze.

"I think I have you exactly where I want you."

They were safely tucked behind the wall. No one could see them here, not even peering through a window, so Adrian stripped out of his tailcoat.

"What are you doing?" She came forward, ready to stop him, he was sure.

"I cannot call myself a gentleman if I allow you to tremble in my company for another second."

When he had the coat off, he approached the lady. She didn't seem inclined to assist, so he pulled her away from the wall and settled his jacket around her. She had slender shoulders and a willowy frame, so the coat draped around her like a blanket.

"I cannot take your coat, you will catch a chill. I think it best if we made our way indoors before we are missed."

"I am quite accustomed to the cold and find the weather invigorating. And I suspect neither of us wishes to join the party."

"Thank you for your coat," she said in a small voice, huddling deeper into the material. "How, as the host of the party, can you ignore your guests?"

"My guests?" he chuckled. "This ball was my father's harebrained scheme, so the guests are his. I'm enjoying your company far more than I will enjoy the lot in there."

"But we have only exchanged snippets of conversation. Hardly enough to form any sort of bond."

"I believe we will make great allies tonight, my lady."

"Is that so?"

"Yes. You see, I don't wish to marry any of the women in there, and you seem intent on avoiding me at every turn."

"I fail to understand how that makes us allies."

"I believe we can assist each other."

She was quiet a moment before she asked, "How so?"

"You do not wish to marry me, and I never expected to be in a position quite like the one I find myself in. We could make a very agreeable match."

"How precisely would we do that, when you don't even know who I am?"

"So you admit to knowing me?"

She turned away, not responding. Adrian wracked his mind over who she was, and why she was familiar.

"Our standards on the perfect marital partner may vary," she finally said. "What traits are you even looking for in a wife?"

"She should be passably pretty."

Except the woman standing before him was far too beautiful to only be considered pretty. His companion made a derisive sound in her throat.

"You do not approve that there should be some physical attraction?"

"I don't believe that a comely face should be your biggest worry in finding a bride."

"Fine, then I will say that I want someone who has at least experienced life."

"Are you suggesting that I'm a spinster?" She wasn't insulted by the insinuation, for she was smiling.

"Simply more mature and flavored than the swarms of eighteen-year-old would-be brides in attendance tonight."

Her disposition brightened, and she took a step toward him. She perused him carefully from head to toe—assessing him. The way she studied him had him shifting on his feet to hide his growing . . . affection.

That was not the kind of reaction he expected, having only just met her.

"So you wish to find a bride who is more . . . *mature.*"

He nodded. There was something about her smile, about the way she spoke. He knew her, but for the life of him, he could not think from where.

"Where did we meet before?" he asked. He needed to know.

"If I reveal that, it will spoil the mystery of our moment."

Her quick response had him returning her smile.

"I'm not so sure," he responded. Admittedly the woman before him intrigued him, but he doubted that would change should he discover her true identity. "Might I escort you on an evening walk?" He held out his arm, and to his surprise, she hesitated for only half a second before opening up his coat enough to slip her arm through his.

Chapter Three

SOPHIE TOLD HERSELF for the tenth time that it was impossible for him to guess precisely who she was. She couldn't say why she didn't want to reveal that tidbit of information, just that she didn't want to ruin the flirtatious exchange between her and the duke.

Not just the duke but Adrian, she thought wistfully; she'd always called him by his Christian name when they were children. Doing so now would be the height of impropriety, not to mention that it would reveal just how well she knew him.

While she had very little interaction with men suitable for marriage, her stepmother having kept her away from any possible suitors, Sophie did not engage in flirtation as a general rule. Flirtation led to innuendo, which could very well lead to acting recklessly, which always led to all other sorts of trouble.

Trouble she was not willing to gamble on, except . . .

She *had* taken the duke's proffered arm. And she had let him lead her farther down the path of the delectable—and she was sure sinful—unknown.

This was her first ball, so why couldn't she be reckless this once?

"I would pay a great sum to know what has snagged your thoughts."

"Only that you might be whisking me away to seduce and sully my good reputation, Your Grace. It would be a simple end to your night, after all, to have to declare the spinster on your arms your fiancée and have your task completed."

She pinched her mouth shut to keep from saying more, though he chuckled low and deep, a sound totally agreeable and not to mention swoon-worthy to her fast-beating heart. While she was on occasion outspoken, she typically thought her words out before speaking bluntly.

"And what if I were doing just that?"

"Are you?" She pulled them both to a stop before they could fully descend the stairs and enter into the maze of hedges that she could find her way through with her eyes closed. How many times had they played hide-and-seek in this very maze? Or hidden deep in the center when their governesses had called them back for their lessons?

This place brought back memories of a much better time in her life, a time when her father was still alive, before he'd ever met her stepmother, before her whole world had shattered and been left empty.

She tipped her head back and inhaled the cool, crisp night air. It smelled of winter, like the Christmas season of her childhood, with all the coniferous trees and tall hedges still showing their green.

"I love this place," she said, her voice breathless, and full of emotion she was having difficulty tamping down.

"Don't worry." He patted her hand and pulled her farther down the path, and what she couldn't help but think might be her certain ruin. "I won't do anything without your consent," he said.

"Not the kind of reassuring words I should like to hear, Your Grace."

"I would apologize for my forwardness, but I am convinced we already know each other." He leaned in close to her ear, his breath hot against her nape. "Perhaps quite well."

She couldn't stop the thrill that raced through her whole body and made her sway into his side. He was there to steady her, his body firm and strong as his hand pressed low on her back to keep her moving forward.

"What kind of woman do you take me for?"

"A sensible one, even though you've let me steal you away from the ball."

"Some would call it the ball of the century."

He laughed at that, though it lacked a certain quality of humor. "Because the duke will find his wife before midnight? Like some bloody fairy-tale prince. This ball was not how I expected to find my duchess."

"Then why go about it in such a grand fashion?"

"A prying question, my lady."

"I seem to have struck at a sore spot." She stopped walking again. This time she slipped her arm out from under his and turned to face him. "If you want my help, you'll have to reveal more of the truths you are hiding."

"You cannot guess?"

She looked up at him quizzically, though it was difficult to make out his features in the dark of the maze. They could no longer see the lights from the house—it was them, the hedges, and the stars above that dotted in and out on a cloudy night. A breeze whistled around them, lifting some of her curls and dragging them over her shoulder.

The duke caught one and held it between his finger and thumb. She could guess very well what his intentions were.

"Why do people prefer to pursue what they cannot have?" she asked.

"Because that is always what is most desirable."

"I cannot marry." It was almost the truth.

"You are promised to another?" Surprise laced his question.

She saw no way of answering untruthfully. "That is not what I meant."

"Then I see no reason not to go after what I want most in this moment."

He tugged the curl he still held, twirling it around his finger, pulling her closer. While it might appear he drew her in, she knew she went of her own free will.

"There are a hundred reasons I should pull away," she whispered the closer his lips got to hers.

"And a thousand reasons to at least see if the spark between us still exists after one solitary kiss."

"One kiss cannot tell you that."

He reached beneath the folds of his coat and fished for something in the pocket. While his hands sought one thing, his knuckles grazed the undersides of her breasts in a not-so-innocent touch. The stays she wore were paper thin and suited for the Grecian style of her dress. Did he feel the tremor that ran through her body with that one forbidden touch? Had he heard the hiss of her inhalation? A sound that indicated she was not unaffected by his forwardness.

"My argument makes perfect sense?" he said, pulling free something small and raising it above their heads.

She looked up, trying to make it out in the dark, but all she saw was a twig with leaves. "What is that?"

"Mistletoe."

She couldn't help herself, she laughed. "Do you carry mistletoe wherever you go?"

"Only should the occasion require it."

He hooked his arm around her back, beneath that coat, pulling their bodies close enough that they touched breast to chest. Her nipples pebbled and poked into him, the sensation not exactly unpleasant. And though she had an insatiable and inexplicable need to rub herself harder against him, she held herself completely still.

"Have you been kissed before, my lady?"

"And if I have?" she asked, her head tilting back, her body arching tighter into his. Their noses brushed, back and forth, back and forth. She was entranced, snared, caught in the trap he'd woven around her with his wickedness.

"Have you ever felt the burn of passion sear you from the inside out and all from a mere press of your lips upon another's?"

She was not able to respond, for his lips brushed over hers and suddenly nothing else mattered. No answer, no quip, nothing but the gentle rub of his mouth across hers was what she wanted.

His lips were surprisingly soft, yet demanding, as they parted hers. Her breath rushed out of her, which he caught and gave back to her before her next inhalation. Their mouths carefully melted together, learning every contour. This was nothing like the innocent kiss he'd given her when they were twelve; then it had only been a press of lips and as innocent as it had been quick and gentle.

This . . .

This was sinful. Much more, better even, than she could ever have imagined a *mere kiss* could be. While she could not claim this as her first kiss, it was by the only man she'd ever cared for aside from her father. When Adrian pulled away, she followed, not wanting their stolen moment to end just yet, wanting to pretend she could actually be his bride.

His choice for the night.

The repercussions of such a joining would be monumental and historic in the house of Kinsley. Kinsley women did what they were told, when they were told. And she'd had it drilled into her from the time of her father's death until only last night that she would never marry. That she would be her stepmother's companion for the rest of her days.

None of that mattered anymore.

The firm caress of his thumb brushing over her lips had her eyes opening. It was over far too soon for her liking.

"I could swear I've felt these lips upon me once before."

It was then that she realized the foolishness of everything she'd not only let happen but had been an active participant in tonight. She pulled out of his hold, his coat falling to the stone path at their feet. She was too heated from his touch to feel the cold.

"It was unwise of me to have walked with you," she stammered out in an anxious voice. It would be the height of idiocy to stay now that she'd come to her senses. She turned to leave.

He caught her hand and spun her around so fast that she slammed into his formidable body. The air whooshed out of her lungs the moment his mouth seized hers in a kiss that was much, much more than the one he'd teased her with moments ago. There was no dancing or testing the waters as he dove right in, his tongue sliding past her lips to twist around her tongue. Their breaths fed off each other's as they tasted and teased, as they devoured and claimed.

What she did know was that this was a kiss to end all kisses.

This would be the end of her.

This *was* the end of her.

No one would fill the place this man had carved out in her life. Not only had he been a friend and her teacher where her ladies studies had lacked but now he was her . . . her what? She couldn't think. She only wanted more of his kisses. To be locked in his arms forever and forget everything else except the two of them.

The palm of one of his hands rested low on her back, his fingers kneading tight circles that made her body warm and lax; she had surrendered into his hold, given herself over to a man she couldn't really claim to know anymore. His other hand curled into her hair, holding her head at an angle he most desired for their kiss. She did not struggle, she did not move. Afraid to show him just how desperate she was to be his, she clenched her fists around his shirtsleeves and held on for dear life as he tilted her head back, arching her over his arm to kiss her deeper.

She hated that she had to walk away from him after this. Hated that she couldn't be the one to steal his attention and his affections and become his bride.

It was the fact that she wasn't supposed to be here tonight that had her stiffening in his hold. Her eyes opened, and she gave a cursory glance to their surroundings to ensure they were still alone. He released her slowly, his tongue caressing her lips, instead of tasting deeply of her mouth before their lips pressed together again like they had the first time. His lips parted from hers, she felt the loss of intimacy and excitement between them being squashed out of existence, like a fire under a bucket of water.

Why did reality have to come crashing to the fore?

Sophie found her footing, only now realizing he held her completely off her feet. She cleared her throat delicately, at a loss for words. Everything she wanted to say seemed inadequate and trite.

The duke was breathing heavily as he stared back at her. She felt like a doe caught in the sight of a predator. If she attempted to run again, she knew he would catch her without any effort. She closed her eyes, put her shoulders back, and tried to compose herself, which was hard to do when her heart was racing, her breathing was erratic, and her body practically trembled to be held by his again.

He seemed to compose himself quicker than she did. Picking up his coat, he dusted it off and put it back on. He straightened the lapels to ensure he looked the part of duke and not a scoundrel who'd just thoroughly seduced one of his guests.

"I recall you enjoying that kiss as much as I, so if I am a scoundrel, that makes you my minx."

Sophie slapped her hand over her mouth. "I hadn't meant to say that aloud."

"I did not think so." He held out his hand, which she eyed wearily. "I won't bite."

"I find that hard to believe." And to prove her point, she did not take his hand. Really, she didn't want to end up kissing him again, because that was exactly what she wanted to do. Oh, good Lord, how had she gotten herself into this predicament?

ADRIAN COULD HARDLY believe he'd lost all control of the situation with his mystery woman. He'd meant to give her nothing more than a chaste kiss. But there was a fire burning under his skin that had been ignited the moment he'd taken her into his arms.

And he wanted more.

None of what had happened negated the fact that he found something familiar in her. He just couldn't place where he knew her from.

He'd been tempted to remove her mask during their kiss, but he'd been just as lost as she'd been from the moment he had hauled her into his arms, afraid that their moment would be lost had she actually gotten away from him. While he knew they could not remain out here for much longer, he was reluctant to see her out of his company.

"I promise to be a perfect gentleman from here on out."

"Then you take half the fun out of the danger you present to me."

He grinned, and before she could hesitate, he took her hand and tucked her arm against his side. She was shivering again, but he could not offer his coat if they were to return to the ball. Instead, he placed his arm around her shoulders and held her tight, rubbing his hands along her arm to bring some heat to it. She did not complain, so he continued to do it.

"While it's warmer than it's been in nearly a month, I underestimated that this gown could contend with the winter season."

"The most beautiful dress I have seen tonight. And I'm more than happy to keep you warm. Soon you will pray for the cold again."

She gave him a sidelong look, curiosity clear in her expression. "And why should I do that?"

"Because I plan on dancing with you for what remains of the evening."

She halted, as though her feet had suddenly stuck to the ground.

"You cannot monopolize my time." A thread of worry filtered through her voice.

And then it dawned on him. She did not wish to be discovered.

"I must confess to something," she continued. "Or really, I should explain that I rarely attend these types of social functions. I'm afraid I know only a handful of people here tonight. Most I do not recognize or could not make out beneath their costumes and masks."

"So you *are* vying for my duchess's seat."

"That, I can promise you, is not my intention. I could not miss an opportunity to see this house once more—"

So she'd been here at least once before.

"You make marriage to me sound like an unfavorable task."

She inhaled sharply, horrified to have suggested such a thing, he was sure. He was not above using that to his advantage.

"You mistake my meaning," she said.

They were walking up the stairs, and regrettably, he knew he had to release her. Adrian was not willing to put any one of his guests—especially someone whose company he enjoyed—under the scrutiny of the *ton* and the dozens of gossips in attendance hoping to be the first to announce his nuptials.

"I jest in poor taste. Forgive me."

"There is nothing to forgive." She looked at him for a silent moment. "I must get back, my cousin will be looking for me."

"I haven't forgotten that you owe me a dance," he called after her as she reentered the ballroom.

It would be noticed if they entered together, so he gave her some time before slipping in behind her. Why should he care what anyone thought if he was enjoying his evening and had found the only company he intended to wile away the evening with?

His uncle Albert stood by the entrance, one eyebrow raised above the silver mask he wore. Censure from his uncle was a rare thing.

"It is a bit cool this evening to be spent outdoors," his uncle mused aloud.

Adrian made no remark; it was his business what he did at his own ball. And he would not pretend he hadn't met someone who interested him above all others.

"Do you know who she is?" Adrian nodded in the direction of his mysterious lady. She held the hands of another young woman, leaning in close to whisper something in her ear. This had to be the cousin she mentioned.

"I do not know her. But that is Miss Isabelle Kinsley she speaks with."

"Kinsley?" He wanted to laugh at his own stupidity

and inability to recognize who the woman was. "You don't say."

"Yes, that is precisely what I said. I can only assume that is Lady Sophie she converses with. She has the look of her mother about her. It's my understanding she rarely leaves the old cottage her father owned."

Sophie and he had been the best of friends as children. They'd lost touch when he'd been sent to Eton. At first they'd written, but as time had passed, they'd lost contact with each other.

Adrian slapped his uncle on the back of the shoulder before walking toward his not-so- mysterious lady friend. The women broke apart and curtsied at his approach.

"You must be the infamous cousin, used as an escape from my poor company."

Miss Kinsley turned her head to the side inquisitively. "Your Grace?"

In a bold move he knew would be noted and whispered about, he took Miss Kinsley's hands familiarly in his own. "I heard of your engagement. Let me be the first to congratulate you tonight."

When she tugged her hand free of his, he held on tighter and smiled brightly. Miss Kinsley leaned in closer to him. "You are making a scene, Your Grace."

"Should old friends not greet each other fondly?"

The young woman blushed, embarrassed. "Of course. I assume introductions are unnecessary for my companion?"

He turned to Sophie. She was stark white beneath her mask, as though she might faint from being put in the center of attention. "We've already had the pleasure of re-acquainting ourselves."

He held out his hand. "I do believe they are starting up a waltz, my lady. Would you be so kind as to dance with me?"

She looked around the room, to the crowd of eyes focused on them. "You know I cannot refuse."

"Just the words I wanted to hear."

He took her hand and led her toward the other dancers in the middle of the room.

"Do you enjoy the waltz?" he asked.

"This is probably not a good time to admit this, but I learned the steps before my coming out. Being more . . . mature, it's been a few years since I have had the opportunity to enjoy this particular dance."

"I will not let you falter."

"And that is not what I'm afraid of," she mumbled under her breath.

"Was I meant to hear what you said this time?"

"As a matter of fact, yes, you were. While you are barely the boy I recognize, you have not grown less obstinate over the years."

"I will take that as a compliment. You should know I'm generally a man who gets what he wants."

"Except your pick of a bride."

"That was a low hit, but I perhaps deserved that."

He placed his free hand over the middle of her back. "Do you remember the basic steps?"

Her brown eyes snapped with something close to annoyance.

Chapter Four

Did she remember the steps to this dance?

Of course she did.

Sophie had this inexplicable need to step on his toes to prove a point. But what point would that be? There were too many eyes on them as it was. So she would not get any satisfaction in making a fool of herself. No, she must make her next move carefully, because this would be her last dance of the evening. There was no other way for the night to play out now that everyone stared at her, wondering about her identity.

For the first time tonight, she hated that she'd run into Adrian at all . . . well, not really. What she hated was the fact that her stepmother could come forward at any moment and ruin the night and her memories forever.

"I would have approached our public meeting differently had you given me your name."

"And what purpose would that have served, Your Grace? Nothing will come of this dance."

"I disagree."

"I was not lying when I said I could not marry."

"Are you dying?"

That caught her off guard. "Pardon?"

"The only reason I can think for you to be unattainable is that you are sick and will die any day now. Let me rephrase that question, are you knocking on death's door? Because you certainly do not look ill."

She couldn't hold back the smile. "What an absurd question. And the wrong assumption."

"It is a valid one when we have a common interest."

"And what interest would that be?"

"To begin,"—he leaned in closer—"another kiss. I think we would both like to disappear into the darkness of the maze and explore just what another kiss feels like."

She looked away. Many of the guests had stopped dancing to watch the path they cut across the ballroom floor. Her body stiffened; she wanted nothing more than to fall back into the shadows and be another nameless girl to whom no one gave a second glance.

"I hardly think the direction of our conversation appropriate," she said.

"Then tell me why you cannot marry."

"You'll think my reason silly."

"No reason is silly if you would force me to find another potential duchess."

"So you would throw me over for another if I insisted we could not be a match?"

"I was hoping to incite jealousy or envy, something to give me reason to win your affections this night."

She sighed.

What girl didn't want a man to utter those kinds of words to her at her first ball? She moved into him, wishing to be close, to give their lips reason to touch.

She caught herself and turned her head away.

It would only be a matter of time before everyone figured out who she was if she stayed in the duke's arms for more than one dance. She could already hear the soft din of whispers starting up around them.

Who is she? Where does she hail from? Who did she arrive with?

Her heart beat at a tempo so fast she felt light-headed.

"You seem nervous." The duke took his eyes off her to look around the room. "Are you hiding from someone? Have we given away too much by dancing together?"

She gave him a sad smile. "I'm not supposed to be here, so when this dance ends, you must let me leave."

"I cannot."

"You must," she said on a frustrated breath.

"I can see you are distressed and that my dancing skills cannot even keep your attention, for your feet have faltered twice."

She stepped on his foot. Intentionally this time. "What was that about my dancing skills?"

"I was teasing you."

The duke grinned and placed his hand more firmly over her back as he turned them around the room. "I'm glad to have your full attention again. You do us both a disservice when you look like you would rather be anywhere but here dancing with the duke of the ball."

"I would rather be where no one could see us," she mumbled.

"We could go back out to the maze."

"You are still frustrating when you are determined to have your way."

"Ah, so you do recall our time together as children."

"It is rather hard to forget. You were always finding trouble for us."

"It was all the good kinds of trouble we found ourselves in. The mischief of twelve-year-olds."

"My father's reaction was to marry and give me the mother he thought I needed to temper my firm will."

That had happened shortly after Adrian had left for school. Her life had never been carefree and wild again and had become one of strict rules and regimented lessons.

"By the tone of your voice, I take it you dislike your stepmother."

This was a conversation she did not wish to have with Adrian. Their dance, thankfully, was coming to a close. When it ended, she pulled her hand away from his and curtsied. "Thank you for the dance, Your Grace."

Other attendees drew closer, likely hoping to foist their own daughters upon the duke for the next musical set. Before he could reach for her or ask her to stay, she stepped back into the crowd and turned away. Of course luck would have it that she plowed right into her stepsister, Esther.

They both tumbled clumsily to the ground in a heap of blue and yellow chiffon. Sophie knocked her hip hard into the floor but managed to get her feet under herself before her stepsister did. Sophie reached for Esther's hand, not saying a word, as she knew her voice would give her identity away.

"You should be more careful of where you're going," Esther said, fixing her crooked mask.

Sophie didn't stop to apologize; she slipped through the crowd like a mouse trying to find its freedom after being spotted where it should not be. She found her cousin by the punch table.

"We have to leave, Isabelle. I was nearly cornered by my stepsister. If she finds out we are here . . ."

"Say no more." Sophie's cousin took her arm, and they all but ran back to the entrance of the house, where footmen waited at the ready. Once their mantles were retrieved, they stood outside and waited for the carriage to come around. The temperature had dropped somewhat, and they both huddled close together to share their warmth.

"Are you going to tell me about your duke?" her cousin said in a teasing tone.

"He's not my anything. We were discussing our childhood, nothing more."

"You danced far too close for it to not be an intimate dance. I think half the ladies were fanning themselves and wishing they were in your slippers tonight."

Sophie climbed into the carriage first, eager to be out of sight. "The ball will go on for some hours yet, so they'll all have a chance to dance with him."

Her cousin lounged back in the seat, as though exhausted. "Don't pretend you are unaffected by his appearance at your side tonight. I saw the look on your face when he introduced himself to me. And when he realized who you were."

Sophie untied her mask and placed it in her lap. "I kissed him, Isabelle. I kissed him before he knew who I was."

Her cousin's mouth dropped open. Isabelle practically jumped on her lap, shaking her in her own excitement to know more. "When did that happen? Where was I?"

"I went out for a moment of fresh air, and he was suddenly there. He just sort of found me standing there, trying to hide against the wall. I'm sure I made a sorry sight."

Isabelle squealed. "You kissed the Duke of Helmsworth and we are running away from the ball? I'm of a right mind to turn this carriage around and head back right this second. This could be the moment you've wanted for so long . . ."

"We will do no such thing. Remember we were never here tonight."

"So what if we were?"

"One, there is no guarantee the duke will propose marriage to anyone tonight. Two, I cannot face my stepmother if she finds out what I've done. I have never had a coming out, if you'll recall."

"Do you really think that if the Duke of Helmsworth proposed marriage, your stepmother would say no?"

"I do." Sophie rubbed her hands over her face, feeling suddenly tired and exhausted from their night out. "I just want to find my bed and hold this memory for as long as I can."

THE MINX HAD left. Adrian wasn't sure when, only that she was nowhere to be found after the next four dances, during which he had banal conversations about the weather and, of all things, the eggnog being served. He thought maybe the lady had imbibed a little too freely.

It had been two hours since his waltz with Sophie. He couldn't blame her for leaving, but he had hoped she would remain, that they could pass the rest of the evening with conversation that seemed to flow naturally between them. Perhaps that was because of their shared past, or perhaps Sophie was the exact woman he was looking for.

Damn it. This was not how he wanted the night to end.

He found his uncle after midnight, standing watch over the crowd, which grew more obnoxious the longer they stayed.

"How many rooms will we have to make up tonight?" Adrian asked, watching the revelers below.

"A dozen or so. They are being made up now."

"Would you consider tonight a success? Would my father be proud of this Christmas ball?"

"I did not see you holding out the mistletoe."

Adrian turned away from his uncle so he wouldn't see the smile lighting Adrian's face. "I still have another week before Christmas."

"Tonight was your chance."

"Leave this with me, Uncle. I will not let my father

down just yet. Will you ensure all the revelers not staying the night are gone by three?" he asked, already turning to leave.

"Where are you going?"

"I have an errand to run."

Before his uncle could ask him to explain, he excused himself and went in search of his valet. First, he needed to change out of his evening attire, second, he needed to find out where Miss Isabelle Kinsley resided. Surely Sophie was staying with her cousin, since they had come to the ball together.

Adrian wasted no time in readying a mount—it was too late to wake one of the stable boys, and besides, the fewer the people in the household who knew his purpose, the better.

Isabelle Kinsley's cottage was five miles away, and easy enough to find. It held a two-story house made of red brick, with evenly spaced, lead-paned windows on both levels.

There was one tried-and-tested method that would have to do in figuring out which room Sophie was staying in.

Adrian went in search of some rocks, hoping luck would have him finding Sophie's room before he woke anyone else in the house.

Chapter Five

THERE WAS AN incessant noise tapping at Sophie's window, like a bird trying to find its way in. She cracked her eyes open. She yawned and stretched under the multitude of blankets she'd buried herself beneath when she'd climbed into bed. Sophie closed her eyes, so tired she couldn't remember why she wanted to wake up.

Tap, tap, tap sounded again at her window.

She threw off her blankets and reached for her dressing robe at the end of the bed. Slipping her arms into the heavy material, she stumbled toward the window and stubbed her toe on the bottom of a chair. She fell into the seat with a curse.

Tap. Tap.

The door to her bedchamber creaked open. "Are you awake, Sophie?"

Her cousin entered her room, quickly shutting and locking the door behind her.

"I am awake now." She glanced in the direction of the tapping, which had ceased for a moment. "It sounds as though someone is throwing rocks at the window."

"That's because that is precisely what is happening." Isabelle went over to the window, released the latch that kept it locked, and started to lift it.

"Come over here and help me, would you?"

Sophie made it to her feet and helped her cousin. "Are you going to tell me what is happening right now?"

"You, my dearest cousin, have a visitor."

"Adrian." He wouldn't dare . . . would he?

"You're on a first-name basis, are you? I had no idea it was as serious as this."

"You're reading too much into it. The Duke of Helmsworth would not throw rocks against my window. That little troublemaker Adrian of Helmsworth most certainly would."

"Ouch," her cousin squawked when she stuck her head out the window. She pulled away and rubbed at her cheek.

"Sorry, Miss Kinsley," Sophie heard the duke whisper none too quietly beneath her bedchamber window.

Sophie pulled her cousin away from the opening and inspected her cheek in the moonlight. Isabelle's soft skin only appeared to be reddened by the impact of the rock, but Sophie leaned out the window with what she hoped was a disapproving look.

"Have you lost your mind?"

"Perhaps my heart, my fair lady."

"You have gone mad."

"I need to speak with you rather urgently."

"Hush," she hissed, afraid he would wake up the house. "Come around the servants' entrance, I'll open the back door for you."

"Like a thief in the night."

"Much worse, I'm afraid." She ducked her head back into her room and shut the window. Turning to Isabelle, she said, "You told him which room I was in, didn't you? That's why you are here."

"He seems so sincere. Hear him out, Sophie."

"That's what I'm going below stairs to do, isn't it?"

Her cousin wisely chose not to respond, but she practically grinned ear to ear. Sophie only shook her head.

"Wait," Isabelle said and tried to pluck the mobcap from Sophie's head.

Sophie stepped to the side. "I don't care if I look like an old maid right now, Isabelle. He should have had the decency to call in the morning."

"The gesture wouldn't be nearly as romantic had he done that."

Sophie shook her head as she opened her chamber door, peeking around the corner to make sure the tap of rocks on glass had awakened no one else. As luck would have it, not a soul stirred in the house. All was quiet, except for the fanning of her cousin's breath on the back of her neck.

Sophie turned to Isabelle. "I'm going down alone."

"What if he should try to take advantage of you?"

Sophie gave her cousin a droll look. "I will knock him on the head with the rolling pin Cook keeps out. I will be all right, Isabelle. Had you not wanted this outcome, you should have told him to leave and come back tomorrow."

"Then we wouldn't be up to a grand adventure."

Sophie rolled her eyes and slipped down the hall, her cousin two steps behind her. Once they were outside Isabelle's bedchamber, Sophie swung the door open and gave her cousin a warning glance. Her cousin's shoulders sagged, but she resigned herself to ending her adventure here and went inside, shutting the door behind her.

Sophie tiptoed down the stairs and through the house. No one was awake, which told her it was far too early to be out of bed after their night out.

She contemplated not opening the kitchen door, but gave in after a whole two minutes.

"I thought you'd changed your mind," he said, sounding amused, though the expression on his face was one of worry.

"Tempting as that was, I didn't feel like listening to you throw rocks at my window all night."

A rush of cold winter air came in with Adrian, and she stepped back, chilled to the bone. Embers from an earlier fire burned in the hearth, so she made her way toward the warmth and let Adrian close the door behind him. He took off his hat and set it on the kitchen table.

"Why are you here?" she asked.

"The ball was a dreadful bore without you to enjoy it with me."

"Surely you've attended enough of those types of functions to have found a set of friends to best pass the time with."

"I have attended a few mandatory balls and danced with a few debutantes in my day, but aside from that, I prefer more intimate gatherings."

"So why arrange a ball to find your bride?"

"As I said earlier tonight, my father demanded it."

"Your father passed away last year. How can he demand anything?"

"My inheritance is locked in trust until I marry."

"I wondered why you would look for a bride at a ball. When did your father want you to marry by?"

"Christmas. Before then, if at all possible. He had hoped I would announce who my fiancée was at the ball, but I hadn't picked her yet."

Sophie stopped rubbing her hands together and raised one eyebrow in his direction.

"You can't seriously be asking me."

He pulled off his heavy winter coat and settled it around a chair.

"I am."

"Adrian—" She sighed, not sure what to say.

He reached for her hand and pulled her closer. She stood in the circle of his arms, much like she had when they'd kissed earlier. "We were once the best of friends. That is as strong a foundation as any in a good marriage."

"I told you I cannot marry. My stepmother will not allow it until her daughter is wed." And even if that day should come, she doubted her stepmother would ever consider Sophie's feelings.

Adrian made a derisive sound in his throat. "Do you think she'll refuse me?"

Sophie stepped out of his embrace and lowered her head. "I know she will. Her greatest accomplishment in life, which she has told me on many occasions, has been stripping the wild out of me. She did not even present me to society when I came of age. I'm to remain her companion for the rest of her days. She will not give her permission in any union I should attempt to make."

"I can be rather persuasive."

She reached for his face and rested her palm on his cheek. Stubble had started to form along his jaw. She rubbed her fingers through the short scruff, liking the new sensation.

"We haven't known each other for fifteen years, Adrian."

"Yet you address me familiarly."

She lowered her hand. "Old habits. You should go before we are discovered."

"You seem to think that would be a bad thing."

"Please, don't make this any harder on me. If my stepmother finds out about any of this . . . let's just say it will be awhile before I see the light of day again."

Adrian's brow furrowed, but he did not back up; he approached her, his hand outstretched so he could tug her braid where it fell over her left shoulder. It was a gesture he'd done on so many occasions when they were children that it struck a deep chord in Sophie, and she swayed a little closer. He released the braid to rub his knuckles along her cheek more intimately.

"Aren't you willing to fight for what we felt earlier?"

"It was one kiss," she whispered. "We shouldn't have done it."

"I don't regret it, not for one second."

Sophie turned away so he was no longer touching her.

"You shouldn't say such things."

"Then prove me wrong."

That caught her attention. Her gaze slammed into his with a smoldering intensity that caused her breath to hitch.

"How?"

"Kiss me again, prove it meant nothing to you."

"I do not think that's wise."

"I think it's the best decision I have made all night."

He caught her hand again, and this time, he pulled her right into him, giving her ample time to step away, but she was curious about his theory. Could their next kiss hold as much passion as their last? Would it feel the same? Would it be all-consuming?

Her lips parted before his even touched hers. As his face slanted over hers, neither closed their eyes, focusing on each other as they drew nearer and nearer, until finally, the soft give of his mouth molded around her lips, parting them, sucking them into his mouth. She licked at his lips, because it felt like the most natural thing to do. She felt silly standing in the middle of the kitchen meeting clandestinely with the Duke of Helmsworth.

But Adrian didn't seem to care—his only goal was giving her a kiss she would never forget. There were kisses like the one they'd shared at twelve, there were first kisses like the one they had shared in the maze, and there were kisses that made your heart swell and your body heat up in need, like hers did now. This was a need she had never before felt the likes of in all her life. Her breasts felt heavy, her lungs seemed as though they lacked air . . .

She no longer wanted to be wearing her heaviest and warmest dressing robe—or her mobcap, for that matter. She wanted to be closer to him, feel his warmth infusing her body. Adrian's tongue slipped into her mouth and twisted around hers. The move was sensual and far more erotic than it had been in the maze. Their bodies were pressed tightly together along the front, Adrian's hand resting against her hip, keeping her steady when she wanted to rub up against him.

She wore only a few layers of cotton and cambric; there were no stays or bindings to get between them. She wanted the heat of his skin against hers.

What was she thinking?

She tore her mouth away from his, her lips swollen and wet, and tasting slightly of mint. She placed her hand on the kitchen table to steady herself, and to keep herself from flying back into his arms. What in the world had gotten into her? She usually had better control over her emotions than this.

One kiss was all it seemed to take to awaken some sort of succubus inside her.

"Sophie, say something."

"I don't know what to say. Is it always like that?" She was panting. *Panting!*

"Only with you."

Right answer. But that put her in a bit of a predicament.

"This does not change the fact that my stepmother will never give her approval."

"Then leave with me. We'll obtain a marriage license in the morning."

"The scandal . . ."

"I suspect it would make my father proud that I found a bride on his terms."

She gave a weak smile. He was likely right in that regard.

"Do you really wish to marry me, or do you only want to save your estate?"

"I'm a greedy man. I pick both. But if I had to choose, Sophie, you're the one gamble I would take."

"Do you think we can make it to Gretna Green?"

Adrian chuckled. "I think you read too many novels. We're three hundred miles away from Scotland. No, what I have in mind will have us married much sooner than a week from today. Are you saying you agree to be my wife?"

"Tell me what happens if I say yes."

"We will leave for my residence in London. There are too many people staying on at Helmsworth Estate this evening. I'm sure half of them are still dancing and feasting in the ballroom. And I'm not willing to share you with anyone until we are married."

She chewed on her lower lip, contemplating the offer. Knowing that for one moment in her life, she wanted only to think about herself and what she wanted. "When?"

"Now."

"Now?" she said in a squeaky voice. But it made sense; they would have to act quickly. If her stepmother ever became the wiser, she would find a way to drive a wedge between Sophie and the duke.

"Get a change of clothes. We can be in London before morning."

"I have to tell Isabelle."

Sophie opened the door, and her cousin fell into the room with a screech.

"Isabelle," Sophie said as she helped her cousin off the floor.

"I had to make sure you were in good hands."

Sophie released Isabelle and crossed her arms over her chest. "I told you to stay in your room."

"Would you have done the same?" her cousin challenged.

"You're right, I would have followed you down here had our positions been reversed."

Isabelle eyed the duke. "So we will become cousins."

Adrian was smiling. "Indeed, we will."

Isabelle squealed louder and slapped a hand over her mouth as she jumped on the spot. Her laughter was infectious, and Sophie embraced her cousin, caught up in the excitement.

Adrian cleared his throat, and brushed his hand over Sophie's arm. "We need to make haste, Sophie."

She released Isabelle and turned back to the duke. "I can pack quicker now that I don't have to write a note for Isabelle. I won't be more than ten minutes," she promised, giving him a very brief kiss on the lips.

Adrian waited for her in the kitchen while she went upstairs and packed a satchel with whatever she could carry.

Isabelle went with her. As soon as they got to Sophie's

room, Isabelle began pulling items from the wardrobe and tossing them on the bed. In the end, Sophie packed her best morning dress for the actual wedding ceremony. She changed quickly out of her night rail into a riding habit, forgoing her stays, though she did stuff them into her bag.

Once Sophie's belongings were packed, Isabelle pulled her into a hug.

"What will you tell your mother in the morning?" Sophie asked.

"That you think you've come down with something and are sleeping in late."

Sophie hugged her cousin one last time. "Thank you."

"You would do the same for me, Sophie. Now off with you, *your duke* is waiting for you."

Sophie wanted this. She really wanted this. There was no way to change her mind now. This was the right thing for her and Adrian.

More importantly, this was something her stepmother could not control. It was like an early Christmas present to herself. She still couldn't believe she'd agreed so easily to the idea. So she stopped overthinking the situation the moment she stepped back into the kitchen and ran into Adrian's open arms. He hugged her close, and she stood in his arms for a few minutes, enjoying the embrace, and the masculine scent that was a little sandalwood, a little horse, and all Adrian.

"I was worried you wouldn't come back."

"Had I not, I have no doubt you would have come looking for me."

Adrian chuckled low and deep. "I don't doubt it either." He put her at arm's length. "Are you ready?"

She nodded, afraid her voice was lost. He grabbed her hand and led her outside to his waiting horse.

Chapter Six

THEY GAINED ENTRY to Adrian's London town house
through the back entrance. He didn't want to take any
chances on being discovered, especially considering half
the *ton* had been at his ball only last night. It was the early
hours of the morning, and the housekeeper was up when
they came through the door, carrying Sophie's valise.

"Good morning to you, Your Grace," she said, taking
in the sight of their disheveled state without batting an
eyelash.

"Tell no one I am home, Mrs. May." Adrian took Sophie's hand, pulling her farther into the house.

"As you wish, Your Grace." The housekeeper asked
no questions as she went on her way, as though seeing
Adrian sneaking a woman through the servants' entrance was a regular occurrence. Sophie remained silent
until he closed his bedchamber door behind them and
breathed a sigh of relief.

"I would provide separate accommodations if I were less worried about discovery. Now that I have gotten you here, I'm reluctant to let you out of my sight."

She smiled up at him, her expression trusting and calm. If she knew where his thoughts had wandered, he doubted she would still be smiling. But he was fit only for sleep.

She looked around his room, which was really more like an apartment with a sleeping area, writing wing, partial library and sitting area, two change rooms, and a bathing chamber where the hipbath and other washing accessories were kept. This was his only residence in London, a house that had been in his family for eight generations of Helmsworths.

"It's as big as my cottage," she said, turning around to take in the whole of the room.

"You can take the bed. We'll need a few hours of rest before I see the archbishop about that license."

Her eyes widened at the suggestion. "I couldn't. I don't mind napping on the chaise longue in the corner."

Adrian approached her, his hand caressing her face, lingering on the softness of her skin. "My fiancée will do no such thing."

"I will only be your fiancée for a few short hours. We will be husband and wife before the day is through." Sophie looked between the bed and him. "There is room enough for us both."

Her offer, while it seemed innocent, sent all the blood in his body rushing toward his cock. An inconvenient time for such a reaction. Instead of answering, or rebuking her offer, which most gentlemen would do, he angled his head over hers and rubbed his lips back and forth over hers. She allowed him entry without hesitation, and their kiss took on a life of its own. Before long, they were both crashing down onto the mattress, their limbs tangling and their hands wandering in not so innocent exploration.

He had promised her marriage, not seduction without the safety of matrimony. It took a force of will he didn't think he had to release her. He hovered over her on the bed, his arms braced around her shoulders.

"I did not mean for that to happen. And as you have probably surmised, I do not want to take advantage of the situation we find ourselves in, sharing a bed with you when my guard is down and my mind is not as sharp as it could be because of a lack of sleep."

"We both agreed to this." Sophie pressed her palm against his face, her thumb brushing across his lips. "I want you to share this bed with me."

He sucked her thumb into his mouth, rolling it around on his tongue and licking off the salt on her skin. "Do you really know what you are asking?"

"You said earlier that I read too many books. You are right, and I've found a number of naughty books that make me blush. I know what I'm asking," she said, reaching for the buttons on her jacket, slipping them carefully through the holes as he watched, fascinated, to see what she'd reveal.

The dress she wore now was far more modest than the one she'd worn to the ball the previous night, and far less revealing. Still, his attraction to her had not waned even when she had donned modest clothes; it had only grown the closer their bodies had rubbed as they'd shared his horse to London.

While he liked to consider himself a patient man, patience was the last virtue he seemed able to hold on to when her lips and body were pliant beneath him. He wanted to feast on her, strip her bare and taste every inch of her.

She raked her nails along his neck with just enough pressure to have him hissing in a breath. He thrust into her skirts, wishing they were skin to skin.

"I think I want to know more about these books you've been reading," he murmured against her lips.

"I can read them to you, but first . . ." She released the buttons on his waistcoat. She was as eager for him to be rid of his clothes as hers, but if she wanted this, it would be done on his terms. Naughty books aside, she was still a virgin, and he would make this a night to remember.

"We will be married before the day is through. We can wait to share a bed until later tonight," he said.

"I want this, Adrian."

"You can stop this at any time should you change your mind." He stood and threw off his waistcoat.

"I don't want to wait, Adrian. If we do this, if we consummate our union, even before marriage, no one can rebuke our claim to each other. No one can stop our marriage. I want to be with you." She reached for his shirt, pulling the material from his trousers. "Lie with me tonight. Make me yours as only a husband can claim his wife."

He stripped out of his shirt, and watched Sophie's expression change from one of awe to one of wicked promise. Her nails scored a path down his navel to the edge of his trousers, twirling in the path of hair that led to the root of his manhood.

"Our bodies are so different," she whispered, her fingers skimming the edge of his trousers now. "Will you remove them for me?"

The innocence of her question had his prick as hard as a pillar of stone. He looked down her, at the way she licked her lips, at the heaving of her bosom, at the way she panted out her breaths in excitement. He took her hand and made her stand before him.

"You first," he said, pushing the open jacket off her shoulders. The bodice beneath matched the hunter green of her skirt. The pieces joined at the waist in a series of ties, half of which were only tucked into the skirts. That made his job easier.

"Turn around," he said so he could unhook the eyelets that kept the top portion of her dress on. She didn't hesitate and tried to help him, but he pushed her hands away, revealing the delicate line of her spine one hook at a time. While there was a chemise beneath, she wore no corset. "You dressed in haste."

When the material gaped forward, Sophie crossed her hands over her breasts, holding the material as she faced him. "I wanted back in your arms and away from Kent before I could change my mind. The stays are in my valise."

He quirked one eyebrow. "And have you changed your mind?"

She shook her head. "My resolve has only grown firmer with each passing minute."

She released the material and it fell between them, revealing the low, square cut of her chemise. Her nipples were pebbled and tight beneath the white muslin. Begging to be sucked. He swallowed and gave his head a little shake. First her skirts needed to be removed, which she was already working on.

"You look as though you are going to eat me alive," she said nervously.

"It is in reciprocation of the look you are giving me."

She pushed her skirts down and stepped out of the heavy pleated layers that had kept the last of her hidden from him. She wore no drawers either, and he could see the dark outline of her mons beneath the short chemise, which would have to come off in short order.

When he reached for her, to pull her close, to feel her curves smashed against him, she danced out of reach. "I believe it's your turn."

There would be no hiding his state of erection once his trousers were removed, not that he was doing a good job of it now. He removed the remainder of his clothes and stood ready for her inspection.

Her eyes widened the lower they traveled on his form. She took him all in, and the only thing he read in her expression was unfulfilled desire. "If you continue to look at me like that, I will not be able to hold myself back."

"I don't want you to hold—"

She was in his arms before she could finish her sentence.

SOPHIE COULDN'T BELIEVE she was actually going through with this. She could not believe she stood mostly naked in the Duke of Helmsworth's bedchamber, and a marriage ceremony was only a few hours away.

More astonishing, she couldn't believe she was staring at a fully naked and aroused man for the first time in her life. She saw his intentions before he even moved. She barely got her chemise off before he caught her up in his arms and edged her back toward the bed. In theory, she could well guess what came next. In practice, well, she had no practice at this sort of thing, and there was nothing to do but hand the reins over to Adrian so he could show her just what she had asked for.

His hand skimmed over her back, his knuckles grazing the cheeks of her buttocks. A shiver of delight overcame her and had goose pimples raising the little hairs on her arms. When his hand cupped her bare breast and rotated around her nipple, she thought she was done for. Her knees were weak and barely holding her up as it was.

"What do you want most right now, Sophie?"

His hand rotated around her breast, the caress methodic and meant to arouse her senses to the fullest. "I don't know," she replied.

"What would happen in one of your naughty books right now?"

"The man would suck—"

Again, the words didn't make it past her lips. Adrian leaned her over his arm, arching her chest up, and sucked her nipple gently into his mouth. The cool, wet sensation of his mouth there had her legs rubbing together to try and assuage the ache building deep inside her womb. His teeth scraped her gently, his free hand squeezed and tickled her breast.

"I cannot stand for much longer." She was afraid she would fall over as she melted against his wicked mouth.

Adrian released her and she cried out at the sudden absence of his mouth. He grabbed her by the waist and tossed her onto the bed, following her in all his naked glory. His manhood was heavy and brushed against the hair at her center, then rubbed along her lower stomach. He picked up where he'd left off, giving her other breast the same treatment as the first.

Sophie arched off the bed, the sensation too much and not enough all at the same time. She'd never expected this. Never expected to want something so carnal and so perfectly sexual that he robbed her of all modest thoughts.

Her legs opened to him, wanting to hold him in the cradle of her thighs.

"I need more. I don't know what I want, but I need more."

He blew a cool stream of air over her nipple as he released it. His hand lowered between them, parting the folds of her sex. Her eyes widened. To be touched so intimately stole her breath away.

Adrian said something under his breath when he found the wetness between her thighs. "You are ready for me."

Her legs were scissoring, desperate to be touched harder, heavier, with more force than his hand could provide. He was off her before she could protest, his shoulders forcing her legs to open wider. She swallowed back a protest when the first touch of his tongue against that private part of her nearly shattered her. His tongue was wicked and unrelenting as he tasted her, sucked her, and swirled around a sensitive part of her that seemed to swell with need. Whatever he did to her, she clasped onto his head, unsure if she was going to push him away to give herself relief from the delicious onslaught of his mouth, or pull him in closer.

Mewling sounds of pleasure fell from her throat. When she thought she couldn't take it any longer, he thrust a finger deep inside her sheath, and she felt herself let go. There was no other way to describe the feeling that filled her breast and made her body explode from the inside out. Her voice was stuck in her throat, as was her breath. She pressed toward him, never wanting the sensation he'd given her to end.

When she came down from the high of her euphoria, she said, "I need you, Adrian. Make me yours, please."

His mouth landed on hers as he positioned himself above her, and she could taste herself on his tongue, could feel the wetness on his face as their mouths melded. He wedged himself between her legs, stretching her open, his tongue thrusting deep, tempting her tongue to play along, and it did.

The first press of his penis against her entrance was a foreign feeling, but not an unpleasant one. She squirmed in his hold, desperate to be closer. He took hold of himself and spread the wetness that had gathered at her entrance, thrusting through the delicate flesh of her mons, heightening her pleasure with every touch.

Her hands tangled in his hair, holding his mouth close as he entered her slowly at first, letting her get used to his size. His arms flexed where he held his weight from her. He was tense, and looked as though he barely held on to the last of his restraint. Sophie wrapped her legs around his lean hips and locked her ankles behind his buttocks. Before she could think better of it, and in the height of her passion, she pulled him forward hard and fast until he was fully seated.

He tore his mouth from hers. "Sophie."

There was a twinge of discomfort, but it dissipated with every second.

She looked up at her fiancé. "I am not as delicate as you are treating me."

"No, you're my minx."

"Only when the occasion calls for it."

He smiled down at her before pulling partially out and reseating himself. She arched into him, liking the sensation more than she ever thought possible. Their bodies strained to be closer. Sweat eventually dampened their skin. And all too soon, Adrian was stilling inside her, his seed pumping hot along the walls of her sheath. He rolled to his side, bringing her with him, his breath heavy, his eyes drowsy.

She gave him a chaste kiss on the mouth.

"I never expected that. I never knew it could be like that."

"We are hardly done." The promise of those words had a sigh leaving her lips.

And for three more hours, he taught her more than one way two people could make love.

Chapter Seven

Christmas Day

"SOPHIE, WHAT DO you think of this angel for the top of the tree?" Adrian asked his wife as he turned from the crates of decorations they'd spent the morning sorting through in the main parlor of the house.

The angel wore a gown of gold and burgundy, a wreath around her long blonde locks. She looked more like a child's doll than a Christmas ornament.

Sophie's smile was bright and cheery as she faced him, and her cheeks held a hint of color from their earlier exertions. She scrunched up her nose. "I think she is too grand for our modest tree. She will tip the top right over."

While they had picked the tree and it had been brought to the house three days ago, neither of them had seemed willing to leave their bed to decorate it before now.

Adrian looked up at the tree, which was at least nine feet tall and three and a half feet wide. Modest only in the sense that it didn't fill this room like the Christmas trees had when they were children.

Adrian plucked a smaller angel from the crate. The

painted porcelain face had a small chip on the cheek, and the lace hem of her dress was pulled loose at the back. "Do you remember this one?"

Sophie set down the paper wreath she'd been wrapping around the tree. She reached for the angel, taking it from his hands to hold it up and run her finger over its face. "Do you remember how she got that chip?"

He smiled. Of course he remembered, that was why he'd pulled it out of the box.

"You tossed her to me, expecting me to catch her. We couldn't have been more than ten at the time."

"And you dropped it," he said.

Sophie's mouth opened on a breath. "I did no such thing. You called my name *after* you threw her in my direction."

"Would I dare?" Adrian winked. He'd loved teasing Sophie when they were young. He enjoyed it just as much now.

"My young mind thought you'd cursed Christmas," she said.

"I made you cry. I felt terrible and vowed that would be the last time I made you sad."

"I don't remember that part."

"You were distraught. To turn your mood around, I kept pulling on your braids until you swatted at me. That was the last Christmas she adorned the top of the tree."

"I think for sentimental reasons she should hold that place going forward."

"I couldn't agree more."

Sophie leaned in and kissed him on the lips. Somehow

they ended up in each other's arms again, the angel held between their bodies crushed together.

Sophie pushed him to arm's length, and held the angel out to him, which he took.

"You make a wonderful distraction."

"As do you, dearest husband." Sophie walked back over to the tree. "If we don't set this up before our guests arrive, I fear we will make a bad impression."

"I think they'll believe I've kept you in bed for the past week. It is what married couples do."

Sophie blushed a fierce shade of red. "When we take the tree down in the New Year, I'll make her look new again, and she'll be perfect for next year."

"She is perfect now," he said, staring at his wife. He could still hardly believe they were married. He walked over to her with the angel in one hand and a chair in another.

Setting the chair down, he stepped up onto it. The chair gave him just enough height that he didn't have to stretch as he settled the angel over the top of the tree.

"Now we are officially almost done," he said, admiring his handiwork with the angel placement.

"I can hardly believe we pulled the tree together in two hours. All we have left is a few more glass balls and the candles to light."

"We will light the candles when our guests arrive." When he came off the chair, he asked, "Are you nervous to see your stepmother?" he asked.

"I wish I weren't." Sophie worried her bottom lip. "She has had so much control over my life that it feels strange to stand defiant against her."

Adrian lifted both her hands and pressed a kiss against her knuckles. "I regret that we do not have time to arrange for a proper wedding ceremony."

"We can have another celebration and wedding in the summer when the weather is more agreeable."

"A fantastic idea." Adrian leaned forward and kissed her again.

Sophie was smiling as she turned her head away. A blush stole up her neck and across her cheeks. He was desperate to be alone with her again, but they couldn't lock themselves in their room just yet.

He looked at his lovely wife. She wore a simple morning dress that was a pretty shade of pink, trimmed with lace at the shoulders and at the vee over her breasts. Simple yet perfectly Sophie.

He could hardly believe his luck in marrying his best friend. She was still his best friend. When they talked, it was as if no time had passed since their last round of troublemaking as youngsters.

He took her hand in his and brought it to his mouth to press a kiss against her hands. "It feels like no time has passed, like we are the same people we were as children."

"Only it is different," she said. "While I cared for you deeply when we were younger, I don't think I felt this kind of love."

That made him smile. He felt much the same way.

"Our friendship has only grown deeper in our years apart. My fondness for you is like nothing I have ever felt for another. Is it possible to love someone from afar?

Without realizing it?" he asked, though he knew the answer to that.

"I think we are living proof that love only grows stronger the older you grow."

Adrian kissed her hard on the mouth, wishing he could sweep her off her feet and escape to a private place. Their breathing was erratic as they broke apart. He was going in for another kiss when his uncle Albert entered the room.

"Uncle Albert," Adrian said, taking Sophie's hand to bring her toward the entrance of the parlor. "We are delighted to see you on this fine Christmas day."

His uncle eyed him up and down. "Marriage agrees with you, nephew. Duchess," he said, taking Sophie's hand and pressing a kiss to her knuckles. "It's a pleasure to see you again."

His uncle had been a witness at the wedding. Adrian and Sophie had headed straight back to Kent after the ceremony and hadn't seen anyone since.

"I'm the first to arrive," his uncle noted.

"We thought you could help smooth out the meeting with Sophie's stepmother and stepsister, so we asked you here a little early." Before he could say that Sophie's relatives would arrive any moment, the butler gave entrance to two women wearing gaudy dresses better suited to a carnival. Adrian was glad they'd arrived at the same time as his uncle, as their tightly screwed-up shrew faces looked anything but pleasant.

Without releasing Sophie's hand, Adrian stepped forward when she hesitated. "We are happy to welcome you into our home on this special day."

"Your Grace," they said in unison as they both curtsied.

They both turned to Sophie, hatred clear in the stepsister's eyes.

Sophie released his hand and walked forward.

"We are so glad you could join us. I feared we parted in bad blood and was not sure how our first meeting since I have married would be." He could tell by the waver in Sophie's voice that she was nervous.

Adrian offered her a steady hand at her back. He felt the slight tremble that wracked her body, and he rubbed his hand in small circles over her lower back. Sophie's stepmother shot him a murderous glare.

"You stepped out of line, Sophie. Your father is surely rolling over in his grave, disappointed that you went about marrying the way you did. He expected obedience from you," her stepmother said.

Adrian cut in before Sophie could respond. "I don't agree. I remember Sophie's father well, and the last thing he would feel is disappointment toward his daughter."

"Your Grace, while I was not married long, I knew my husband well," Mrs. Kinsley said.

"Did you know Sophie and I played together as children? We have known each other for so long that marriage seemed . . . natural when we were reacquainted. So natural we could not wait to wed, and while we did not have a long engagement, we do hope to have a repeat of the ceremony in the warmer months. I'm sure Sophie will require assistance." He doubted she would want assistance from these two women, but his only purpose was to calm the bad waters stirring up between them, which was visibly causing Sophie great distress. "Mrs. Kinsley, Miss Kinsley, may I introduce my uncle, the Earl of Trawley."

Adrian's uncle stepped forward, bowing to both women with a sidelong look at his nephew.

Their firm expressions of reproof toward Sophie melted away the second Uncle Albert took Mrs. Kinsley's hand and kissed the back of it like he had with Sophie's.

"I believe the pleasure is all mine," Albert said.

Sophie breathed a sigh of relief and slipped her arm behind Adrian's back. She stood on the tips of her toes and kissed his ear before whispering, "Thank you."

"I would do anything for you, Sophie, surely you know that." He pulled his wife in front of him and kissed her full on the mouth.

Mrs. Kinsley said something reproving and covered her daughter's eyes.

But Adrian didn't care, because the only thing that mattered was that Sophie was now his duchess. And Christmas was a whole lot brighter with her by his side.

"I love you, Adrian. May we fill this house with the laughter of children conspiring against the adults once again."

Holding her in his arms, he said, "I have loved you my whole life, Sophie. And you in my arms is the greatest Christmas present I could ever have hoped for."

The Duke's Christmas Wish

By Vivienne Lorret

For Heather

Chapter One

IVY SUTHERLAND GRIMACED at the sight of *another* long, winding corridor inside Castle Vale. She might never reach her room. Worse, she might never stop regretting the second cup of tea she'd drunk before leaving the inn this morning. "Do you suppose we're still in Hertfordshire?"

From beside her, Lilah Appleton lifted a gloved finger to her pursed lips. Silently, she shook her head and gestured to the imperious Lady Cosgrove, who walked ahead of them. It was a well-known fact that Lilah's aunt Zinnia did not possess a single shred of humor.

Of course, Lilah's disapproval might have been more believable if not for the subtle lift of her cheeks. Amusement brightened her brown eyes and caused her dark lashes to tangle at the corners. "I'm certain the view from our windows will be of the incomparable grounds of this estate."

That notion still did not appease Ivy. The Duke of Vale's estate reached as far as Bedfordshire. Upon their arrival, they'd been given ample time to admire the vast grounds with the queue of carriages extending nearly a mile. At the time, a light dusting of snow had begun to settle upon the rolling hills and stands of evergreens, creating a portrait backdrop for the duke's party, leading up to a Christmas Eve Ball. Even so, while Christmas was only a sennight away, Ivy wasn't entirely sure they would reach their rooms by then.

As it was, she and her friend, along with Lady Cosgrove and a pair of footmen, followed a maid down another corridor within this stone fortress. Truly, the place was immense. Ivy wished there were benches lining the arched walls instead of battle scene tapestries and empty suits of armor. Then again, stopping for a rest wasn't the best idea. The sooner she reached her room, the sooner she could stop regretting that second cup of tea.

"I wonder if His Grace hired extra servants to find guests who might become lost," Ivy said, only partly in jest. "They might call themselves *The Rescue Brigade,* equipped with food rations and blankets for the long journey."

The comment earned Ivy a snicker from one of the footmen and a laugh from Lilah. Her friend covered the amused outburst with a cough, but not quickly enough. Lilah's aunt Zinnia turned her head, snapped her fingers, and glared—all without missing a step or altering her clipped stride. While Lady Cosgrove was a handsome woman in her middle years, she was also a master of quick, censorious glances.

When that look was turned on her, Ivy imagined that a sense of discomfiture might make most young women blush. She, however, had been told by several people that a blush turned her milky complexion to an unbecoming shade of scarlet and made her pale blue eyes rather dull. Because of that, she refused to be embarrassed whenever possible. Therefore, Ivy answered the look with an innocent lift of her brows. To which Lady Cosgrove responded with a smile . . . *of sorts*. Not many women could affect such a formidable countenance when dressed in a cheerful cerulean traveling costume. An unexpected shudder coursed through Ivy at the skilled display of such a severe smile. It must have taken years of practice.

When Lady Cosgrove faced forward again, Lilah composed herself, brushing wisps of brown hair away from a sloped brow, then silently mouthed to Ivy, "You are incorrigible."

Ivy grinned, tucking a limp lock of her own, whitish-blond hair behind her ear. She'd rather be incorrigible than spend any more of her life trying to be perfect. Those years had been fruitless and exhausting. Even when Jasper—Lilah's brother—had been alive, Ivy still hadn't been enough for him.

More than two years had passed since then, and now, at five and twenty, Ivy was firmly *on the shelf* and not interested in marriage in the least. Well, not her own. She was, however, interested in helping her friend find the perfect match. While Lilah might be willing to marry any man who could satisfy the stipulations of her father's will, Ivy wanted her friend to find a man who loved her, as well. And their bachelor host might be that man. After all, there was rampant speculation about the reason the duke was hosting the party. Many wondered if he might be in search of a bride. That was the sole reason Ivy was here at Castle Vale.

That, *and* to find the nearest chamber pot. *For mercy's sake, they'd been walking corridors for an age!*

Ivy shortened her stride to quick, small steps. She also curled her fingers into her palms and squeezed, hoping to send the signal to the rest of her body. *Stay clenched,* she begged, *and do not think about tea.*

"Here we are, my lady," the mobcapped maid said as she turned the key in the door. Bobbing a curtsy, she gestured them inside the elegant room furnished with rose-colored silk wallpaper, bedding, draperies, and accented in peridot-green pillows and upholstered chairs. "Your ladyship's suite is the larger chamber. Miss Appleton and Miss Sutherland share the smaller one on the other side of the dressing room."

The maid led the way past the white stone hearth in the corner, then through a shorter, arched doorway. The dressing chamber was more like a parlor, large and elegant, equipped with velvet-cushioned chairs, a low table for tea, and a vanity table near a slender window. The view overlooked an inviting garden path lined with snow-speckled topiaries. Further inward, the doorway to the smaller bedchamber waited. But in between the vanity and the door, a slender, square stone outcropping stood. Ivy imagined it must have been a garderobe at one time.

In her youth, Ivy had toured a few older castles and found similar structures built against outer walls. Typically, the inside would hold a stone bench with a hole cut out of the center, nothing more than a festering pit beneath it. Although it seemed primitive to her, years ago, people would hang their clothes in such rooms, believing that the stench would ward off insects and whatnot. *The stench on the clothes likely warded off people as well,* she thought.

Thankfully, that practice had been abandoned. From what she'd witnessed, the old garderobes were sealed off or transformed into closets, *sans* festering pits, of course.

When the maid opened the door to the small stone room, Lady Cosgrove let out a gasp. "What is this—this *thing* in the closet? Where are the chamber pot and the washbasin?"

Blocked by the maid and Lady Cosgrove, Ivy could not see the *thing* that had earned such censure. She shuffled to the side in order to peer between the pair. First she saw only sprigs of lavender hanging from the ceiling in front of a window slit. Then, following the line of Lady Cosgrove's shoulder down to the hand she had pointed at the offending object, Ivy saw what resembled a large copper cauldron, fixed to the floor.

"It is a *plunger toilet,* my lady," the maid said with obvious pride, standing straighter. "His Grace has installed these in three of the castle's former garderobes. The Dowager Duchess wishes for your ladyship to have every luxury and convenience. Her Grace placed you in the finest chamber."

With the mention of the dowager duchess, a friend of Lady Cosgrove's, her ladyship's visible disdain gradually dissipated. She lowered her arm and cleared her throat. "You may inform Her Grace that it is a fine room, indeed—though to my mind, a chamber pot is far simpler and less offensive. Nevertheless, I'm certain we can all adapt to this modern . . . *contraption*."

Ivy knew that these *plunger toilets* had been around for decades, but they had not yet gained in popularity. Only the most affluent houses had them, and sometimes not even then. While she'd heard of them, this was Ivy's first time seeing one in person.

Rumor stated that the duke was a modern-thinking man and something of a scientist, naturalist, and mathematician. In fact, his latest *Marriage Formula*—it had been said—was designed to obliterate the need for courtship before marriage. His proposal had both intrigued the gentlemen of the *ton* and earned the disdain of the women.

Ivy didn't care a whit either way. Because, with all of Lady Cosgrove's talk about chamber pots, Ivy was all too aware of her current state of discomfort. She shifted from one foot to the other and tried not to think of chamber pots. Of course, not thinking about chamber pots made her *really* think about chamber pots.

"It would, however," Lady Cosgrove continued, unwittingly and *mercifully* interrupting Ivy's train of thought, "ease my mind somewhat to know where the washbasin was located." Turning her back on the *toilet,* she gave it one last cursory flip of her fingers before stepping aside.

The maid sighed in relief and gestured to the cabinet on the opposite side of the spacious dressing chamber. "Right this way, my lady."

Now that Ivy had an unobstructed view of the *toilet*, she realized it was far more oval-shaped than a cauldron. To her, it looked like a giant copper egg, hollowed out and served up on an ornate, curvaceous dish.

"I've never seen one before," Lilah said, sidling up to her. "It's rather large and somewhat off-putting. Imagine stepping in here in the middle of the night. You might hit your leg on it and trip, bashing your head against the wall, while losing a slipper inside, and there it would go, down to . . . places unknown. Oh, but what if it did *not* go down all the way? Then it could be trapped and—"

"You worry too much." Ivy bumped Lilah's shoulder with her own. Although understandingly, it was no wonder that Lilah worried, with all the weight on her shoulders, the urgent need to find a titled husband to satisfy the codicil to her father's will. Still, Ivy was determined that her friend would enjoy the next week and find a husband, even in the unlikely instance of a ruined slipper.

Lilah leaned forward on her toes and peered down into the shallow water as if it had been the great abyss. "Mother says that I haven't been worrying enough. Which is precisely the reason I have begun to think of every terrible thing that could occur."

As they spoke, Lady Cosgrove finished perusing the cabinets and returned to the first bedchamber, maid in tow. The sound of other voices drifted into the dressing room, likely Lilah's aunt directing the footmen where to place the luggage.

"If you ask me, it's all a matter of perception," Ivy said, pointing toward the bowl. "Let's say you do trip, bash your head, *and* lose a slipper."

Lilah straightened her spine and frowned. "Aren't you supposed to be allaying my fears?"

"*Pfft,*" Ivy said with a shooing motion of her hand. "Not when they are preposterous. Now play along. What is the worst thing that could happen?"

"I don't know, Ivy," Lilah said on a breath, her exasperation clear in the way she lifted her brows, shoulders, and hands in one simultaneous twitch. "I suppose the worst thing would be that the duke would discover that I've *ruined* his plunger toilet with my slipper."

"Precisely."

Lilah's slender brow furrowed. "And why are you grinning as if this would be good news?"

"Because then the duke would notice you, *obviously*. Not only would he know your name and face but he would think of you every time he went to his own garderobe." Ivy nodded in encouragement, only to have Lilah shake her head.

"That is not how I would wish him to think of me."

Ivy dismissed her friend's concern with a half shrug and a tilt of her head. "You could work on that later. Alter his perception."

Lilah sighed, but there was a hint of a smile on her lips. "You truly are incorrigible, you know."

"Surprisingly, that doesn't discourage me in the least."
Ivy reached out and embraced her longtime friend.

Then, suddenly, a twinge speared through her with
great urgency. Ivy shifted. Standing back on her heels,
she crossed one foot over the other. The second cup of tea
forced her to study the *toilet* with an even more critical
eye. "It appears sturdy enough, don't you think? Far more
resilient than a porcelain chamber pot. In fact, the more I
think on it, this large copper *egg* makes perfect sense. It's
rather brilliant."

Of course, her judgment might have been influenced
a bit by a need to use it *tout de suite*.

"I quite agree, Miss Sutherland," someone said from
just outside the dressing room. "The Duke of Vale only
wishes that the plunger toilet were his own invention."

Ivy turned to see the Dowager Duchess of Vale step
through the archway. In that instant, Ivy realized that
Lady Cosgrove had not been directing the footmen after
all. Instead, she spoke with a gentleman who was partially hidden from view by the door. Ivy could not iden-
tify him from his profile. All she could glimpse from here
was a crop of short, dark hair, the edge of a thick eyebrow,
a well-formed ear, and the shadows lining the underside
of his cheek and jaw.

"Your Grace," Ivy and Lilah said in unison to the
dowager duchess, and each dipped into a curtsy. With
Ivy's legs still crossed, however, rising gracefully proved
to be a challenge.

"Miss Lilah Appleton," the dowager duchess began,

directing her smile to Lilah first. "I'm thrilled that your mother could spare you over the holiday for this party. I do believe you were introduced to my nephew at the Ruthersfield Ball last May."

In the exact moment that the dowager duchess said the word *nephew,* the gentleman in the other room inclined his head toward Lady Cosgrove and pivoted on his heel. Out of the corner of her eye, Ivy watched as Lilah bowed her head and dipped once more. However, quite inexplicably, the majority of Ivy's attention fixed upon the Duke of Vale. His perfunctory gaze skimmed past the dowager duchess to Lilah, and he bowed his head once more.

Strangely, Ivy couldn't breathe. Her breath was caught somewhere between an inhale and an exhale, in the same manner that a sudden fierce wind stole one's breath. Yet there was no breeze. There was, however, the rushing swish of her pulse in her ears. She couldn't imagine what was causing this peculiar reaction.

It certainly couldn't have been due to her first glimpse of the duke. After all, he was not a handsome man. Not the way Jasper had been, with a face sculpted by angels and fleecelike waves of golden hair upon his head. No, the duke was too angular, as if forged by a blacksmith. His aquiline nose and square jaw were too harsh. His shoulders, too broad for his tall, narrow frame. In fact, if she were to trace his silhouette from head to toe, he would look exactly like one of those suits of armor in the hall.

Yet there was something arresting about him. Something that kept her staring at him, waiting for the moment when his eyes would rest on hers. The notion, and the waiting, were as disconcerting as they were absurd.

"And Miss Ivy Sutherland," the dowager duchess continued, "I'm simply delighted by your presence, as well. You abandoned soirees and society all too soon, and I don't believe I've had the pleasure of introducing you to my nephew."

"No, ma'am," Ivy said, garbling the words as she fought to breathe properly. Then, expecting the exchange to follow immediately, Ivy dipped into a curtsy. Only she forgot that her legs were crossed and ended up teetering slightly. With all of her weight balanced on one foot, she wobbled. For an instant, she must have looked like a teapot tipping over. Or worse, she must have appeared a *trifle disguised*. Yet there was no polite way to explain her lack of grace. With the garderobe in such close proximity, she'd just as soon confess to imbibing spirits as say she'd drunk far too much tea.

Needing an excuse, she quickly added, "Your Grace, please excuse my clumsiness. These slippers . . . *er* . . . pinch."

Regrettably, between the words *slippers* and *pinch*, Ivy lifted her gaze from the duke's camel-colored waistcoat and white cravat to his darkly intense eyes. Those eyes resembled two hematite stones and drew her in like a flake of iron to a blacksmith's magnet. Those eyes, fringed with thick, black lashes, seemed to swallow any surrounding light, but while reflecting it at the same time. She felt as if she were wobbling again, or that the room was tilting beneath her feet. She did not like the sensation in the least. It made her impatient to end this introduction.

Yet the duke said nothing, to either end it or begin it. Instead, he furrowed his brow and stared at Ivy as if she were a madwoman.

"You are fortunate, indeed, Miss Sutherland," the dowager duchess said, her voice sounding distant through the din in Ivy's ears. "My nephew has invented a device to assist with such a problem. How serendipitous it is that you should have tightly fitting slippers."

Slippers. At once Ivy recalled her conversation with Lilah from a moment ago. The sole reason for attending the duke's party was to find a husband for Lilah. And who better than their host? With great relief, an idea sprang to mind that would potentially rescue both *her*—from this dreadful situation—*and Lilah*—from being too easily forgotten by gentlemen, as she had in the past.

"Then the fortunate one is Miss Appleton, because I'm wearing her slippers, ma'am," Ivy said in a rush. Everyone knew that if you told a lie quickly, your voice wouldn't waver and give you away. Not only that, but Ivy counted on Lilah's good breeding to keep her secret. She knew that Lilah wouldn't put forth an argument until they were alone. Even with this announcement, however, the duke's gaze did not waver from Ivy's. And oh, how she wished it would, because she remained ensnared by those magnets. "Miss Appleton has quite the inquisitive mind. I'm certain she would be delighted to see such an invention, sir."

The duke frowned. Then, from the doorway, a feminine throat cleared.

"Forgive the interruption, ma'am, but you wished to know immediately if any circumstances arose that would require your attention," said the woman, who was likely the housekeeper. "Lady Granworth has arrived."

The dowager duchess gasped. "How delightful! I must welcome her at once. And my dear Lady Cosgrove, as her relation, you must accompany me. I'm certain you are as curious as I about what prompted her return to society after so many years away."

"What a coup, Duchess! Not even I have been able to draw her out of Bath," Lady Cosgrove exclaimed. "I daresay the tongues will wag, and you will be the envy of all."

"Zinnia, you flatter me," the dowager duchess answered, adding a trill of laughter, "but I am not opposed to such an honor. No, indeed. And when Lady Harwick arrives, we shall all have tea in my sitting room and— *Good gracious*! I nearly forgot. Miss Appleton and Miss Sutherland, I regret to cut our visit short. I will see to it that a tea tray is brought up to your room at once."

"Thank you, ma'am," Lilah said as she moved out of Ivy's peripheral vision.

Ivy parroted her friend, albeit distractedly, because she was still caught by the duke's gaze. Even though it likely had been fewer than two minutes from when she'd first spotted his profile—and less than a minute since they'd been introduced—it felt like substantially more. Even more peculiarly, she'd apparently incurred his disapproval. She could think of no other reason why he would stare at her so intently.

"Nephew," the dowager duchess called from the other room, "I wonder if you would be so good as to accompany us?"

Then, without any hint that he'd heard his aunt at all, the duke brusquely nodded his head, turned, and strode out of the room.

The moment the door clicked shut, Ivy doubled over, clutching her middle as she fought for breath and balance.

"*The fortunate one is Miss Appleton because I'm wearing her slippers? Miss Appleton has quite the inquisitive mind?*" Lilah scoffed as she stormed into view. Coming to a sudden halt, the hem of her fawn redingote swirled around her ankles, revealing the unpolished toes of her half boots. "We both know those are your slippers on your feet. In addition, I haven't the least desire to see the duke's slipper-stretcher."

"Whyever not?" Having caught her breath, Ivy straightened and hurriedly moved toward the garderobe. "I think the invention sounds interesting."

"Of the two of us, you are the inquisitive one. After all, you were the one who wanted to see how fast the gardener's flower cart would roll down the hill . . . with you inside of it, no less."

Ivy closed the door and started to lift her redingote and skirts, talking to Lilah from the other side. "I was twelve years old. *Of course* I wanted to know how fast the cart would roll. Besides, Jasper dared me. And I don't recall hearing your words of warning before I climbed in it—only your peals of laughter."

Oh! Ivy gasped as her backside and legs met the cold toilet. Then . . . nothing happened. That demanding second cup of tea was being stubborn. After trying for so long to stay clenched, she was now facing the real possibility that she'd forgotten how to *unclench.*

"Shortly thereafter, we all knew better," Lilah said, the annoyance fading from her tone. "You were lying in a heap on the ground, your head bleeding from the stone that you hit. Even my brother was frightened."

"*Don't be dead, Ivy. Don't be dead,*" the thirteen-year-old Jasper had whispered over and over as he'd knelt beside her in the grass. "*I promise I'll never dare you to do another foolish thing as long as we live. Just don't be dead.*"

The moment Ivy had opened her eyes and seen the worried tears streaking through the dirt on his cheeks, she'd fallen in love with him. She'd known right then that she would never love anyone else the way she'd loved Jasper. And until he'd died three years ago, she'd done everything she could to prove it to him. Sadly, it had never been enough.

She sighed, weary from thinking about how difficult it had been to pretend that she was careful and perfect for all those years. That was over now. She needn't worry about garnering anyone's approval in order to appear marriageable, because she wasn't going to marry. She wasn't even going to worry about what the duke might think of her. All that mattered was what he thought of Lilah.

"At least our introduction was a success," Ivy said, her voice echoing around her. "Surely the duke will think of you often."

Lilah laughed with more mockery than mirth. "Indeed, whenever his shoes pinch. Such is the dream of every debutante."

"Then we shall wish ill-fitting shoes upon him for the duration of the party." Ivy grinned, and with that thought, felt at ease for the first time since meeting the duke. Perhaps her reaction to him had been nothing more than a product of an overactive imagination and that second cup of tea.

NORTHCLIFF BROMLEY KNEW he wasn't going mad. There was no record of insanity in his lineage. His own parents had been of sound mind. While he had no siblings to provide further study, his cousins were seemingly reasonable individuals. Even his uncle, from whom he'd inherited the dukedom, had been perfectly sane.

Knowing this, however, did not explain why his logical mind had suddenly abandoned him. Or why his thoughts were as unpredictable as a wooden cube tripping down a spiral staircase.

Alone in his private study, he flattened his hands on his desk and glared down at the ledgers spread before him. Not one of them held the answer.

"Nephew, have you heard a single word I've said?"

North jerked his head up at the sound of his aunt's voice. He glanced around to find the room virtually the same as it always was, in orderly disorder. Towers of books teetered on tables. Unfiled patent papers were strewn about. Gadgets, inventions, and more books littered the shelves. There was a rather comfortable chair and hassock beside the hearth, but it was currently serving as the foundation for a scale bridge he was designing for the stream that cut through his land. Most importantly, however, the door to his small sanctuary was closed. It was always closed because he did not like interruptions when he was thinking. Yet for some reason, his aunt was now standing on the opposite side of his desk, and he hadn't heard her approach.

"Aunt Edith, how long have you been in here?"

"I've been scolding you for the past five minutes," she answered, the fine wrinkles around her mouth drawn tight as she pursed her lips. Her silver-lashed eyes flashed in annoyance.

Since she rarely scolded him, and rarely disturbed him in his study, he supposed he owed her the courtesy of listening. At least for a moment. "Pray tell, what have I done to earn this reprimand?"

"Weren't you listening?" She tsked, glaring at him. Then, on a heavy exhale, she shook her elaborately coiffed head in a manner that suggested she'd answered her own question. "I've never seen you so distracted as you were when we met with Juliet Granworth earlier. Not to mention, directly before that, you were quite rude to Miss Appleton and Miss Sutherland."

"Rude? I've never been rude in my life." He followed the rules of society with exactitude. In fact, he engaged in most introductions by rote, all the proper words spilling from his lips without fail, even while his mind was engaged elsewhere. To him, most people fit into two categories: dull or wholly uninteresting. During these introductions, he allowed his mind to move on to matters of estate business, familial obligations, weekly schedules, and, more importantly, to ideas for inventions.

"You didn't say a word to either of those young women," Edith claimed.

"Of course I did." With a father who had been ostracized from the family because he'd married a commoner, North had encountered opposition when his late uncle, the former Duke of Vale, had named him as the heir apparent. Since the duke had had no children of his own, no surviving brothers, and North was the eldest of the nephews, the title had naturally fallen to him. Even so, North had always felt the need to prove that he was the rightful heir. Therefore, his manners were always impeccable.

"Not a single word. Not even a murmur of acknowledgment," Aunt Edith continued. "I thank Mrs. Humphreys for saving us all by coming to the door when she did."

This news was odd indeed. He thought for sure that he'd made an obligatory greeting. His brain was like a machine in perfect working order. Yet even he had to admit that he'd felt something inside of him go drastically wrong the moment he'd heard Miss Sutherland speak.

It was as if his entire world had come to a sudden, grinding halt. He could think of no matter of estate business that needed attention. No familial obligations had come to mind. His weekly schedule had suddenly gone blank. Worse, a keen sort of panic had assailed him in regard to his invention of the *Marriage Formula*. And when he'd looked at her, his brain—the machine he relied upon the most—had failed him. The only part that remained working was a voice that kept asking one question over and over again: *Why isn't Miss Ivy Sutherland's name in one of the ledgers?*

In order for his formula to work, he needed to know every marriageable person in polite society. One single error or miscalculation could risk his Fellowship with the Royal Society. He was hosting this party for one purpose—to reveal the validity of his *Marriage Formula*. Not only to his guests but to two persons who could assist him in gaining the Fellowship he wanted more than he'd ever wanted anything before. In fact, he'd purposely invited Lord Basilton and Lord Pomeroy from the Royal Society in order to calculate matches for their unwed offspring. If everything went as planned, Basilton and Pomeroy's approval—by way of their votes in the New Year—would earn him a Fellowship.

Gazing at his aunt, who was ineffectively attempting to tidy the corner of his desk, North swallowed his pride. "Forgive me. I was distracted earlier. Though it is no excuse, I'd realized suddenly that I had an unmarried guest at my party whose name was, until that moment, unknown to me. Under the current circumstances, surely you can understand my appearance of rudeness."

Surprise lifted his aunt's penciled brows before her

expression fell to something of a disappointed pout. "Oh, is that all? For a moment, I'd thought Miss Sutherland's understated beauty had you tongue-tied."

If one could call blue eyes that resembled the pale perfection of a winter sky *understated*. Or a complexion as flawless as moonlight. Or hair the white-blond color of a candle flame. Or lips tinged pink as if brushed by madeira. *Understated*? No, her beauty was quite evident.

He meant to laugh, but more of a growl came out instead. "I am not a man ruled by baser impulses. If I were, then my formula would mean nothing and every hope I have of becoming a *Fellow* would be for naught."

"Nephew, I had no idea that Miss Sutherland's attendance at this party could jeopardize so much. When Zinnia wrote and asked if her niece's friend could attend, I saw no harm in it. *Clearly* I underestimated the power of one unmarried young woman."

North eyed his aunt. There was more than a trace of mockery in her tone and expression. "Miss Sutherland holds no power over me. You give her far too much credit. Besides, she cannot be overly marriageable if I'd never met her."

"She has been out of society for the past two years," she said, appearing distracted by her attempts to straighten the papers on the corner of his desk. "Which, as it happens, was when you garnered interest in society in order to begin your formulaic calculations."

He opened a drawer and pulled out a fresh sheet of parchment before dipping a quill pen into the inkpot. "Then Miss Sutherland must be at least four and twenty."

"Five and twenty."

He jotted that down. "Of noble birth?"

"Her father is a country gentleman. He earned a knighthood in the war, years before he married. Her mother is a cleric's daughter. They reside in Surrey. Norwood Hill."

"Such a meager connection to earn Miss Sutherland the opportunity to marry into the aristocracy." Still, it was more of a connection than his own mother had had, he mused, dipping his pen once more. "Has she a fortune, a wealthy relation, or dowry property?"

"None. She is educated, however. Her parents employed a tutor and a dance master for her instruction before her debut."

"Perhaps she descends from a hearty lineage— multiple sons born on both her father and mother's side? How many brothers does she have?"

Edith clasped her hands and offered him a patient stare. "Like you, she is an only child, as were her parents."

Huh. Studying the parchment, he released a breath he didn't realize he'd been holding. He felt . . . relieved. Beyond relieved, actually—*elated* was more precise. "Then she is of no consequence. Her presence will not disrupt my ability to prove my formula in the least."

Eager now, he opened one of the fresh ledgers, which he'd begun solely for this party, and scribbled her name on the page. *Miss Ivy Sutherland of Norwood Hill—no consequence.* Then he underlined the last two words for good measure.

Aunt Edith huffed in obvious exasperation, drawing

his attention. From that disapproving purse of her lips, he already knew what she was going to say.

"Nephew, I wish I could admire your uncanny ability to write down a name and summarily disregard the person who carries it."

"I do not disregard either the person or the name," he argued, while softening his tone. "The names in each of my ledgers are the means that will gain me a Fellowship. I value them a great deal."

She pointed down to his disorderly desk. "If only you'd spent as much time figuring love and happiness into your equation."

"A man should be happy on his own without needing another to spoon-feed it to him. As for love," he said while sprinkling sand over the fresh ink in the ledger so that it wouldn't smear, "it is an emotion invented by the idle-minded."

When he heard no response, he lifted his gaze from Miss Sutherland's name and saw his aunt's disappointed frown.

He released an exhale. "Very well. Will it soothe your ruffled feathers if I promise not to ignore Miss Sutherland or her friend with the pinching slippers for the duration of the party?"

Appearing to mull this over, Edith took a moment before nodding curtly. "Dinner will be in one hour."

North had other plans for this evening, such as organizing his ledgers and making sure every person here was accounted for. He felt the flesh between his brows furrow. "This morning, you'd said that we would not be having a formal dinner this first night, since so many of our guests would be tired and want trays taken to their rooms."

"Yes, but we must think of those who are not tired. Besides, we have many more guests in attendance than we'd originally anticipated. Perhaps you have finally earned a measure of acceptance from those dreaded purists."

"It is more likely that they believe I aim to make one of their daughters a duchess."

"Then let them think what they will." As if the matter had been settled, she made her way to the door. "Tonight's gathering will be an informal dinner in the Great Room. The footmen will carry trays of cheeses, tarts, and hors d'oeuvres, allowing you the freedom to move about, thereby giving you the perfect opportunity to make amends to Miss Appleton and Miss Sutherland."

As the door clicked shut, leaving him to his solitude, North's gaze drifted down to the name in the ledger. As before, all other thoughts stopped, suspended like a pendulum in a clock paused at the crest of the oscillation. It was unnatural. Illogical.

The only reason for his current state of mind had to stem from the inordinate pressure he was under to prove his formula. *Yes, that must be the reason.* And with that reassuring thought, he bent down, blew the dust from the page, and closed the book.

North was certain that his next encounter with Miss Sutherland would be a matter of rote behavior and nothing more.

Chapter Two

"FOR AN INFORMAL dinner, this is quite the crush," Ivy said from beneath the wide stone archway of the Great Room.

There were at least one hundred guests, she surmised. The finest array of satins, silks, and lace crowded elbow to elbow in the vast space. If not for the green and gold brocade draperies along the far wall, and the wide tapestries adjacent, the clamor of conversation likely would echo to deafening proportions. Instead, prattling, laughter, and the occasional clink of glassware all rose overhead to the vaulted wood-beamed ceiling.

Beside her, Lilah nodded. "It's a veritable sea of coiffures, tiaras, and feathers."

"Yes and beware the waves of gossip," Ivy said, charting a course toward the footman with the red wine on his tray. She needed something to settle her unexpectedly raw nerves. For some reason, she could not stop mulling over her encounter with the duke and wondering if the next would unsettle her just as much. From this vantage point, however, she hadn't spotted him yet.

"Gossip, I can take. It's the wine I'm worried about." Lilah smoothed her gloved hands down her pristine white dress.

As a woman on the shelf, Ivy's wardrobe wasn't restricted to a muted palette. This evening she wore her favorite red satin petticoat beneath a gauzy silk tulle sheath. Earlier, she'd had the maid prepare the blue muslin, trimmed in velvet, yet blue was too calming a color. Inside, Ivy was anything but calm. Therefore, she needed to wear something that made her feel confident, and even a bit pretty.

Belying her self-assuredness, however, she caught herself fidgeting with the cuff of her long white glove. Abruptly, she stopped. "If you do happen to encounter a spill of wine, just be sure it is from the duke's glass."

"I do not know why you are fixed on seeing me married to the duke. As you well know, any titled gentleman of noble birth will do," Lilah whispered.

To Ivy, the answer was obvious. "Yes, but one can easily assume that the duke invited unwed debutantes to his party for the sole purpose of finding a bride for himself. The same cannot be said of the other gentlemen in attendance."

"After your performance earlier, the duke is likely to see me and then instantly glance down to my feet and inquire about the comfort of my shoes."

"I fail to see the problem in a man recalling you from a previous encounter."

Lilah sighed. "Because his recollection would be of my shoes, not of me, Ivy. You don't know how many times Aunt Zinnia has reintroduced me to a gentleman within minutes of a first introduction, only for him to behave as if the second time was new to him. Just once, I'd like a gentleman to remember *me*."

Ivy threaded her arm through her friend's and squeezed her companionably. "And I am here to make certain that your wish comes true."

From the far corner, Lady Cosgrove lifted an arm and beckoned both Ivy and Lilah to her. As they entered the room, the crowd seemed to undulate, each group of attendees moving to and fro. If the center of the room could be compared to a tidal pool—filled with the shiniest of stones—then the cluster of society's premier elite fit there perfectly. Their ostentatious display of jewels gleamed beneath the light of an immense wrought-iron chandelier. Chaperones and their pastel-clad charges formed the first ring, turning their ears toward the center of the room while their eyes followed the unmarried gentlemen. In groups of only two or three, those gentlemen caused surges, altering the form of the gathering as many angled for their attention. Along the outer rim were the matrons. It was no surprise that this group positioned themselves to oversee the entire room at a glance. Everyone knew that these women held the most power. The dowager duchess and Lady Cosgrove were among them.

Also within their midst was a woman too old to be a debutante but far too young to be considered a matron. Her hair was silken gold—a shade darker than Ivy's—

the thick waves styled into an elegantly simple twist. Her peach silk gown was the same, elegant and simple. As was the diamond pendant she wore. In her slender carriage, she possessed a regal quality that one could never learn. One had to be born with it. Ivy, unfortunately, had not been.

"Miss Appleton, Miss Sutherland," the dowager duchess began the instant they arrived. "I should like to introduce you to an honored guest, Lady Granworth."

The name sparked a recollection for Ivy as both she and Lilah offered the obligatory curtsies. This time, Ivy managed to be somewhat graceful.

"Of course, since Lady Cosgrove and Lady Granworth are cousins through—Zinnia, is it your mother's side?" The dowager duchess turned to her friend. In receiving a nod, she continued. "No doubt you have heard mention of her, Miss Appleton."

"I have, Your Grace," Lilah said. "In fact, Aunt Zinnia, Lady Granworth, and I have exchanged letters during the past year."

It was in this moment that Ivy recalled hearing Lady Granworth's name in conversations with Lilah. Juliet Granworth was Lilah's third cousin. Apparently, there had been a split at one time in their family. When Lady Granworth's husband had passed a year ago, however, Lady Cosgrove had reached out with an olive branch.

"After so many letters, you must call me Juliet. It is a true pleasure to meet you in the flesh, at last, cousin." Extending a gloved hand to Lilah, Juliet Granworth smiled. When the light caught her sapphire-jeweled eyes, her delight was evident. Then she turned to Ivy. "Miss Sutherland, please call me Juliet, for I am certain we will be friends as well. From Lilah's letters, I feel as if you and I are already acquainted."

"I assure you that I'm not nearly as wayward or impulsive as Lilah has likely expressed," Ivy said with a grin.

This comment earned a cough from Lady Cosgrove and a silent smirk from Lilah.

"I believe the descriptions I read were quite complimentary of an admirable determination to live by one's own rules," Juliet replied with all the appearance of sincerity.

Even though Ivy was touched by the compliment, at the same time she noted Lady Cosgrove's disapproving glance toward Lilah. Deciding it was best to save her friend, Ivy added, "A careless endeavor on which only a woman resolved never to marry should embark." She managed the words without the slightest of grins. *Contrition, thy name is Ivy*, she thought, congratulating herself.

"A truth well spoken, Miss Sutherland," Lady Cosgrove said, her stern agreement a clear warning to her niece. "Gentlemen of noble birth prefer accomplished, genteel brides."

Lilah laughed wryly. "What good are accomplishments or manners if there is not a single gentleman interested in them? We are tutored to speak French, to read Latin, to dance, to exhibit poise, to draw, and to sew, but none of that matters if . . ." Her words trailed off as her eyes widened.

Surprised by her friend's outburst, Ivy couldn't speak.

Lilah often spoke her mind to Ivy when they were alone, but this was the first time she'd ever said anything in direct contradiction to her aunt. As Ivy watched her, Lilah's lips parted and her gaze darted to her aunt as if she'd just realized the same thing.

"That is to say—"

"I quite agree, cousin," Juliet interrupted. "I've met no gentleman who has any real interest in needlework. Otherwise they would all be dressed in coats with thistle flowers embroidered on the cuffs, and keep a ready needle tucked away in a waistcoat pocket."

Ivy laughed, liking Juliet Granworth despite her enviable beauty. "Indeed. Now, whenever I see a gentleman with a monogrammed handkerchief, I will not assume he has a sister but more so that he embroidered the square himself."

"That must be the true reason gentlemen do not want ladies in their clubs," the dowager duchess said cheekily, stunning the group. "They fear the competition."

This time they all laughed, even Lady Cosgrove.

"I wonder what has become of my nephew," the dowager said after a moment, searching the crowd. "Regrettably, he is often late when distracted by a new invention. I do believe that his *Marriage Formula* is currently occupying his mind."

"A formula for marriage, ma'am?" Juliet asked, her wispy brows lifting. "I don't believe I've heard of such a thing. Are men and women so easy to enter into an equation?"

The dowager duchess tsked. "I am not in full agreement with my nephew on this notion of his. However, he did alter his original title for my sake—which was *The Matrimonial Goods Exchange*— therefore, I feel obligated to support him."

"Ghastly title, Duchess," Lady Cosgrove said under her breath.

"I concur," the dowager duchess answered. "His former title made it sound as if marriage were part of a bartering system, which—of course—it has been for centuries. I believe, however, we've risen above that archaic notion. In our modern day, more and more marriages are decided on by matters of mutual regard and fondness, as they should be. I'm sure you would agree, Zinnia."

Lady Cosgrove was silent for a moment. Ivy imagined that at any moment, she would employ another infamous look. Instead, a wistful smile graced her lips.

"You and I were fortunate, Duchess," Lady Cosgrove said with an uncharacteristic softness. Then, looking to Lilah, she cleared her throat. "Though not all young women can afford romantic notions."

Perturbed, Ivy spoke up in defense of her friend. "Everyone deserves a chance to find love, no matter their circumstance."

She would have said more, too, but suddenly, a wave of dizziness spiraled through her. She closed her eyes for an instant to recover. Then her gaze swept to the door, as if instinct directed her to the cause of the ailment. She didn't understand how she knew the duke would be standing there. But he was.

And he was looking directly at her.

"At last, there is my nephew," the dowager said, lifting a hand to beckon him forth. "You were good to spot him first, Miss Sutherland. Had I not noticed the shift of your attention, his arrival might have escaped my notice."

Ivy wanted to deny that her attention had shifted in any way. She wanted to think of a lie to excuse her sudden absorption in the area surrounding the archway. At the very least, she wanted to be able to turn away. Yet she could do none of those.

The duke hesitated, reluctance etched on his features in the way his dark brow furrowed. Then his nostrils flared as he drew in a breath, deep enough to expand those broad shoulders and the wide chest beneath a dark gray coat and silver satin waistcoat.

And when he took his first step, Ivy was certain she felt the quake of it beneath her feet.

"For his tardiness," the dowager duchess continued, "we should question him ceaselessly about his formula."

"Duchess, I fear we should not antagonize your nephew," Lady Cosgrove said, likely in the hopes of making a favorable impression for Lilah's sake.

Earlier, it had seemed that neither Ivy nor Lilah had made any impression on the duke at all. He hadn't spoken a single word of acknowledgment. In contrast, Ivy had spoken far too much. While she'd blamed that dratted second cup of tea before, now she was beginning to wonder if it was something else. She tended toward verbosity when she was nervous. Yet what reason could she have for being nervous? She didn't care what the duke thought of her. All she wanted was to ensure a match for Lilah.

"If there is any person used to criticism, it is my nephew. And he is a stronger man for it." The dowager duchess's voice lilted with obvious pride.

Criticism? From what Ivy had heard, he'd inherited the title at the age of fifteen. And from what she saw, he wore the ducal title like a second skin. His stride was sure and direct, his hematite gaze disarming. Who would dare criticize such a man?

That thought aside, however, Ivy wished he would look away, or that a footman would offer him a glass of wine, a wedge of cheese, a fig tart . . . *Anything.* A frisson of fear dowsed the dizziness, though fear of what, she wasn't certain. All she knew was that her heart was beating faster now. Moreover, she had the uncanny desire to bolt from the room.

"Ivy, I beg you not to mention my shoes or spill wine on my gown," Lilah whispered from beside her.

He would be upon them any moment. Even from half the distance of the room away, he stared at Ivy as if she were completely insane. Or possibly as if she'd offended him in some manner. Truly, he looked entirely too bothered by her presence.

"Of course I won't," Ivy said, her voice thready and quivering. She was in a state of panic now. "Lilah, please tell me that you see a friend in the crowd—someone with whom you must visit this instant."

Lilah released a quiet, sardonic laugh. "Whyever for?"

"Pray, do not ask me, because I do not know." Then, like an answer to a prayer, a footman crossed in front of Ivy, breaking the spell she'd fallen under. Hastily, she took Lilah's hand, turned, and curtsied to their party. "Forgive me, ma'am, but I only now spied a drop of wine on Lilah's gown. We must make haste to the retiring room before it stains."

Even before being dismissed, Ivy hauled her friend away in the opposite direction. She had no idea where she was going, but she started to feel better immediately.

It wasn't long before Lilah wrenched out of their clasped hands. "What has come over you today, Ivy? And more importantly, why must *my* dress be the one with the stain? Yours would be equally ruined by an imaginary splash of wine."

"But not as noticeable." Ivy smoothed her hands down the front of her gown, more out of a need to calm herself than to make her point. Her left glove had slipped down her arm again. Drawing it up, she fought the urge to glance over her shoulder to see if the duke had noticed their abrupt departure. "Besides, I needed to ask you what topics you would like to discuss with the duke. There must be certain things you'd want to know about your future husband."

"Have you gone mad?" Lilah squinted, her brown eyes flashing daggers. "Please tell me now before your *assistance* in seeing me wed goes any further."

Ivy drew in a breath. She knew her actions of this day were questionable. Not even she could guess how to explain herself. All she knew was that she needed to keep her distance from the duke until she figured it out.

She drew in a breath, preparing to exhale a slight fabrication of the truth. "I'm almost entirely positive that I'm not mad. However, I have realized, quite suddenly, that I have been neglecting to consider the other gentlemen in attendance. Given the freedom of an informal dinner, we really must take advantage and mingle around the room."

Lilah's eyes softened somewhat as she studied Ivy. After a moment, she nodded. "That is perfectly sound reasoning—though perhaps you could have used that as your excuse for our departure instead."

"If you'll recall, that was my first attempt when I asked you to find a friend," Ivy pointed out, lifting a finger as she adjusted her glove once more.

"You gave me *two seconds* to examine the entire room."

Ivy offered a half shrug and a grin. "Very well, I forgive you."

"You are lucky that I am fond of you, otherwise I might accidentally spill an entire glass of wine over your head," Lilah said all too sweetly.

"Tut tut. No need for theatrics, dearest. From this moment forward, I shall be perfectly sensible." *As long as I stay far away from the duke,* Ivy thought. The only problem was, if she continued to avoid the duke, then how could she steer him in Lilah's direction?

NORTH SPENT THE next hour mingling, just as Aunt Edith had intended. He welcomed nearly all of his guests—all except two. Thus far, Miss Sutherland and her friend with the pinching slippers remained elusive. However, not so elusive that he was unaware of their placement in the room at any given moment.

Even so, while his mind was diverted, he displayed the proper amount of interest in various topics of conversation. During this time, he heard no fewer than four dozen castigating reports on the state of the roads. At least thirty criticisms regarding the inconvenience of house parties at such a time of year. And yet, an unending list of the accomplishments possessed by the debutantes in attendance.

The reason for the last was that many assumed this party was for the purpose of finding a bride for himself. Whether or not they thought his half-commoner blood was inferior to theirs, his title made him irresistible. Once he revealed his true purpose—the final proof of his *Marriage Formula*—he would soon prove his worth on his own terms.

His guests would be more than delighted. Well, at least the men would be. They were, after all, the ones put upon by all this Season nonsense and pointless courting rituals.

Two years ago, at the club, North had overheard Basilton and Pomeroy speaking of the expenses and inconveniences of each Season. That was what had first given North the idea for the formula. He knew there had to be a simpler method for a gentleman to find a bride whose person and dowry appealed to him. And once North proved his formula, he would finally earn his Fellowship.

To his mind, the formula and his plan provided a universal benefit to society. Edith, however, was not at all convinced that women would want to be partnered by way of a formula instead of a series of parties and balls. He hoped his aunt's sentiments were not shared by too many others of her sex. He knew that if women gave his formula a chance, they would soon see the brilliance of his plan.

"Why does Aunt Edith appear so cross with you, cousin?" Beside him, Liam Cavanaugh, Earl of Wolford, plucked a fig tart from the tray and ate it in one bite, leaving time enough to reach for another before the footman could get away.

North glanced over a half dozen heads to Edith. Her narrow-eyed gaze was already upon him, and it abruptly snapped to another person in the room—or persons, rather—before it returned to him. This was Edith's way of pointing out that he'd neglected to greet Miss Sutherland and her friend.

He offered his aunt a nod of understanding. Then, as his gaze skimmed over the crowd, it lingered for a moment on Miss Sutherland, standing not two strides from him. She was turned away, but only just. From his vantage point, he noted the tension in her jaw and the way her eyes darted around the room, searching. He wondered if there was cause for her restlessness, or if she was forever in motion, unable to be still.

While he pondered this, she shifted. The line of her shoulder tilted, drawing his attention to the movement of her arm at her side, and to the glove that slipped down her slender arm. His gaze fixed on the small expanse of milky flesh it revealed.

The tips of his fingers tingled, making him aware that he'd left his chamber before taking his gloves from his valet. Typically, an idea for a new invention made him absentminded. This time, however, his preoccupation had been Miss Sutherland's fault entirely.

After a moment, he forced himself to turn back to Liam. "How do you know Edith isn't glaring at you instead?"

His cousin failed to subdue the amused smirk that creased one side of his mouth. North and Liam resembled each other enough for one to presume a familial connection. Both were of the same height, build, and age. Both had the same dark brows and dark hair, but that was where their similarities ended.

Liam wore his hair at a length befitting a man of leisure and overindulgence. More than that, his reputation for excess was well earned. He was fortunate that dissolution had not marred his more refined features. Or dulled the glint of mischief ever-present in his green eyes.

Most important, however, was their final dissimilarity—if Liam had been born just one month sooner, he would have become the Duke of Vale without the barest hint of disapproval.

"Because she likes me better," Liam said, nudging North with his elbow.

North had always suspected as much. After all, he did not possess what some might call a warm, engaging personality. "Where is your usual coterie? I thought both Thayne and Marlowe expressed an interest in the ascending room I've built in the east wing. Of course, with

Burton and Hormer's design marginally flawed, I felt the need to modify the pulley system to my standards."

"Had I half your brain, all of London would be my playground." Liam shook his head and tsked as if in regret.

North lifted his brows. "You mean to say that it isn't already?"

"*Hmm* . . . a third, perhaps," Liam said with a thought-ful nod. "As you might have guessed, Marlowe will not attend. Once he learned that the Earl of Dovermere was due to attend with the eldest of his eight daughters, he changed his plans."

It was common knowledge that Jack Marlowe was Dovermere's illegitimate son. Born on the wrong side of the blanket, Marlowe had never had the acceptance of society. Criticism over a less-than-acceptable birth was something both he and North had in common. "An oversight, though I'm sure Edith meant well. Since Do-vermere was a friend of our late uncle's, she merely wants father and son to reconcile."

"As for the *estimable* Marquess Thayne, he and his mother will arrive on the morrow. As of yet, he does not know that Lady Granworth has chosen your party to re-emerge into society. Something tells me that Thayne will be quite surprised. After all, everyone remembers the scandal between the two of them . . ."

North barely heard his cousin speaking. Like earlier today, his mind abruptly stopped. Everything around him slowed, voices merged into a collective murmur, the room seemed to darken everywhere but where Miss

Sutherland stood. And for an instant, he caught her staring in his direction.

Even from this distance, he saw her shocked expression clearly—a delicate movement in her throat, the widening of her pale eyes, and the first tinge of bright red to her cheeks. In the way her lips parted, he saw rather than heard her small gasp.

All of a sudden, he wanted to hear that sound. Taste it. Feel her breasts rise on a swift intake of air as he hauled her into his embrace. The weight of arousal dropped swift and low inside him, like the sudden plummet of a sandbag at the end of a rope. She turned away quickly, but the result didn't alter. He still felt that inexplicable, heavy desire for her.

Before he returned his attention to Liam—who now, strangely enough, spoke of a pair of draft horses he'd purchased solely for the journey on the off chance of a heavy snowfall—North watched Miss Sutherland pull up her glove once more.

That glove. Watching it slip down, inch by inch, was like the veil dance he'd witnessed during his travels to India. Only this was much slower and, surprisingly, more erotic. He was becoming obsessed with the flesh hidden beneath that glove. He wanted to dip his fingers inside and peel the garment from her arm.

"What are your thoughts on the matter?" Liam asked.

North didn't hesitate to respond. "I wonder why you didn't purchase a sleigh instead. The vehicle's performance on snowy terrain is unsurpassed."

"Hmph. I thought you weren't listening," Liam said

with a smirk, his gaze skimming to Miss Sutherland's general direction and then back again.

She slipped her arms behind her back and thrummed her fingers together. Once more, her glove slid down. North grabbed a glass of merlot from a passing tray, downed it in one swallow, and replaced the empty glass before the footman was out of arm's reach.

North made sure his expression was perfectly bland. "Have I given the appearance of rudeness or preoccupation?"

"No," his cousin answered, scrutinizing him. "And you never do. It's just that most of the time, I have the feeling that your mind is busy on other tasks."

An astute observation, North mused. Perhaps both he and Liam shared another similarity. However, North wasn't about to admit anything. He didn't have to—*he* was the duke. "I believe that we should speak with Edith and find out which one of us has earned her censure."

"I already know it isn't me," Liam said with a grin before he set off on a direct path toward their aunt.

North, however, took a slight detour.

Unable to fight the urge, he walked in Miss Sutherland's direction. At the same time, he calculated the nearest footman's route. Just as he'd anticipated, both the footman and he arrived in the narrow path behind her in the same instant. Then, in the second that transpired, he graciously allowed his servant to pass, while he himself skirted within a hairsbreadth of Miss Sutherland, his front to her back.

There was no time for an exchange. Or even for him

to make his presence known. There was only time for a breath—filled with the sweet scent of persimmons perfuming her simple coiffure—and a single touch.

The pad of his index finger grazed the warm, soft flesh of her arm and dipped, ever so slightly, *beneath* the cuff of her glove.

A hedonistic shudder wracked him in that briefest of moments. And he was already several steps away before he heard her gasp.

Chapter Three

"I DO NOT wish to be late to the concert," Lilah said from the door to their chamber the following evening. "Aunt Zinnia would not be pleased. She left a quarter of an hour ago."

In the dressing room, Ivy hunted for her other slipper. It had to be here, somewhere beneath the array of petticoats, stockings, and chemises strewn about. She'd seen it only a moment ago . . . "Since your aunt prides herself on pedestrianism, she must leave inordinately early. We, on the other hand, have no qualms over employing a quick pace when the need arises."

Ah ha! She spotted the blue silk toe peeking out from beneath the chair in the corner. Rushing over, she snatched it and slipped it on as she hopped toward the bedchamber.

"It may sound strange to your ears, Ivy, but some of us prefer not to arrive winded and gasping for breath . . ."

Lilah's friendly scolding stopped when Ivy appeared. "I thought you asked the maid to press your sea-green gown for this evening."

Ivy smoothed her hands down the fine blue satin and adjusted the darker velvet sash beneath her breasts. That same velvet trimmed her sleeves, hem and bodice. Where the red gown last evening had helped her feel confident, this gown made her feel calm. Right now, she needed as much calm as she could manage. "I changed my mind. Sea green is such a turbulent color. I don't think it suits me."

Lilah laughed but kept her comment to herself. "You will be wearing gloves this evening, won't you?"

"Of course." Yet at the mention of gloves, Ivy felt her face heat. She turned away from Lilah and crossed the room toward the bed. Surreptitiously, she withdrew the folded pair of evening gloves that she'd tucked beneath her pillow last night. Slowly, she and slowly pulled them on.

All day long, she'd been trying not to think about the duke's inadvertent touch last evening. The problem was, not thinking about it turned into thinking about it. Often. And in those moments, she'd come to the conclusion that his touch had not been an accident. The swift, warm graze of his flesh against hers had felt entirely too purposeful. Not to mention intimate. Especially when he'd delved *beneath*.

Ivy glanced down at the underside of her arm, certain that a mark had been left behind. She could still feel the path his finger had taken. Still feel the hot frenzy of tingles beneath her flesh. Incomprehensible though it seemed, her pale skin was unmarked by anything other than the appearance of a long blue vein. That vein must, assuredly, lead to her heart, because its rapid palpitations kept tempo with the tingles.

When Ivy walked to the door, Lilah eyed her with speculation. "Do you always keep your gloves beneath your pillow?"

"I didn't want to misplace them. After all, I knew you'd be in a rush," Ivy answered on a single breath, hoping to distract her friend. Then, linking arms with Lilah, she made haste down the corridor. If they didn't hurry, they would surely be late for the concert.

"That *I'd* be in a . . ." Lilah stopped on a huff, slipping free of Ivy. "You know very well that I value punctuality, whereas you are the one making us tardy."

Ivy tossed a grin over her shoulder. Occasionally it was easy to fluster *and* distract her friend at the same time. "If that is true, then why am I four steps ahead of you?"

Lilah wanted to be cross—Ivy could tell by the set of her jaw—but in the end she rolled her eyes to the ceiling and mouthed the word *incorrigible,* giving up a smile in the process. Yet there was something altogether mischievous in that small curl of her lips. "Perhaps because you are heading in the wrong direction. Again. Therefore, I am four steps—*now five, six*—ahead of you."

This time, Ivy was the one who stopped. Sure enough, she peered down the corridor in the direction she was heading and saw a narrow window in the distance. *Drat!*

This castle had her turned completely around. "Perhaps I know of a shortcut."

"Like the one we took last night? Thank you, Ivy, but no. I'd prefer to arrive at the concert tonight, not in the wee hours of tomorrow morning."

That wasn't entirely fair. Last night she'd been far too preoccupied to remember the way to their chamber. She blamed the duke. It was his fault. Completely. His errant touch had addled her. Even thinking about it now, she caught herself rubbing her palm over that place on her arm.

Abruptly, she dropped her hands to her sides. "Very well. We'll take your way."

Lilah laughed as they began their trek down the corridor that would eventually lead them toward the stairs to the ballroom. "Likely it is the *only* way. I'm glad one of us paid attention to the housekeeper's tour of the castle this afternoon."

"While you were studying architecture and listening to the history of the Norman Conquest, I was searching for your future husband." Unfortunately, Ivy had not caught a single glimpse of the duke all day. Part of her— the confused, tingly part—was relieved. Yet the rest of her was still determined for Lilah to marry the most eligible bachelor here. Vale was the obvious choice.

Ivy decided that she would just have to put her strange reaction to him aside, conquer her inexplicable dizziness, and resume the focus that had brought her here in the first place.

"As the maid informed our group earlier," Lilah

began, "the gentlemen had gone on a hunt early this morning. Therefore, searching for one would have been a futile endeavor."

One thing that had always confused Ivy about house parties was the fact that gentlemen and debutantes were, more often than not, kept apart. Supposedly, these gatherings were designed for the purpose of matchmaking. Yet the only moments the sexes spent together were typically before and during dinner. Ivy wondered how anyone managed to find a suitable spouse at all. "Our host was still here."

Lilah shook her head. "Ivy, I truly wish you would cease your pursuit. The duke is not going to marry someone like me."

"Well, he won't if *that* is your attitude," Ivy scoffed.

"It has nothing to do with attitude and more with interest. The duke is more likely to marry you than me."

Ivy tripped over her velvet hem and nearly stumbled into a suit of armor.

"Whyever would you say a thing like that? I'm not the least bit intrigued by the duke, and I certainly harbor no romantic notions about him. Not a single one." This time, when she said the words in a rush, her throat constricted. She tried to swallow, but the sensation would not abate.

"I didn't mean to suggest that you did . . ." Lilah hesitated, her eyes turning doelike and sorrowful. "Oh bother, Ivy. I know that asking you to attend this party was a selfish indulgence on my part. I should have realized how difficult it would be for you to be surrounded by marriage-minded debutantes, especially after what happened with my brother."

Now Ivy felt guilty for the way that her denial had sounded more like an outburst. "Don't be silly. You have no reason to apologize. I don't mind it here at all. In fact, the castle is lovely. If the party were to last ten years, then perhaps I could even tour it in its entirety. However, if you insist on being at fault for a nonsensical offense, you can make it up to me by inviting me to live here with you and your duke."

Lilah released an exhausted sigh as they reached a fork in the corridor. Automatically, Ivy turned left, certain that was the correct path. Everything inside of her told her to turn left. Behind her, however, Lilah cleared her throat. "The ballroom is this way, Ivy."

Ivy caught a glimpse of a man striding down the hall, heading in the direction she wanted to go. Even before her eyes recognized his form and his sure, purposeful stride, a jolt dashed through her, setting her off balance. In an instant, she knew it was the duke. Part of her wanted to flee to the ballroom. Yet another part knew that this was the perfect opportunity for Lilah. "We must go this way, for I believe that is the duke."

Beside her now, Lilah squinted. "At this hour, it is more likely a servant. Furthermore, the light is too dim. You cannot be certain."

But Ivy was. Even that path on her arm tingled again. "Our host is alone. There is no better time to make an exceptional impression on him."

"Thus far your methods have been far from impressive," Lilah grumbled.

"Think of those instances as part of a process. We

keep going until we find one that works." Although Ivy hoped the process wouldn't take too long. Once the duke started to show clear interest in Lilah, Ivy could return home, where she could forget about errant touches, tingles, and dizzy spells.

"His Grace is walking in the opposite direction of the ballroom. I am certain he has no desire to be accosted. Please come away," Lilah begged. "We must attend the concert. I know we are very late."

Ivy took a breath, preparing to use her most persuasive tone. "Your aunt will surely forgive you once you have secured a duke. Such a boon would reflect well on her, also."

Lilah glanced down the hall once more, appearing to waver. Then she shook her head succinctly. "No, for he has already turned that corner."

Oh, for mercy's sake! "He cannot have gotten too far. We could still—"

"I am leaving, Ivy," Lilah interrupted. "Are you joining me?"

NORTH WAS A man of science and purpose. He was not allowing an uncharacteristic reaction to Miss Sutherland to dictate his actions. The reason he was not seated in the ballroom, awaiting the concert to begin, was that he'd forgotten his gloves. It had nothing to do with the fact that Edith had arranged for him to sit next to Miss Sutherland and her friend all evening.

Nevertheless, he was thankful that he'd discovered

the seating arrangement before he'd entered the ballroom. Moments ago, he'd stood in the hall at the back
of the room, peering through a slivered opening of the
French doors. The concert had already begun. Wall
sconces and chandeliers had bathed the room in golden
light. His guests had been seated in rows of cushioned
fiddle-backed chairs, their lorgnettes poised—more for
the purpose of gossip than for musical admiration, he'd
been sure. That had been the reason he hadn't stepped
inside. That and because there'd been three empty seats
in between Edith and Lady Cosgrove. *Three*—most likely
one for him, one for the tardy Miss Sutherland, and one
for the equally tardy Miss . . . *whatever her name was.*

He never should have told Edith the truth earlier
when she'd asked if he'd spoken with Lady Cosgrove's
niece and Miss Sutherland yet. *Damnation!*

Even now, striding away from the concert, he felt his
pulse thicken at the thought of sitting beside Miss Sutherland. Just imagine the damage that could befall his plan
if one of those lorgnettes spied him taking an indiscreet
glance at a certain Miss Sutherland. Or worse, saw him
touch her again.

That was precisely the reason he'd had to return to
his study to don a pair of gloves. The fabric would likely
be barrier enough to remind him of his position. If it
did not, dire consequences awaited him. Tongues would
surely wag. Some might even assume he was attracted to
her beyond his control.

However, he knew the truth.

The epiphany had come to him a short time ago. Of

course, this was after he'd caught himself requesting that the cook add a persimmon jelly to the menu for this evening. After he'd spent hours tinkering with his slipper stretcher. And after he'd found himself searching a map of Surrey for Norwood Hill in his private study —which was likely where he'd left his gloves.

Upon realizing his preoccupation, he'd summarily dismissed the cause as being linked to Miss Sutherland. It was far more likely that his fixation stemmed from his desire to prove his formula. His Fellowship was at stake, after all.

In the past, when he'd been on the precipice of revealing one of his own inventions to the Society for review, he'd usually found a minor flaw that would prevent him. The reason then had been that he hadn't been fully prepared. In his excitement, he'd rushed a few previous inventions. Yet with his formula, he'd taken his time. It was too important to rush. And in the end, his equation was flawless. Therefore, the obvious conclusion regarding his preoccupation with Miss Sutherland was that it was a form of self-sabotage. Nothing more. This time, however, he had proof that his formula worked. And over the course of the party, he would reveal his greatest achievement.

Now, on the way down the hall, North decided to test the stabilizing bars he'd added to the ascending room track to make for a smooth ascent and descent. Removing the key from his pocket, he opened the door. It was safer to keep a locked door in front of it, otherwise—if the room was not on the same floor—a gaping hole would greet you. That could be disastrous for anyone to happen upon.

Then, just as he stepped inside, he heard a rush of footsteps coming from around the corner. Holding the door open with one hand, he peered over his shoulder in time to see Miss Sutherland emerge, but she wasn't looking in his direction. Instead, she was looking over her shoulder.

"Tell your aunt that I will be late because I decided to wear the sea-green gown after all. And do not worry. Everything will be fine," she called out, and a voice replied in an indistinguishable murmur.

North opened his mouth to warn her, but he was suddenly preoccupied by the thought of her slipping out of this blue dress. He *could* offer his assistance . . .

By the time he cleared his head, Miss Sutherland was taking a few hurried backward steps. When she turned around, she ran headlong into him with a surprised *Oh!* and then an *oof!*

North stumbled back into the ascending room. He did everything he could to remain upright. Planting his feet wide, he was forced to hold her against the sturdy column of his body. Forced to grasp her arms. Which, incidentally, were bare between her velvet-trimmed cap sleeves and elbow-length gloves. Bare beneath his hands. Bare, warm, and softer than goose down.

A shudder—that was more about untamed desire than preoccupation—quaked through him to his very core. Staring down into her almond-shaped eyes, he watched as they widened and swept over his features, from brow to chin. Her gaze lingered a fraction longer on his mouth, as if she was waiting for him to speak or, perhaps, waiting for him to kiss her.

He took a moment to speculate whether it was the former or the latter. In the seconds that passed, he catalogued how her hands were *resting* against his chest, not pressing as if she wanted to gain her freedom but curled slightly as if trying to capture the beat of his heart in the cup of her palms. Also, she made no movement to separate from him. Her breathing was rapid—though perhaps that was the result of running down the hall. When she wet her lips, however, she provided an irrefutable answer.

Another surge coursed through him. It was a shame he could not act upon it.

"Good evening, Miss Sutherland." As if by rote, he set her apart from him and lowered his arms. Instantly, he wanted to haul her back. Yet he did not. He knew he should say something inanely polite and send her in the direction of the ballroom. Yet he could think of nothing. His mind had ceased to function once more.

Chapter Four

"GOOD EVENING, MISS SUTHERLAND."

Even though Ivy knew that the duke was bound to speak at one point or another, hearing him now left her a bit dazed. His tone matched his countenance perfectly—rough-hewn and darkly mesmerizing. His enunciation lived up to ducal standards, she was sure, but there was something of an underlying growl to each word. The sound of it made her want to close her eyes and hear it whispered to her. "Your Grace. At last, we complete our introduction."

Instead of him staring at her as if she were a mad-woman, her impertinence earned an unexpected smile. That smile formed two distinct creases alongside his mouth, like a tutor's brackets marking an important passage in a lesson. She was inclined to agree with this imaginary tutor, because the duke's broad mouth was certainly worth further study.

He inclined his head. "Northcliff Melchior Bromley, the fifth Duke of Vale, Marquess of Edgemont and Viscount Barlow, at your service. Forgive me for not introducing myself properly yesterday. I was . . . unaccountably distracted."

"With a name like yours to remember, I'd have been distracted as well," she said, the words tumbling out heedlessly.

His smile remained, deepening to three creases on each side, and his magnetic eyes crinkled at the edges. *Oh dear.* The combination did far worse things to her equilibrium than mere dark intensity had. "Are you lost, Miss Sutherland?"

"Lost? No, I—" Still standing near him, she didn't feel lost at all. Nor had she been lost when she'd chased him down in the hall. However, she could admit to neither. "Actually, yes. I believe I am. Though I imagine you employ a servant rescue brigade below stairs, whose sole purpose is to aid wayward guests."

He shook his head, his expression turning thoughtful. "Alas, they are all on another mission at the moment, so you are left with me. Luckily, I hardly ever get lost."

Surprised by his quick wit, she laughed. "*Hardly ever* is better than I have managed thus far."

"I'll tell you a secret, Miss Sutherland," he said, leaning in a fraction. He lifted his hand to her elbow and turned her to face the hall at her back. "Each hallway is comprised of a specific décor. The one leading to your chamber is, I believe, host to suits of armor. The one leading to the ballroom is adorned with statues in various dance poses. Others have urns, marble busts, paintings, topiaries . . ."

"That's actually quite brilliant," she said, turning to face him.

She might have said more to that effect, too, but she ended up breathless instead when he flashed those creases at her again. Reaching out, she placed a hand against the door frame. That was when she looked around at their close quarters. It appeared that they stood inside a closet. With the only light source coming from the hall behind her and a single lamp suspended from the ceiling, all she could see was unfinished walls with vertical tracks of metal and dangling ropes exposed, along with a small bench secured to the floor. A floor which—alarmingly enough—shifted beneath her feet. "Either the floor is moving, or your spell-casting abilities are even greater than I first imagined."

Wait a moment, did I say that aloud?

His gruff laugh was answer enough. "The floor is indeed shifting. A degree of movement allows for subtle changes in the frame and structure, providing a smoother elevation or descent—much like a carriage ride is smoother because the supports bounce and give instead of remaining rigid."

Ivy felt her cheeks heat, doubtless with that unfortunate scarlet color. It was less about embarrassment over what she'd said aloud and more about the alteration in him. His enthusiasm for his subject matter was obvious. The amount of passion in his voice enthralled her, stirred her, heated her. So much so, in fact, that it took her a moment to grasp what he was saying. "A carriage?"

"The term being used for the one being built in Regent's Park is *ascending room*. Essentially, this room is an elevator like those used in coal mines . . ." During his explanation, he never once looked away from her. He seemed as eager to tell her as she was to learn of it. Then he held out his hand. "Would you care to join me?"

She slipped her fingers into his palm without the barest thought of refusing. Had she still been a debutante, such an act could have ruined her. She had no chaperone, and to be alone in a gentleman's company was strictly forbidden. Even *on the shelf*, the same fate could befall her. With all the guests distracted by the concert, however, she doubted anyone would know. Unless . . . "Will it take long?"

He lifted his brows as he drew her farther inside toward a small cushioned bench. "Are you always in a rush, Miss Sutherland?"

"Always," she answered immediately, which earned her another chuckle.

"Then I will have you at the concert before you are missed." His grasp lingered for a moment before he released her.

Ivy's stomach trembled when the floor shifted once more. Her legs shook, too, forcing her to sit down on the bench. Even though she had an impulsive nature and enjoyed trying new experiences, it did not mean she never felt warned against them. Usually when she ignored this feeling, it tended to transform into one of exhilaration. She rather liked that part.

He moved to the door and turned the key in the lock,

closing them inside. Anticipation swelled. Still, she felt compelled to ask, "Should there not be an inner door as well?"

"I'd thought of that, but it might give some the feeling of being caged in." He shifted to the right and opened a wall-mounted box that contained a lever.

While his statement made sense, when she looked around the small, dimly lit room, she could see how easy it would be to get a hand or foot trapped between the space between the floor and the wall. *Stop it, Ivy. You're beginning to worry like Lilah.*

Nevertheless . . . "Some might say that the purpose of a cage is to offer a semblance of security, while giving the illusion that one's freedom is within reach."

"You are quite safe, Miss Sutherland. The steam engine is not directly below us. Besides, this time of year, the water used for cooling the condenser is quite cold, thereby limiting the possibility of explosion. Plus, I have installed a series of bumpers to slow down the carriage should the supports give way."

"*Explosion? Give way?*" she gasped, having second thoughts.

Too late. The room jolted into motion. A harsh metallic clacking sound accompanied it. Her gaze lifted toward the sound to find a flat, black ceiling overhead. The room suddenly resembled a coffin. The candle flame cast undulating shadows on the unfinished walls, but the ceiling seemed to devour the light, reflecting nothing.

"Fear not," he said gently, drawing her gaze. "I have operated this room dozens of times, including twice today, without a mishap. I've run through every conceivable catastrophe and put forth methods of prevention."

Something Lilah would appreciate, Ivy thought absently. He sounded so sure of himself that she felt foolish for being alarmed.

Then another sound rang out above them. This time it was a grinding metal on metal, and a high, piercing shriek. Perhaps like a rope stretched to the point of snapping.

The carriage jerked to a stop with enough force that she bounced on the bench. "Please tell me that was supposed to happen."

The duke did not answer. He faced the lever instead, feet planted wide as if bracing himself. A series of clicks followed the up and down movement of his arms. Lifting the lever up—*click*. Down—*click*. Again and again. His broad shoulders strained against the seams of his coat. His breathing became harsh. He expressed an oath. Then suddenly he turned, took her by the shoulders, and lifted her to her feet.

"Hold onto me," he growled in her ear. His arms snaked around her waist and tucked her head into the crook of his shoulder. Then another marrow-chilling grinding sound ripped through the room.

Ivy clung to him. The first instant of their descent, her feet lifted off the floor. Time seemed suspended by a mutual intake of breath. The metallic shrieks grew deafening. Her feet returned to the floor, but her stomach was still elevated, held aloft by the force of their sudden fall. She remembered a similar feeling from when she'd raced down the hill in the gardener's wheelbarrow. It had been truly terrifying and then exhilarating, but only *after* she'd awoken and found herself still alive.

She closed her eyes now, hoping for the same result.

The carriage jerked on a groan and the crack of splintering wood.

"First bumper," the duke whispered, tightening his arms around her.

Another jerk followed. *Groan. Crack.*

"Second bumper. We're slowing now."

Slowing? How could he tell?

Another jerk. *Groan . . . crack.*

"Third bumper. Hold tight."

The carriage jerked. Hard. *Groan . . .*

She waited to hear the *crack.* When it did not come and their descent paused, she lifted her head. The candle flame had flickered out, enshrouding them in darkness. "How many bumpers are there?"

"Four. We are resting upon the last now, but fear not, it is quite sturdy and not a great distance from the bottom of the shaft." The nod of his head brushed her temple. "A survivable fall."

She should have been furious. She should have railed at him for putting her life in danger. Yet right that moment, a cool, tingly feeling of exhilaration poured through her. *I am alive,* she thought. *I'm alive, and his arms feel wondrous around me.*

Ivy drew in a deep breath and tilted her head back. She absorbed every sensation. Her heart pounded hard, like horses galloping over a moonlit path. The air smelled cold, damp, and delicious. The superfine wool of his coat was warm and soft beneath her fingertips. And where he cradled her body against his stomach, hips and thighs, it felt hot and right. She never wanted it to end.

He cleared his throat and shifted, drawing himself apart from her. He took the tantalizing heat with him, too. "I think perhaps we are out of danger."

Since his hands were slowly leaving her waist, she supposed that was a hint to stand on her own and release him as well. On a disappointed breath, she did. Yet now she had that tingly feeling trapped inside her without any way to purge herself of it.

It was a dreadful feeling to keep inside. It made her feel edgy and irritable. Perhaps she was too old and out of practice to enjoy the elation after surviving an ordeal. Or perhaps if the duke would simply pull her into his arms once more, she might not feel this way.

"Regrettably," he began, "it appears we are between floors."

That meant they truly were blocked in. *No!* She was imprisoned here, when she would much rather run through all the corridors of this castle until she was bent over and breathless.

"It is my understanding that actual carriages are equipped with brakes," she grumbled. "For what is a smooth ride if there is no way to stop it?"

In the moment that passed, he exhaled audibly. "Duly noted, Miss Sutherland. For your information, I did employ a brake. Unfortunately, the speed of our descent caused it to fail."

The warmth vanished from his tone. Hearing him speak each word with cold, precise enunciation only added to her irritation. "Then perhaps it would be wise to design one that *reacts* to a rapid descent."

"I am all eagerness to hear your design modifications. A scientist never has enough ideas on his own," he drawled, not sounding the least bit eager.

She ignored his sarcasm. "A clamp of sorts would do the trick."

He did not respond, leaving her in this battle alone. The silence seemed to drag on and on until she could no longer stand it.

"I do not like this confined space," she said after a full minute. "I prefer to move about. Taking the staircase would have been a much better option."

"And yet *you* accepted my invitation." He scoffed at her. *Scoffed!*

"Do not make it sound, sir, that it is *my* fault we are in this predicament."

"That was not my intention." The accusation edging his tone did not convince her that he was in earnest. To her, he sounded as irritable as she was. But what could be his reason?

It was only then that she realized she might have wounded his ego. It was his ascending room, after all. And from what she had gathered from his aunt, he was rather proud of his modern contraptions. Not only that, but apparently he'd endured ample criticisms in his life.

A small twinge of guilt pinched her conscience.

"I'm somewhat impulsive, and you are rather persuasive. It is a dreadful combination," she explained.

He murmured a sound of agreement.

Then they were silent for another minute or two in the darkness. She could feel that he was close, because the space in front of her was warm, but she dared not reach out for fear of clinging to him once more. "What do we do now?"

"Wait for Mr. Graves," he said. "Someone from below stairs would have heard a crash and notified him."

Sure enough, within seconds a man's voice called down to them from above. "*Your Grace! Are you hurt?*"

"I am fine, Mr. Graves, though"—the duke hesitated—"I am not alone. Please fetch a ladder but with the utmost discretion."

Mr. Graves summarily left, promising to return in due haste.

The enormity of what had happened was starting to settle upon Ivy. Sure, she'd survived the clutches of death, but what now? If anyone should find out she spent any time alone with the duke, her reputation would be ruined. Worse, Lilah's would be tainted. No doubt Lady Cosgrove would ask Ivy to leave . . . and just when the party was starting to get interesting.

"I'm dreadful at waiting," she said.

"Somehow that does not surprise me. Have you always been impatient *and* impulsive?"

"Even as a child, I'm afraid," she admitted, nodding to herself. "I could not wait for the next footrace over the hill, or the next adventure. I could not stand to linger in bed when I was wide awake, even when it was before dawn. Nor could I tolerate being kept from my slumber when that was the only thing keeping me from beginning a new day."

Caught in a memory, she continued. "There was one summer, many years ago, when my aunt, uncle, and younger cousin came to stay with us. She had a pet frog that she kept in a box by her bedside table. She had an absurd notion that if she gave him a kiss, he would turn into a prince, but she was waiting for the day when she had the courage to find out. Apparently, the sound of constant croaking did not hinder my cousin's sleep. Across the hall, it had the opposite effect on me. Therefore, I decided to liberate the frog from his confines.

"In my own defense," she said after a short pause, "I never thought the frog wouldn't be able to hop from such a distance."

"What was the distance?" the duke asked, his tone warmer and suspiciously amused.

"A third-floor window," she murmured. "Over a stone patio."

Vale laughed, a hearty, rough-hewn sound that shook the small room. Automatically, she reached out for support and, as luck would have it, he was the closest thing to seize. His hand settled on her hip, steadying her. Gradually his laughter died, but she could still feel his warm puffs of air against her cheek. "Your cousin never had the chance to see if her frog was a prince in disguise."

"Oh, he wasn't. I made sure of it . . . just in case," she whispered. The obvious path of her thoughts would be to remember the moment that she'd held the bleating, wriggling frog in her hands as she'd kissed that cold, wet mouth. Instead, Ivy could think only of how close she was to Vale. So close that she could stand on tiptoe and press her lips to his. And she would, too. She was certainly impulsive enough. However, Ivy didn't want to break the spell.

The two kisses in her life had both yielded unpleasant outcomes. The first was the slimy frog, and the second was when she'd foolishly kissed Jasper, just weeks before his death.

With an angry swipe of his hand, Jasper wiped her kiss away in front of her. "No, Ivy. That is not done," he scolded. "A young woman does not kiss a man. If his passions are stirred, then he will kiss her. I have given you no indication that you stir mine! And now your actions have disappointed us both."

Thinking about that now, Ivy took a step back. It was the last thing she wanted to do, but it couldn't be helped. The duke's pleasant grasp disappeared. Unfortunately, she forgot about the bench directly behind her and she stumbled against it. Reaching out, she braced her hand against the wall—then felt a sharp prick pierce her thumb through her glove.

She drew back on a hiss.

"What has happened?" As if he had no trouble seeing in the dark, the duke returned her to his embrace.

Like before, she felt the heat of his hands on the bare flesh below the sleeve of her dress. For a breathless moment, she forgot the question. Then when the pad of her thumb began to throb, she remembered. "I touched the wall. I think . . . I have a splinter in my thumb."

"Then we must remove it." Already his hand shifted to cradle the elbow of her left arm, as if detecting which hand she was protecting. His fingertips brushed the exposed flesh above her glove. "This one?"

Her breath caught in her lungs. The thrill-seeking, impatient aspects of her nature wanted to strip off her glove and toss it to the floor so that she could feel more of his touch. *Now*. Her pulse began to purr in her ears, swift and hot. Yet it was the quieter and more prudent part of herself that spoke. "Yes, but it is likely nothing."

Of course, she said the words without trying to free herself. She might have even turned her arm in order to feel his finger travel down the same path as last night.

"Hmm," he murmured. "I am of a nature that certainty is paramount."

He delved beneath her glove, his movements gradual and cautious. The heat and slight roughness of his flesh elicited a flood of tingles throughout her body. Her flesh, blood, and bone all quivered in unison. He took his time, slowly drawing the soft leather down her arm, baring her flesh, inch by inch. Every subtle shift felt like a new caress. Even though the reason for his thorough examination was likely to keep from alarming her, for some reason, she had the sense that he was enjoying this.

Then one of his fingers traced the same path as last night. The touch was so reminiscent that she suddenly knew it had been no accident. That knowledge sent another rush through her, fluttering low in her stomach.

"This room is too dark. You'll never be able to"— the glove slipped from her fingers—"find it." A soft mew of surprise escaped her. She felt naked, as if he'd stripped far more than her glove from her flesh.

His hand cupped her elbow, and another grasped her wrist. His thumb slipped naturally into the center of her palm. Unable to help herself, she rolled her hand forward, rubbing against his touch. The hand at her elbow skimmed upward to capture her, gently holding her hand immobile.

"Your skin is incredibly delicate, soft as orchid petals," he said, his low voice rougher now, hoarse as he gradually lifted her hand upward. "These gloves are too thin to offer a proper amount of protection." His heated breath coated her palm. If not for the evident concern in his tone, his suggestion might have riled her. Instead, it warmed her.

"Ah. That explains it. You were bothered by my ill-fitting glove last evening," she teased, her voice nothing more than a purr in her throat. More than anything, she wanted to curl her fingers closed, hold each breath he released into her palm, and keep them. But he held her hand open, exposed to him. It made the sensation almost unbearable.

"Bothered? Yes, but not in the way you mean." His throat issued a rumble of amusement that licked her flesh. "I notice that you are wearing the same pair this evening."

"I only brought the one pair—likely ruined now."

"The flesh beneath is far more important." And then, he pressed his lips to her palm.

Ivy gasped but did not pull away. She was too eager for more. "What are you intending to do?"

"A purely scientific examination," he said as his lips grazed her, trailing a path from the center of her hand up the slender length of her thumb. "Our mouths are quite perceptive. Have you ever noticed how infants first put things to their mouths in order to unlock the object's mysteries? The same principle works in this circumstance. If you have a splinter, I will be able to detect it easier this way."

He sounded so confident that it was impossible to argue. Then again, she doubted she would have argued regardless. Her eyes drifted shut as he brushed his lips over the pad of her thumb. It was no longer throbbing. Likely, her injury had only been a small depression from the head of a nail and had not broken the skin. She'd suffered enough stumbles to know the difference. Yet she couldn't seem to find the words to tell him.

IF NORTH WERE a man given to foolish romantic notions, then he might have imagined that fate had a hand in placing Ivy Sutherland at his party. Of course, he was not such a man.

His momentary lapse in rational thought, not to mention his actions, stemmed from an escalation in his pulse, he was sure. Not to mention, the heightened sensitization of his nerves was the likely result from the sudden plummeting of the elevator. It was all perfectly understandable.

So why, then, was he finding it difficult to release her?

He brushed a kiss over the flesh of her thumb, examining her closely. The sweet citrus scent that he'd noticed from her hair last night was here as well. A low, hungry sound growled in his throat. In response, she rolled her wrist once more, pressing her thumb to his mouth, inviting him to draw her in. He did, reveling in her gasp and the feel of her body molding against him. His hand splayed over her back while his tongue explored her unmarred, silken flesh.

Under the circumstances, his actions were quite reasonable. How else would he be able to detect a splinter, here in the dark? Of course, Mr. Graves would likely arrive with the ladder at any moment and North *could* examine her then . . .

However, everything inside of him was compelled to hold her this closely and to press his lips to her. Any part of her. Every part of her.

Unfortunately, Mr. Graves chose that moment to arrive with the ladder.

The commotion heard overhead was enough to remind North of his position in society, not to mention his purpose for hosting this party. He was supposed to be proving his formula, not allowing his baser instincts to wreak havoc with his careful plan.

As the sound of footfalls began to near and a sliver of lamplight bled through the seam in the hatch on the ascending room's roof, North set Ivy apart from him. She, however, kept her thumb to his lips, curling her impossibly soft hand around his jaw. What else could he do but press one more kiss to her palm?

"I detected no splinter or the faintest mark on your flesh." He should know, he'd been quite thorough.

As if his statement jolted her, she drew back quickly. "Oh, yes. Of course. I am quite . . . relieved, as I ought to be, and not the least bit disappointed that further examination is unwarranted."

North grinned as her words tumbled out in a rush. A ready quip was on his lips, but to release it would be to extend their flirtation and venture into dangerous territory. This wasn't merely a physical attraction, after all. She was clever, too. A brake clamp that reacted automatically to a rapid descent? He should have thought of that himself. But if he had, his fall with Miss Sutherland would have been all too fleeting.

If logic hadn't conquered his romantic notions earlier, hearing proof of her brilliant mind might have sent him over the edge.

Fortunately, Mr. Graves lifted the hatch before North could reach for her once more. Lamplight spilled down into the small chamber, illuminating Ivy's bright eyes and flushed cheeks. Any other woman might have become pale and drawn from the harrowing fright. Not Ivy. Instead, she seemed even more vivacious.

"Miss Sutherland, I should like to introduce you to Mr. Graves," North said, standing at her side. He noted that she kept her hands at her back, one gloved and the other bare. By chance, the other glove was tucked neatly into his own pocket. "You may not realize it, Graves, but you are standing in the presence of a genius. Miss Sutherland has come up with an impressive idea for a braking system for passenger elevators such as this."

Graves possessed a single, thick black eyebrow, and

it rose at this information. "My sister's boy would love to hear of it, miss. He is forever making inquiries about His Grace's inventions," he explained to Miss Sutherland. "Young master Otis dreams of being a master builder and inventor some day. And if it would keep Sir safe, then I would like to learn of your idea, too."

"By all means. Although I'm afraid my *genius* has been overstated." She glanced up at North, her expression tender. "I have far more knowledge of falling than of preventing it."

Mr. Graves assured her with a nod. "Sir has a sense about these things."

Right now, North wasn't certain he had a sense about anything, because he wished they were still trapped.

Yet, without a word of confession, he assisted Ivy to the ladder.

Before she mounted the first rung, she looked over her shoulder at him. "This was quite the adventure, Your Grace."

"It was indeed, Miss Sutherland." A stranger now stood in his skin. North wondered if he would ever feel like himself again, or if he'd been changed forever.

Chapter Five

THE CHRISTMAS EVE BALL was only a few days away.

Ivy, Lilah, and the debutantes had spent most of the following day gathering greenery to decorate the hall. Red apples and white ribbons adorned garlands of pine and fir boughs over doorways and along the main stairs. Holly branches tied with silver bows made wreaths for wall sconces. The leftover pieces were clustered together with sprigs of rosemary to form a ball that hung from the foyer chandelier. Some of the young ladies even set about on a hunt for mistletoe, hoping for a kiss that might bring about a wedding within the year. Unfortunately for them, there was none to be found.

Ivy was a bit disappointed, but only for Lilah's sake. Claiming a kiss and a mistletoe berry could have done just the trick. Especially since Ivy hadn't done her part in securing a husband for her friend.

Even when she'd had the perfect opportunity to catalogue Lilah's innumerable qualities last night, Ivy had neglected to do so. In fact, while alone with the duke last night, she'd completely forgotten her entire purpose for being here. Worse yet, she hadn't behaved as an unmarried women in society ought to have done. Instead, she'd been herself, which likely didn't bode well for Lilah either.

This evening, however, she was determined to make amends. She would forget about the events of last night. She would forget about the connection she felt. And she would forget about—

Ivy's thoughts abruptly veered backward. Had he felt a connection, too? Or had his actions merely been dictated by circumstance? What if, like with Jasper, the duke now was ashamed of his actions and hers? And what if, upon seeing her this evening, the duke pretended not to know her?

Awash in these turbulent thoughts, Ivy donned her sea-green gown for dinner and stepped out of the dressing room in search of her slippers. "I was sure I left them by the bed."

"You have been preoccupied all day." Lilah smoothed the front of her cream-colored gown and pointed to the marble console by the door, where a pair of green satin slippers waited. "Are you still unwell?"

Spotting the gold-tasseled slippers, Ivy realized that she must have left them on the table when she'd dropped one of her earbobs on the floor. Inexplicably, the thumb on her left hand—the one that he'd kissed—hadn't ceased tingling today, which had made it difficult to accomplish certain tasks, donning earbobs among them. "The very blossom of health. As you know, it is not unusual for my thoughts to drift."

After the ascending room experience, she'd come to this chamber and sent a maid with a note stating that she was ill. Yet in truth she hadn't been able to imagine sitting still for a concert, not with her entire being over-brimming with exhilaration. Nor would she have been able to sit still beside *him*, pretending nothing had happened between them.

Then, later, she'd hardly been able to sleep. She'd still been awake when Lilah had returned from the late supper that had followed the concert. Still awake and dreaming of the duke.

Ivy slipped into her shoes as Lilah pulled on a pair of gloves. That was the moment Ivy recalled that she only had one of her gloves. *Oh dear!* She'd left the other one behind last night. She'd brought other gloves, of course, but they were of the shorter variety. She'd only had her maid pack one pair of long evening gloves. Quite honestly, she'd never imagined needing another pair.

"I overheard Aunt Zinnia and the dowager duchess speaking of how our host was equally distracted last evening," Lilah said absently. "Though, from my own observations, His Grace appeared no different than he has been since our arrival."

Hearing the barest mention of the duke sent a wondrous thrill through Ivy. It started in her stomach and speared straight through her heart on its ascent. "You said nothing of him all day. Tell me, did he speak to you?" *Did he ask about me?*

Lilah shook her head. "Not a word. He did, however, glance down at my shoes once or twice. I don't think he remembers my name."

"Oh." That thrill turned into a hard lump of guilt. Ivy swallowed. How could her conscience permit her to wonder if the duke had asked about her when her sole focus should be Lilah?

Surely she could have thought of one thing to say on behalf of her dearest friend last night. An interesting tidbit that would have enticed him. Perhaps while standing in his embrace and plummeting down the shaft, Ivy could have mentioned Lilah's bravery—spiders never had bothered her one whit. Or perhaps when he'd tenderly stripped the glove from Ivy's arm, she could have mentioned how lovely Lilah's hands were—her fingers were quite elegant, and she played the harp beautifully.

Yet Ivy did not want to think of the duke's lips on Lilah's thumb.

The duke. After what had transpired between them, she should call him Vale, perhaps. At least in her mind . . . but no. The nature of her thoughts demanded more intimacy. *Northcliff*, perhaps, or simply *North*. She wondered which he preferred. Then again, asking him such a question assumed an intimacy between them, and if there was one thing that made Ivy timid, it was making an incorrect assumption.

She wondered—if Mr. Graves had returned just a few minutes later—would the duke have kissed her? And if he had, would he have been as disappointed as Jasper had been? Would North ultimately have discovered that she did not stir his passions either?

Ivy tried to clear away the clutter of depressing thoughts in her mind. "I will think of something, Lilah. Surely tonight he will speak to us." *Unless,* Ivy thought, *he regrets every moment last night and desires to avoid me. . . .*

In the mirror, Lilah sighed and adjusted the coral comb in her coiffure. "If I begged you not to, would it make a difference?"

Ivy thought about her guilt and knew her answer. She was here for one purpose, and from now on, she would try harder for Lilah's sake. "Likely not, but there is always a chance."

Lilah said nothing, while Lady Cosgrove's voice called out from the other room. "Miss Sutherland, would you come here, please?"

Lady Cosgrove sat at her vanity, having her hair dressed. With an elegant, though minute, lift of her hand, she pointed to the door. "One of the maids left a mended glove for you on the table by the door. Though I did not know you tore your glove last evening. I thought you'd been ill."

Ivy drew in a sharp breath and fixed her gaze on the long white glove across the room.

"Yes, my lady, I . . . I had a dizzy spell, and when I reached out to steady myself, I snagged my glove." The statement was true enough, but she stumbled over the words regardless. Had North sent her glove to be mended?

She wanted to rush across the room and press the soft ivory leather to her lips, but her trembling legs kept her pace slow. Lifting her glove from the table, she noted the fine stitching on the thumb. When she slipped it on, she realized something was inside. Withdrawing it, she held a short stickpin, like a cravat pin, with a bit of cork around the point to keep it from piercing her glove. She looked closely at the small design on the other end and nearly laughed. It was a jade frog wearing a tiny gold crown.

A frog prince . . . Even though she dared not allow it, something tender and shivery swirled beneath her breast, making her feel lighter than air. Surely such a gift meant something. In the very least, that he would acknowledge their acquaintance.

Now, more than ever before, she dearly hoped that she would not see regret on the duke's face this evening.

DURING DINNER, NORTH had decided that having a single table capable of seating over one hundred guests was more hindrance than a point of pride. Miss Sutherland had been seated at the opposite end, near Aunt Edith. At such a distance, he'd only been able to make out the bluish green hue of her gown—nothing of her expression, or whether or not she'd turned her head in his direction.

He'd found himself glancing equally as often at the clock, calculating the duration between courses and the interim period where the ladies would retire to the parlor in the west wing, leaving the gentlemen to their port and cheroots.

Now, dinner was over and a suitable time had passed for the requisite separation of the sexes. When a footman notified him that the ladies were awaiting them, North was the first out the door.

"Your step is rather eager, cousin," Wolford said from beside him in the archway leading to the parlor, his green eyes glinting with mischief. "Tell me, is there a certain debutante who has caught your fancy?"

North had endured enough of his cousin's teasing over the years to know better than to take him seriously. Yet a frisson of apprehension rolled over him as he wondered if his countenance gave anything away.

He collected himself, hesitating on the threshold. Upon first examination of the room, he noted Miss Sutherland's absence. A keen sense of disappointment trudged through him. "Such a development would be to the detriment of my formula. It is far more likely that the reason for my haste is simply to bring the evening to a close, sooner rather than later."

"What with Baron Cantham's snide remarks about your bloodline, it is no wonder," Wolford growled.

His cousin's defense of him caused North to forgive his more annoying characteristics. "Though he may be a purist, it is rather telling that both he and his daughter accepted my invitation." After dinner, he'd paid little heed to Cantham's thinly veiled slander. North had had far more important matters on his mind, like clock watching and—

Suddenly, Miss Sutherland emerged from a connecting doorway at the far side of the room. She stood arm in arm with her friend—whose name he could never seem to remember. Ivy's gaze darted around, seeking, until it collided with his. And held.

Something akin to elation stirred within him when she did not look around for anyone else. His chest grew warm and tight at once. Perhaps the port in the glass he still carried had turned. Although when her smile appeared, tentative and questioning, he forgot all about his drink. Instinctively he knew that she wondered if he would acknowledge their acquaintance. In order to protect her reputation, their time in the ascending room had to remain a secret. Therefore, he could do nothing more than hold her gaze as a measure of reassurance. Yet that was not enough for him. So he inclined his head a fraction as well.

She smiled in earnest now. If the sun dawned behind her this very instant, the star would appear dim and cold by comparison. And were he elevated to king right then and there, with all of England at his feet, the feeling could still not compare to this.

Suddenly, he felt like the most important man in the entire world. Every cell in his body told him to go to her. Now. To plow through the obstacles between them, seize her, and—

"At last, you are caught," Wolford said in a conspiratorial chuckle. "I see that your gaze is fixed on that cluster of blushing maids by the door."

North stiffened. "Is a host not meant to acknowledge the presence of his guests?"

"Even more damning than that, I was speaking all manner of nonsense, and you gave no reply."

North's heart thudded in his chest. He was still focused on the idea of taking Ivy Sutherland in his arms. It was not like him to entertain such thoughts. Not only that, but acting upon impulse was not something he did. Ever. Discounting, *of course*, last night's compulsion to invite Miss Sutherland into the ascending room. He was a methodical, planning sort. If he behaved in a manner so out of character, his guests would likely assume that he was ill. Or worse, that he'd been carried away by a romantic notion.

For his formula to have any merit at all, he could never do such a thing. Yet knowing this still did not remove the unexpected, consuming desire.

"I have turned a deaf ear to your nonsense," North readily explained. "As you know, I am not a man ruled by passions. Nor am I of an impractical nature."

"Aye. We are the same in that," Maxwell Harwick, Marquess Thayne, drawled as he sidled up to their small group just inside the parlor. He set down his empty snifter on a rosewood wine table with enough force that he nearly sent it toppling. "Leave the romantic notions to the women who want to marry a title and riches. They deserve what they get in return."

With a slow shake of his head, Wolford clucked his tongue at Thayne. "Apparently, you are forgetting that you are now a man with a title and riches. Worse yet, your mother is determined to find you a bride. Perhaps even here at this very party."

North allowed himself to expel a breath of relief when Liam's keen attention turned from him to their mutual friend. Now that the other gentlemen were filing into the parlor, it would not bode well for North's formula if his cousin's deliriums were overheard.

As for Thayne, North felt a sense of commiseration with him. Thayne had never expected to inherit a marquessate from a distant fourth cousin. Since receiving his title, he, too, had fallen under scrutiny. Every event of his past was analyzed beneath a microscope.

Thayne offered a none-too-friendly grin. "Do not look now, Wolford, but you are also a man with a title and riches."

Wolford made a show of brushing off the reminder from his waistcoat. "Like my father before me, I will marry at the ripe age of one and sixty, and no sooner."

While Thayne and Wolford continued their repartee, North abandoned them and crossed the room toward Aunt Edith. Fortuitously, she stood within a group that included Miss Sutherland, her friend, and Lady Cosgrove.

"Nephew, your hearing astounds me," Edith began. "Not a moment ago, I made the comment that I wished to gain your attention. Then, before I had even finished the sentence, you were striding toward us."

"How serendipitous," he said with a polite bow before greeting each of them in turn. Miss Sutherland's name was the last to leave his lips, and it lingered there for a moment. The hue of her gown turned her blue eyes stormy and dark. He noted the subtle parting of her lips on a breath that lifted the creamy swells of her breasts, and desire flooded him. "I was heading this way to make amends for being an abominable host. I could not allow another evening to go by without offering my sincerest apologies to both Miss Appleton and Miss Sutherland for my inattentiveness. From this moment forward, I will make every effort to ensure your enjoyment."

Edith patted his hand and smiled adoringly. "That pleases me, nephew, though with nearly three dozen debutantes all vying for your attention, I fear you will wear yourself thin."

"Never fear, Aunt Edith. I'm quite resilient." He glanced at Ivy, then down at the small jade pin she'd placed in the center of her bodice. It was nestled there so perfectly that he felt a pang of jealousy. "Rather like a . . . frog that has frozen in a pond for winter, but at springtime hops away."

At the mention, Ivy lifted her gloved hand to touch the pin.

"You always were fond of frogs," Aunt Edith said. "Your mother even taught you to speak German through a folk tale about a frog. I seem to recall that 'Der Froschkönig' was your favorite as a child."

"Yes, 'The Frog King' was my favorite." North watched Ivy's eyes widen and a blush color her cheeks. "Though, in the English translation, he became a prince. I'd always felt sorry for him when he was thrown against a wall. Now I suppose he was fortunate to have found the one girl who was not annoyed by his incessant croaking, or else he might have been dropped from too great a distance instead."

A bubble of laughter escaped Ivy. "It could have been a much different tale for our poor prince, Your Grace."

"Ah, Miss Sutherland," the dowager duchess said with delight, "only now have I noticed your pin. Are you also fond of frogs?"

"Inexplicably, yes, ma'am," Ivy answered without hesitation, keeping her gaze fixed on his. "Very much so."

Elation expanded inside his chest, drawing it so tight that he could hardly bear the sensation. It caused a wave of panic to wash through him. He knew he should not have been feeling this way—whatever *way* this was. His sole focus needed to remain on gaining a Fellowship. Only proving his formula mattered.

Therefore, he forced himself to turn away from Miss Sutherland, at least marginally, in order to concentrate on the others within the group.

"I find it rather surprising that frogs are considered good omens for a happy marriage, don't you? After all, they are not the most romantic of creatures," Edith offered to the group, though with a sly glance toward North. When he cleared his throat in warning, she continued and discreetly fluttered her hand in a gesture over his shoulder. "With the use of my nephew's *Marriage Formula,* however, luck is not needed, I can assure you, Lord Basilton."

The man in question joined the group just as she spoke. He was of a short, solid build, with wiry brows and a carefully groomed beard.

"Yes, indeed, ma'am," Basilton said. "That is precisely the reason I ambled this way."

North stepped to the side to allow more room. The fact that he moved closer to Ivy was nothing more than happenstance. The sweet fragrance of persimmons filled his every breath. Mere inches separated them. He switched his port to his other hand so that he might accidentally brush her arm when he lowered his to his side. And when he did, he cursed the barrier of gloves between them. Yet at the same time, he noted with pleasure that Ivy did not pull away.

Unable to resist, his index finger discreetly arced out to capture her pinky, all too briefly, before he renewed his focus on the task at hand. "Basilton, I've been told that your daughter is quite the accomplished violinist."

Miss Basilton emerged from behind her father and looked down shyly. As of yet, North had heard nothing more than a quiet murmur from her, and only when prodded. He found that he preferred young women who could not contain their thoughts. And, perhaps, those who had a penchant for impulsive decisions.

Basilton's mustachios twitched in something of a grin. Puffing out his chest, he hooked a thumb between the buttons of his waistcoat and thrummed his fingers over the copper-colored silk. "We've had our share of exceptional musicians in our family. I'm pleased to add Hortencia to the list. Say, are musical abilities factored into your formula?"

North had waited years to gain Basilton's interest. This was the first real indication that the *Marriage Formula* might gain him a Fellowship. "They do, yes. The formula is designed to focus on the important factors of monetary assets, including property as well as dowries; lineage; *and* interests."

The moment he said *lineage,* North heard a snort of derision from Baron Cantham, who stood within a separate circle, which seemingly had their ears carefully tuned to *this* circle. North ignored the reaction, knowing that a number of his guests were purists when it came to noble blood.

Oddly enough, North had a place in his formula for men like Cantham. The sole purpose of the result was to benefit all parties involved—a pure and basic exchange of marital goods of monies, property, and lineage security. Adding in the *interest* portion of the formula had been an afterthought to appease his aunt.

"How does it work?" Ivy asked, turning to North and casting a perturbed glance over his shoulder to Cantham.

North felt a lump of guilt swell in his throat. Because— while there was a place for men who cared only for matters of lineage—the equation as it stood now never would have produced a match for Ivy.

It had never been intended for the names in the red ledger. There was simply too little data to analyze.

"It's a matter of filling out a card where each individual would rank their preferences," he began. "From there, it becomes a matter of calculation. That is when the *Marriage Formula* truly takes form. The resulting answer corresponds to another party's similar result. It's actually quite—"

North intended to finish his oration with the word *simple.* However, when he paused to clear his throat and gage the reaction of those around him, he heard Ivy whisper, "Brilliant."

And he was not the only one who'd heard. Her declaration earned a few turns of the head. Her eyes went wide. "Do go on, Your Grace."

"I won't allow it. I must hear more of Miss Sutherland's opinion," Wolford said cheekily when he and Thayne found their way into the group. Wolford angled himself in such a way to effectively separate North from Ivy. "Surely, most members of your sex would not agree with the *brilliance* of my cousin's formula. Other young women rant endlessly on the merits of a gentleman's charm, character, and money. Only the last of the three can be determined on a card."

North glanced at Basilton long enough to see his speculative frown, then North turned a glare on Wolford. Unfortunately, he only received the back of his head.

"A wise young woman is not fooled by charm, my lord," Ivy said to Wolford. "My own mother has said that what might first charm you in a ballroom can become tedious after more than twenty years of marriage."

Edith snickered and tapped Lady Cosgrove with her fan as they shared a nod. Basilton chuckled, the sound more like a wheezing cough. And North felt that pressure again in the center of his chest, expanding more and more.

"In addition," Ivy went on, seemingly oblivious to the eager attention she'd gained, "if a gentleman has a dishonest character, then who is to say that he would not be dishonest in filling out a character question on his card?"

"I couldn't agree more." Juliet Granworth joined their ever-increasing group and settled a hand on Ivy's shoulder, as if in support. "There is no judgment of a gentleman's character better than witnessing it firsthand."

"The same could be said of women," Thayne said as he set another empty glass on the nearest table. Uncharacteristically, he'd been drinking more than his share, and North wondered if it had to do with Juliet Granworth's presence. After all, few could forget the once-famous kissing scandal that had involved Juliet and Max shortly before she'd married another man.

"Though with Vale's formula," Thayne continued, his voice rising, "at least there is a better chance of marrying for what truly matters in the end."

"And what truly matters is character." Juliet squared her shoulders.

Thayne laughed without humor and gestured with a sweep of his hand to encompass the flattering gold silk gown she wore. "Or perhaps ascertaining *character* is merely an excuse to indulge in a Season, to wear new gowns each year, and to promenade through ballrooms in order to collect scores of fawning admirers."

"As usual, you are making assumptions on my character. I see the years have not changed you," she said quietly. Then her gaze turned cold and remote, and she turned her head, as if she could not bear to look at him.

Instantly, Wolford—charmer that he was—offered a wry laugh and clutched Thayne's shoulder. "I daresay it is easy to guess which pair would never find a match, formula or not."

"Without a doubt," Thayne grumbled in agreement.

Basilton appeared oblivious to the exchange and

turned fully to North. "To prove your formula, do you plan to use it to find a bride for yourself, Vale?"

The group—in addition to a few of those mingling along the outskirts—fell silent. They were eager for his answer. All except for Ivy, it seemed.

Without even a glance in his direction, she slipped away, disappearing into the music room. The urge to follow her ran rampant through him. His legs jerked in preparation, his left foot lifting off the floor. North had to force himself to think of the consequences. Force himself to ground his foot firmly to the floor.

Drawing in a breath, North returned his focus to the question at hand. He knew that if he chose to marry Basilton's daughter, a Fellowship would likely follow. Call him old fashioned, but North would rather succeed on his own merit. "Of course I will use my own formula. When the time comes."

Chapter Six

"EVERY GIRL MUST take a turn and stir the pudding,"
Miss Pendergast said. The spinster chaperone clapped
her petite hands with maniacal enthusiasm, rousing Ivy
from a trance. The kitchens of Castle Vale were burst-
ing with debutantes this afternoon. Yesterday, Miss Pendergast had spoken of a tradition that any unwed maid
who stirred the Christmas pudding would find her true
love in the new year. As an alternative, Ivy suggested that
they could all take part in the tradition and then deliver
the puddings to the duke's tenants. Miss Leeds had been
quick to offer her agreement.

The only problem was, Ivy had had no idea that
making a pudding would be so difficult. The eggs, milk,
and treacle were not mixing well with the suet. Adding
the flour turned into a disaster of lumps. She must not
have stirred fast enough. Looking over her shoulder at
Lilah, her pudding partner, she sheepishly shrugged.

"Perhaps whoever receives our pudding will believe that the lumps are currants."

"I just hope the person owns a pig to feed it to," Lilah said with a laugh. Tomorrow, on Christmas Eve, they would set off for the village in order to deliver them to the duke's tenants, along with a fat pheasant or goose, whichever the gentlemen were able to kill today while on another hunt.

Staring down at the soupy mess in the bowl, Ivy was glad that Lilah hadn't pinned all of her marital hopes on the magic of the pudding. Obviously it hadn't worked to gain Miss Pendergast a husband. Then again, perhaps Miss Pendergast *had* been in love once, only to have been spurned most cruelly. Such a trial was difficult to overcome, Ivy knew. Likely it was terrifying even to think of falling in love again. And Ivy feared it was happening to her.

She couldn't stop thinking about North . . . or Northcliff. Worse, she'd taken to wearing the frog pin each day, but tucked in the folds of her chemise, close to her skin. Close to her heart.

"Ivy, you are going to spill the pudding," Lilah warned in her ear. "We do not want ours to come up short."

"I'm sure Miss Sutherland doesn't think such traditions matter, since she favors a mathematical equation over a chance of marrying for love," Miss Leeds sneered from across the oak plank table. Those around her wore similar expressions.

Ivy had not earned much favor with the debutantes in the past two days since the duke had explained his formula.

Her support of his idea had not been well received. As for the duke, however, the gentlemen had inundated him with questions. In fact, the constant flow of interested parties had left no room for her to stand within his circle, as she had the previous night. Knowing how much his formula meant to him, Ivy was pleased for his sake. Anyone could see it in the passionate way he expressed himself.

"I do not see why His Grace's formula cannot coexist with tradition. Nothing within it states that parties are forbidden. And wouldn't it be nice to know that your dance partner was a potential *perfect match*? It would allow you to see him in a wholly new light." At her words, some of the debutantes showed interest, offering tentative nods and curious murmurs to their pudding partners. However, a number—bearing frowns and crossed arms—still firmly demanded their Seasons, their parties, and, most importantly, their new trousseaux.

"One has to wonder how lineage is even a factor when nobility runs so thin in . . . *certain* people." Miss Leeds sounded very much like her father, Baron Cantham.

Ivy's hand curled around her spoon. She desperately wanted to hurl a clump of suet and flour at Miss Leeds's head. "None of us know the specifics of the equation, but the result is for the benefit of us all."

"*All*? What does it matter to you, Miss Sutherland? From what I understand, you have no interest in marrying."

"Not that it is any concern of yours, Miss Leeds," Lilah said, her shoulders as stiff as a stair tread, "but she is here to support *my* endeavors."

"Don't you see?" Miss Pendergast said gently. "Miss Sutherland's circumstances might very well have been changed if the formula had been in existence before she was past the marrying age."

While the chaperone's intentions were kindly meant, Ivy suddenly felt a weight settle over her breast. It was as if someone had stacked all the pudding crocks on her at once. She could hardly breathe. And, to her horror, the sting of tears pricked the corners of her eyes. Deep down she knew that even if the formula had existed when Jasper had been alive, he still wouldn't have married her. More than that, she feared that the formula wouldn't have found anyone for her to marry.

Hastily, she turned around under the pretense of gathering a bowl of dried plums and currants for the pudding, then dabbed the moisture from the corners of her eyes. Unfortunately, her actions did not go unobserved. For in that same moment, she saw the duke standing in the doorway, his gaze missing nothing.

NORTH WATCHED IVY quickly lower her hand and brush her damp fingertip over her apron. She offered something of a smile before she dipped into a curtsy.

"Your Grace, what an unexpected pleasure," Miss Pendergast said, following suit. As did the rest of the room.

He felt unaccountably annoyed at the lot of them— all except Ivy, of course—and for what he'd overheard. Unfortunately, it wasn't true. His formula would not have found Ivy a match of any sort. Part of him was glad of it—glad she was here and not making Christmas pudding in another man's home—glad even though it made him a selfish monster.

Selfish or not, he still wanted to comfort her. Wanted to pull her into his embrace. Wanted to kiss those damp lashes and then her mouth. Ever since leaving the ascending room the other night, he'd regretted not kissing Ivy. He'd squandered an opportunity that he might never have again.

Not able to do that, however, he stepped past Ivy. Surreptitiously, he held his folded handkerchief behind his back where only she could see. Her fingers brushed his as she slipped it out of his grasp and whispered a soft *thank you* for his ears alone.

He cleared his throat. "Ladies. I heard tale that dozens of puddings were being made and will soon find their ways into the homes of my tenants. For that, I wanted to offer my appreciation to each of you."

A collection of smiles and tittering commenced, most of the debutantes expressing their desires to *only be of service, Your Grace*. At least he assumed that was what Miss Basilton had murmured, gaze fixed to the table while she blushed.

Seeing her reminded him of his conversation with Lord Basilton earlier this morning. Because of the formula, Lord Basilton and his daughter—the only female born into a family with seven sons—were now gravitating toward Baron Nettle, a widower with four daughters and desperate need of a well-dowried bride who was young enough to produce a son and heir.

In addition, Lord Pomeroy's eldest son was turning

his attention toward Miss Bloomfield, who recently inherited a goodly sum from a late grandmother.

North knew that gossip and the natural progression of information might have eventually led Basilton and Pomeroy on this same paths. However, once North had worked out the formula with the few guests who'd filled out cards, he was able to make the process much simpler. Now, his Fellowship was closer than ever.

Everything was going according to plan. So then why wasn't he thrilled?

Perhaps it was because his formula was working too well. He had proof of its validity, which meant that he had been right all along. It also meant that he'd earned this on his own merit. Most men would find comfort in that. A week ago, he would have been one of those men. Now everything that was supposed to be good and right suddenly felt wrong.

"We are all looking forward to this evening's play, Your Grace," Miss Leeds said, squinting at him in an attempt to bat her lashes. "You've provided us with such a wealth of entertainment during this party that it saddens me to know it must end."

North found himself nodding in agreement, but his thoughts were of Ivy leaving in a matter of days. "Castle Vale will be empty without each of you. I daresay Mrs. Thorogood will be saddened to have fewer visitors to her kitchens as well."

Standing with her hands on her hips and shaking her head at the disastrous mess upon her work table, the cook in question raised an eyebrow at him and huffed.

"Oh dear me," Miss Pendergast exclaimed, "I imagine it's well past time for these young ladies to rest before dinner. Not to mention, time to allow the cook to boil our puddings. We are ever so grateful, Mrs. Thorogood."

Grumbling, the cook picked up the first pudding and walked through a narrow hall that led to the main kitchen with the ovens and stoves.

Gradually, the girls filed out, one by one, each pausing to curtsy, blush, giggle, or bat her eyes—with the exception of Miss Leeds, who did all four. He also overheard Ivy telling her friend that she would follow as soon as she added the currants and dried plums. Her friend hesitated, yet at the same time Miss Leeds intervened.

"Miss Appleton, since we have both been invited to tea with the dowager duchess, we should walk together." She sidled up to Ivy's friend and linked arms with her before maneuvering to stand before North. "Will you be coming to Her Grace's sitting room as well, sir? We would be eager for your escort."

North recalled his aunt inviting him to this tea. Now, however, he believed he would rather linger in the kitchens. "Alas, I must forgo the pleasure of your company, as I have business with Mrs. Thorogood."

Miss Leeds offered another curtsy-blush-giggle-bat, then pulled Miss Appleton away before she could finish her curtsy. Mrs. Thorogood trudged in for another pudding before disappearing again.

As he moved toward Ivy, she frowned in puzzlement. "I thought you wanted to speak with your cook."

Likely, he could think of something to tell Mrs. Thorogood, but the truth was, the only reason he'd come down to the kitchens was to see Ivy. "It can wait."

"Oh, then you must be waiting for this," Ivy said and reached under her sash to hold out his handkerchief. "Thank you. I don't know what came over me a moment ago. It must have been all the flour dust."

As guilt trampled through him, he said nothing but merely closed his fingers over hers. He held her hand in his for a moment, feeling the combination of her soft skin and a smudge of wet pudding. It took everything within him to resist lifting her hand to his lips and tasting her. Briefly, he wondered if their entire acquaintance would only be the sum of a few errant touches. He wanted so much more.

They stood in silence—all except for the constant clunking of pots and pans, the chatter and shuffling of a dozen kitchen maids and sculleries in the adjacent room.

When he heard the clack of Mrs. Thorogood's sturdy shoes, he reluctantly released Ivy's hand but put his thumb to his lips to taste the remains of the pudding. It was sweet and creamy, rather like her flesh. "Mmm . . . I'm certain this particular pudding is the most delicious of all."

While the cook came and went, Ivy's gaze dipped to his mouth and lingered. She wet her lips as if she, too, wanted a taste, but not of the pudding. North shifted nearer until he could feel the brush of her skirts against the fine buckskin of his riding breeches.

"You are too kind," she said, her voice a mere whisper. Then she shook her head and turned back to her bowl.

"This pudding is the worst of the lot. I don't know what I did wrong. Lilah and I added all the same ingredients that the others did."

For the first time, North looked down at the runny brown liquid sluicing down the sides of the bowl as she vigorously stirred. The strange part was that the end of the spoon had a clumpy white mass stuck to it, which left the mixture interspersed with lumps. "Well, perhaps after it is boiled . . ."

She gave a wry laugh. "It will need to be boiled until Twelfth Night."

"Then I will have something to look forward to," he said honestly before a solemn truth struck him. He would not have until Twelfth Night with her. The day she would depart was fast approaching.

There was a commotion in the other kitchen, the crash of crockery and Mrs. Thorogood's grousing at the maids. All of which meant that he had a fraction of time alone with Ivy.

"I suddenly feel that now is not the most opportune time to ask the cook about my lumpy pudding." Ivy glanced at the doorway. "Besides, I really should be off . . ."

Without wasting a moment, North pulled her out of the room, stopping in the vestibule between the door and the hall. There were too many servants milling around.

Making no attempt to separate from him, Ivy lifted her face. "May I ask you a question?"

"You may ask me anything you wish." He turned her hand over and rubbed the pad of his thumb into the center of her palm, where it was warm and dewy.

"Do you prefer *Northcliff* or *North*?"

He grinned. The question was more revealing than his answer could be.

Then, as if she realized it as well, she went on in a rush. "It was only because I was thinking of you earlier—well, not thinking of you but more so *wondering*—if you had a preference. Not every name can be shortened, after all. Certainly not mine. And besides, you might have been scolded with your full name. Your mother might have said, 'Northcliff Melchior, what have you done with my curling tongs this time?'"

That wondrous, inopportune, elation returned to North. He wanted to take her away with him to the nearest dark corner to kiss those rapidly moving lips and slow them down. "Curling tongs serve multiple purposes. They work wonders for holding a book open."

Curiosity brightened her expression, lifting the corners of her mouth. "I hadn't thought of that. But what of the binding?"

"*That* was when I would hear my full name, along with my father's reminder of how those books had once belonged to my fourth great-grandfather—Melchior had been his Christian name."

"It's quite fitting that you were given the name of one of the three wise men, though I imagine you heard the word *incorrigible* a time or two in your youth," she said fondly. "But you still haven't told me if you prefer North to Northcliff."

Because he wanted to delay their parting for as long as possible. "First you must tell me your full name, Miss Ivy Sutherland of Norwood Hill."

"You will laugh," she warned. "I arrived in this world early, you see. My mother told me that she'd once had great hope that my impatience would be fleeting. Therefore she named me Ivy *Patience* Sutherland."

Something shifted inside him, and that too-full sensation in his chest began to burn and ache with a ferocity that demanded a cure. Unfortunately, he feared this particular ailment had no cure whatsoever. "What is it, Ivy Patience Sutherland, that makes you so impatient?"

She swayed closer to him, as if something had shifted inside her, too. "It's difficult to explain, but I am sometimes overcome with an urgent need to find out what will happen next."

"I understand. I have been overwhelmed with eagerness in the past, rushing headlong into a new invention. Over time, however, I realized how much more I enjoy the process than the result." His gaze drifted to her lips. "Therefore, taking my time, savoring what I enjoy, is the greatest reward."

Drawn in by that alluring citrus scent combined with the spices from the pudding, he wanted to lean forward. When Ivy's free hand fanned out over his lapel, he realized he had. And that he'd tilted his head in preparation to capture her lips.

"Your advice is sound, I am sure. But right this moment, all I want to know is what will happen next."

North did, too.

At the sound of footsteps nearby, North straightened immediately and released her. For a moment, he'd forgotten about the servants and the possibility of tainting her reputation. He could only think about how much he wanted to taste her, explore her. "I would hate to make you tardy for my aunt's tea," he lied. If he could do so without damaging her reputation, he would haul her away this instant. "As for me, I am assuredly late for a meeting with Baron Cantham."

Ivy's nose wrinkled. "Miss Leeds's father?"

"I was surprised by the request to complete an equation for her as well. Cantham comes from a lengthy descendancy who all possess the Leeds surname. He is a staunch advocate in bloodline purity."

"*His own*," she said with a shudder. "Though how insulting for you to endure his public scorn even when, it appears, his prejudice can be pushed aside if his daughter were to become a duchess."

Her defense of him warmed North. "Such comments are not the barbs they once were."

She tilted her head, gazing at him with tender scrutiny. Whether she believed his lie or not, she said nothing. Instead, she drew in a breath. "I wish you were attending your aunt's tea. F-for Lilah's sake, of course. You've not had much of an opportunity to become acquainted with her."

He grinned, loving the way she ran out of breath while saying things she likely didn't mean. "Unfortunately, this evening I have private appointments with others who share Cantham's way of thinking. I will likely not attend the play."

"Oh," she said, her gaze mirroring his own longing and disappointment. "It is wonderful, though, that your

Marriage Formula has gained such a following. How proud you must be." He offered a nod, but before he could make a comment, she continued. "Then I will simply see you tomorrow evening at the Christmas Eve Ball?"

Time was slipping away too quickly. He was at odds with his desire to spend more time with her, and his desire to take the steps to earn his Fellowship. "Perhaps I should request your first dance now before anyone else has the chance."

"And perhaps, before you come to your senses, I should say yes."

Chapter Seven

THE CHRISTMAS EVE BALL at Castle Vale had begun. As usual, Ivy was running late. This time, however, she was not looking for her slippers. She was looking for the duke's study instead.

She hadn't passed a single servant here in the east wing, but when she saw that the hall was lined with paintings of scientists at their worktables, she knew she was on the right track. Hesitating at an open pair of glossy walnut doors, she smoothed her hands over her skirts.

This evening, she wore layers of silvery gray silk organza with little puffed sleeves that rested at the very crests of her shoulders. Her pale, straight hair had been curled, coiffed, and secured by silver combs. Unfortunately, the small oval mirror in the hallway reflected that a few strands had unwound and now lay limply against her temples. Not only that, but her cheeks were flushed as well.

She made a face and shrugged. At least when she arrived later to the ball, her unrefined appearance would only corroborate the story she'd told Lilah about feeling a trifle ill.

Now was not the time to be worried about her appearance, however. Ivy needed to decline the duke's offer for the first dance. What business did she have dancing with him, when she needed to help Lilah win him?

Stepping over the threshold of the study, she prepared to do just that. Yet after a glance about the room, she realized the duke was not here. Disappointed, she was about to turn around when she saw him emerge from a narrow doorway on the far side of the room near the fireplace.

For a moment, he stilled and blinked at her, as if he was as surprised as she. Then those creases appeared on the side of his mouth.

He crossed the room, leaving the narrow door behind him ajar. "Miss Sutherland, what brings you to the east wing? Shouldn't you be patiently waiting for the first dance?"

At the word *patiently,* she knew he was teasing her. Yet as he neared, she felt a tremor of apprehension. What if her plan worked too well? Could Ivy's heart bear to see North marry her friend? "Actually, I was hoping to speak with you about that."

"Oh?" He stepped past her and peered into the hallway before closing the door.

Ivy knew that being alone with him, *again,* wasn't at all proper. His closing the door was even less proper. Perhaps she should mention it. Perhaps they should hold their conversation in the open doorway . . . yet when he gestured for her to accompany him into the other room, she forgot to mention it.

"It was Lilah," she began along the way, "*Miss Appleton's* idea to take the puddings to your tenants, though I'm certain Miss Leeds would like to take the credit." If Ivy had to endure the sight of him marrying anyone, she would rather it be Lilah than that dreadful Miss Leeds. Though neither thought made her happy.

A smirk appeared, looking perfectly at home on his lips. And when she drew close enough to pass through the narrow doorway, something hot and pleased shone in his eyes. "Actually, Mrs. Thorogood told me that the idea was yours."

"Well . . . it was Lilah who whispered it to me," Ivy said quickly, forgetting all about the cook being present for her idea. *Drat*! Continuing, she tried to make up for all the times she'd missed the opportunity to bring Lilah to his notice. The way she should have been doing all along. "As you might have guessed, I have the propensity to say whatever idea is on my mind, even if the idea isn't mine in the first place. Lilah is incredibly kind and generous. Not only that, but—like you—she is fond of numbers and equations."

"Is she?" He grinned in earnest now as he closed this second door as well.

Most assuredly *this* was not at all proper. Yet Ivy said nothing to reproach him. She wanted to be here. It was a cozy space, cast in the glow of firelight. Floor-to-ceiling shelves lined the semicircular walls. Unevenly stacked papers and leather books with worn bindings poked out in complete disarray. A few jars were tucked in here and there, along with assorted sizes of microscopes and other scientific paraphernalia. Yet all the clutter appeared to have function and order. There were no plates with half-eaten dinners. There were no forgotten teacups. The room was not a dirty mess. It was a sort of organized chaos. It felt like stepping into the mind of a genius. *His* mind. She realized quite suddenly that this room was an extension of him. "Do you often bring your guests here?"

"Never," he said as he moved toward his desk and leaned back against the one place that wouldn't cause papers to topple. "My aunt has invited herself on few occasions, and Mr. Graves is permitted at my request."

Those intense, magnetic eyes held hers in an unspoken communication that Ivy felt in the center of her heart. She hadn't been imagining the uniqueness of their connection. He felt it, too. Which made what she had to do all the more difficult.

"Lilah has quite the head for figures, indeed. Since her brother and father passed away, she's been overseeing her family's estate ledgers," Ivy said, drifting toward his desk, where an assortment of contraptions rested. The first one looked like a miniature ascending room, built out of wood. Picking it up, she toyed with the button-sized pulley and small ropes.

"Hmm . . . and what other accomplishments does your friend possess?" As he spoke, North reached over and compressed the pulley. The action sent the miniature ascending room on a swift descent, slipping down a few inches until it suddenly caught and held. Then, flipping the contraption over, he brushed his fingertip over what looked like four diminutive clamps.

Ivy beamed. *Brakes.* Somehow he'd come up with a design from her suggestion in only a matter of days.

"That's ingenious. However did you—" Lifting her gaze, she found him staring at her. Another moment passed in silent communication that made her want . . . *everything.* She wanted so much more than she could ever have.

"I was inspired by a fascinating and brave young woman," he said, setting aside the model to take her hand, drawing her to stand before him.

She cleared her throat and went on with her task. "Lilah is brave. Do you know that I've never seen her flinch in the presence of a spider? She has other fine qualities, too."

"I'm certain she does." He expelled a rasp of air that was just shy of a laugh. "Miss Sutherland, I am not going to marry your friend."

"That isn't what I—" Ivy stopped, already seeing in his perceptive expression how easily he'd read her intention. "Whyever not?"

Something tender softened the flesh around his eyes and the creases around his mouth. "I suppose the simplest reason is that Miss Appleton and I are not in the same ledger."

Ledger? Before she could ask what he meant, he reached behind him to a stack of ledgers in three colors on his desk and held them up, one after the other. "You see, for my formula, there are certain people who automatically enter the black ledger—those with high-ranking titles, a good deal of property, and wealth. The brown ledger contains members of the lower-ranking aristocracy and the landed gentry." He stopped then, his gaze fixed on the trio.

"And what about those in the red ledger?"

He shook his head. "They have little, if any, hope of marrying at all."

"Please do not tell me that Lilah is in the red ledger."

He blinked at her. "You needn't worry. If my formula is correct, your friend would find her match among those in the brown ledger."

No. That couldn't be right. Ivy wanted Lilah to be in the black ledger. After everything she'd been through, her friend deserved the very best. "Have you finished her equation? Isn't it possible that her number would pair with yours?"

"I have not, but I already know the answer. And I think you do, as well." He set the ledgers back down. Gently, he took her other hand as well. "Now, tell me the real reason you want me to marry your friend."

She didn't like thinking about the past, and she certainly never spoke of the life-altering incident, yet she found herself wanting to tell North. It would be better for him to understand.

Ivy exhaled. "It's because of Jasper, her brother."

North's brow furrowed. "I don't recall the mention of his name."

"He had an unfortunate . . . accident and died a couple

of years ago." Reluctantly, Ivy released North's hands and turned away. "You see, since we were children, I'd always planned to marry Jasper."

"And he is the reason why you are not married now?"

She nodded even though the answer was more complicated. She began to amble around the room, stopping at a bookshelf full of sideways stacked books, and jars filled with all sorts of things. She picked up one that contained a green branch dotted with small white berries that looked suspiciously like mistletoe. "I'd always planned to take care of Lilah, too. Her parents were not very kind. After Jasper died, they became worse.

"Within the year, her father died as well, and for a while I thought she might have a reprieve from the demands put upon her. However, then came the reading of her father's will. After Jasper's death, Lilah's father added a codicil, stating that the line had to be preserved. Lilah has to marry a man of noble blood, or she will essentially lose everything. Worse yet, if she doesn't find a titled gentleman to marry by the end of this coming Season, she will be forced to marry her licentious cousin, who holds her father's estate."

When she turned around, North was there beside her. He lifted a hand to cup her jaw. "I am sorry for your friend. If you like, I will work her equation and find a match for her. In addition, I will introduce her to as many of my unmarried friends as possible. You must know that I would do anything . . ."

His touch stirred so many sensations within her. She wanted to lean against his hand and close her eyes. Fighting the impulse was next to impossible. "Anything other than marry her yourself."

"I am sorry, Ivy."

He wouldn't marry Lilah. Ivy's entire purpose for attending this party was to save her friend, and she had failed. So then why was joy leaping inside her heart?

"No. I am the one who should be sorry, because hearing those words from your lips fills me with blissful relief, when it should fill me with agony instead." It was no use. She lifted her hand to cover his, to urge him to linger. "I am a terrible friend. I failed Jasper, and now I have failed—"

"How did you fail?" North shook his head, his gaze frank and earnest. "Even in the short duration of our acquaintance, I feel as if I know you. You cannot fail at anything, because you are the kind of person who does not give up when something matters to you. I know you, Ivy, to the very core of my being. You weave the world around you into a fabric of light that blankets anyone who stands near. Your vivacity is as charming as it is infectious. Your heart is warm and open. And your curiosity might even rival my own. There is nothing within you that could fail."

Embarrassed, she wanted to look away so that she wouldn't have to face the truth. She even attempted to step back but found herself against the bookcase. Yet even with North so close, his hand still curled beneath her jaw, she did not feel trapped. Surprisingly, she found his nearness comforting. If ever there was a time to admit her dreaded secret, now was it.

"But I did fail," she said. "For years, I tried hard to be perfect. To let Jasper know that I was the bride for him. I was patient. You may not believe it, but I was. Nearly ten years went by before my impulsive nature finally consumed me. And when I kissed him on that last night we ever spoke, he scolded me and told me that I did not stir his passions."

North slowly shook his head, his gaze drifting to her mouth, lingering. "That is not possible."

"It is true, I tell you. I must have done it wrong. All I know is that I wasn't enough for him. And there you have it."

"Not possible. I simply do not believe it." His thumb swept against the underside of her bottom lip. "Your mouth is far too perfect."

Ivy held her breath. "Apparently not."

"It is a matter of simple mechanics." His gaze lifted to hers. He edged closer by degrees. With one hand propped on the shelf beside her head, and the other sliding to the back of her neck, his fingertip dipped into the hollow at the base of her skull. A riot of tingles traversed her spine, plummeting all the way to her toes. "I'll show you."

And then he kissed her. Her lips parted on a soundless gasp of pleasure. The press of his mouth was brief, but warm and pleasantly firm. When he withdrew, the sensation of his lips upon hers lingered. A current zinged through her. She imagined that she knew what an electric coil felt like, all tingly and warm.

Reeling from it, she was almost afraid to ask his thoughts. Instead, she prolonged the moment. She licked her lips to see if she could taste him, and the barest hint of port teased her tongue.

His gaze darkened. The hand at her nape tightened ever so slightly. His nostrils flared and his breath rushed against her lips, but he said nothing.

Surely something that felt so wondrous to her couldn't have been a complete failure. Could it? Ivy closed her eyes before she asked, "Well?"

"I'd say the experiment was a complete success. However . . ."

Her eyes snapped open. "*However*?"

"It was only *one* kiss," he said with a slight lift of his brow, as if uncertain. Yet one of those creases made an appearance beside his mouth. "A scientist must experiment multiple times in order to come to a definitive conclusion. I believe we should make another attempt, for further study, of course."

He hesitated only long enough for her to agree with a nod before he took her mouth again. This time, he angled his head the other direction, kissing her once—*twice*, nuzzling the corner of her mouth. By the time he concluded, she was out of breath and clinging to his shoulders.

"Hmm . . ." he murmured, the low sound vibrating through her. "Another successful experiment."

She moved closer, her hands sliding down from the breadth of his shoulders beneath his coat to wrap around his torso. This new position molded her body to his. Beneath the solid wall of his chest, his heart pounded. Her breasts ached and her back arched so that she felt the firm rise and fall of his breaths. And lower, she felt the unyielding, intriguing heat of him. "Though . . . perhaps further study is in order."

"In great depth." His hand abandoned the shelf and settled on her hip. He shifted, his feet on either side of hers. "I must warn you—this may take a while."

This time, he did not wait for her response. Instead, he kissed her again. But it was more than a kiss. Their entire bodies were involved. While their mouths eagerly fused, nipped, devoured, she could not stop the impulse to arch against him. His hand splayed over her lower back and pulled her closer, lifting her. In the same motion, his stance altered, his foot sliding in between hers. Her skirts made a shushing sound as their legs tangled and their hips connected like interlocking pieces.

"*North*," she moaned, her head falling back as his kisses continued down her chin to the column of her throat. The feel of his heated lips on her flesh did terrible, wondrous things to her, making her breasts throb and ache, turning her body liquid where their hips aligned. "Or do you prefer Northcliff? You never told me."

"When you are in my arms, you may call me whatever you like," he said, his lips tracing the line of her collarbone. The hand at her nape drifted down to tease the edge of her gown, nudging it off the crest of her shoulder. He stroked the newly exposed flesh with the pad of his thumb. Lifting his head, he captured her lips once more.

At the first touch of his tongue, a soft murmur of surprise escaped her, jolting her. He drew back a fraction to look at her, as if gauging her reaction. He must have seen something that pleased him, because he grinned and slowly sampled her again. Taking his time, he delved past her lips in leisurely strokes.

This was all new to her. She mimicked his actions, tentatively slipping her tongue into his mouth and gliding sinuously over his flesh. He issued a low, hungry groan of approval.

The sound fed her impulsive nature and made her eager to further her own studies. She sucked the tip of his tongue, swirling hers around to feel the variant textures, from the ridged top to the silken underside. Wanting to explore more, she suckled him deeper into her mouth.

North responded with a growl. Matching her eagerness, he tilted her head back, claiming her mouth. His hips rolled against hers. A swift shock of desire speared her, sending hot tremors throughout her body. Even her mind quivered, making her dizzy. She clung to him tighter still, her hands finding his shoulders again as the full-body kiss went on and on.

Unfortunately, she needed to catch her breath. From the sound of his deep inhales and exhales, North did, too. The motions of his hips stilled, though he remained firmly pressed against her where the pulse of her body throbbed incessantly.

She broke away, pressing her cheek against his, her fingertips skimming the soft, short hair at the back of his neck. "I wish you had a sofa in here."

"A sofa?" He laughed, the sound rough, as if it caused him pain.

"I feel dizzy and everything inside of me is telling me

to lie down. And then we could continue . . . with our experiment."

North's fingertips curled over her hips, and the soft flesh waiting beneath the layers of her gown. He rocked against her once more, then eased away and released a slow exhale. "I would need hours with you, Ivy. Days. Weeks. Months . . ."

With a nod, she rose up on her toes to kiss him. She agreed to his terms unequivocally, willing to give anything to continue just like this.

He laughed softly, pulling back far enough to brush her hair from her forehead and to press a kiss there as he cradled her face. "Dearest Ivy, even if I were to take just a few more hours with you, I would be forced to marry you."

She flinched at his choice of words.

He seemed to notice and quickly continued. "Or rather, *we* would be forced to marry."

"*Forced*"—as in, against his will—"I see."

"Perhaps *expected* is more accurate."

A gradual numbness began to settle over her as she saw his expression alter from passion to something that looked like regret. She'd seen Jasper give her that look. A ghost of the pain she felt that day came to haunt her now. "I would never force you to do anything against your will."

"Nor I you, which is precisely why I never should have—" He didn't finish. Then again, he didn't have to. Ivy already knew. *I never should have kissed you. . . .*

She slipped away in the space between the duke and

the wall, keeping her gaze averted. When she shifted to put her sleeve back in place, she felt the tines of that frog pin scrape against her flesh.

He stepped in front of her and grasped her arms, his gaze imploring. "So much is at stake for me. I've worked hard for the Fellows of the Royal Society to acknowledge me. I cannot afford to lose my head, or my heart, and behave irrationally. My entire formula is proof that none of that nonsense is necessary. Don't you see? I could lose the one thing I want more than anything else."

"More than anything" actually meant, *more than I want you*. North wanted his Fellowship, just as Jasper had wanted someone else. Anyone else, as it had turned out. She'd been fooling herself to imagine that the duke was one person who could want her *more than anything else*.

However, she couldn't fault him for it. Because, up until a moment ago, she hadn't even realized that was what she wanted. Up until a moment ago, her only worry was that Lilah might be in the red ledger. Now she worried that her own name was there.

"I wouldn't want to ruin your chance to gain a Fellowship. Resentment would be sure to follow, and for what? A few hours of kissing that would likely never be repeated?" She shrugged, and his hands dropped to his side.

He closed his eyes and scrubbed the side of his fist over his forehead. "Ivy, I don't think you understand what those hours would entail—"

"Besides, you and I would never suit," she interrupted, not wanting to hear about what might have been if only she had never mentioned the sofa. Restlessness filled her, forcing her to move around the room or risk feeling the pain inside her heart. It was a slow pain—a terrible, squeezing ache. She knew her heart wouldn't survive long under the pressure, but part of her wished it would just shatter in a flash so that she could be done with it. But apparently, a breaking heart had all the time in the world.

"You need someone who will tenderly scold you about your disorganized mess of a study." Ivy attempted a laugh in order to sound worldly, as if things like this happened all the time and she was used to it. "Yet if you were to see the chaos I left in the dressing chamber upstairs, you would realize that I would have no right or inclination to scold you. Not only that, but I would constantly want to inspect your inventions—which might very well lead to their destruction. Even our names are opposites. Surely a man named Northcliff should never be forced to marry a woman whose surname is Sutherland."

"Now you're just spouting nonsense," he hissed, his words clipped.

Surreptitiously, she dabbed at the sudden well of moisture along the lower rim of her eyes. "I do that frequently. Yet another one of my flaws."

"Ivy . . ."

She didn't know what he was going to say, but somehow she knew she couldn't bear to hear it. "Most of all, you need a person who fits into your formula, a person who possesses the qualities that matter to you. You need someone who doesn't suddenly wish that, all along, you'd set out to disprove your own theory, to prove instead that there is more to someone's worth than lineage, property,

and wealth. And, perhaps, that matters of happenstance—
like a fateful pairing of hearts in a single moment—might
have been the truest answer all along."

She didn't know why she hesitated at the door. Perhaps
she thought he might want to stop her. After a moment,
however, he didn't say anything more. Ivy left the room
without looking back.

Chapter Eight

NORTH CROSSED THE room and closed the door, letting Ivy go. He didn't know what else to do. Because if he stopped her, he didn't know what he might say. A number of irrational phrases filled his head, and he was afraid of them spilling out.

"Don't go. Forgive me . . ."

"You make me question my sanity. I might already be accustomed to the madness. I crave it . . ."

"I need you in my life. Stay. Forever . . ."

He pressed his forehead to the door as more thoughts continued along the same vein that ran directly to his heart. They twisted knots inside his mind. The pressure within his chest now felt condensed and weighted, crushing him. He preferred the elation, no matter how uncontrolled and incalculable it was. But as he straightened and moved away from the door, he suddenly knew he would never feel it again.

At his desk, he lifted the scale model of the ascending room, remembering Ivy's smile of pleasure when she'd seen the changes in his design. He'd done them for her. The errand of a romantic fool. She was his inspiration. He'd worked on it without sleep for an entire day, stopping only to see her at dinner.

He pulled on the strings to elevate the diminutive room once more. Yet the pulley string snagged. He tugged again. Then, before he could stop it, the top of the model cracked, collapsed, and crumbled.

He stared down at the broken pieces as it fell apart in his hands. It was useless now. The entire model would have to be rebuilt. Yet this wasn't even *his* invention. It belonged to someone else. North was merely modifying it. The pointlessness of it hit him hard.

Suddenly angry, he closed his fist and crushed the model further. Yet that was not enough. So he hurled it into the fire. The flames flared, leaping up in a shock of orange, consuming the wood in an instant.

A rush of primal satisfaction tore through him, feeding this inexplicable rage.

Striding back to the desk, he snatched up the model of a guillotine and hurled it into the flames as well. He crossed the room to the shelves. The slipper stretcher went next, landing with a clunk against the other logs. It was too solid to incinerate in a flash, so he began crumbling papers and tossing them into the fire. Heaps and stacks of designs and potential patents went up in flames. Everything he'd worked on for years.

He grabbed the jar of mistletoe, his arm reeling back,

preparing to smash it to bits. But then he remembered her kiss—*their kiss,* those moments of utter contentment— and suddenly, he couldn't release the jar.

"This is madness!" he shouted to the empty room. "My formula is what matters. *All that matters.*"

Then, seeing the ledgers on his desk filled him with a mixture of purpose and loathing. *You need someone who doesn't suddenly wish that, all along, you'd set out to disprove your own theory, to prove instead that there is more to someone's worth than lineage, property, and wealth. . . .*

He gripped the black ledger, his fingertips white from the force. Then he hurled it into the flames.

The brown one followed.

Picking up the red ledger, he shook it at the ceiling. There was only one name on its pages. One single name that should be of no consequence. "This was a brief aberration that is over now. She was not my match. It could not have lasted. *Ha!* It was never meant to begin."

At once, he lowered his arm and stared at the red ledger in confusion. *Lasted?* Why had he said that? It wasn't as if he'd given any thought to marrying Ivy Sutherland of Norwood Hill. Or any thought to spending hours, days, weeks, *years . . .* kissing her, touching her, listening to her ideas, having her rush impatiently into his arms, feeling elation each and every day for the rest of his life. No. Not a single thought. He was a rational, scientific man. When it was time for him to marry, he would use his formula to find a suitable candidate.

Taking up the quill pen, he dipped it into the inkpot and worked Ivy's equation, needing her number. He already knew it would yield nothing, because she met none of the criteria. She only had insubstantial goods to bring to a marriage. Only her vivacity, her winter-blue eyes, her warmth, her heart, her mind, her laugh . . .

His formula was an insufficient tool to measure these qualities. His formula . . . was lacking in everything that mattered.

Suddenly, he realized that he was a complete fraud.

All the breath left North's body as he sank to his knees. His formula didn't work.

WHEN IVY HEARD the door to the other room open, she leaped up from the window seat and rushed across the room to douse the lamp. She didn't want Lilah to see that she'd been sobbing like a complete idiot.

"Are you feeling better—" Lilah stopped cold the instant she spotted her. "Oh, dearest, what is the matter? You've been crying."

Ivy shook her head. "Nothing more than a headache."

Carefully, Lilah looked over her shoulder and closed the door to the dressing chamber. "I hope this doesn't have anything to do with the duke."

"Of course it doesn't have anything to do with . . . Why would you even think that?"

Lilah sighed. "I know you wanted me to marry him."

"Oh." Ivy pinched the bridge of her nose and sat heavily on the bed, playing the part of a headache victim, and certainly not someone with a broken heart. "You must forgive me. I did not realize how foolish my notion was until this evening."

Apparently she was convincing, because the concern lifted from Lilah's expression.

"Then you have heard, as well." Lilah tsked as she plucked her gloves off one finger after the other. "I cannot believe our host would abandon his own party. There were whispers that he rode away on his horse."

Ivy lowered her hand, her attention riveted. "The duke left in the dead of night?" That did not sound like something he would do.

Lilah nodded and removed her combs from her hair, shaking it free before she sat down beside Ivy.

"I don't understand," Ivy said. "Why would you think it had something to do with his not wanting to marry?"

"Either his interests lay elsewhere, or he has no intention of marrying any of us. If he did, he would have attended his own Christmas Eve Ball."

Thinking of what he wanted *more than anything,* Ivy offered a solemn nod. "I believe you are correct on both counts."

"There now, it is done. You mustn't think of him anymore, and you must stop hoping that he will marry me."

Ivy's shoulders slumped forward, and she settled her face in the cup of her hands. "Lilah, I've been such a fool. I never really wanted him to marry you. Not since the moment we were introduced."

"If it's because you thought his manners abominable, then I certainly agree."

"No." Ivy shook her head and turned toward her friend. "My failing is much worse, and I hope you can forgive me."

"Of course. What is there to forgive?" Lilah smiled and squeezed Ivy's shoulder.

"I think . . . for just a moment"—Ivy drew in a breath and slowly released it—"*I* wanted to marry him."

Lilah covered her mouth on a gasp. "You wanted to— But that means that you— Is it possible that you've fallen in love?"

Not love. Whatever this was, it was much worse and it had no name, only a combination of symptoms: dizziness, exhilaration, bliss, consuming desire, misery, pain, heart-wrenching agony, despair . . . "You must know that I could never love again after Jasper."

"But that was not love, silly." Lilah offered a tender smile. "That was one of those childhood dreams we hold onto for far too long. You thought of him as your Prince Charming, no matter how many times he proved otherwise. But he remained a boy who was determined to gather as many hearts as he could, filling his pockets with them until they overflowed and fell to the dirt at his feet."

Jasper had enjoyed women. That had been one of the reasons why his unequivocal rejection of Ivy had hurt so much. Why hadn't he wanted her, too?

"Right before he left with that married harlot," Lilah continued, "I begged him to set you free, once and for all. It wasn't fair the way he kept you . . . forever in his pocket."

"You asked him to set me free?" Ivy stared, agape. She

replayed the set-down he'd given her and how it had left her feeling like a failure. She'd never heard Jasper sound cruel. In fact, he'd sounded more like his father in that moment. Now, Ivy understood why.

"I suppose he did set me free," she said. "That was his last noble act, only I was too stubborn to see it. Perhaps Jasper did love one of the women whose hearts he collected. He loved his sister."

"Of course he did," Lilah said on a watery laugh, wiping away a sudden sheen of tears. "I'm an incredibly loveable young woman. And one day I might even find a man who realizes it."

"I will make sure of it," Ivy vowed as she hugged her friend.

"Oh, please, Ivy. Don't."

Ivy was in the midst of convincing her friend of a perfect plan for her upcoming Season, when the door from the dressing chamber suddenly opened. More surprising than that was having the dowager duchess step inside the room.

"There you are, Miss Sutherland. I am in a fretful state, to be sure," she said, wringing her hands. Strands of silver hair stuck out from her coiffure. "I am taking it for granted that you have already heard the rumors of my nephew's leaving this evening. Let me say that over the years, he has disappeared into his study when working on an invention, but he has never left the house without a word. Worse, he did not pack a bag, inform his valet, or even order a carriage. It is now very late, well past two o'clock on Christmas morning, and still he has not returned."

Ivy stood, her own alarm mounting. She hadn't entirely believed that he'd left, but was likely in another part of the castle. What errand could have sent him out of doors on Christmas Eve? Glancing at the starlit night beyond the frost-rimmed window, she worried that it had something to do with the agitated state she'd left him in. "Do you have any idea where he could be, Your Grace?"

The dowager duchess shook her head. "I was hoping you would shed some light on the situation."

"Me, ma'am?"

"His study is in complete disrepair. Many things destroyed, or burned in the fireplace."

Ivy gasped. "Was there an assault? Did someone break into his study? Is he hurt?"

"I have been assured by the groomsman who saddled his horse that my nephew was alone and appeared unhurt, though disheveled. When asked where he was going, my nephew responded that he needed to clear his head." The dowager duchess stepped forward, lifting an object in her grasp. "My only clue is inside this red ledger, which sat squarely in the center of his desk."

"I don't understand. What does that red ledger have to do with me?" Ivy asked as a sinking feeling settled into the pit of her stomach. She wanted to step back from it.

"Perhaps if you looked inside, you could offer your insight."

Reluctantly, Ivy took the ledger, her hands already cold and trembling.

"You'll see that there is only one name in that entire ledger, and it is yours."

Numbly, she opened the book. True enough. The first page read: MISS IVY SUTHERLAND OF NORWOOD HILL—<u>NO CONSEQUENCE</u>.

"And what about those in the red ledger?" she'd asked him a few hours ago.

"They have little, if any, hope of marrying at all."

"Mr. Graves found the remains of the other two ledgers in the ash," the dowager duchess said. "I know they were an integral part of his formula. One can only presume that some dire result caused such destruction."

Dire, indeed. For the third time in her life, her kiss had brought about a calamity. Only this was the worst of all. Where could North be? Was he hurt? Or did he clear his head enough to forget her entirely?

Miss Ivy Sutherland of Norwood Hill—<u>no consequence</u>. It was true. She possessed no title, no property, no dowry—none of the things that mattered to North.

"You don't understand, Ivy, we would be forced to marry."

The grip around Ivy's heart intensified until she felt it shatter beneath the pressure. Strangely, she remained composed on the outside. Inside was a wholly different story. Inside, she was on her knees, sobbing. "I wish I could help, ma'am, but I do not know where the duke is, though I pray for his safe return."

And she did, even when he saw no redeeming quality in her existence.

"Pray . . . Yes, we must all pray. If my nephew has not returned by dawn, then I will send out a search party."

Chapter Nine

NORTH WAITED IN the hall outside Jack Marlowe's rooms in his lavish estate. After riding on horseback for four hours in sleet, North was wet and cold to the bone. But this was a matter of importance that he could not delay one moment longer.

After a short interval, Marlowe emerged from a gilded doorway, securing a blue silk banyan around his waist as he swaggered, barefoot, into the hall. With a careless rake of his hand, he pushed back a golden mane of hair from his forehead. "Vale, do you have any idea what time it is?"

North didn't want to waste time by answering unimportant questions. "Marlowe, what do you think of my formula?"

They'd been friends for years, and he trusted Marlowe to speak plainly. He would have spoken with Wolford, but his cousin tended to laugh too often when the matter required severity. Thayne had been too distracted since

Juliet Granworth's return to society. And as the bastard son of the Earl of Dovermere, Marlow hadn't wanted to attend the party, knowing that his father was there. So it had been up to North to come to him instead.

Marlowe's tawny brow furrowed. "You rode all the way here in the dead of night for me to stroke your ego? Come now, Vale, I must get back to"—he turned his head toward the bedchamber door—"darling, what is your name?"

"*Minerva,*" came the singsong reply, along with a giggle.

Marlowe shrugged. "I must get back to Minerva. She's an opera girl and was just showing me how long she can hold a single note."

"This won't take long," North said, losing his patience. He started pacing around the marbled hall, his booted steps echoing around him. "I want my formula to have merit and lasting value. What I've created is a simpler, surer method than the notion of marrying for love would be."

"I agree. Love has no place in a marriage. Marriages are all about drawing new lines on old maps and ensuring that blue blood continues to bleed from inbred veins for generations to come. At least with your formula those *highest of high* on the ladder rungs needn't marry their cousins. And there you have your answer," Marlowe concluded with a brush of his hands.

North stopped pacing. "We don't all marry our cousins."

"Enough of you do it to put a stain on the whole lot.

Want a drink?" Marlowe poured from a decanter sitting atop a mahogany and gold inlaid secretary along the far wall.

Absently, North shook his head. There was something in the words Jack chose that sparked his interest. "Even though you think love has no place in marriage, you still believe it exists?"

"I fall in love all the time. Ask any of my paramours." He nodded toward the bedchamber door as he tipped back his glass.

"I'm speaking of true, honest, soul-deep love. The kind that takes you by surprise and changes the entire course of your life in an instant."

"Vale, the night air has gone to your head. You are speaking of supposition and theory instead of facts. At school, I bore witness to many of your recitations against *prattling poets* whose craniums were—in your opinion— *overflowing sop buckets.*" Marlowe laughed and poured himself another drink. "Why are you really here? Why come all this way when you likely already knew my answers to your questions?"

"I needed to hear from a fellow analytic. To feel grounded once more."

"Hmm . . . And you couldn't have found a single one beneath your own roof? It sounds as if you've stumbled on an error in your calculations."

"No. The equation is flawless," he admitted, feeling a sense of despair roll over him.

"Then congratulations are in order. Soon you will have scores of the unwed who want to remove the risk of being wrong. You must be thrilled. I know you've worked hard on this for a while now."

North scrubbed a hand across his brow. "I am thrilled."

"It's strange, though. Your jubilation looks rather like disappointment," Marlowe said on a wry laugh.

North lowered his arm and glared at his friend, agitated. "You're wrong. *This* is what elation looks like. I set about to create a formula that provides clarity and simplicity instead of needless frippery and feelings. *Disappointment*? You make it sound as if I'd wanted to disprove my own theory all along—"

Then it hit him.

All the years of criticism regarding his common blood, of having to prove himself worthy of the dukedom and wanting desperately to gain a Fellowship, but to what end? He never would have been satisfied. His brain would have continued to turn with whatever invention he could begin next. The only time he'd ever stopped to live in one single moment—the only time he'd felt a true purpose in his life—had been during those moments with Ivy Sutherland of Norwood Hill. "*Damn.*"

"Well then, I'm glad I could help. Next time, be a chap and wait until calling hours." Marlowe paused on his way back to his chamber. "Say, do you need a room, a fresh horse?"

"A fresh horse, I'll take. As for the room"—North paused to calculate his next move—"I won't know until I've concluded my business."

Marlowe walked to the bellpull and rang for a servant.

"What business could you have on Christmas Eve? The only other estate for miles belongs to Lady Binghamton, the archbishop's sister."

North had already been aware of that before he'd left Castle Vale.

"Your horse. My business." Then, before Jack could slip away, North held up a hand to stay his friend. Withdrawing a pencil from his pocket, he took out a card. "Do me a favor, Marlowe? When you're back in London, send a bouquet of flowers to Miss Lilah Appleton. I wrote her street on this card."

Marlowe took the card and flashed a smile. "Is she my Christmas present?"

"No, and I only want you to send her flowers. Just the once, and make no other contact with her. Besides, she is far different from the type of woman you prefer. She is respectable."

Marlowe made a sour face. "Then why are you bothering with the flowers?"

"*You* are sending the flowers," North corrected. "And the reason for that is because I promised her friend that I would do whatever I could for her."

"You have me intrigued."

"No, Marlowe, I absolutely forbid you to be intrigued. For the sake of our friendship, I need to know that I can rely on you to behave with honor."

"Send her flowers. Leave her be. Understood. Now I must get back to . . . to . . ."

"*Minerva*," the woman huffed from the room beyond. "Ah yes, the opera girl. She was quite interested in acquainting herself with a man in possession of an *immense*"—Marlowe's brow arched suggestively—"fortune."

With a reluctant laugh and a shake of his head, North turned away and called out, "Happy Christmas."

"Indeed, for the rest of the chorus will be arriving later today," Marlowe said before disappearing into his bedchamber.

As for North . . . he was feeling rather impulsive, but completely certain as well. He hoped to find the archbishop in a particularly giving mood this Christmas morning.

Chapter Ten

"THE DUKE HAS returned! The duke has returned!" The pageboy's joyous shouts rang out through the corridors of the castle.

Tears welled up in Ivy's eyes, and a stuttered breath of relief left her. Yet, knowing that Lilah was studying her closely, Ivy turned toward the window. A fresh dusting of snow had fallen in the wee hours of the morning. The first glimmer of Christmas touched her heart, but the ache deep inside remained. "Then he is safe. That is good news. I'm certain the dowager duchess is quite glad."

Before she allowed herself to dwell on pointless musings, she went to the basin and splashed frigid water onto the swollen, tender flesh around her eyes. In the looking glass, her complexion appeared too pale against the sable trim of her red dress. It could not be helped, she supposed. A broken heart hardly aided one's complexion.

Lilah came up beside her, her reflection tinged with

sorrow. "Ivy, when are you going to admit that you're in love with him?"

She shrugged. "Whatever for? Love serves no purpose. If it did, it would be in the duke's formula."

"Well . . . saying the words might cheer you up."

Lilah looked so hopeful that it was hard not to indulge her. More than that, however, Ivy wanted to say the words aloud, to get them out of her heart so that the pain would subside.

"All right, then, I love him." *Cheer* did not make an appearance. Nor did her heartache lessen. She wasn't surprised. "We don't want to be late for chapel. I am impatient to finish this day so that we may leave tomorrow."

Lilah said nothing more about love as they donned their redingotes and bonnets in preparation to walk to the small chapel on the grounds. Nor did she say anything about the fact that they were likely the last ones to exit the house because, as usual, Ivy had made them late.

Outside, the sunlight glanced off the freshly fallen snow in a blinding display. A blast of cold, crisp air sent a few flakes swirling over the path, glistening like diamonds being strewn over the ground. That same blast of air turned toward her and Lilah.

Ivy's breath arrested in her lungs. She closed her eyes as tiny ice crystals washed over her, clinging to her mouth, nose, and eyelashes. A shadow crossed in front of her, blocking the sunlight for a moment. Reaching up to brush the snowflakes away, she was surprised to feel the warmth of a hand touch her cheek, her brow, her lashes. A man's hand. A familiar hand. There was a certain thoroughness to the caress that could belong to only one person. *The duke.*

"Happy Christmas, Ivy," he whispered, his tone surprisingly cheerful.

She felt as if he was mocking her pain. Her eyes snapped open, and she took a step back. The only thing that kept her from walking away was the fact that he looked terrible. His pale complexion and the purplish bruises lining the underside of his eyes told her that he hadn't slept either. A tender warmth filled her heart.

However, before she could allow herself to feel a semblance of hope at this knowledge, she remembered the true cause of his lack of sleep. And it had nothing to do with his having a broken heart.

"I hope you enjoyed your escapade. Though you might have had more consideration than riding off in the middle of the night and worrying"—she drew in a stuttered breath—"your aunt."

It was only then that Ivy realized she'd raised her voice. She looked around to find that Lilah had slipped away and the courtyard was empty. The bell in the chapel tower rang, startling her. "The service has begun. I must go, Your Grace."

She offered a perfunctory curtsy, never expecting him to reach out and take her hand.

"I prefer *North*," he said. "And I would like you to sit with me in church this morning."

A moment passed when he gazed at her with a mixture of trepidation and expectation. Such a request was not a matter to be taken lightly and quickly forgotten.

"I cannot." She slipped her hand free and took *two* steps back this time. "The front pew belongs to you and the dowager duchess. Your rank—your lineage—dictates your place. As you know, those of no consequence sit many rows behind you. I saw the red ledger. I know my place."

She strode away before she gave in to either anger or tears. Neither would serve her.

He kept pace beside her. "Then I shall sit in your row."

"To do so would risk what matters most to you."

"Hmm . . . then how else can I speak with you? You are walking at such a fine clip that we will be within the chapel before I have said all that I planned."

On a huff, she stopped and turned to him. "Then say it now and be done."

"I've been thinking a great deal about our frog and his chances of survival—should he have chosen the wrong young woman—and I have come to a conclusion."

She blinked, confused. "Pardon me?"

"I believe there was more to it than happenstance," North continued, as if he was making perfect sense. "After all, it was quite a risk on the frog's part. Especially if you take into account the damage that can be caused by a tremendous fall."

"Are you speaking of the fairy tale?"

He lifted his brows in a way that suggested she already knew the answer. In that moment, she realized that it was their tale he was telling.

North took a step closer. "I believe that all his concerns and calculations were cast aside when he first beheld a pair of winter-blue eyes and first heard her speak about something as absurd as pinching slippers. In that instant, his entire world changed. He knew that he had to risk everything and reveal himself to her in the hopes that she wouldn't throw him back without at least giving him a kiss first."

"In the tale, she *did* throw him," Ivy reminded. "What she needed was to find a frog who would be transformed by the fall."

"You're absolutely right. I've recently discovered that falls of all kinds can do that. The most transforming of all is falling in—"

"*Cousin!*" Before North could finish, the Earl of Wolford rushed down the path, the snow crunching beneath his boots. "I received the most interesting missive from Jack Marlowe just now. He wants to know if you've altered your formula."

"You may tell Marlowe *yes, I have,*" North said without removing his gaze from Ivy.

"He also asked—strangely enough—whether or not you found the archbishop agreeable or—"

"*Wolford,*" North interrupted, "please take your seat in the chapel."

The earl departed without another word. A stunned awareness began to creep upon Ivy. "Did you ride off in the middle of the night to see the archbishop?"

"I did."

This time, she took a step closer. "Whyever would you do such a thing on Christmas Eve?"

"I can think of only one reason."

So could she, but it made no sense. Not unless . . . "I was never going to speak of our kiss. As I said last night, I would never force a man to marry me." Hearing her own words rekindled the hurt and anger she'd felt last night. "I am perfectly content as I am. I certainly do not need to resort to tricks in order to claim a husband. I may be of no consequence to you, but I have wonderful traits that are worth more than a fine lineage, vast property, or any amount of wealth. Your formula was wrong about me."

"I know. I am a fraud, Ivy." North took her hands, tugging off her gloves so that he and she were flesh to flesh, and lifted them to his lips. "You were right. I wanted someone to disprove my formula. You made me see what truly matters, perhaps not for anyone else, but for me."

When another gust of wind stole the warmth from her, she pulled her hands free. "That is a fine, pretty speech, and I thank you. I will be able to leave here without any bitterness in my heart."

"I am in earnest," he said. "And though my method is somewhat disorderly, when I asked you to sit beside me in church, I wasn't just asking for today. I want you there beside me always."

A lovely thought. However, that, too, was a fairy tale. "Even if I could, there would be no other opportunity. I leave on the morrow."

He laughed. "Ivy, I am asking you to marry me."

She couldn't have heard him correctly. "But your formula . . . the red ledger . . ."

"I failed to calculate the one factor that overrides all others—*love*. I fell in love with you in that first moment.

I've come to love you more and more in each moment since. You are my perfect match in every way."

Dumfounded, she didn't know what to think or how to respond.

"I can see that there is only way to convince you," he said, glancing toward the chapel. He drew in a breath and nodded. "You are all that matters, Ivy."

He walked away from her and into the chapel. Then Ivy found herself standing at the open doors. The melodic sounds of hymns drifted out into the courtyard. At the front, the vicar had yet to climb to the pulpit. And she watched as North strode down the center aisle and faced the congregation.

"Good morning, all," North said. "Before we begin to celebrate this glorious day, I have a confession to make. As you know, I invited you all here to learn of my *Marriage Formula*. This formula was originally designed with an honest desire to enhance our society by simplifying matters of marriage down to the basic desired elements . . ."

Numbly, Ivy walked forward. Awareness crept over her as she realized what he was saying. And more importantly, what he was risking. She couldn't let him do it.

"However," he continued, ignoring the fervent shakes of her head, "I have recently discovered that my calculations were—"

"Frog!" she shouted, drawing startled gazes in her direction, along with a few gasps. She pointed to the floor, gesturing beneath the pews. "I saw one just there."

As luck would have it, Ivy was standing near the corner of Lilah's pew. "Please pretend there is a frog in your lap," Ivy whispered.

"Why must— *Oh, Ivy,* you truly are incorrigible." Lilah sighed in exasperation, then suddenly leaped up from her seat. "Frog!"

Beside her, Lady Cosgrove stood, but likely only out of necessity. Nevertheless, it started a reaction among the guests. A few squeals erupted. They all began to stand, scatter, and search the floor. Even the vicar shook out his robes.

Ivy rushed to North's side. "I couldn't let you do it."

"Why not?" While the creases on the side of his mouth revealed his amusement, there was a measure of trepidation in his gaze.

She could tell him how she believed that his formula had merit and that, with a little tweaking to include the names from the red ledger, it would be even better. However, instead of saying all that, she simply told him, "Because I love you."

Without warning, he picked her up and spun her around in a circle. Right there, in front of the entire congregation. When her feet returned to the floor, she suddenly realized that the frog hunt was over. Everyone was staring at them. She even heard a few people whispering unsavory things about *common blood*. That was when it occurred to her that he could still lose the Fellowship he'd worked so hard to gain.

"And this is because I love you," North whispered, smiling down at her before he addressed his guests. "As I was saying before, I have recently discovered that my formula—"

"Is a success," Ivy interrupted. Again. Boldly, she took his hand. "The results of the duke's formula brought us together."

Which wasn't a *complete* fabrication and, therefore, was acceptable to say in church. The only thing she would have to repent was the small lie about the frog. . . .

An odd, warbled bleating sound interrupted her thoughts, and she looked down. Much to her surprise, a fat green toad hopped into the aisle. Then the melee began once more.

Ivy looked up at North. He seemed equally shocked. Then his gaze slid to the doorway, and he grinned as the Earl of Wolford bowed. "My cousin is rather resourceful in a pinch. He had to have sprinted all the way to the warm springs by the hillside."

This morning, she never would have imagined her heartache transforming into the happiest day of her life. "Riding off in the middle of the night to see the archbishop was rather impulsive of you. Not only that, but you automatically assumed that I would be equally as impulsive to marry you by special license."

He flashed those creases. "Call it a *leap* of faith."

"After all this, I suppose I should say yes." She laughed, overflowing with that wonderful feeling of exhilaration. "If a frog is a good omen for a happy marriage, then it would be a shame to waste a perfect opportunity."

About the Author

USA Today bestselling author **VIVIENNE LORRET** loves romance novels, her pink laptop, her husband, and her two sons (not necessarily in that order . . . but there are days). Transforming copious amounts of tea into words, she is proud to be an Avon Impulse author of works including: *Tempting Mr. Weatherstone*, The Wallflower Wedding Series, and the Rakes of Fallow Hall series.

Discover great authors, exclusive offers, and more at hc.com.

One Magic Season

By Ashlyn Macnamara

I can hardly write something Christmas-themed
without dedicating it to my husband,
who starts decorating in early November
and leaves the lights up until . . .
well, he still hasn't taken the ones
in the dining room down!
Cheers, darling!

Chapter One

Three miles from Worthington Manor
Christmas Eve, 1816

THE CARRIAGE WHEELS ground to a halt on the snow-covered road, a soft crunch followed by heavy silence. Something about that sound replayed in Lady Patience Markham's mind long after it had ceased. A delay already. At this rate, they'd never make it to her brother's estate until long past dark. They'd had a late start because she'd decided to pack a few extra warm woolen gowns.

The flakes of snow dancing past the window justified that decision, at least. The sight raised gooseflesh at the back of her neck, and she drew her pelisse more tightly about her. At the age of nine and twenty, she was young to be styled the Dowager Countess of Worthington, but neither youth nor title could shield her against the cold creeping into the cab.

From outside came the dull thump of the coachman jumping from his perch. The carriage shuddered at the sudden relief of a fourteen-stone burden. Shouts echoed through the frosty air.

Across from Patience, the steady clicking of her maid's knitting needles halted. "Do you think—?"

Linnet broke off, but her round eyes and the whiteness of her wrinkled cheeks beneath the shadow of her bonnet completed her thought.

"Any highwayman with sense would stay indoors in this weather." There. That sounded confident enough, though it didn't speak for brigands of the senseless variety. Heaven forbid they encounter one of those.

Another glance outside revealed a wild whirl of snow tumbling at the mercy of a persistent wind. A gust buffeted the carriage, causing it to shake and creak. No doubt about it, the storm was worsening. They'd set out to mere flurries, but now . . .

Wisdom would send even the most hardened criminal indoors to huddle near a roaring hearth with a cup of something bracing and hot. Quite apparently, highway robbers possessed a great deal more sense than dowager countesses of any age.

In a burst of snowflakes and icy wind, the door opened. The red-faced coachman poked his bulbous nose into the cab. "A delay, my lady. One that cannot be helped."

Instinct pressed Patience's feet into the wrapped flat-irons Linnet had prepared for their comfort. The irons had long since given up their last parcel of warmth. "Good heavens, what's happened?"

"Another coach is blocking the road. Looks as if it's broken down."

"Can you not drive around?"

"I might try, but with this storm, the snow's piled awfully deep."

Patience pressed her lips together. At the rate the snow was falling, they'd have to dig themselves out if they stayed here too long. "What do you advise?"

She knew the reply before he gave it. It was the only sensible solution. "Turn for home, my lady. If I'm to risk stranding us in a drift, I'd rather it happen because we were using good judgment."

"Yes, let's do. At this rate, we'd never have arrived before midnight." Assuming they arrived at all.

She tamped down a wave of disappointment. She'd so been looking forward to spending the Christmas season with her brother's family. Peter's wife had given birth to a daughter the previous summer, and Patience had yet to make her new niece's acquaintance. Add a pair of rambunctious boys, and the holidays had shone with lively promise. She'd especially anticipated the cries of delight when her nephews opened their gifts.

But it couldn't be helped now, not with the choice becoming clearer and clearer—turn for home or freeze.

Voices carried on the howl of the wind—shouts, calls, some familiar, some not.

Patience stretched a hand toward the coachman. "My goodness, is the other carriage still occupied?"

"They've asked our men to help dig them out, but I fear if we do that, we'll become stuck ourselves."

"We cannot leave them, not in this weather." Patience hugged herself beneath her pelisse. Its heavy velvet and the wool of her traveling costume had seemed sufficient protection against the elements this morning. "The least we can do is offer them a ride." Another body in the coach might help provide warmth, if nothing else.

The coachman glanced at the leaden sky. How much colder would he be, exposed on his perch, and that despite his caped overcoat, woolen hat, and thick gloves? "Nearest inn's in Stroud, but I doubt we'd make it so far. At any rate, I don't think the other fellow would find the accommodations to his liking. Seems he's a duke."

A duke. In spite of herself, she exchanged a glance with Linnet. But then Patience shook the thought away. Heavens, how many dukes did England contain now? She tried to count on her fingers but quickly lost track. Wasn't it at least twenty, counting the Duke of Wellington? What were the odds they were about to take on her particular duke?

He's not your duke, she reminded herself firmly. He hadn't even been her marquess a decade ago. His family had ensured that. In its own way, so had hers.

"Doesn't the Duke of Kingsbury have an estate near Gloucester?" Apparently Linnet's thoughts were running in the same direction. "One of your mother's upstairs maids ran off with a Kingsbury footman, if I remember aright."

Patience quelled a spur of jealousy at the thought. Maids and footmen all stood on equal ground, unlike the daughter of a baron and the heir to a dukedom. "It's probably some stuffy old goat, but either way, that's no reason to refuse help." She turned to the coachman. "Offer him what comfort we can provide. If he's willing, he can shelter at Worthington Manor."

As for Patience, she wouldn't even have to see Kingsbury—if the occupant of the other carriage was, indeed, Kingsbury—beyond the time it took them to return home. She'd be safely ensconced several hundred yards down the hill from the main manor in the dower house.

"It's a pity about the Worthington servants," Linnet said as soon as the door closed behind the coachman. She made the statement casually enough, but even so, the comment bordered on insubordination. But Linnet had acted as Patience's maid for so many years now that she was nearly family. During Patience's one aborted season, Linnet had seen her through many a tearful night, dispensing more motherly advice than Patience's own mother ever had.

If Linnet felt she could speak plainly now, it was only a result of long habit.

"What do you mean?"

Linnet resumed her knitting, her fingers flying despite the cold and a pair of thick gloves. "They'll be holding their servants' ball tonight, and tomorrow many of them will have made plans for Christmas with their families. Now they'll have to lay all that aside because you've decided to foist a duke on them."

"Oh." Patience bit her lip. Clearly, she hadn't thought this through. The servants at the main manor had no doubt expected an easy time of it through Twelfth Night, with the current earl—Patience's brother-in-law—deciding to spend the holidays with his wife's family. Besides, Patience had little authority over the manor staff. She employed Linnet and a maid-of-all-work, who saw to the cooking, cleaning, and fires at the dower house. "Then what do you suggest? We can't leave the man out here to freeze."

The door whipped open on another blast of frigid air and snow. "I concur most heartily."

Patience gasped. That voice. How many times as a young lady had she imagined that voice asking her to a reel or a turn about the room? How many times over the intervening years had its echo vibrated through her dreams? How many times had she awoken to an empty pillow and the bitter reminder that she would never be his?

But she wasn't dreaming now. She was very much awake, and her heart was pulsing a heavy beat, working its way toward her throat.

The duke who entered the carriage was the furthest thing from a stuffy old goat. Not if the laugh lines radiating from his eyes indicated anything. Time had etched those marks slightly deeper than she recalled, but they still framed the bluest irises she'd ever seen.

The cold had reddened his sharp cheekbones and the straight nose that overshadowed a firm, strong chin. And that lower lip. Every bit as full as she remembered. She diverted her gaze before she fell into her old habit of speculating just how that lip would taste. Since her marriage, and his, she'd lost the right to such diverting thoughts.

What she couldn't ignore was the sheer impact of his presence. She might as well have been standing out in the storm, the gale scouring her skin raw, for her heart was experiencing a similar sensation.

As he stared at her, his smile faded, and his laugh lines melted into shallow furrows. "My God, is it you?"

Thank the heavens he'd spared her the sound of her name in that quiet, almost reverent tone. She inclined her head, hoping the gesture would mask the wash of heat that poured over her cheeks. "Your Grace."

He sank into the seat next to Linnet. Was he just as shocked to see her? In all the intervening years, she hadn't avoided him, at least not deliberately. She'd simply arranged her life so as to sidestep the *ton* and live as quietly as possible. Even during the four years of her marriage, she'd been as content to remain in the country as the earl had been to leave her there.

The carriage shook beneath the weight of a trunk being loaded in the back, then further, as the coachman took his perch and the tiger boarded. The harness jangled, the wheels creaked, and with a great effort against the wind, the carriage pushed forward, working its way into a slow circle as it came about.

Kingsbury's stranded coach floated past the window, already axel-deep in drifts. The ducal crest complete with coronet burned into Patience's vision, a harsh reminder. *Yes, this is who he is. Too high for one such as you.*

Then she noticed the absence of his team. "What of your driver?" she asked.

"I sent him on with the horses." He leaned across Linnet to peer out, and his very presence seemed to fill the space of the cab. "Yes, there he goes with my tiger.

They ought to make the next village at least and shelter in the pub until the storm lets up."

"You might have gone with them." Part of her wished he had. Then she might have avoided this feeling of an old wound being torn open, and she might have avoided the sheer breathlessness he conjured from her even after all these years.

He shrugged, his broad shoulders settling deeper into the squabs. "I might have. We were just deciding what to do when your coachman offered me a ride. It was clear, though, that you couldn't accommodate all of us."

No, not in the small conveyance she'd been allotted for this trip. The current earl had taken his larger coach to Hampshire.

"I do thank you for your kindness in allowing me to ride with you," Kingsbury added. Such perfect courtesy, just as she remembered from him.

"You do know we're making for Worthington Manor." Obligation forced her to point out their direction, which would lengthen his journey in the end, if indeed he'd been headed toward Gloucester.

His smile chased the shadows from the cab. "A dashed sight better than freezing in my own coach. Or even sheltering in some dingy village public house."

"I wonder if you'll agree when we arrive."

"Why?" The lines about those blue eyes crinkled as his grin broadened. "Have the servants all fled?"

Patience suppressed an urge to place her hand over her heart. His low, friendly tone, as if they'd been sharing some private joke, only made her pulse trip over itself.

"Something like that. The earl is not in residence, but I can put you up in the dower house."

The steady clicking of Linnet's knitting needles broke off for a moment, and she sniffed, turning a stiff-lipped glare on Patience. Patience raised her chin and met the stare head-on. She was no longer some green girl a handsome young man of high station could dazzle.

If Kingsbury noticed Linnet's reaction, he made no comment. "I shall be grateful for whatever hospitality you can offer. Despite my title, I am not utterly dependent on an army of servants at my beck and call every moment of the day. In fact—" He captured Patience's gaze and held it. Her heart, blast it all, fluttered just as it had when she was nineteen and easily dazzled. "I shall look upon this as an adventure."

THE LAST THING Nathaniel Westlake, the seventh Duke of Kingsbury, had expected for Christmas was a punch to the gut. Not only that, but one delivered by a lady.

But that was exactly what it felt like to see Miss— *No.*

She was Lady Worthington now. He must remember that, even if the rest of her matched the image she'd graven in his mind. Black hair, hidden beneath a staid bonnet, and flawless pale skin set off a pair of striking green eyes and lush lips. The years had been kind to her. If anything, she was more beautiful now than when he'd first met her. When she was a young baron's daughter from the country who had just made her bow.

She sat across from him, her spine straight, one might

even say rigid, her hands folded, holding some manner of silent conversation with her maid. No doubt the maid disapproved, if the jerky movement of the woman's knitting needles indicated anything.

No doubt, as well, Lady Worthington would win this particular argument. The set of her jaw told him as much.

And thank God for that. Nathaniel had no eagerness whatever to knock about an empty manor house waiting for the weather to clear, when he might spend a few hours renewing an old acquaintance—and if he was completely honest with himself, an old, unrequited desire. One he'd thought long buried, but it roared to life now, a spark set to dry tinder.

"Where were you headed in such a storm?" That Lady Worthington broke the silence came as a shock. He'd sensed a hesitancy in her demeanor, one increased with the heavy burden of what might have been.

"I was called to Town on a personal matter, but I'd hoped to make it back to my estate to surprise my boys on Christmas morning."

At the mention of his twin sons, her smile became fixed, deuce take it. "So they weren't expecting you?"

"No, thankfully." One small blessing in this mess. He'd hate to disappoint a pair of small children on so important an occasion as Christmas morning. Instead, he had to face a decade-old disappointment, one of his own making. "You said before that the earl is not in residence. I must confess my surprise that he didn't include you in his Christmas plans."

"Oh, he offered." She waved that thought away with

a gloved hand. "I turned him down in favor of spending the holidays with my brother. I'd presents prepared for my nephews, but I suppose they'll have to wait to open them. My old governess would approve. She firmly believed that denying oneself built character."

The maid's snort temporarily drowned out the steady click of her wooden needles.

Nathaniel cleared his throat. "How have you been keeping?"

She inclined her head. "Just as you see me."

"I mean it. I'd really like to know."

Those grass-green eyes widened. Clearly she'd interpreted his question as a social sort of device whose reply did not matter so long as it was given. But it *did* matter. Greatly.

"I've a quiet enough life, as you shall see. I am content."

Content. There was a telling word. Not happy, merely content. But then, he couldn't state any better for himself. "I am imagining you playing the doting auntie to your nephews."

"My governess would despair," she said. "This Christmas aside, I've quite spoiled them. I suppose it's for the best that I never had any children of my own." A shadow seemed to pass across her face, there, then gone in an instant. "They'd be regular little scamps."

She looked hard at him, giving him the impression she was trying to communicate with him wordlessly, as she had with her maid. *If nothing came of our association, if we both married elsewhere, it was for the best,* her green gaze said. *I left Worthington with no heir, and his title passed to his brother. I failed in my primary duty.*

If Nathaniel had secured his succession, he'd failed at marriage in his own way. God only knew he'd made an honest attempt with his wife, Olivia, despite her being his family's choice. Miss Patience Wentworth had become Lady Worthington by then, to Nathaniel's everlasting regret.

And just as it had with Miss Wentworth, he'd run out of time when it had come to Olivia. They'd been wed less than a year when she'd succumbed to childbed fever within a week of presenting him with an heir and a spare. Fewer than twelve months was hardly sufficient to learn all there was to another person.

Yet he'd spent even less time with the woman sitting across from him now. Less time and in less intimate circumstances, with chaperones—indeed, with the rest of society—scrutinizing his every move. How was it, then, that he felt he knew this woman far better than the one who'd shared the marriage bed with him? How did such a thing occur?

For if he'd failed with Olivia, it was possibly because he'd never been able to push past the fact that she was not Miss Patience Wentworth.

Now he found himself seated in a carriage, trundling through a snowstorm with a woman he'd thought lost to him forever, as if God, or fate, or whatever higher power oversaw his life had given him another chance.

A chance to get it right.

The only thing he needed was to determine if the lady still returned his interest.

Chapter Two

THE FIRST TIME the future Duke of Kingsbury had placed his hand on Miss Patience Wentworth's, the contract had electrified her. Even through the barrier of gloves, the touch had shot through her like a spark popping up a chimney. Surely that couldn't have been right. Surely it couldn't have been proper. But the next time the dance had brought them together, it had happened again. And then again.

Surely such an event shouldn't repeat itself ten years later before her front door. But the moment the duke handed her out of the carriage, she once again experienced that old, familiar jolt. For a moment, she was back in that ballroom, twirling beneath the chandeliers in a white satin gown, her skirt belling about her ankles. Anticipating the next touch. Hoping he'd ask her for another dance once an appropriate interval had elapsed.

Now, watching his reaction from beneath the brim of

her bonnet, she pulled her hand away. Had he felt it, too? Indeed, had he ever felt more than a passing attraction for her? That shatterproof façade of correctness made it all the more difficult to read him.

Oh, he'd danced with her, often enough to raise eyebrows and set tongues wagging. Enough that after several social events during which he'd sought her company, his sister had pulled her aside and warned her off in no uncertain terms.

"A future duke and the daughter of a country baron?" Lady Diana Westlake had waved a very expensive fan before her nose, as if to wave off an unpleasant scent. Patience had to think the gesture had been a comment on the cleanliness of her hems and the soles of her dancing slippers. "It simply isn't done. Put the thought from your mind this very moment."

But Patience hadn't been able to. By the end of that very first reel, she'd been certain of one thing—she was completely and utterly smitten with the marquess.

For all the good it had done her.

The door to the dower house flew open, pulling her from her memories.

"Oh, my lady. Thank the heavens." Heedless of the blowing snow, Jane bolted over the threshold. She bunched her apron in her fists and gave the innocent fabric a hard twist. "When the wind started t' howling, I was that certain ye'd overturned into a ditch."

Patience placed her hands on the maid's shoulders and gently pushed her back into the entrance hall. "Why are you not up at the manor enjoying the servants' ball?"

"Oh, I couldn't've. Not with this storm and my worriting over yer fate 'n all."

Patience encouraged her maid to advance to make room for Linnet and the duke. "As you can see, we're perfectly fine. The carriage didn't turn over once."

Jane craned her neck to peer past Patience. "'Tis a good thing I'm here though, when ye've brought company back with ye."

A very good thing. The soft glow of a fire beckoned from the sitting room. In a few hours, the feeling might even return to Patience's toes. "Yes, Jane. We'll need to make up the guest room. The Duke of Kingsbury will be staying with us until the weather breaks."

Jane let out a screech and backed up, nearly tripping over her feet in her haste to drop into a curtsy. "Yer Grace. My stars, ye'll forgive me, but I'm sure as we haven't anything fit for a duke's table. And at Christmas."

Smiling, Kingsbury stepped forward. "Anything you were planning on having yourself will be splendid. I shall be indebted to your mistress for her hospitality."

"If you'd put the kettle on for some tea, I'd be grateful," Patience said, though her mind was already preoccupied with the contents of the pantry. "We can sup on one of the meat pies I was taking to my brother's." Accompanied with some cheese and pickles, the fare would be simple but filling. "Linnet, if you'll see about the guest bedchamber, we might vacate the hall and let the coachman bring in our trunks."

"If it please you, my lady, I should like to consult you on that very matter."

If it please? Patience blinked. After so many years, Linnet almost never behaved this formally, and unlike Jane, she wasn't about to allow a title to turn her head. Linnet stared back, a telling glint in her eye.

With a nod to Kingsbury, Patience waved her hand toward the sitting room. "You'll pardon me for a few moments. Please, make yourself comfortable. Jane will bring you tea. Or perhaps we ought to send up to the manor for the good brandy?"

"Do not trouble yourself," Kingsbury replied. His rich baritone settled into her chest, more warming than any fire. "I wouldn't dream of complaining about the accommodations, and that's before I consider the alternative."

Patience found herself returning his smile. How easy it would be to slip back into the skin of that bedazzled young girl from the country. She pulled herself away and mounted the stairs, catching up with Linnet in front of the linen cupboard.

"Since when do you need to consult with me on a matter of clean sheets?" Patience kept her voice low for fear it would carry down to the ground floor.

Clearly in no need of advice, Linnet turned, a pile of bedding in her arms. "Just what do you think you're about?"

Patience gaped. All that was missing was the *young lady* on the end. "What gives you the idea I'm planning anything? The man was in a pickle, and we extended him some kindness. It was the least we could do."

Linnet looked away for a moment. "Your pardon, my lady. I forget myself. It's only that I've been with you so long."

"And since you know me to be of good character and reputation, you ought to think nothing scandalous will come of his staying with us."

"Under normal circumstances I would agree with you," Linnet insisted. "But I haven't forgotten what that man meant to you, and I haven't forgotten the way he broke your heart."

"Do you think I have? I am no longer that naïve little chit."

"I am not entirely certain." Linnet hugged the pile of sheets to her chest. "I couldn't help but note the way you looked at each other in the carriage. If that man's intentions are honorable, I'm the Prince Regent."

A wash of heat rushed up Patience's cheeks. She ought to reply. Ought to set Linnet down, but the words refused to come. At any rate, she could hardly come up with a convincing counterargument. She'd been unable to tear her gaze away from Kingsbury, and he certainly hadn't passed the journey home staring out the window either.

Thankfully, thuds on the staircase announced the imminent arrival of the coachman. He heaved the duke's trunk to the landing. Patience stared at the Kingsbury crest emblazoned on the top. That his private belongings were in her house, about to disappear into the spare bedchamber . . .

Well, the intimacy of the situation was not lost on Patience. In fact, the import of all she was considering struck her straight in the midsection. Kingsbury would occupy that bed tonight, mere feet away from her. Almost as if they'd married.

Linnet's expression softened. Once the coachman thumped back down the steps, she said, "I'll allow as to how you never had a chance to learn the true pleasures of marriage."

The last thing Patience wanted to recall was her husband's fumbling. Her marriage bed had known discomfort at best without even the joy of motherhood to compensate. Deep in her heart, she knew her notions of conjugal bliss would be more than vague ideas if Kingsbury had offered for her hand.

Something devilish in her prodded her to respond. "Perhaps now that I'm a widow, I should reap the benefits."

Linnet sighed. "But can you do that and yet guard your heart? I'd hate for you to go through that sadness a second time."

"So would I," Patience admitted.

By the end of her one London Season, she had hoped to receive an offer. But after a month of routs, balls, social calls, and flowers, the future duke's family had voiced their disapproval of the match through Diana. Their relationship might have surmounted that obstacle, but it had not survived her father's death.

With a heavy heart, she'd overseen the packing of her ball gowns and returned to the country. With each passing day, she'd hoped for a letter or, indeed, any sign that Kingsbury had developed the sort of affection that led to a proposal.

The day of the burial had come and gone with no sign. A month later, Diana had sought her out one final time to voice words that had echoed through Patience's mind like the thump of a coffin's lid closing.

He never cared for you. The words, spoken in a false, friendly tone, as if Diana had been feeding her tidbits of the latest gossip, had burned through Patience's brain, cold as acid. *You were nothing but an amusement to him. A trifle. He's gone, you know. Gone to amuse himself in Italy with our brother.*

After that encounter, she'd faced reality and laid aside, along with her dolls and the other trappings of childhood, her dream of being styled the Duchess of Kingsbury.

She could only live up to her name for so long, after all. It had been time to grow up. Time to do her duty. And that had meant forgetting silly notions like infatuations, no matter how much it had hurt.

LADY WORTHINGTON WAS too young to be a widow. The thought first took hold of Nathaniel at supper, and it continued to peck at him throughout the meal. He focused on the smoothness of her hand as she lifted her wineglass and noted the soft fullness of her lips as she swallowed a bite of her meat pie.

He knew of her situation the way one knows a fact one learned in school. Paris is the capital of France. Half one hundred gives fifty. Twelve pence make a shilling.

A woman should not be widowed at twenty-nine—not any more than he'd expected to lose his own wife so soon after their wedding.

On a cold, intellectual level he knew.

But her youth didn't strike him in the gut until he followed her from the dining room to take a seat on the most stiff-backed settee he'd ever encountered. He glanced about her sitting room: murky green wallpaper flecked with chinoiserie and peeling about the edges, faded brocade upholstery, heavy velvet draperies over the windows. It was a place for an old lady to pass her remaining years in peace.

He raised his glass of brandy to his lips, and the liquor coursed into his belly on a wave of warmth. Lady Worthington sank into a shield-backed chair— Hepplewhite, if Nathaniel wasn't mistaken, and every bit as uncomfortable as this damnable settee. She gazed into the fire, the flicker from the hearth gilding her flawless complexion.

Too young, but that was what happened when a chit not many years beyond the schoolroom married someone thirty years her senior.

She should have married you.

He drowned that particular annoying voice in more brandy, because he might have lost her, as well, after too brief a time. Olivia's passing had been heart-wrenching enough. He could not have borne losing a wife he'd chosen himself.

He shifted his weight. Whatever poor excuse for padding had been built into this torture device had long since worn away. "I knew the late Lord Worthington."

A gasp. No, she wouldn't expect this topic. Why would she, when they'd managed to navigate supper conversation with the usual social inanities?

"I'm sorry I couldn't save you from that," he added.

Her gaze snapped to his, her mouth rounded into an O. "It wasn't so bad."

Her reply rang false in his ears.

"Truly? I've just told you I knew him." Nathaniel had seen the man at White's on a regular basis, telling bawdy jokes with his reactionary cronies, drinking too much, laughing too loud, smelling of stale tobacco smoke and sweat.

"I was quite content when he went up to London to take his seat in Parliament." A hint of a smile played about her lips. "I always prayed some hotly contested matter would come up at the end of the session and necessitate an extension."

Once again, he adjusted his hindquarters, bracing himself against her potential reaction to his next question. "Might I ask why you did marry him?"

"Why do you believe that is any of your affair?"

There it was, the verbal slap he'd been expecting. He deserved it, too. "Call it curiosity, if you like. It's my curse."

"Is it not enough that he had a title? And that he *offered*?"

He winced at that one, but it was no less deserved than her first set-down. "Don't forget, I know you as well."

"Perhaps not as well as you think."

He rose to his feet. His aching arse thanked him. "The girl I recall was not chasing after a title."

"That is not how your family viewed it."

The devil take it, this was going all wrong. And he

could not make excuses for his family. He knew quite well how the situation had appeared to them. And he, damn his own eyes, had not fought hard enough. "Your pardon. I did not intend to spend the evening disputing the past. We all have our regrets, I suspect."

She watched him out of the corner of her eye. "What is it you regret?"

The hopeful note behind her question gave him the courage to approach. "Many things where you are concerned."

"Many?" That came out on a whisper. "Such as?"

"For one, we never had a chance to waltz."

"Waltz?" Her brows shot up. "The waltz hadn't yet come into fashion when we were younger."

"More's the pity. I would have caused a great deal of gossip asking you for every set."

A becoming bloom of pink spread across her cheeks. "As it was, you caused enough talk with the number of times you asked me to dance."

He held out a hand. "Have you ever waltzed?"

"No." Of course she hadn't. By the time the dance had been admitted to Almack's, she'd hidden herself away in the country.

"I wonder if you'd indulge me now?"

Her mouth opened halfway, and she shook her head. "You cannot be serious. We've no music."

"We could pretend."

She was tempted. He could tell from the way she drew her lower lip between her teeth, biting down slowly. Damn, but he wanted to do that—and he wouldn't stop with her lip.

Muttering something that sounded suspiciously like *incorrigible,* she rose from her chair. "If I tread all over your feet, it would be roundly deserved."

"You'll not hear a word of complaint." He set his left hand at her waist, enjoying the way her lips parted on a small breath of air.

If he pulled her closer than polite society would have deemed appropriate, she would not protest. She didn't know the difference. Besides, she felt curiously right in his half embrace, just as he suspected she would.

He took up her free hand, setting the bare flesh of their palms together. A tingle of warmth spread up his arm at the contact. "Now you set your other hand on my shoulder."

"I'm not at all certain this is proper," she murmured. Still, she followed his direction, the weight of her arm resting on his biceps and her fingers curling round his shoulder muscle.

"It's not, according to some. My mother considered this quite the scandalous display when it first came into fashion." For good measure, he pulled her an inch closer. "And now you let your movements mirror mine."

He took the first step, and she moved with him, hesitating only a moment.

"That's it. Step with me. In rhythm. And step and turn." On the next beat, he twisted his hips. She came with him, her fingers tightening about his.

She caught on quickly, and soon he was whirling her about the room, the tips of her breasts grazing his chest on every turn, while her hold tightened. Just the way the waltz was meant to go—in his head, at least, and with this particular woman.

At last he came to a stop. Her cheeks were pink, her eyes alight, and she laughed, a beautiful, full-throated sound that sent his blood rushing south. Good Lord, she would have scandalized all of polite society the way she took to this dance.

"It's even better with music." His words emerged on a husky tone.

"Thank you for showing me. It was diverting." Sadness tinged her statement, leaving him with the impression a long time had passed since she'd done something purely for amusement.

"Then it was worth risking scandal." He couldn't stop himself from raising a hand and setting it against the softness of her cheek. "There's something else I regret."

Her eyes darkened, as if she knew what was coming. Her body recognized the overture, at any rate. Her entire being leaned toward him. "What?"

"That I never got to do this." And he let his lips descend to capture hers.

Chapter Three

UNTIL KINGSBURY'S MOUTH took hers, Patience did not know the true power of a kiss. It possessed the ability to erase the past, to make her forget the lack of feeling his sister had claimed of him. When his mouth moved on hers, she had to believe in *this* reality. *These* were his true feelings. Here.

Now.

Thank heavens she'd never before experienced the force of his kiss. If she'd known the way he could enflame her senses with his lips and tongue, she might never have borne her husband's attentions. What Kingsbury was doing to her now combined every conversation, every dance, every furtive touch they'd ever shared and multiplied the effect a thousand times over.

She savored the taste and scent of him—the bitterness of brandy enmeshed with the man himself, expensive sandalwood mixed with his musk. As with the waltz, she followed his lead, opening when he opened, touching tongue to tongue along with him. The press of his palms against her spine gave her hands permission to explore the muscled plane of his back and the contours of his shoulders.

As with the waltz, every movement stole her breath and made her cling.

Scandalous, that's what this was, because he drove her thoughts straight to the bedchamber. He provoked her brain to call up shocking images of them moving together in a more intimate dance, completely naked on tangled sheets.

The benefits of widowhood indeed. She hadn't realized the full extent of what she'd missed, but somehow her body recognized and demanded what it had never had. An aching hollowness took up residence between her thighs, clambering to be filled, to be stretched beyond endurance.

The thought drove her to press herself against him like some wanton, her breasts crushed to his chest, her fingers speared into his hair.

With a groan, he tore his lips away to trail hot, urgent kisses along her cheek, her jaw, her throat—all the skin he could reach, but it wasn't enough. She wanted that mouth on places yet covered.

God, she wanted. And so did he, if the hard thrust against her lower belly meant anything. She arched her neck in offering. *Yes. More. Show me where this leads.*

His fingers slipped to her nape, lingering at the fastenings of her gown. But then he raised his head, and his hands glided up to her jaw. His caress grazed her cheeks; his breath expelled in hard little puffs.

Her eyes opened to meet his searching blue gaze. Good Lord, he wanted assurance. She read that much in his expression. He wouldn't simply take what he wanted. This highly placed, powerful man needed confirmation that her hunger was as strong as his.

She tightened her fists about the lapels of his topcoat. She ought to tear it from his shoulders and let him know in no uncertain terms that she accepted him. Accepted this. Only the smallest sliver of doubt stopped her. In the back of her mind echoed Linnet's warning to guard her heart.

How difficult a task that was proving, especially when he was studying her with such intensity. Waiting. They'd done nothing but wait for each other, for this moment, yet he would wait more if she asked it of him. That, as much as anything, put the lie to Diana's words. Patience was more than a mere trifle to him. She had to be.

Her heart gave another dangerous lurch in his direction.

She smiled to fend off the inevitable. "Why did we wait so long to try this?"

He'd never tried to lead her astray when they were younger. A good thing, because she would have followed him onto the nearest darkened terrace and tripped happily toward her downfall.

With the pad of his thumb, he traced a cheekbone. "I think on some level, I sensed it would be like this. I wouldn't have been able to stop. I'd have ruined you."

"You've stopped now." She couldn't prevent herself from pointing out the obvious.

"Only because I do not wish you to do anything you'll regret." Suddenly he yanked himself out of their embrace to stride across the room, his hand tearing through his hair. "Damn it. I should have done it then. I should have ruined you."

"What?" Patience stood rooted to the spot, shaken. What he'd just proposed did not jibe in the least with the man she'd known. As for the man he'd become—no, it wasn't right for him either. Not when he'd stopped himself to assure himself of her feelings.

"If I'd gone through with it. If I'd ruined you . . ." He turned, his expression bleak. "I would have had to make you an offer. No one could have stopped me."

"Are you so certain of that?" She asked the question carefully. His family would have stopped at nothing to keep them apart. After her father's death, his parents had leaped on the opportunity to invent an excuse to send him on an extended trip to Italy with his younger brother. The war had prevented a grand tour, but they'd claimed his brother had needed to see something of the continent and had required a guardian to keep him out of trouble.

Or, at least, that was the tale gossip had made of his fate.

Kingsbury had returned only after she was safely married to Lord Worthington.

"I would have taken you to Scotland."

His vehemence struck deep. "I'd no idea you felt so strongly then."

Perhaps if she had, she would have worked harder at encouraging him. At the time, she'd thought they disposed of sufficient time to allow their feelings to take their natural course. But then, if they had married, Diana would have made her life hell.

"I can no longer be certain of my affections then," he admitted. "They may be influenced by what I'm feeling now."

She bit her lip. She ought to demand clarification, but part of her held back. Whatever tender feelings they acted on tonight did not change the fact that his family would surely protest any permanent relationship between them.

And she refused to allow herself to be kept as a mistress. Then she *would* become his plaything. That was a line she would not cross, not even for Kingsbury.

In the hallway, the case clock whirred before striking twelve solemn chimes. They sounded like the intrusion of reality. "My goodness, it's Christmas already."

"Indeed." His tone was clipped, his jaw firm. "Happy Christmas." He glanced about at her bare walls. "Just look at what we've accomplished without mistletoe."

She returned his smile, but she could not shake off the echo of the clock striking. Perhaps it was time for a little circumspection. She might have made some trite observation, something expected. She might have mentioned the late hour, but he might have misconstrued that as an invitation to her bed. Any number of conversation options paraded through her mind, but she rejected each one, until the quiet weighed heavy on the sitting room.

With a nod, he indicated he understood the meaning behind her silence. She wasn't ready for more. Not yet.

He crossed to her, and the warmth and softness of his lips brushed her cheek. "However long you require, I will wait for you."

WITH THAT FINAL comment to Lady Worthington, Nathaniel buggered himself. Or at least he condemned himself to a sleepless night. He passed the long hours waiting for the sky to lighten, straining his ears for the gentle pat of a naked footfall on the carpet, the snick of a door latch, the creak of a floorboard.

Anything.

But of course, she didn't come. As much as she'd responded to his kisses, as much as he suspected he'd awakened her passions, she was too proper, too well bred to blithely set convention aside and fall into his bed.

No matter how much he longed for her. No matter how much she might desire that outcome for herself. She'd returned his kisses with all the sweetness and wonder of a woman discovering for the first time the boundless joy that might be shared with another. The give and take of pleasure.

How much greater might that response be when she lay beneath him? When he was buried so deep inside her he'd never wish to come out.

The vivid nature of those mental images haunted him while he rolled out of bed, knotted his cravat without a valet and made his way below to find Patience already at the breakfast table. He wished her good morning and took his place, but the particular shade of pink staining her cheeks sent his mind in all manner of scandalous directions. What would that blush look like on her breasts and belly once she'd taken her fill of pleasure?

Suppressing a groan, he set down his teacup with a dull *thunk*. He had to stop thinking about bedding her while she sat across from him spreading apricot jam over a piece of toast.

Yes, and wasn't this a domestic little scene? They might have sat like this on any number of mornings long since if only he'd possessed the courage to defy his family. But he'd been raised to do his duty, just as much as the lady facing him had.

And he'd done that duty. He'd married the young lady his parents favored, but her perfect bloodlines hadn't saved her.

Sitting here now, he realized the full scope of what he'd sacrificed to society.

Lady Worthington bit into her toast. "The snow appears to have stopped in the night."

When in doubt, mention the weather. Had their interactions been reduced to the mundane? Or worse, was she reminding him of his impending departure?

"I doubt the roads will be practicable today." He reached for his teacup, but the liquid inside had turned cold.

"Oh, certainly not, but you can't let your family worry over your whereabouts." She traced the rim of her saucer with a forefinger.

He suppressed a stab of envy for the china. "Nor yours."

"I'd send a messenger, but I'll arrive just as quickly myself, I suspect." She pushed back her chair and stood. "As I recall, you noted the lack of mistletoe last night. If we're to spend Christmas here, we might do something to rectify that situation."

Last night, yes. He'd much rather talk about that than the inevitability of their separation, especially if the discussion involved mistletoe.

"I'm not sure we'd find any mistletoe now," she added to his disappointment. "But we might do something to add a little holiday cheer to the place. Holly and greenery and such."

"I shouldn't mind a constitutional. It ought to be bracing." He pushed his chair back. "Just so long as you don't expect me to cut you a Yule log. I'm afraid I've never had the opportunity to hone my skills with an axe."

And if they got cold enough, perhaps he'd persuade her to share her body heat with him.

"I'll get my bonnet and wraps. Jane will bring your overcoat."

Before long, they were breaking a path through ankle-deep snow, headed toward the thick woods behind the dower house. Their breath plumed from their mouths in white clouds that dissipated into the cold, crisp air.

Beneath the naked branches of oak and birch, woodland creatures had already left their own tracks since the storm had ceased. Here and there, a spruce or fir peeked between the trunks, a dark smudge on the landscape beneath its mantle of frosting. But for the crunch of their feet, the woods lay blanketed under silence. Not even a birdcall disturbed the calm. Kingsbury glanced about him, seeing nothing but trees and the odd forms created by snow-covered bracken.

Lady Worthington paused in her tracks. "There's a stand of holly somewhere back here."

"Do you walk this way often?" His voice seemed loud to his ears.

"It's cool and pleasant in the summer. A stream runs through a bit farther on, but it's likely frozen over. If you venture that far at twilight, you might even come across deer—as long as you're quiet."

Quiet, just like these woods. Almost too quiet. "You don't have any troubles with poachers, do you?"

"Why, no." Her brow furrowed. "At least, I wouldn't think so."

"Didn't you say the earl had gone for the holiday? If anyone wished to try, now would be an excellent occasion."

"They're welcome to try if they like." Lady Worthington shrugged beneath her pelisse before marching off again. "It's Christmas, after all, and the harvest was poor." She strode on a few paces, then pointed. "No one's going to catch a deer in that."

He followed the direction of her finger. Rabbit tracks marked a trail through the undergrowth. Almost hidden beneath a bush, a thin wire circle appeared between the bare twigs. A snare, but so far the rabbits seemed to have escaped the noose. "No, they use rifles for deer."

"I haven't yet heard a gunshot on one of my walks, even when the earl was holding a shooting party. Ah, there we are." Her strides lengthened as she made for a dense row of bushes.

Bright red berries dotted curling green leaves, their color in defiance of the surrounding wintry grays and whites. From the basket she carried over her arm, she produced a pair of secateurs and snipped off a few branches. Then she turned from her task to contemplate him.

The corners of her mouth stretched with humor. "It's a good thing I brought my basket, else we'd have to make crowns of holly and carry them home on our heads."

He shook off his misgivings. "Would you have me decked out like Father Christmas?"

"Or the Lord of Misrule." Her impish smile widened into a promise of sin and pleasure.

"I'll give you misrule."

He gave in to temptation and reached for her, his hands grasping her by the waist. Her basket swung from her arm, its contents threatening to spill onto the frozen ground.

She responded with a yelp that turned into a throaty laugh as he pulled her closer. The cold had brought out a becoming bloom of pink across her cheeks. He dipped his head, but the instant before their lips touched, a great quantity of something cold and wet slipped down the back of his neck.

With a roar, he sprang back. The lump of snow only slipped farther down his spine. "Good God, woman. I'd expect someone as well bred and quiet as you to play fair."

She laughed again, and despite the cold dousing, the sound spiked straight to his groin. "Goodness, what do you think I did? I cannot control the wind or even the trees if they decide to drop their weight of snow."

"I call the timing of the action rather suspect."

"Think what you will, I had nothing to do with that. This, on the other hand . . ." Quick as lightning, she scooped up a handful of snow and lobbed it at him. It splattered across his chest.

"If that's the way you wish to play it, I shall demand satisfaction." He bent and prepared his own weapon.

As the projectile left his hand, she ducked before coming back to stand with her own handful of snow and a wicked glint in her eye. "Satisfaction, is it?"

The battle was on, snowballs flying fast and furious. Like a pair of children, they pelted each other, Lady Worthington's shrieks breaking the silence of the woods. By the third time she got him in the face, he was forced to admit that this woman, one whom he'd thought perfectly well brought up and even on the quiet side, possessed not only a surprisingly forceful arm but also a deadly aim.

Right. He was going to have to change tactics if he expected to emerge from this encounter with his pride intact. Though the action meant eating more snow, he worked his way closer, defending against her onslaught all the while. When he was near enough, he lunged, pinioning her arms.

"Now who's not playing fair?" Her eyes were bright, her cheeks red, her mouth lush and inviting.

"Didn't Cervantes have something to say about that?" He caught his breath and pulled her nearer. "Love and war are all one. It is lawful to use sleights and stratagems to attain the wished end."

She gaped for a moment before pulling her lower lip between her teeth. "And which is this?"

Damn it all, he wasn't prepared to face a question like that, not with his blood practically singing with emotion. He couldn't have named the last time he'd had fun with a woman, though. Not like this; perhaps not ever. Not something that was pure innocence.

The frigid air, the laughter, the merriment—complete honesty would force him to admit this wasn't as good as bedding a woman. But with this particular woman, these things merely made him want to bed her more, if only to hear her sigh and cry out the way she had just now. If only to experience her intensity in the midst of battle in a far more intimate setting.

The devil take those feelings that had prodded him to act the idiot and quote *Don Quixote*.

"Can it be a little of both?" he hedged.

She struggled against his grip, her hand coming out to smack him on the shoulder.

"War, definitely," he confirmed. "Why don't you tell me where you learned to fight like that?"

"I have a brother." A tendril of dark hair had worked its way from beneath her bonnet to straggle down her cheek. "I thought you were aware. I had to learn out of self-preservation."

"Ah, but did he teach you to preserve yourself against this?" He lowered his lips, but, once more, fate stood in his way.

Another snowball hit him on the side of the head, and this time, it couldn't have come from her. Or from the branches above.

Chapter Four

PATIENCE STEPPED BACK. Kingsbury was scrubbing snow out of his right eye, but the culprit's identity concerned her more. She looked beyond his shoulder. The snowball had come from somewhere over there.

A bush rustled, and the sound of muffled laughter met her ears. Or had she imagined it?

"Who's there?" she called. "Show yourself."

The branches stilled. She strode over to investigate. A young boy huddled among the twigs and dried leaves left over from the previous autumn.

"Jamie." She crossed her arms. "Up you get."

His gap-toothed smile faded, and he straightened. At the sight of his sunken cheeks and ragged clothes that hung loosely on his thin frame, Patience's heart swelled.

Still, she forced her brows into as stern a line as she could manage. "What do you think you're about?"

He stole a wary glance at Kingsbury before replying.

"Beggin' yer pardon, me lady, but yer scarin' off th' rabbits."

The snare. Of course. Lowering herself to the child's level, she softened her tone. "Don't tell me you were trying to catch Christmas dinner."

As bad as the season had been, the notion should hardly shock her. Ever since the previous summer—or, more accurately, what had passed for summer, since the weather had refused to warm—rain and frost and all manner of disasters had led to crop failures across England. Beggars were common. The poor in the cities were starving.

Before setting out for her brother's estate, Patience had sent what food she could spare to the Worthington tenants, but clearly supplies hadn't been sufficient.

Jamie stared at the snow-covered ground. "Ain't nothin' t' catch."

"And you're not helping matters by adding to the commotion," Patience pointed out. If the boy meant to snare something for his supper, he needed to rethink his strategy.

"Who have we here?" Kingsbury came to a halt next to Patience.

"Jamie belongs to one of the tenants." She straightened. "And Jamie, I believe you owe the duke an apology."

The boy's face blanched. "Duke?"

"Yes, this is His Grace, the Duke of Kingsbury, and you've hit him with a snowball."

"It weren't any less than you were doin'."

Patience's lips twitched, but she refused to let them

stretch into a smile. "That was different. If we were having a snowball battle, it was by mutual agreement."

"Was it?" Blast Kingsbury and his confounded eyebrow. "I don't recall any particular negotiations about the terms of our snowball battle. It just happened. In fact, you started it."

She glared at him. "I did not."

Jamie sniggered.

Kingsbury crossed his arms, but his blue eyes twinkled. "I am prepared to listen to your excuses. I will consider them at my leisure and let you know if they're acceptable."

The urge rose in her to reach for another handful of snow. Instead, she dropped into an exaggerated curtsy. "I most humbly beg your pardon if my behavior has not met with your standards. I shall endeavor to comport myself with the strictest decorum in the future."

Kingsbury cleared his throat. "I don't know if it's necessary to take matters quite that far."

Good Lord but the man knew what it took to call a blush to her cheeks. A piercing look, a certain tone, and the heat rose from deep inside her.

Jamie tugged at her skirts. His eyes were round, his brow puckered. "I can't say all them fancy words."

"That's quite all right, my lad," Kingsbury said. "I shall consider the matter closed, unless Lady Worthington decides to fire another salvo."

Patience pressed her lips together. "The proper reply is 'Yes, Your Grace,'" she prompted.

Jamie eyed Kingsbury. "What is it that makes ye a duke, er, Yer Grace?"

"An accident of birth."

Patience looked sharply at the duke, but he concentrated on Jamie, his expression giving away nothing. Still, her chest tightened with something that felt suspiciously like hope. She forced her mind to call up an image of Linnet.

Guard your heart. Yes, she had to. If only she could.

She shook off the moment. Her basket lay where she'd dropped it in favor of a snowball fight. The sprigs of holly she'd already gathered were spread over the ground. "Jamie, how would you like some hot chocolate?"

The boy's eyes widened for a moment, sparking with the same sort of longing Patience had just tamped down, but then he schooled his features. Lord, but he was too young to know how to do that. "I can't. Me mum told me not t' come home without Christmas dinner."

Her heart swelled further, but for a completely different reason. The situation was more desperate than she realized if his family had gone through the food she'd given them a few days ago. "Well." She strove to inject a note of cheer into her tone. "Why don't I give you a job and see if you can't earn something for dinner?"

His jaw dropped, and the hope returned, along with a healthy measure of joy. "What do ye need me t' do?"

"You can start by collecting this holly." She gestured toward her abandoned basket. "And if you know where to find me a few pinecones, that won't go amiss either." She handed him her secateurs. "And if you're very careful, you can cut me some evergreen boughs."

He brightened, and with an excited "Yes, me lady," he took up her basket and darted into the deeper woods.

Kingsbury stepped closer—she sensed his presence as much as anything. "That was well done of you."

The sheer admiration that rang through his voice provoked a wave of heat, both inside and out. If he didn't stop, one way or another, he was going to make her melt the snow, but then, of course, he'd be free to leave.

Another step and he lifted her chin, compelling her to meet his gaze. "Have I embarrassed you?"

"No." That came out too forcefully, and her cheeks warmed further.

"You've no reason to feel bad, you know." He shook his head slightly. "Damn it, but my sister was wrong about you. All wrong."

"Please, I'd rather not talk about her." The last thing she needed was for thoughts of his sister—his family—to intrude on their little interlude. As long as they stayed at the dower house, it was like they'd stolen this slice of time together.

"Yes, you're right," he muttered. A furrow formed between his brows, and he looked away.

He might have said more, but Jamie ran out of the trees, shouting. Evergreen branches trailed over the side of the brimming basket, and pinecones spilled out to mark his path.

Patience smiled at the boy. "Now you can come into the house and help us make something of all this."

THE WORTHINGTON DOWER house greeted them with succulent scents wafting from the kitchen below stairs.

Spices, meat, butter, baking. At the mingled aroma, Nathaniel's stomach growled.

A similar rumble came from Jamie.

They took their bounty into the sitting room, where Lady Worthington's maid sat by the fire, a sock forming under her rapidly clicking knitting needles.

"Good Lord," Lady Worthington said. "Does Jane think we're having His Majesty's army to Christmas dinner?"

The maid cast a look in Nathaniel's direction. "Jane is under the impression His Grace requires a sumptuous repast. She's been fluttering around all morning making all manner of things."

Nathaniel cleared his throat. "I can assure you I require no one to go to any bother on my account, but since it's been done"—he nodded in Jamie's direction—"I'm certain we can put the spare food to good use."

Lady Worthington graced him with a smile that set her entire face alight. "That is an excellent idea. Would you ask Jane to set something aside for young Jamie here to carry home? And while you're at it, ask if it would be too much trouble to send up some hot chocolate?"

The maid bustled out. Before long, Lady Worthington had installed Jamie at a small table with a needle and thread and asked him to string holly and berries along the length. She settled herself beside the boy and began to form pinecones into a complicated pattern.

"Don't think you can just stand there and oversee." She sent Nathaniel a sharp glance. "You may be a duke, but you can lend a hand."

He watched her wield her needle. "I doubt I possess the required skills."

"Nonsense. You can string berries along with Jamie."

And so the afternoon passed with holly and evergreens and pinecones formed into garlands, while they gorged themselves on fluffy scones washed down with generous amounts of hot chocolate. At some point Lady Worthington began humming a carol, and it wasn't long before everyone else joined in. The day outside was beginning to grow dark when they sent Jamie on his way bearing a basket of food, some extra decorations, and a pair of the maid's woolen socks for good measure.

Lady Worthington stood arranging some evergreens over the mantel. While she adjusted each branch just so, she crooned under her breath, "'Now the holly bears a berry as white as the milk.'"

"I wonder where that comes from," Nathaniel said. "Holly berries are red. Mistletoe, on the other hand . . . those berries are white."

"Well, we haven't got any mistletoe, it seems. Not unless Jane collected some in the autumn and laid it aside without telling me."

He crossed to stand next to her. The heat from the hearth warmed him through, but the lady standing next to him sparked an altogether different flame within. She had from their very first meeting.

He curled his fingers about her waist. "Would I be horribly in breach of tradition if I kissed you without mistletoe?"

She folded her hands in front of her and looked down.

"Perhaps. I would like you to explain something to me, though."

"What's that?" He leaned closer to breathe her in. She smelled clean, like the outdoors, fresh as the pine boughs they'd brought into the house.

"What you said to Jamie earlier about being a duke by accident."

"It is an accident, don't you think?" He sighed. He normally endured his burden without complaint, but suddenly the weight bore down on his shoulders. "Jamie didn't ask to be the son of a poor tenant any more than I asked to be a duke."

She looked up at him, her gaze steady. Her eyes reflected the flames like the sparks from emeralds. "Or any more than I asked to be the daughter of a simple country baron."

"That boy may possess nothing in the way of wealth, but do you realize he has something that I don't?"

"What's that?"

"A choice." He stepped back and raked a hand through his hair. Frustration exploded in his gut. "Someday that boy is going to grow up and wish to marry a maid. He'll be allowed to pick someone to his liking and not have to worry if she'll be acceptable to his family." He tried but failed to keep the bitterness from his voice. "And do you know who will stand in his way? No one."

She stood very still, watching him carefully. Gaging his every reaction, if he didn't miss his guess. "Unlike us."

Yes, Lady Worthington had married elsewhere, but only due to his own lack of courage. He might have prevented that if only he'd defied his family's wishes. And perhaps he'd listened to his sister once too often. "She doesn't really care for you. She only wants to be styled Your Grace," Diana had told him more than once.

He hadn't wanted to believe his sister, but when he'd returned from Italy to learn the young lady he'd courted was now a countess married to a much older man, the news had struck a painful blow. Was she so desperate for a title that she'd consign herself to a life of unhappiness?

But then he might have suspected that any woman who showed an interest in him longed only to become a duchess. And faced with Lady Worthington now, he still didn't wish to believe her to be merely after status. Had that been the case, she surely wouldn't have holed herself away in the country all these years.

"It's my fault," he admitted. "All of it. My family didn't approve of my choice, and to my everlasting regret, I let them sway my opinion."

"Was your wife so bad, then?" Lady Worthington asked the question with more gentleness than he deserved.

"She was perfect." At least according to his family. Perfect reputation, perfect connections, perfect manners, perfect breeding. "I hardly knew her."

The wedding had followed fast on his return from the continent. He'd considered it a blessing when Olivia had discovered she was increasing so soon after the wedding, a sign of hope for the future and for his marriage. Perhaps in time he might even forget the country chit whose mere touch had electrified him, whose face he'd seen every time he'd bedded his wife. But there, he'd failed, and the childbed had robbed him of a second chance—with Olivia, at least.

"I grew up in the awareness of one thing first and foremost," he added. "My duty to the dukedom. It granted me power and wealth, yes. But it demanded payment in return. Too high a price."

Chapter Five

Too high a price.

Kingsbury's statement echoed through Patience's mind long after their conversation had drifted to safer topics. It was still throbbing in her brain like a constant pulse as they sat down to dinner.

Duty and sacrifice. Her own marriage had taught her those hard lessons. If only she could be certain he'd been referring to *her* when he'd mentioned the price he'd paid. The words might have rung with the truth to her ears, but she had to be certain she wasn't merely hearing what she wanted to hear.

Heaven only knew she longed deep in her bones that he'd meant her, for it put the lie to his sister's words. With every passing hour in Kingsbury's company, Diana's claims seemed less and less credible.

But that only meant it was becoming more and more difficult for Patience to guard her heart. She was softening, melting like the snow outside beneath the sun's steady rays, a slow drip that dissolved her defenses.

"I wish to lodge a complaint." From his place at the head of the table, Kingsbury set his goblet down with a decided *thunk*.

Patience looked up from her plate. Lost in her thoughts, she'd been absently separating her roast goose, mince pie, and vegetables into neat little piles. "Is it the wine?"

Along with the meal, she'd barely touched her glass.

"Not at all. The claret is quite excellent."

Thank goodness. She'd sent up to the manor for one of the earl's better vintages. It was the least she could do when receiving a duke for Christmas dinner.

"Are you ready for something stronger? Port, perhaps?" Beneath the cover of the table, she crossed her fingers. She'd neglected to request any specific gentleman's drinks.

"Do not trouble yourself. And before you ask, the meal has been lovely. Not that you'd have noticed."

She lowered her lashes. The blasted man saw everything.

"Your cook has outdone herself," he added before wiping his lips with his serviette. Then he pushed back his chair. "No, my complaint is rather more personal in nature. You never answered my question earlier."

"What question?"

He prowled the length of the dining room table, almost casually, but his gaze never left hers. She twisted her serviette in her lap while sifting through this afternoon's conversation for a clue as to what he was hinting at. Certainly not his enigmatic comment about duty and sacrifice. That had not been phrased as a question. Nothing else sprang to mind, but then this man's very presence took up a great deal of room in her thoughts. Was this how a cornered mouse felt when faced with a cat?

"You never informed me if your sense of tradition would be offended if we dispensed with the mistletoe."

"Oh." She dropped the poor tortured bit of linen in her hands in favor of her wineglass. She tipped a fortifying swig down her throat, and the corners of her jaws ached with the claret's dryness.

Duty and sacrifice.

Once more, the duke's words to her threaded through her imagination. She still couldn't make sense of them. A reference to their aborted romance, perhaps—Lord, *please*—and yet he'd called his wife perfect. To him that price could have well been losing her to the childbed.

Patience was hardly in a position to demand clarification.

Guard your heart. Linnet's admonition chased the duke's words through her mind. The problem was, Patience didn't know if she could, despite Kingsbury's description of his late duchess.

If Patience gave in and kissed him again, she knew quite well she wouldn't stop there. Not that he'd demanded rights to her body. No, in a way this was worse. In her current position, she could never hide behind mere duty. If she went to his bed, it would be in open acknowledgment of mutual feelings. Mutual desire. Mutual lust. Mutual hunger. Mutual need.

Looking at him now—that sculpted face, his dark hair emphasizing the blue of his eyes, the broad-chested body—she admitted to herself that she did, indeed, want him. She always had in an earthy, carnal sense that, ten years ago, she'd been too innocent to recognize. She wanted all of him, with nothing held back.

The notion ought to shock her, for she'd never faced her marriage bed with such enthusiasm.

One night. The voice of temptation rose in her, intriguing, tantalizing. She could have one night and yet not call herself his mistress.

Kingsbury picked up her hand and lifted her knuckles to his lips.

Patience gathered her courage. "You spoke of your regrets last night."

"That I did."

"Were those you mentioned the only ones?"

"Oh, my dear." He tugged at her hand, his intent clear. He wanted her standing on a level with him. "Last night we barely scraped the surface of my regrets."

So much quiet reverence fueled that statement that her throat ached. Warmth spread through her chest, while the hopeful corner of her heart sat up and took notice.

The back of his hand brushed her cheek. "But perhaps we should discuss your regrets, as well."

She had just as many as he, but she was only prepared to discuss one of those at the moment. "I regret never learning the true joys of marriage."

His palm settled at the back of her neck. "Do you mean motherhood?"

"And all that leads to it."

His free arm snaked about her waist, pulling her against his chest. Yes, she wanted his body pressed to hers, but not like this. She wanted her skin next to his, their hearts pounding in tandem, as close as humanly possible.

His forehead came to rest against hers, their lips inches apart. "I can show you that. Gladly." He brushed his lips against hers, the kiss light—too light for all her yearning. "I just don't think here is the best choice, unless you'd like to shock the servants and find out how sturdy this table is."

Heat washed up her bosom and all through her. Good Lord, she was blushing like a schoolgirl. Oh, the image he'd conjured in her mind. She'd never considered such things.

The low rumble of his laughter promised all manner of wickedness. "Ah, I've got you thinking about it, haven't I? For a woman who was married four years, you're still quite the innocent."

"You . . . you paid attention to such things?"

"The length of your marriage? From the moment I saw the announcement in the *Times*—months out of date, mind you, since I was on the continent—I cursed every day, every hour Worthington was allowed to have you." His grip tightened at her nape and waist. "I would have saved you had I only known in time."

She placed her fingers over his lips. "I don't wish to talk about our past. Not now. Not tonight."

"No, we've much better things to do. Above stairs."

They made it as far as his bedchamber, barely crossing the threshold before Patience found herself sandwiched between a solid wall and Kingsbury. His mouth descended in a devouring kiss that stole her breath and inflamed her senses. A decade's worth of yearning poured into that single act.

His tongue flicked against hers, and she welcomed its invasion. He possessed her mouth the way his body would possess hers—with his whole self and his full passion.

As she responded, her fingers crept to his neck to slip beneath his cravat and collar, seeking the skin beneath. She needed that warmth as proof this was all real. It was happening here and now.

At long last.

Smooth, heated skin, the roughness of stubble, the softness of his hair, the solidity of bone and sinew beneath. The sandalwood scent of him filling her nostrils, filling her being, yet soon that wasn't enough. Her body craved his entire person, not the duke but the man.

She tangled her fingers in his cravat, and he pulled away with a groan.

"Why have you stopped?" She went on trying to work the knot loose.

"If I don't, I'm going to have you here and now against this wall." A most devious grin spread across his face. "Unless—"

"I've never done such a thing, if that's what you were hinting at." The swath of linen came free in her hand, and she went to work on the fastening at his collar. "There are so many things I haven't done. I've never wanted to do them." She caught his gaze and held it. "Until now."

"What things?" The question emerged as a raspy whisper.

"Would you prefer I told you?" She let her hand slip down his firm chest, bypassing, for now, the buttons on his waistcoat, until she reached the falls of his breeches. Until she clasped the whole, hot length of him through heavy fabric. "Or showed you?"

A tremor passed through him. "You're going to kill me."

"I doubt it." Good heavens, where was this wantonness coming from? Her husband had attempted to convince her to perform such acts as she was now contemplating, but she'd never desired them before. With Kingsbury, her body demanded she explore.

A gentle squeeze, and his eyes fluttered shut. "I'll finish too soon. I'm no longer a lustful lad of sixteen who can stiffen every other moment."

"We've the entire night." Her fingers drifted upward, releasing one button after the next. "Is not part of the joy between bed partners in the giving of pleasure as well as receiving?"

His only response was a shudder and a groan. His erection leaped into her hand, and she ran her palm down the heavy shaft. Soft skin slid over a steely inner core, impossibly hard. Her internal muscles clenched with the need to be filled.

She sank to her knees.

NATHANIEL HISSED OUT a breath at the sight of Patience—at such a moment he could think of her by nothing other than her given name—at his feet, cheeks flushed, breasts heaving, full, rosy lips parted to take him in. The wet heat of her mouth engulfed the head of his cock, while her hand slid to the base, her grip firm. God, so perfect. Her tongue circled the ridge of flesh; then she plunged deeper.

Blood pumped to his groin and, with it, an urge to thrust into her throat. Better to grit his teeth and let her have her way. He'd last longer—he hoped—perhaps long enough to savor the full embrace of her body. Not just her mouth but her nails on his shoulders, her thighs clasping his hips as he drove them both to completion.

Soon.

He threw his head back and stared at the ceiling while, in his imagination, he tossed her onto the thick feather mattress and listened to the bed ropes groan as he mounted her. God, yes, and he'd draw every last bit of pleasure from her.

Over and over, she pulled back, her tongue circling, lapping at the beads of moisture that formed on the tip of his erection, before taking in more of his length. Ever hotter. Ever deeper. He grazed the velvety skin at the back of her mouth, and his bollocks tightened. He needed to stop her before he spent, before it was too late.

He threaded his fingers through her hair, his palm cupping her scalp, but her rhythm only increased. Her cheeks hollowed, the pull sweet and hot and eager. Sweat prickled on his brow, and pleasure burned at the base of his spine.

"God, stop, before I spend."

Her mouth released him with a pop, but her fingers still curled about the base of his cock. He shuddered at the sight of her, kneeling before him, looking all too pleased with herself. If he didn't miss his guess, she knew quite well that she'd nearly brought him to his knees, figuratively if not literally.

Her grip slackened, fingers slipped away, and he nearly sighed with relief. He drew her to her feet, swept her into his arms, and placed her in the center of the mattress. Never taking his eyes from her, he tore at his garments, discarding them heedlessly on the floor. His valet would have a fit of apoplexy to see the mess Nathaniel was making, but he was past caring.

He needed Patience the way he needed air. He needed to hear her cries as he wrung every last drop of pleasure from her.

She sat up to ruck out of her gown, and he held his breath at the hints of rosy skin she bared to him. Naked, he climbed onto the bed to help relieve her of her stays and chemise. Then he stretched out beside her to indulge in the sight of her lush body. His gaze followed each curve, her neck, her shoulder, her rounded breasts, to the flare of her hips and the length of her thighs.

Then he pulled her against him, flesh to flesh, and took her lips once more.

Chapter Six

KINGSBURY'S TONGUE INVADED her mouth to twine with hers until she was mindless with the ache to be filled. Patience wrapped her arms around him and gave over to the sensations he aroused. The taut muscles of his back tightened and jumped beneath her fingertips. His breath wafted hot over her neck as he trailed his lips along her throat. His tongue darted warmth and moisture in its passing, and deep inside, a sensation of emptiness throbbed.

Her hips shifted restlessly against him in a demand for something she'd never before asked for. Something she'd never thought possible. With Kingsbury, though, it would be. Her body knew as much, if her mind did not.

He shifted downward, and his lips closed about her nipple and drew—drew on the bud, drew a heavy gasp from her throat, drew the knot of need in her belly ever tighter. His tongue circled the peak, and she arched into the caress in an unconscious demand for more.

He raised his head, caught her eye, while his lips stretched into a truly wicked smile, wolfish and knowing.

"Don't— Don't stop." The words burst from her lips on an airy note of longing.

"I wouldn't dream of it. Not when you beg so sweetly." He dipped his head once more, and a dark lock of hair fell across his forehead. He trailed his tongue over her breast, flicking at the nipple, and sending hot currents of hunger shooting through her veins.

Her fingers dug into his shoulders until she was sure she bore a sliver of skin beneath each nail. He repeated the motion, and this time, his hand slipped across her belly to her hip, trailing fire in its wake, a fire that raced through her limbs.

He paused once more, and a whimper escaped before she could clamp her mouth shut. A low chuckle rumbled up from his chest, the tremor passing through her as well, so closely were they pressed together.

And yet, not close enough. "Please."

"Please what?"

She canted her hips, needing his fingers, or better his staff.

"No, no, you want something. You've got to tell me. Otherwise, it will be my pleasure to tease you until morning just so I can listen to those lovely sounds you make."

She swatted at his back. His fingers were so close to where she wanted them. "Your Grace—"

He pressed a finger to her lips. "Nathaniel. You're lying beneath me in my bed. The least you can do is drop the title nonsense."

She drew in a breath. Such a seductive tone that it compelled her to comply. But if she did—if she obeyed—it would tear down a barrier between them. If she allowed him the humanity of his given name, how vulnerable might that simple familiarity leave her? How open and raw and hopeful her heart?

"Patience." Her own name taunted her, tempted to reply in kind. How easily he stripped her of formality.

"Nathaniel."

"God, yes. Say it again." His fingers slipped farther, sketching the line where her thigh met her body, close, so close.

"Nathaniel."

His touch eased between her legs, parted her folds, and trailed moisture from her entrance to the bud at its crown. "I'll make you scream it yet."

He traced a lazy circle about the tiny peak until she wanted to scream for another reason altogether. She pressed her hips into his touch and arched her back, but he seemed determined to spend the remaining hours until morning toying with her.

Unable to stand the torment, she skimmed her hand along his chest, across his belly, until she gripped his length. His breath expelled on a hiss. She pressed forward, spreading her fingers down the length of his shaft until they encountered the springy curls at its base.

His head sagged against her, and a shudder passed through him, strong enough that she felt it in her own body, as though he'd coaxed the reaction from her. With a grunt, he shackled her wrist and pulled her hand away.

"I'm not about to take that chance again," he panted. "I won't let you have me off and take nothing for yourself." He bent her arm back until he held it above her head, the back of her hand pressed into the pillow. "I wonder, though, how many times I can bring you to crisis before you beg me to take you?"

Good Lord, the very idea. A moan parted her lips at the thought of everything he'd try to do to her.

He pressed his lips to the fleshy undercurve of her breast, then his teeth abraded the spot, just hard enough to send a jolt of pleasure to the center of her belly. His fingers circled once again, more insistent, driving her along an ever-climbing spiral of heat and need and sensation.

Yes, Lord, yes.

She arched into the touch. He trailed kisses down her body, and she shuddered with the anticipation of him treating her as she'd just treated him, his tongue branding her most sensitive flesh, marking it as his. The warmth of his breath wafted along her inner thigh, and she trembled.

Soon now, soon he'd show her true pleasure. She threaded her fingers through his hair. The soft strands slipped against her fingertips. Their ends tickled her inner thighs. His fingers shifted and he parted her, exposing her utterly.

At the first burning touch of his tongue, a moan escaped her lips. He licked a path from her entrance to the tiny bundle of nerves at its crown, and her palm fitted itself to his head, holding him in place. *Just there. Oh yes, there.*

He slipped two fingers into her, thrusting to match the rhythm of his tongue. She clenched about him, quivered, her head back against the pillow, moaning into the dark while he drove her on. Each flick of his tongue against that sweet, sweet spot sent her spiraling upward through flame and joy.

For a moment, he held her at the brink, her feet dangling over a void, as if he was determined to wring every last ounce of pleasure from her. Then he applied full force to his thrusting fingers while sucking that sweet, sweet spot, and she plummeted, screaming, into oblivion.

NATHANIEL CAUGHT HIS breath. He felt as if he'd run for miles, yet he'd only watched Patience fall apart. His cock throbbed a painful reminder that he had yet to join her in that semblance of paradise. Soon, but he wanted to savor her for a moment while he basked in a certain measure of masculine pride that he'd satisfied this woman.

Her eyes fluttered open, bright in her flushed face, and he smiled. She looked utterly bemused, lost, really—lost in an exquisite afterglow he would damned well make her experience again. And again. As many times as he possibly could.

He reached to frame her face with his fingers, tracing the delicate line of her cheekbones and jaw. "That's one."

Before she could reply, he captured her lips and demanded a response, demanded a renewal of her arousal, as he settled himself between her legs. When she opened to him and twined her fingers through his hair, he thrust home.

At last.

He groaned into her mouth. Such warmth surrounded him, drew him into her depths. He wanted to lose himself completely in her tight sheath, pound away until both of them ceased to exist as separate people.

A red haze of lust began to descend, and he fought for control even as he withdrew and pressed in again. Her hips rose to meet his, and a groan tore from his throat.

Smooth, so smooth. So wet and tight. She moved with him in perfect rhythm, her breathing rapid, her swollen lips parted and emitting such lovely sounds of passion.

She murmured something incoherent. His passion-addled brain struggled to make sense of it, but the most he could decipher was encouragement. He pushed himself onto his elbows, changing the angle of penetration and thrusting deeper.

She arched beneath him and hummed a drawn-out note of pleasure. He trembled and burned with the need for release. His entire body tightened with it. He gritted his teeth and refused to give in.

Not yet. Not until he'd experienced her contracting about him, squeezing him dry as she reached another peak.

She was close. Her internal muscles rippled along his length. So good. So hot. So utterly perfect.

Her thighs gripped his flanks, her fingers tightened on his shoulders, and her nails bit into his flesh.

"Come for me, love." His words were ragged, low, and harsh, a sensual command.

Her eyes fluttered open. "What?"

Right. He'd forgotten himself and used a term no lady of her station should know, but he'd no idea how to explain. Not now. Not in this moment. So he made his reply physical, increasing his tempo, thrusting deeper.

She hitched in a breath, the sound nearly a hiccup. A tremor wracked her body, then another. She opened her mouth in a long, keening cry, while inside, she pulsed about him in rhythmic waves of ecstasy.

He gritted his teeth against a violent urge to come. Not yet, not inside her, not until she was done. Her climax fluttered onward, at once pleasure and torture from not giving in to instinct. A drop of sweat trailed down his jaw. He closed his eyes, and a tremor wracked his body. His entire being tightened, starting in his bollocks.

"Oh God." He wouldn't last. Not a moment longer. With a shudder and a groan, he pulled out of the sweet haven of her body and let his release shoot into the sheets.

Spent, unable to support himself any longer, he collapsed onto her. Her arms tightened about him, pulled him against her. The soft peaks of her breasts flattened beneath his chest. He expelled a breath in a sigh of contentment, of utter completion.

HOURS LATER, NATHANIEL stared at the ceiling, watching the light change from midnight's shadows to the grays of impending dawn. Patience lay sleeping in the circle of his arms, her hair spread over his chest like a blanket, her head pillowed on his shoulder. Right where she belonged.

God only knew he ought to have drifted off long since.

Over the course of the night, he'd lost count of how many times he'd made this woman cry out. He'd certainly proved himself as lustful as he'd been at sixteen. Perhaps even more, but then, he had so many lost years to make up for.

He tightened his embrace and pressed his lips to the top of her head. Lord, to sleep like this—or not—every night, in a small corner of paradise here on earth. But then some part of him had always suspected lovemaking would be different with this woman.

The reality had surpassed his wildest imaginings.

He glanced at the window, praying for a wall of white, another snowstorm to strand him even longer. If he was certain of anything, he was certain of this—a single night wasn't nearly enough to learn all there was to Patience, Lady Worthington. A year wouldn't comprise enough time, nor a decade—and he'd already sacrificed that much on the altar of duty.

He'd lost her once. He couldn't stand for it to happen again.

Noises echoed from somewhere in the house—the quiet thumps of footfalls, the servants preparing the grates and starting fires. With any luck, he'd have another day and another night with her. Heaven let it be.

A sudden tapping at the door startled him from his thoughts.

"Your Grace?" The thickness of the oak muffled a feminine voice. Not the one who cooked, the other one. Linnet. "Your pardon for the disturbance."

Did he detect a note of disapproval? He ought to be

thankful for the woman's assumptions, for they were the only things preventing her from entering. To be safe, he pulled the blankets over Patience.

"What is it?" he called.

Patience stirred and raised her head, blinking the sleep from her eyes.

"Someone's come asking for you," Linnet replied through the door.

"Who?" But even as he asked the question, the answer rose in his mind. No one else knew his whereabouts.

"Your coachman, sir." No one but him. "He set out as soon as he could to collect your carriage, reckoning you'd like to continue on your journey. He says the roads are clear."

Chapter Seven

PATIENCE WASN'T READY for the idyll to be over, not after the heights Nathaniel had shown her last night. He'd taken her places she hadn't known existed. Though she'd behaved in an utterly wanton manner, she wished to continue the exploration. Good Lord, what woman would refuse such pleasure? But with him. Only with him.

Worse, her desire went beyond the bedchamber. She longed to pass more days in his company, drinking tea at breakfast, walking in the woods, casting snowballs. Laughing. Simply enjoying each other.

Yet he was leaving. She could hardly stop him, though. His family was expecting him. Just as hers was expecting her.

Your families will always stand between you. His especially. Though the admonition rang in her head, she clearly heard Linnet's voice.

She pushed the thoughts aside and busied herself with

repacking her things in preparation for setting out to her brother's once more. Anything to keep her from focusing on Nathaniel and the fact that he was walking out of her life. Again.

Blast. Her throat tightened suspiciously, and the backs of her eyes stung. She should have staved off *that* particular thought.

The door to her bedchamber burst open. "Good Lord." Linnet quickly dropped into a curtsy. "Your pardon, my lady, but what are you about?"

Patience glanced at the piles of gowns on her bed. In her effort to occupy herself, she'd rather made a mess of things. "I thought I'd reconsider which garments to take to my brother's."

Linnet strode to the bed and lifted a pale yellow confection in filmy muslin. "Were you planning on staying until next summer?" She shook her head. "You've gone and put your foot in it, haven't you?"

Patience returned her maid's gaze steadily. It wasn't as if Linnet couldn't work out for herself what had transpired last night. Clearly her statement referred to more than Patience taking pleasant advantage of her widowhood.

"If I have, I am well beyond the age where I might be expected to bear any consequences for my actions." She managed that reply with far more confidence than she felt.

Linnet gathered a few more summery gowns and stored them in the dressing room. "Will there be consequences?"

Only the scars on my heart.

She'd wanted one night, and one night was what she'd received. It wasn't enough. Not nearly. But any resulting wounds would have to be borne with quiet composure.

"There were never any in my marriage," she replied. "I shouldn't think there'd be any now." Not when Nathaniel had taken a gentleman's precautions and finished in the sheets, but Patience was not about to divulge that kind of detail.

"Men," Linnet spluttered. "They do love to blame their shortcomings on women whenever they can. How can you be sure your lack of children was not due to your husband?"

"I cannot, but there's no sense in discussing the matter. I doubt I shall have occasion to repeat any indiscretions that may have occurred." Not when she and Nathaniel led such utterly separate lives.

Linnet threw her a look that all but shouted, *I wouldn't be so certain.* "His Grace sent me to fetch you."

This was it then. This was good-bye.

"Yes, I suppose he's eager to be off." Patience unclasped her hands—she'd been twisting them in her skirts without realizing—and strode for the staircase. She'd nothing left to do but hold up her chin, straighten her spine, and wish him well. Any tears could wait until she was alone.

He stood by the front door, dressed in his caped greatcoat and holding his hat in gloved hands, by all appearances a man ready to affront whatever winter might throw at him. His gaze swept over her as she descended to the entrance hall. Intense appreciation sparked in the blue depths of his eyes.

Yes, he might well enjoy the sight of her, but that wasn't preventing him from leaving.

"We find ourselves back where we started two days ago." He took her hand and bent over it. "I am bound for my estate on the other side of Gloucester."

He paused for her reply, his gaze still heavy with scrutiny, but what response could he possibly expect from her when he'd stated the obvious? Did he intend her to take hope from the sort of inanity he might utter over tea at a social call?

A new thought struck a horrifying blow to a heart already scraped raw by a night beyond her wildest imaginings. What if all his pretty declarations yesterday had been nothing more than calculated seduction? A game, a trifle.

She thought back to the young buck she'd met ten years ago, but, beyond Diana's declarations, Patience could not recall any rumors that he made a habit of breaking hearts. But then he'd been the heir to a dukedom. The eyes of society would forgive such a man a great deal based on his social standing alone.

If he merely wished to seduce you, why would he wait an entire decade? an annoying voice in her head argued. *Surely he'd have found another outlet for his passions in the meantime. More than one.*

No, no. She couldn't afford to let that voice sway her. If she convinced herself he harbored feelings for her, it would only make this separation more painful. And would he not have broached the entire parting differently? He wasn't making the slightest attempt to stay on.

"You should be on your way if you wish to arrive before dark." She'd meant to reply in kind, but to her own ears, her reply carried far more ice than she'd intended.

Something hardened about his jawline. He hadn't expected that frosty reception either. What was more, he didn't like it. At all. Good Lord, what had happened to her over the past couple of days? First she behaved like a complete wanton, and now she was deliberately provoking a duke.

Well, good. He—no, his entire family—needed provocation. Someone should have shown them all long ago that an accident of birth was no reason to lord themselves over the rest of the world.

Accident of birth. The exact words he'd used with Jamie. The memory of the duke's interaction with a small boy only compounded her inner turmoil. Blast it all, she no longer knew what to think.

"I'd hoped," he said so tightly that she could hear his clenched molars, "that last night meant enough to you that I'd at least merit a good-bye kiss."

Before she could respond, he reached for her, taking her by the wrist this time, his grip merciless. His lips crushed to hers, harder and more demanding than anything he'd asked of her in his bedchamber. It was as if he wished to leave a permanent imprint of himself on her—like a brand.

All too soon, he released her, and she staggered back, gasping for breath. She touched her fingertips to her mouth, half expecting to encounter blisters.

"I'd hoped," he went on, "last night meant enough to you that I might convince you to come with me."

Her knees wobbled, and she reached for the wall. "I . . . I could not possibly . . . How would it look for me to arrive in your company unannounced? I would not have your family say you've insulted them by lodging your mistress beneath your roof."

"Is that what you think?" His tone was downright dangerous.

"Of course not." Not based on his reaction, at any rate. "But I know what your family will make of me." Her mind echoed with the verbal darts his sister used to aim in her direction, terms like *countrified* and *upstart* and *aiming far too high*. Oh, they'd never been direct. Diana was far too polite to make a scene, but she knew the effect of a well-placed stage whisper. "In any case, my brother expected me two days ago."

"There is your solution. Arrive in his company, and no one can make any claim of scandal. In fact . . ." His expression relaxed into a smile. "Come for Twelfth Night, all of you. I will inform my mother and add you to the guest list."

His mother presented merely one obstacle. His sister, on the other hand, was an entirely different matter. "I don't know if I'd dare eat in front of them."

"Why on earth not?"

"The one time I happened to be invited to the same dinner party as you, I had the misfortune to be seated across from your sister." Of course he wouldn't recall. His place had been exactly ten places away and on the same side of the table. Patience had stolen enough glances in his direction to have counted.

"I know my sister can be difficult, but why would you term it a misfortune?" Now he sounded merely intrigued. Perhaps they could part on better terms, at least.

"I had the distinct feeling she took the seating as a personal affront."

"Ah, yes, she has her moments of pomposity."

Patience crossed her arms. "If you want to term it that. She took advantage of her location in the end."

"How so?"

"She watched the entire meal to make certain I used the correct fork at every service."

"And did you?"

Good Lord, how his teasing tore at her heart. If only her husband could have offered her companionship like this. She returned his smile but feared the expression was forced. "I didn't dare not."

His gloved hand touched her cheek. "I must go, but do come. All of you."

"I'll think on it." She couldn't force any more words past the sudden knot in her throat.

Eyes closed so she wouldn't have to watch him depart, Patience listened to the door latch click behind him. Through the heavy plank, the creak of the harness somehow reached her ears. A horse snorted. The coachman chirruped, and with a slap of the reins, Nathaniel was gone.

Right, and now she ought to see about leaving herself. Off to Peter's before he worried any further about her whereabouts. Heaven only knew she wouldn't be able to tolerate remaining in this house for much longer. Not when Nathaniel had seemingly left an imprint behind him. If she set out today, at least she wouldn't be able to do anything foolish, like sleep on the sheets she and the duke had set aflame last night.

At last she opened her eyes and turned for the stairs.

"My lady." Hair askew beneath her mobcap, Jane trundled down the passage. "Has His Grace gone? He forgot this." She held out a small box wrapped in plain brown paper.

"Yes, it's too late." Somehow Patience summoned the fortitude to speak normally. "He's already left."

As she reached for the package, her instincts twinged. Had he left it behind on purpose? To give to her or to ensure she followed? But she could send this on if necessary. She wouldn't *have* to deliver anything personally.

A separate sheet of paper crinkled beneath her fingers. She scowled at Jane.

"I didn't read it, my lady," the maid replied, all innocence.

Patience lowered her brows further for good measure. The package might have been wrapped roughly, but the message was written on proper vellum. She unfolded the note.

My dear—

At the mere greeting her eyes clouded. Yes, he'd called her that. His words to her echoed through her mind. *Oh, my dear. Last night we barely scraped the surface of my regrets.* Heartfelt words. Tender words, fraught with emotion. She forced herself to read on.

It is a season for thinking of those who are less fortunate than we, and so I hope you will fulfill a small request for me. Enclosed is one of the gifts I had thought to present to my sons to remember this Christmastide. It is a mere trifle to them, and upon due consideration, I feel it is better conferred on young Jamie. Will you ensure that he receives it?

I am ever yours,
Kingsbury

NATHANIEL STARED OUT at the snow-covered landscape, but in his mind, he was back at Worthington Manor—or, more precisely, at the dower house—trying to work out what the hell had just happened. After the night they'd just spent, he'd rather expected Patience to fall into his arms.

But no, she'd gone and speculated on his family's reaction to him turning up in the company of a female. What was more, she had them dead to rights. They would look down their noses at Patience even if she had been born well enough to wed an earl. Yes, and she was correct in her assessment. She couldn't afford the appearance of scandal.

He understood her reluctance to face his family. He only prayed that hesitancy didn't extend to him, personally. Because if he knew anything, he knew he had to see her again. He couldn't stand to pass the rest of his life living on the memory of a single night. He wanted more with her.

Good God, when had he gone and done something so foolish as fall in love with Patience? Certainly not anytime during the past two days. No, that event dated back much, much further, even if he hadn't realized in the moment.

If he was completely honest, it had happened in an instant, the moment he'd spotted her across a crowded ballroom, one young lady clad in white silk and a feathered headdress among so many others, but for some inexplicable reason she'd drawn his eye. And she'd been conversing with one of his school friends, which had given him an excuse to beg an introduction.

He'd asked her to dance, she'd accepted, and the moment she'd laid her hand in his had been like the crackle of lightning in a summer storm—electric, awe-inspiring, and terrifying all at once. He'd been a goner, even if he hadn't known it.

But he knew now. He had ten years' worth of experience to compare her to. But Patience didn't compare, and that was the problem. For him, she stood above all other women he'd ever met.

He'd lost ten years with her. He wasn't about to lose another decade. He wouldn't lose another week if he had his way. No, on Twelfth Night, she would bloody well come to his estate, and then he'd have only to convince her.

The rest of his family be damned.

Chapter Eight

Kingsbury's Estate
Twelfth Night, 1817

THE MOMENT PATIENCE entered one of the numerous receiving rooms, she remembered why she despised social gatherings. Ladies dressed in exquisite ball gowns and glittering jewels gathered in flocks, chatting and laughing with gentlemen clad in stark black. The fashion plates from *La Belle Assemblée* come to life.

Though she'd donned her best gown, Patience felt like a wren next to these peacocks. Once dinner was announced, she could only pray she wasn't seated next to someone *too* insufferable.

She edged closer to her sister-in-law, grateful that at least one of the ladies present would deign to speak with her.

"Odd." Constance pulled out her fan and waved it before her face. "I thought we must have been asked here as a curiosity. Country gentry on display."

Patience suppressed a smile. Thank heavens for Constance's sharp wit.

Peter snorted with laughter, though he quickly covered the reaction with a false cough. At the sound, heads turned in their direction. Several sets of eyebrows rose. Several more pairs of heads tilted toward each other. Whispers were exchanged behind fans. A few of the faces triggered her memory. A decade ago, she'd met some of these ladies who had conspired to make their own brilliant matches. She might have even traded pleasantries with them over tea. But since her exile to the country, she'd turned back into a stranger.

Patience bore the weight of their scrutiny in silence.

Constance pulled a face. "What do you suppose they're saying about us?"

"Perhaps they believe we've become lost on our way to our true destination," Peter replied with a wink. "Still, we're in the company of a countess. That must count for something."

Patience jammed her elbow into his ribs. She could get away with it. No one was paying her the least bit of attention now. Just as well. "I regret mentioning the invitation at all."

When she'd finally arrived at her brother's, she'd waited a day or two before approaching the topic. Even then, she'd eased into it carefully so as not to provoke too many questions.

"I beg your pardon." Her brother pulled on his sleeves. "When a duke summons you, you respond." He'd said as much days ago.

"Summons? It was hardly a summons." And if she kept on repeating that to herself, she might come to believe it. "As I told you, I had a note. If we were in the area, we might consider . . ." She trailed off. Even to her own ears the story sounded weak.

"*I* received a summons," Peter admitted.

"*You* received . . ." This was the first Patience had heard as much.

"No uncertain terms." He turned a penetrating gaze on her. "I should like to know what that's all about, actually."

"I confess myself quite intrigued, as well," Constance added. "I seem to recall ten years ago Kingsbury was quite smitten with a certain young lady. Yet how he's suddenly remembered your existence, I can never guess."

"He wasn't Kingsbury then." Another lame response, but it was the best Patience could muster. She couldn't possibly go so far as to tell them the real reason behind this invitation. Not that she knew for certain, but whatever Kingsbury's reasons, they traced back to the previous week.

Thankfully a footman chose that moment to appear with a tray of wassail. She chose a cup of the steaming, spiced liquid and raised it to her lips.

The drink spread warmth through her, or perhaps that was due to the sudden presence at her side. She hardly needed to turn and see for herself who had joined them. Her body seemed to sense his on an elemental level now. She took a larger swallow, the aroma of cloves and allspice briefly masking Kingsbury's sandalwood scent.

Kingsbury shook hands with her brother and inclined his head to her sister-in-law before addressing Patience.

He picked up her free hand and bent over it. "I'm so happy you've come."

You may be the only one. She stopped herself before she blurted something stupid, but even as she gave the expected reply, she caught sight of Diana eyeing their group.

"I wonder if you'd indulge me," Nathaniel went on.

Patience wafted her fan before her face. Perhaps it was the drink, but the room had suddenly become overheated. "Indulge you how?"

"Simple curiosity. How did young Jamie enjoy his present?"

"Oh, do tell," Constance put in. "Start from the beginning. Who is Jamie?"

Patience's face flamed as hot as the sun. She might be thoroughly in love with Nathaniel on account of that blasted Christmas present, but right now she wished only to smack him. "He's the son of one of Worthington's tenants."

"Indeed?" said Constance. "And how would someone like His Grace know of the child, let alone give him a gift?"

"Did Lady Worthington not recount her adventures?" Nathaniel asked. "She is too modest. She came to my rescue when my carriage became stuck on Christmas Eve. She was kind enough to offer me shelter from the storm." He recounted the story so smoothly, as if the previous week's events had transpired in complete innocence.

"And we happened across Jamie," Patience finished. "His Grace was kind enough to leave the child a bilboquet." She made it sound like a mere trifle. No doubt to Nathaniel it was. But the wooden cup and ball had been cunningly carved, the deep golden wood sanded smooth as silk. Some master wood-carver had surely made the toy with a great deal of care, and such expertise usually commanded a high price. "Jamie was quite delighted and sends his thanks."

Patience was putting words in the boy's mouth. When she'd taken him the gift on Boxing Day, the duke's generosity had left him at a complete loss. She'd walked back home through the woods, her heart swelling with Nathaniel's thoughtfulness. She hadn't just fallen in love with him, she realized. She'd plummeted straight off a cliff.

The corners of Nathaniel's eyes crinkled as his smile deepened. "It does my heart good to hear it. I hope you'll forgive my lack of manners, but I should like to borrow Lady Worthington for a few moments," he added to Peter and Constance. "I promise to return her before dinner is served."

Constance shot Patience a look that clearly said she'd be explaining everything in detail on the carriage ride home. Patience drained her cup and set it on a side table.

Nathaniel offered his arm.

"What is it?"

"I want to show you something."

"What?"

He steered her into the corridor. "I promise it's nothing scandalous. I will not lead you astray. That is . . ." His voice lowered an octave. "Unless you'd like me to."

The invitation in his tone called up all manner of wicked memories of the joy she'd shared with him. Tempting. So tempting.

He guided her into the entrance hall toward a curving grand staircase. As they ascended, his free hand hovered at the small of her back, its presence tangible as a cushion of warmth in the half inch of air that separated his palm from her gown.

"Where are we going?"

"You'll see."

They climbed a second flight. The bedchambers were on this level. This couldn't possibly be an attempt at a seduction before supper. Along the upper passage to the back of the manor, he threw open a door.

She hardly had the chance to take in the small furnishings, the rocking horse, the rows of tin soldiers, before a pair of boys rocketed into him to shouts of "Papa!"

A nursemaid strode in their wake. "Ye young masters be careful now. His Grace is dressed in his evening clothes."

The nursery. He wanted to show her the nursery.

"Good heavens, why?" She could only think of a single reason, and that reason set her pulse to racing.

He extricated himself from his sons' enthusiastic embrace and smoothed the black superfine of his dinner jacket. "It seemed fitting. In a way, I suppose, these are my versions of Jamie."

That reply did nothing for the state of her heartbeat.

"Colin, Oliver," he said to the boys, "it is time to show how well you've learned your manners. I am about to present you to a lady. Lady Worthington, to be exact."

They stepped back to regard her with round eyes and a certain measure of skepticism. Close to Jamie's age, they bore their father's dark coloring and striking blue eyes. Longing, keen and sharp-edged, pierced her heart like a lance. Had things worked out differently, they could have been hers.

"I'm very pleased to meet you." She forced the words past a knot in her throat and held out her hand for them to shake. "You're the very image of your father."

"Why does everyone say that?" asked one of them. She couldn't have distinguished the two if she'd tried.

Nathaniel ruffled his hair. "Because it's true. And now I shall wish you a good night, for I must return to my guests."

The nursemaid bobbed a curtsy and took the boys in hand. The door to the nursery closed at Patience's back, but she barely noticed. The corridor seemed to be shimmering with waves of heat like those that rose over a summer field. She blinked away the tears.

"What do you think?" Nathaniel asked. Something in his tone betrayed a keen desire to hear her response.

"Of your boys?" By some miracle her voice sounded only a little thick. "They're fine young men. You've every right to be proud."

Please heaven, don't let him note anything is amiss. She couldn't afford to have him asking questions if he noticed that she was upset, for the very reasons made too many assumptions about his intentions.

Or was this gesture his attempt to inform her of his intentions? She hardly knew anymore.

He stepped in front of her. The breadth of his shoulders blocked the light. "Are you all right?"

Or she could fib. She raised her chin and met his gaze dead on. "I have to wonder why you invited me to this gathering. It was clear enough in the sitting room that I am not wanted here."

His fingers brushed her cheek, and he leaned closer. "On the contrary."

"Tell me," she insisted. "I must know the truth. Are you playing games with me?"

But he didn't have a chance to reply, for a new voice echoed down the passage. "Really, is this any way to behave?"

Patience practically jumped back, she moved away so fast. Her heart hammered the way it had when, as a child, she'd been caught doing something naughty.

If she'd thought anyone might interrupt them, she would have wagered her pin money on Diana. But a much older woman appeared past Nathaniel's shoulder, her wrinkled face set in lines of displeasure. The dowager duchess.

"I thought I raised you better than that," the woman added, as if her own son had still been six years old rather than six and thirty. "Stealing off for a tryst before supper."

Nathaniel raised a brow. "Does that mean after supper is acceptable?"

The dowager raised both of hers. "That will do."

"There is absolutely nothing untoward occurring here."

"I should hope not. You are both beyond the age where

I should have to remind you to conduct your affairs with discretion."

"This is not an affair." Nathaniel all but growled the words.

"Indeed? Well, I wish you'd come to me to discuss your desire for another duchess. I might have suggested a few well-connected ladies who might carry off the role to my satisfaction."

"Let us understand one thing." Nathaniel placed himself between Patience and his mother. "If I decide to marry, I shall choose my own duchess this time, and you shall have no say in the matter. Nor shall Diana." He looked about. "Where is she? Hiding in a corner to watch you set me down?"

"The very idea." The dowager duchess waved a hand before her face. "I'm here because you are neglecting your guests. I have been informed supper is served, but we can hardly proceed to the dining room when you are conspicuously absent."

Nathaniel turned to Patience. "Then let us go."

His mother sniffed and headed back down the corridor, but Patience held back. "That is what I meant about not being wanted."

He held out his arm for her to take. "If you will kindly accompany me, we're neglecting our guests."

Our guests. As if she was the hostess tonight. She caught her breath. "But your mother."

"Do not concern yourself." He set off toward the staircase. "One of the first things a duke learns is that he can get away with telling most of the world to bugger themselves, and they very kindly bow and set to."

Patience nearly tripped over her gown.

"Forgive me. Has my language shocked you?"

"No." She'd heard far worse from the earl when he'd been in his cups. And that was to say nothing of her brothers when they weren't. "I just never expected you, of all people, to say something like that."

"Our history together would lead you to think that, wouldn't it? But I intend to remedy that situation tonight. My family be damned."

"Something tells me your mother won't be one to bow."

"I don't plan on giving her the choice."

They reached the ground floor to find the guests gathered, ready to process to the dining room. Diana stood at the front of the group, watching Patience through narrowed eyes.

"Lud." She might have addressed her companion, but her voice carried throughout the hall. "I didn't realize we were going to observe all the old traditions tonight."

Beneath Patience's hand, Nathaniel's arm muscles tightened. "What tradition might those be?" he asked carefully.

"Oh, that nonsense about turning the world upside down and placing one of the servants at the head of the table. Is that where you're planning on seating Lady Worthington?"

A collective gasp went through the crowd. Diana's escort edged away from her. Heat rose to Patience's cheeks. From several feet away, the weight of the dowager's glare bypassed her to settle on Diana. Thank the heavens.

"I ought to send you to dine in the kennels for that remark," Nathaniel shot back. "However, I prefer you remain on hand to witness tonight's proceedings. Now, shall we go in to supper in a civilized fashion, or is that much beyond you?"

Nathaniel led Patience before the entire company into a palatial dining room dominated by a table swathed in white linen, lined with ornate candelabra between the fine porcelain plates. He took her to an opulent, carved chair at the right of his place.

She hung back for a moment. "You cannot mean to seat me here."

"Indeed I do. You will understand why in a moment."

As the rest of the company filed in, Diana glared from her spot much farther down the table—thank goodness. Servants brought in the first course and poured rich red wine into crystal goblets. Patience suppressed an urge to down the contents in a single gulp.

She didn't get a chance at even a sip. Before the meal could begin, Nathaniel rose from his place at the table's head, glass in hand. "Before we tuck into this lovely meal, I should like to request your indulgence while I propose a toast."

Murmurs rippled up and down the table. Both Diana and the dowager duchess scowled, without doubt over the breach of protocol.

"Ten years ago, I made the acquaintance of a certain young lady." Nathaniel nodded at Patience. Her heart beat faster. "One might say I was immediately smitten, and I would not argue with that assessment. But then I made a grave error. I thought I had ample time to press my suit, but circumstances intervened. By some miracle—one might even call it a Christmas miracle—our paths crossed once more. And so I would ask us all to drink to the magic of the season."

He raised his glass, and the rest of the company followed suit. The claret's richness filled Patience's mouth and warmed its way down her throat.

But Nathaniel wasn't finished with his speech. "Lady Worthington and I have renewed our acquaintance, and I have discovered my feelings have not changed. If anything, they have grown stronger."

His blue gaze captured hers. Nothing could make her look away. "I wish to rectify my mistake, here, tonight."

Good heavens, what was he planning?

"I wish to beg Lady Worthington to make me the happiest of men and consent to be my duchess."

Patience's jaw dropped. All around her, the table erupted in sound—breathy sighs from the ladies, outrage from certain quarters, a possible cheer from her brother—but she could barely speak. Her heart had jumped into her throat.

He watched her with a confident smile, but some shadow behind his eyes told her he wasn't altogether certain of her reply.

She took another fortifying drink in hopes that the other guests would attribute her reddened cheeks to the claret. "I hardly know what to say."

"I should like your acceptance," he said, his voice low, "but I will equally understand if you require some reflection."

He was waiting. An entire roomful of guests waited for her answer. Despite their audience, she felt as if she was addressing him alone. "What you said . . . Do you believe it is possible to fall in love at first sight?" Heaven only knew, she'd believed it at one time.

He nodded. "I know it is."

"But can that feeling last?" There it was—her real concern, because they would certainly have to overcome his family's objections.

He took her hand, giving it a slight tug. "Don't you think we've proven that?"

She resisted the pull of his grip, a silent plea to stand alongside him. "I mean for an entire lifetime."

"That is what I intend to find out, for nothing will keep me from you again." He raised his gaze to stare down the table at his mother and sister. "Nothing and no one."

Patience, for her part, refused to look down the table. She did not need to see his family's reaction. "Your sister led me to believe you had no true feelings for me."

"She could not possibly have known what was in my heart then." The love evident in his gaze filled her to brimming. She could not remain in her seat much longer, for the upwelling of emotion seemed likely to buoy her up to the ceiling. Higher. "No more than she does now."

Patience rose to her feet, keeping her eyes on his. She might be giving her reply in public, but it was for him alone. "Then I should be glad to accept your proposal."

"Another toast!" This from her brother. She turned to face a beaming Peter and Constance. "To the happy couple. And may their years and joys be long."

Her lips stretched of their own accord. She didn't think she'd ever stop smiling. All about the table, glasses raised. Even Diana and the dowager could not resist the appearance of not following the crowd, whatever their private feelings.

As the chorus of cheers and congratulations rose about them, Patience leaned closer to whisper in Nathaniel's ear. "I should like to know one thing."

"What is that?"

"Once I'm duchess, will I be permitted to tell certain people to bugger off? Even if they're members of your family?"

His laughter rang over the noise of the other guests. "I would be especially disappointed if you didn't."

Epilogue

Kingsbury's estate
Christmas 1817

THE ONE THING Patience could usually count on in the country was at least one good blanket of snow in the winter. When that snow coincided with the Christmas season, so much the better. She looked on today's covering of white as a particularly auspicious sign. The upcoming year would be a good one.

Her hand in Nathaniel's, she watched Oliver and Colin bound ahead through the frozen parkland and recalled a previous Christmas morning when she and Nathaniel had gone in search of greenery. This year, they had no such need, as the servants had already seen to the decoration of the manor house—mistletoe included. But this day had dawned too beautiful to waste.

One of the boys stooped and gathered a handful of snow, packing it into a furtive ball that he let fly at his brother. The other gave a shout, and battle soon raged.

Nathaniel smiled at them. "What do you say we join them?"

"It's tempting, but given a choice I'd much rather pelt your sister."

He nudged her. "Then you should have invited her for Twelfth Night."

Plans were well underway for another lavish feast, minus a few conspicuous guests. "She's perfectly welcome to attend, as long as she can promise to curb her tongue."

Sadly—or perhaps not so sadly—Diana found it difficult to keep such promises. She'd refused to attend their wedding on principle, and every other attempt at reconciliation had proved fruitless.

Nathaniel let a plume of breath escape into the frigid air. "I doubt we'll be seeing her any time soon, then. The woman is nothing if not tenacious."

"I'd say tenacity runs in the family."

He stopped in his tracks. "Are you comparing me to my sister?"

"In a sense. You're two sides of the same coin. Your particular version of tenacity paid off in the end, I'd say."

"If you mean to say I never gave up hope of winning your heart, I'm not completely certain you have the right of it. We might not have lost so much time if I'd exercised my ducal prerogative sooner."

She leaned closer to whisper in his ear, lest her voice carry in the crisp air. "You mean the one where you tell people to bugger off?"

He grinned. "The same."

"Think no more of it. Things worked out the way they were meant to in the end." She glanced at the boys, safely shouting and laughing and ignoring their father. Excellent. "I think now is the perfect occasion to deliver your Christmas gift."

He glanced at her empty hands. "You don't happen to be hiding a snowball in your pocket, do you?"

"Not quite. But my gift isn't visible just yet. This time next year, however, you'll be able to see and hear it. I daresay you may even smell it if you don't hand it off to the nursemaid fast enough."

Once more, he stopped in his tracks, slack-jawed. "Are you saying . . . ?"

She looked up at him through her lashes. "I have good reason to believe you'll be a father again by this time next year."

In a perfectly undignified display, he let out a shout, threw his arms about her waist, and whirled her about. Just as quickly, he set her back on her feet and backed away, palms facing outward. "Your pardon."

She burst out laughing. "I assure you my condition is not that delicate." To prove it, she laced her hands behind his neck and pulled his lips down to hers. "We can even manage without mistletoe for now."

"We always have," he murmured before closing the final gap between them.

About the Author

USA Today bestselling author **ASHLYN MACNAMARA** writes Regency romance with a dash of wit and a hint of wicked. She considers writing her midlife crisis but reckons it's safer than hang gliding or rock climbing. She lives in the wilds of suburbia outside Montreal with her husband, two teenage daughters, and one loudmouth cat. Although she writes about the past, you can find her in such newfangled places as her website, ashlynmacnamara.net, facebook.com/AuthorAshlynMacnamara, and twitter.com/ashlyn_mac.

Don't miss the next fabulous
historical romance series from
USA Today bestselling author
Vivienne Lorret!

The Season's Original series begins with
THE DEBUTANTE IS MINE
Coming April 2016 from Avon Impulse